THICKER THAN
BLOOD

OTHER TITLES BY MIKE OMER

ZOE BENTLEY MYSTERIES

A Killer's Mind
In the Darkness

GLENMORE PARK MYSTERIES

Spider's Web
Deadly Web
Web of Fear

THICKER THAN
BLOOD

MIKE OMER

THOMAS & MERCER

Text copyright © 2020 by Michael Omer
All rights reserved.

Published by Thomas & Mercer, Seattle
www.apub.com

Amazon, the Amazon logo, and Thomas & Mercer are trademarks of Amazon.com, Inc., or its affiliates.

ISBN-13: 9781542042444
ISBN-10: 1542042445

Cover design by Christopher Lin

Printed in the United States of America

To my parents, who helped every step of the way

CHAPTER 1

Friday, October 14, 2016

Catherine always believed that her soul was weightless. It was a thing made of thoughts, and feelings, and beliefs—all bodiless, as light as sunshine. But the soul also contained a person's secrets. And those turned heavier every day.

If she could carry the weight on her back, perhaps she could go on as usual. She imagined a sturdy backpack, like her uncle used to have, with buckles and padded shoulder straps. She'd put all of her secrets there and adjust the hip belt, spreading the weight uniformly.

Instead, her secrets chose where they lay. They'd settle around her neck one day, dragging her down, making her neck stoop. The next morning they'd crawl into her gut, and she'd constantly bend over with cramps, running to the bathroom every hour. Right now, the secrets lurked in her heart, squeezing it, until it felt like it would shatter, or simply stop.

She'd called in sick that morning, third time that week. Her dad was getting worried, and she circumvented his questions by mentioning "lady problems." It was now late in the evening, and she sat in her living room. The television screen flickering in front of her as she tried to cry.

Her tears had forgotten their way out. They constantly filled her throat, making her voice brittle and whiny, but they hadn't emerged in days. If she only managed to cry, it would be a release. Perhaps the weight of the secrets would become bearable. Her eyes remained dry. Her lips quivered, and that only made her feel childish and stupid.

Secrets were sticky. They could clog your tear ducts if you weren't careful.

She toyed with her phone, as she had many times in the past weeks, opening her contact list, her dad the first one in her favorites. Appropriate, since he was her favorite. Her favorite parent, her favorite human, her favorite thing in the whole world. She could tell him the truth. The weight in her heart would dissipate into nothing. Her finger wavered over the screen. For a second she could almost feel the anticipated relief.

And then the images came. His hurt face. He wasn't a young man anymore. He'd had a heart attack last year, which the doctors called a "near thing." What would this do to him?

The imaginary relief morphed into thorny fear and guilt. She couldn't.

She let out a raw, feral sob. Dry as dust, no tears.

A sudden knock on the door made her heart skip a beat. For a second she couldn't fathom who it could possibly be. It was very late. Her friends or neighbors would text her before showing up on her doorstep, especially at this hour. Then she knew. It was her father. He was worried about her, wanted to see how she was doing.

He'd take one look at her face and know something serious was wrong. That if these were "lady problems," they weren't the kind that happened on a monthly basis. Would she be able to lie to him when he asked her? Not right now. Not this evening. She'd have to tell him everything.

Relief, fear, and guilt flooded her at once as she got up, stumbling to the door. She took a quick glance through the peephole.

"Oh," she said in surprise. She knew this man, but he wasn't her father.

She reached for the dead bolt, more out of confusion than intent, her mind foggy after a long day. As she did it, she felt the sudden wrongness. Her thoughts, scrambling in panic, tried to order her fingers to stop, that this door should remain shut. This man shouldn't be here at all. And something shimmered in his eyes. Something dangerous and unstable.

But there was a moment of disconnect between her brain and her body. As if in slow motion, she turned the dead bolt knob, unlocking the door.

It shoved open, slamming into her face, a sudden blinding pain. She fell back to the floor, the entire right side of her face throbbing, her vision foggy. Tears sprang into her eyes, finally finding their way out. She tried to scream, to speak.

A hand clamped on her face, blocking her nose and mouth. She couldn't breathe. Couldn't make a sound. She struggled, and he hit her.

The world went blissfully dark.

Her eyelids fluttered open. Her mouth felt strange, woolly, and it took her a moment to realize something was stuffed in it. She lifted her hand to pull it out.

"Don't."

The command froze her.

"I need that there. I can't have you screaming."

Her eyes focused on the familiar face, and she blinked, beseeching him mutely to let her go.

"This will only take a few moments," he said, sounding almost apologetic. He held something. A needle.

He pulled her right hand toward him and raised the needle, about to stick her. She let out a muffled scream, tried to pull her hand away. She was weak, and his grip was strong enough to hurt, but the sudden

3

jerk surprised him, and he missed his mark. She gasped as the needle plunged into her arm.

"Look what you made me do!" he snarled, angry, and she saw that gleam in his eyes again. His grip tightened on her wrist, hurting her, and he stuck the needle again. She tried to claw at his face with her other hand, and he slapped her.

"I can't hit your vein like that," he muttered. The needle went in again. He shook his head and mumbled to himself, frustrated.

She wrenched her hand away, a blinding pain flaring through her arm as the needle twisted. Blood seeped from the ragged hole in her arm. She felt dizzy, thought she was about to faint.

"Damn it!" He tossed the needle away in fury, and it clattered in the corner of the room. He looked at her, gritting his teeth in anger. Then he glanced down at her bleeding arm. His eyes widened. His throat constricted as he swallowed.

He lowered his head to her arm and, to her revulsion, licked the blood. The rough feeling of his tongue on her skin made her squirm in disgust and horror. She tried to pull away, but he held her arm tight, making a strange sound. A snarl.

His lips tightened on her skin, and he began to slurp. She stared mutely as he sucked blood from her torn skin. He finally pulled back, a trickle of blood running down his chin.

"I had to." His face twisted in shame. "I'm sorry."

The world faded again.

When she came back to her senses, he was gone. A strange keening noise echoed somewhere nearby. Crying? Yes. It was him. He was still in her home, and he was crying.

The police. She had to call the police. She tried to force herself to move, to get up, but her limbs wouldn't obey her. Blood seeped from her arm, dripping to the floor.

Finally she managed to budge. To pull the gag from her mouth. She was about to rise when a noise behind her made her freeze.

And then a fabric tightened around her throat, choking her. She clawed at it, couldn't get a grip on the noose, her mouth opening wide as she tried to scream. No sound. No breath. Spots danced in her eyes as her vision clouded.

A low chuckle, full of malice, and a growling voice whispered in her ear. "Now for the fun part."

CHAPTER 2

Saturday, October 15, 2016

Detective Holly O'Donnell stood in the hall and watched as the medical staff gently placed Catherine Lamb's body on the stretcher. The body had been zipped in a body bag, out of sight. But the image was seared in her mind. The strands of matted hair, glued to the victim's cheek with dried blood. The bruises on the skin, contrasting with the paleness of death. The torn clothes, Catherine's final unavoidable indignity. Sometimes, O'Donnell could summon a barrier of professional aloofness. Not today.

The two men carrying the stretcher took a moment to maneuver out of the living room, doing their best to avoid stepping in the large smeared stain of dried blood. As they left, O'Donnell gave herself a moment to refocus. The murder scene's atmosphere always changed when the body was removed. Voices grew louder. Officers moved around more freely, their actions businesslike. Someone would crack a joke. A general sense of relief settled over everyone. The dead were gone. It was time for the living to tie up the loose ends.

She scrutinized her surroundings in the soft light filtering through the window. It was a small house, and she imagined that before the recent gruesome events it had been a sweet place. A cozy bedroom, a pleasant living room with a couch and a small TV. The kitchen was a bit cramped, but Catherine Lamb had done wonders with the space, hanging pots and pans on the wall in a way that almost made them seem like part of the decor. Through the window in the kitchen, a glimpse of the backyard could be seen. Lawn gone wild, spotted with weeds and dry leaves.

O'Donnell turned toward Officer Garza, who stood in the kitchen, flipping the pages in his sketch pad.

"Let's do the living room," she said.

He took a second too long to nod, a flash of resentment on his face. She was getting used to those moments of spite. Of cops looking at her like she didn't deserve to call herself a detective, or a cop, for that matter. And as if she *definitely* didn't deserve to be calling the shots.

Well, she called the shots, deserve it or not. Garza would have to deal.

He entered the living room, sketchbook in hand, and waited for her. She hesitated for a moment, the large bloodstain on the floor frustrating her. For someone as tall as Garza, it posed no problem. But she couldn't just step over the stain. She would have to jump over it, like she had twice before already. And with the shoe booties, which *she* had insisted everyone wear, she could easily slip and fall. Not to mention that in her own mind she looked ridiculous, hopping like a rabbit in a cheap suit.

She jumped over it and did in fact slip and almost fall. Then she straightened and eyed Garza, daring him to laugh. He didn't.

Focusing on the job at hand, she began measuring the room with a tape, calling out the measurements to Garza, who jotted the details on the page. Garza and his partner had been first on the scene. When O'Donnell had shown up, she'd asked Garza to be the sketcher, while his partner was in charge of the scene perimeter. They'd already done the bathroom and the bedroom and had waited for the body to be removed before they started with the living room.

She placed an evidence marker numbered eight next to the victim's phone, discarded on the floor. Evidence marker nine was placed by the torn bra. Evidence markers ten to fifteen next to the bloody footprints that covered the floor. On one of her first homicide trials, they'd almost lost the case because they had marked three footprints with only one marker, leading to shoddy photographs. Never again.

"Make sure to point out the direction of the footsteps in the sketch," she said.

"I will." Garza was measuring the distance of the victim's phone to the room's doorway.

"And triangulate the distance of each one separately."

He shot her a disgusted look but said nothing. Of course, he knew how to do his job; there was no need to micromanage him. But it was better safe than sorry. O'Donnell had had enough *sorry* in the past months for a lifetime.

She paced around the room, careful to avoid the bloodstains, searching for anything she might have missed, but found nothing. Then she strode over to Garza and glanced at the sketch. She grudgingly had to admit to herself that the man did a good job. The sketch was tidy, the triangulations careful and methodical.

Loud voices caught her attention. The officer outside was arguing with someone, and the tone got more and more heated. Media already? Or a nosy neighbor?

She jumped over the bloodstain again, not slipping this time. Definitely getting better at bloodstain jumping. Then she marched out of the house, squinting as she adjusted to the sunlight.

They'd cordoned off Catherine Lamb's house and tiny front yard as well as a patch of the sidewalk. Garza's partner, a rookie fresh from the academy, stood on the sidewalk inside the perimeter, the crime scene logbook in his hand. On the other side of the yellow tape were a man and a woman. The woman wore a long beige trench coat, her hands in her pockets. She had a matching brown wool hat and scarf. The man had a black overcoat, which he wore over a gray suit.

The woman's voice rose over the traffic noise as she berated the rookie. "We just need a few minutes. It's in your best interest to—"

"Excuse me," O'Donnell called, striding over, her breath clouding in the cold air. "Is there a problem?"

"Feds," the rookie said. "They want to enter the crime scene."

O'Donnell frowned and turned to face the two feds. The man was black haired, tall, with wide shoulders. His posture was ridiculously casual, almost slouching, like a high school student trying to seem cool. The woman was, to some extent, the complete opposite. She didn't even reach the man's shoulder, and wisps of auburn hair peeped from underneath her wool hat. Her delicate lips were pursed with displeasure, and her entire body seemed poised, as if she was about to lunge at someone. Her nose, long and curved, was pink from the cold. She turned her gaze to O'Donnell, who almost took a step back. The woman's eyes were the color of grass, and their intensity was deeply unnerving. It was as if she wasn't just looking at O'Donnell—she was actually scrutinizing each and every one of her skin pores.

"I'm Detective O'Donnell." O'Donnell forced herself to meet the woman's stare. "And you are?"

"Agent Gray." The man flashed his FBI badge. "And this is Dr. Bentley."

"This is a Chicago PD crime scene, agents. You can't come in. Not until we finish processing it."

"This murder might be relevant to an ongoing case we're investigating," Bentley said. "We just need a few minutes to—"

"Who said this is a murder?" O'Donnell asked.

Gray flashed his partner an annoyed look, which she didn't seem to notice. He sighed. "Lieutenant Martinez tipped us off. He called to tell us a twenty-nine-year-old woman named Catherine Lamb was strangled to death in her home."

O'Donnell maintained her poker face, doing her best to hide her anger. She'd always thought well of Martinez, who, like her, worked in the Area Central detective bureau. What was he thinking, contacting the FBI about a local murder? And giving them preliminary, unverified information, like the cause of death, was a mistake even rookies didn't make. "How is this murder related to your case?"

"We're not at liberty to say," Gray said quickly, just as Bentley opened her mouth.

O'Donnell gave them a tight-lipped smile. "I have a crime scene to process. Have a nice day, Agents."

"Wait." Bentley's voice sharpened, eyes flashing in anger.

O'Donnell turned away. She'd have a talk with Martinez later and figure out what this was all about.

"Detective O'Donnell," Agent Gray called after her. "Two minutes of your time, please? We might have some information."

O'Donnell sighed and walked back. Gray seemed embarrassed, humility creeping in his features.

"Mind if we talk privately?" he asked.

O'Donnell crouched under the yellow tape and stepped a few yards away from the house, out of earshot.

"What is it?" she asked the agents, who'd followed her.

"We're investigating a serial killer named Rod Glover," Agent Gray said. "He lived in Chicago for about ten years, using a fake identity."

"What does he have to do with this murder?"

"We're not sure if he has anything to do with it. But Rod Glover strangles his victims. And his last known address was right in this neighborhood, in McKinley Park."

"That sounds like a very arbitrary connection," O'Donnell pointed out. "Do you show up at every homicide investigation with suspicion of strangulation in the area?"

Bentley snorted with impatience. "Sexual homicides with strangulation in this immediate area aren't an everyday occurrence—"

"*Sexual* homicide? Did Martinez tell you it was a sexual homicide?"

"He said the victim's clothing was torn."

"Why the hell did he tell you all that? This case has nothing to do with him, and none of this is in any reports. He—" The puzzle pieces suddenly clicked together. "Dr. Bentley? You're Zoe Bentley, the profiler. You worked with Martinez on the Strangling Undertaker case."

"Yes."

Three months before, Chicago had been terrorized by a serial killer who murdered and embalmed young women, leaving their bodies posed all over the city. Lieutenant Martinez had been in charge of the investigation, and he'd asked for the bureau's help. Dr. Bentley and Agent Gray had been part of the task force that had finally caught the killer.

"You're not from the FBI's Chicago field office."

"No," Gray answered. "We're from the Behavioral Analysis Unit."

"And you just happened to be in Chicago today?" O'Donnell asked, incredulous. The BAU was located in Quantico, Virginia, half a country away.

"Not exactly. We've been following Glover's tracks. We've been in Chicago for the past week."

"And now you want to take over the case? Just because you think it might be related—"

"We're not taking over *anything*." Gray raised his hands in a placating manner. "We just want to assess if it's possible Glover is related to this case."

"Fine." O'Donnell shrugged. "Talk to your guys at the field office. They can get the case reports from us, and you can take a look."

"It would be much better if I could see the scene for myself," Bentley blurted.

"Better for who?"

"Well, for everyone. We're much more experienced in profiling these kinds of attacks. If we see the scene—"

O'Donnell got impatient with the woman's patronizing manner. "The photos will be in the case file."

Gray touched Bentley's arm, just as she was about to say something, and she shut her mouth.

"Listen," he said. "We can try and help with this case. We can allocate federal resources."

That was what O'Donnell had been hoping to hear all along. DNA tests in Chicago had a ridiculous backlog. But if the feds got involved, volunteering their own labs? O'Donnell could use a lucky break like that.

Besides, she was curious. She'd heard a lot of people talking about Zoe Bentley and the Strangling Undertaker case. People loved talking about Bentley almost as much as they enjoyed talking about O'Donnell and the recent scandal. The profiler was depicted as everything from a sham to a genius. There had been some sort of mess in the Strangling Undertaker case. Bentley had managed to get severely injured during the investigation. She and her partner had possibly held back crucial information from the cops. O'Donnell had even heard an absurd rumor that when they'd arrested the murderer, Bentley had been half-naked. The profiler sure made people talk.

She wanted to see her in action.

"Fine," she said. "You can have a look. But if I ask you to step away, you leave."

"Hey, it's your scene." Agent Gray flashed her a smile.

She led them back to the house. Bentley and Gray signed the log and followed her inside. Garza was still in the living room, sketching. The photographer had joined him and took close shots of one of the bloody footprints. O'Donnell made a note to make sure he got a few wide shots of all the footprints together.

"Gloves and shoe covers." O'Donnell pointed at the boxes by the entrance. She watched Bentley's expression as the profiler noticed the large bloodstain.

"The victim was bleeding," Bentley muttered as she put on a pair of gloves.

So far, O'Donnell wasn't particularly impressed by the woman's deductive skills. "Martinez didn't mention that?" she asked innocently. She knew he hadn't. It wasn't on the initial report of the first officers on the scene.

Bentley ignored her and put on the shoe booties. She approached the bloodstain. Without even pausing, she leaped over it, landing in the living room.

O'Donnell was irked. Zoe Bentley was even shorter than she was, but she had managed to jump over the bloodstain with the grace of a damn gazelle.

CHAPTER 3

Zoe scrutinized the large bloodstain and the footprints that crisscrossed the room's floor. At first, it was hard to make sense of the mess; the footprints were smeared and cut across each other. Slowly she managed to untangle them in her mind. Someone had paced in a circle near the room's entrance several times and had gone to the far corner and back. He'd stepped in the pool of blood several times, which probably indicated he was confused or distraught.

The bra, discarded on the floor, had been torn by force, the metal clasp on the back twisted. What about the rest of the clothes? Torn as well? She tried to keep the obvious question from clouding her judgment. Could this be Glover's work?

If she kept focusing on Glover, she'd invariably morph the facts to match what she wanted to see. But she wasn't sure she could avoid the question. Glover grew and filled her mind like a parasitic vine, crawling into every nook and cranny, suffocating every other thought.

For the past few weeks, she and Tatum had meticulously traced Glover's footsteps, going back ten years, like a movie in rewind. They'd started in the place where he'd last been. An apartment in her own building. He rented it under the name Daniel Moore and stalked Zoe and her sister, Andrea, for over a month. When Zoe left to investigate a case in Texas, Glover struck. It was pure luck that Andrea managed to escape unharmed. Glover was shot in the process and hunkered in his dank apartment, recuperating. The forensic team estimated Glover nearly died but managed to stop the bleeding. And once he could stand on his feet, he ran.

There was more. Glover was dying. Not from a bullet, but something much more mundane. He had a terminal brain tumor, and that made him more dangerous than ever. A dying beast had nothing left to lose.

She turned to O'Donnell. The detective stood on the far side of the room, her dark eyes following the photographer. He half knelt as he took a series of shots of the bloody footsteps.

"Can I see the photos of the body?" Zoe asked Detective O'Donnell.

O'Donnell frowned, contemplating it for several seconds, as if the request was unreasonable. Finally, she asked the photographer to show them the images.

He stood up, straightening his wide-framed glasses with a thin finger. He then began fiddling with his camera, frowning as he scrolled through the images.

Tatum stepped into the living room. "There are some bloodstains in her bedroom." He pointed at the doorway over his shoulder. "More footprints and some bloody finger smears on her night table and on the wall."

"Fingerprints?" Zoe asked.

"I don't think so, not anything I could see with my naked eye—just smears. The forensic guy in the room said it looks like whoever left them wore gloves."

"Gloves indicate planning, but this mess looks like a complete blunder," Zoe said.

"There are also bloodstains on the bathroom sink and floor."

"He washed himself there?"

"Looks like it."

Zoe was trying to imagine the events unfolding, when the photographer said, "There we go." He walked over to them and showed them the screen on the back of the camera.

For a second Zoe had difficulty understanding what she was looking at. "Is that the body?" she asked. "Was it covered?"

"Yeah," O'Donnell answered behind her. "She was covered in a blanket."

"Who found the victim?" Tatum asked.

"Her father, Albert Lamb," O'Donnell said.

"Was he the one who covered her?"

"He said he didn't, that he found her that way," O'Donnell answered. "And the evidence corroborates it. See those stains on the blanket?"

The photographer flipped through the images, finding a close-up of two large brown spots.

"Bloodstains." O'Donnell pointed. "She was covered when the blood was still fresh. But the body was in advanced rigor mortis when we got here and the blood dry. She's been dead for a while. Whoever covered her did it soon after she died."

Did O'Donnell contemplate the alternative? The father could be the killer. He might have covered her body and called the police hours later.

"So he found her covered and just left her like that?" Tatum asked in disbelief.

"No. He took the cover off, saw she was dead and stiff. He still tried to wake her up, according to his initial statement. Then he covered her again and called nine-one-one."

The photographer scrolled through a few more shots of the covered body from various angles. Then he paused. The image on-screen displayed the body without the cover.

It was easy to see why the father had covered her again.

The woman's body was folded, her knees bent backward, her skirt pulled down to her ankles. Her shirt was torn, her left breast exposed. She wore no underpants. Even if the father had wanted to protect his daughter's modesty, he would have found it hard to pull up the skirt, the way the legs were bent.

Zoe glanced at the torn bra that lay on the floor, marked with an evidence marker. "Did you find her underpants?"

"Not yet. We're still looking through the trash."

"If they weren't here, you probably won't find them," Zoe said. "He took them. It's a trophy."

She examined the picture closely. The body's arm was covered in blood, and the woman's face was spattered as well, clumps of her hair clinging to her bloody cheek. Blood was smeared on her left leg, but it looked like it didn't originate from a wound. At a certain point, the victim's leg had probably brushed against the blood on the floor. Bruises marred the woman's neck—possibly ligature marks, but it was hard to be sure on the small screen, particularly in that wide angle.

The photographer kept scrolling through the pictures, speeding the pace, as if he found it hard to look at them, which Zoe found strange. He had taken the pictures himself.

"Wait," she said. "Go back one."

He scrolled one picture back. It was a close-up of the marks on her neck. They really did look like ligature marks, but Zoe still wasn't entirely sure. What had caught her attention was a delicate silver strand on the woman's neck.

"Did she wear jewelry?" she asked.

"A silver necklace with a cross. Her father said she wore it all the time," O'Donnell answered.

"Why didn't he take *that* as a trophy?" Zoe muttered.

"Maybe he's not into jewelry," Tatum suggested.

Zoe nodded. It was possible, though serial killers who took trophies usually took jewelry. Especially if, like in this case, she was strangled, and the necklace was on her neck. Surely the killer would have noticed it. Could he have used it to strangle the girl? She examined the image closely. It didn't seem likely. The necklace would have snapped. It was much too delicate.

"You said there were finger smudges on her night table," Zoe told Tatum. "Any jewelry there?"

"I don't know."

"There was a jewelry box there," O'Donnell said. "With two bracelets."

"Two bracelets and a necklace," Zoe asserted. "The killer probably searched through her stuff, got the necklace, and put it around her neck after she died."

"I doubt it," O'Donnell said. "Her father said she always wore it. Much more likely that the killer was simply looking for anything valuable he could take. The bracelets were cheap trinkets, so he left them. We'll ask the father if she had any valuable jewelry."

Zoe felt a flash of irritation, but she didn't argue the point. She kept looking as the photographer scrolled through the rest of the images, perhaps observing Glover's handiwork again for the first time in a while.

When she and Tatum had found Glover's alias, they'd traced his steps. They already knew he'd lived in Chicago for the past few years. They found his old apartment in McKinley Park, where a couple of students now stayed. They also traced his old job as a support technician, a position he'd lost six months before. They spent a few days just talking to his old coworkers and managers, trying to glean any piece of information. Most of his coworkers said he was a great guy. Always happy to help, quick with a joke or a laugh. His manager had actually used the phrase *full of teamwork spirit*.

Two of his female coworkers had thought there was something creepy about him. But they couldn't put their finger on the reason.

Zoe knew the feeling. She'd experienced it herself when she was fourteen years old, and Rod Glover was her neighbor. At first he seemed like a nice guy, charming and funny. Then, strange, unsettling behavior patterns began to emerge. And around that time, young women began to die.

"That's the last one," the photographer said, lowering his camera.

"Any signs of the weapon?" Tatum asked, turning to face O'Donnell.

"Well," O'Donnell answered. "I'm assuming there were two weapons. The marks on her neck look like ligature marks, so he used some kind of rope or a belt. And the bleeding came from an ugly cut on her arm. So some sort of blade was involved as well. Also, her shirt looks like it was partly cut with a blade. But we found nothing that fits either of those." She pointed at the footprints. "It looks like the killer crossed the room to pick something up from the floor. See how the prints stop just before the wall? I'm betting he stopped to crouch there."

Zoe's opinion of the detective improved slightly. "You think it was the knife?"

"I'm almost sure it was. If you go over there, you'll see a few drops of blood, just by evidence marker sixteen. I think they came from the blade."

Zoe stepped over to the corner of the room and crouched to look at the floor. There they were. Several perfectly round brown stains. Tatum crouched beside her.

"Vertical blood drops," he said. "That's why they're circular and not elliptical. That means it couldn't have been spattered from the other side of the room. It's likely that the weapon was dropped here."

Zoe nodded, trying to imagine it. "He could have walked here, knife in hand. Then stopped for a few seconds. That would account for the drops as well."

"I'm not a forensic expert," Tatum said carefully. "But see how there's no spatter pattern around the drops? If they had dropped from the height of one or two feet, you'd see a small circular spatter around each drop. There's none, meaning the blood dropped from the height of just a few inches. I think Detective O'Donnell is right. The weapon lay here, dripping blood, and the killer crouched to pick it up."

Zoe agreed. It was the simplest explanation. She imagined it. The killer attacked the victim, threatening her with the knife. During the struggle, the knife cut the victim's arm. Then what? Had the victim managed somehow to disarm the killer, throwing the knife to the corner? Maybe.

She straightened and tried to think. There were conflicting behavior patterns in the entire scene. Stepping in the blood, covering the body, leaving blood smears all over the apartment. That all reeked of confusion, fear, maybe shame. But wearing gloves spoke of planning. The missing underwear was a trophy. The necklace fit nowhere. Had the death been accidental? It was impossible to guess; Zoe wasn't even sure if the victim died of blood loss or asphyxia.

Usually she could picture the possible scenarios in her mind quite easily. But here, the different details didn't mesh well.

They were missing something.

CHAPTER 4

Tatum scanned the room again, trying to get a feel for the victim.

In a way, it was his comfort zone. He'd seen Zoe slip into the mind of a killer, as easy as if she were putting on a sweater, and it never ceased to impress and slightly unnerve him. It wasn't the same for Tatum. Sure, he knew the statistics; he read endless research papers and serial killer interview transcripts, had studied serial killer profiles until he dreamed about them almost nightly. But to use his own sweater analogy, for him slipping into the mind of a killer was like putting on a straitjacket two sizes too small. It was uncomfortable, almost impossible to do and left him aching and exhausted.

But a lot of their work revolved around knowing the victim. Understanding the victim's routine indicated what attracted the killer to them. Figuring out how the victim reacted when attacked also helped, and that often had significant implications about the killer's psyche. Some killers became more violent when facing a meek victim, while others became deadly only when the victim struggled. Know the victim, and you were already halfway to understanding the killer.

Catherine Lamb had been distracted, perhaps depressed. There were signs of recent neglect throughout the house—unwatered plants, dusty windowsills, an overflowing laundry basket. Sure, this could also mean she was a slob, but there were endless indications that she wasn't. Her clothing was folded neatly; the bathroom, aside from the recent bloodstains, was clean; the food in the fridge was fresh. The mess and neglect were superficial, recent, a thin layer of unhappiness.

Had she been lonely? She might have been dating, perhaps online. If she'd been extra careless, she might have agreed to an offer to pick her up for a date. That would account for the lack of forced entry marks. But no, that didn't match the torn clothing he'd seen in the images. Catherine hadn't intended to leave home when she was attacked.

He glanced at Zoe, was about to mention the clothing, but she was biting her lip, frowning. It was her do-not-disturb mode: she was thinking something through.

O'Donnell was looking at Zoe too. The detective was blonde, her wavy hair cut just above the shoulders, and she was dressed in gray pants and a dark-blue coat. Her chocolaty-brown eyes were narrowed in suspicion. Tatum loved chocolate and was partial to exotic tastes—salty chocolate, spicy chocolate—but he'd never seen suspicious chocolate before. She tilted her head to the left, as she'd done earlier when she'd met them outside.

O'Donnell looked like a jaded spectator at a magic show. As if she wanted them to pull a rabbit out of the hat, just so she could say it had been there all along, that they'd hidden it in their sleeve. Come see Tatum Gray, the magical profiler. Pick a card, any card. Your card is . . . the Jack of Spades, unemployed, probably white, aged twenty to twenty-five, and he wet his bed and tortured kittens as a child.

She caught him looking at her and said, "So? Do you think it's your guy?"

"It's too early to say," Tatum answered reflexively.

Her eyebrows arched. "Do you see anything in common with his other victims? Does she look similar? Did he take trophies from the other murders? Did he cover the other bodies?"

"Rod Glover didn't cover the other bodies," Tatum admitted. "But there are similarities—"

"So why did he cover this one?"

"There could be several reasons." Tatum shrugged. "Some serial killers cover their targets when they're ashamed. It's also a form of abstraction—turning your victim into an object."

"He covered her for the same reason he put the necklace around her neck." Zoe turned to face them. "He knew her."

O'Donnell folded her arms. She seemed about to say something, when the officer from outside called, "Detective O'Donnell!"

"Excuse me," O'Donnell said and strode outside.

Tatum took another glance at the scene and followed her. A man stood outside, on the other side of the crime scene tape, his eyes bloodshot, his hair disheveled. Tatum estimated he was about sixty, but he looked ninety, his body stooped, hands trembling. Tatum knew this look; he'd seen it many times before. This was a man who'd been pulverized by grief. He was probably Albert Lamb, Catherine's father, who'd found her earlier. He held a small plastic bag.

"Mr. Lamb." O'Donnell's tone transformed, the steely edge from before gone. "I'm sorry, but you still can't—"

"I brought her some clothes," Mr. Lamb said, his voice hoarse. "To dress her. I had some of her clothing at home, and I thought—"

"Mr. Lamb, this isn't necessary right now. Later, you can give her clothes to the funeral home, and they—"

"But her clothes were torn!" Tears were running down the man's cheeks. "She wouldn't want . . . she needs . . . please, the shirt has buttons—it will be easy to put it on her. I can do it myself, and then I'll leave. Just let me in for one minute . . ." He crouched, about to pass under the tape. The officer with the logbook seemed poised to grab him, but O'Donnell stepped forward instead and put her hand on Mr. Lamb's shoulder, as if helping him through, but also effectively stopping him from moving inside the house.

"Your daughter's body isn't here anymore. They took her to the morgue," she said. "And they will perform an autopsy. After the autopsy, her body will be released to the funeral home, and you can give them the outfit to dress her."

He gazed down at his bag helplessly as a tear dropped from his chin to the ground.

"Do you want me to take this to the morgue?" O'Donnell asked. "I can tell them."

Tell them what? Tatum wondered, but he could see the relief in the man's face. He'd heard what he'd wanted to hear, took comfort in the detective's authority and businesslike manner.

"Yes, thank you," he whispered.

"Mr. Lamb, do you think *now* you will be able to answer a few more questions?"

"Yes. I . . . I am sorry about before. I just couldn't . . . couldn't . . ."

"It's quite all right, sir." O'Donnell flipped a page in her notebook. "Can you please tell me—"

"Is that the other detective?" The man gestured at Tatum.

O'Donnell glanced back. "What other detective?"

"Shouldn't there be two detectives? Don't you investigate in pairs?"

"Yes, we do." O'Donnell seemed momentarily taken aback.

There was some sort of issue there. O'Donnell's partner obviously wasn't around, and she didn't want to tell the man that. Perhaps she wanted to avoid the way it would look—as if the police only sent one detective for Catherine Lamb's death. He stepped forward. "I'm Tatum Gray. I'm working with Detective O'Donnell."

Mr. Lamb nodded, distracted. Tatum met O'Donnell's eyes as she frowned at him again—apparently all he could get from the detective were frowns.

She turned back to the broken man. "Can you tell me again what happened this morning?"

"I called Cathy . . . Catherine. She was sick yesterday. She's been sick a lot lately, so I was worried. She didn't answer her phone. I called several times, and she didn't answer. So I came over. I thought maybe she needed help."

"What time was that?"

"Time . . . I don't know."

"When did you call her first?"

"Around eight."

"And how long until you decided to check up on her?"

"Half an hour, I think."

"Right after your last phone call?"

"Yes . . . no. I called her twice on the way."

"So you left around eight thirty, called twice more on your way. And what time did you arrive here?"

"It's a fifteen-minute walk. It must have been around quarter to nine."

O'Donnell nodded, writing it down in her notebook. "You knocked?"

"Several times, and she didn't answer, so I tried the door. And it was unlocked."

"Is it unusual for Catherine to leave her door unlocked?"

"Yes. She always locks her door."

"Go on."

"I came in. It was messy, and there was a blanket on the floor. With stains. And her . . . I could see her hand peeking out from under the blanket."

"Mr. Lamb, are you sure the blanket was on her when you came inside?"

"Yes!" His voice rose, cracking. "It was on her. I pulled the blanket away, and she . . . she was cold, and her clothes were torn. Blood and bruises all over her body. I called her name, and I shook her. She was stiff." The man's eyes turned distant as he recounted the nightmarish moments. "I dialed nine-one-one."

"And then what did you do?"

"They said they're coming. And her clothes were torn. So I . . . I covered her again. And then I got out of the house. I had to get out of the house. I couldn't stay there. I waited outside until the police arrived."

"She had a necklace on when we got here. A silver necklace with a cross. Was it on her throat when you found her?"

"Yes. She almost always wore that necklace."

She kept asking him about his actions, going through the details carefully, while Tatum listened. Albert's demeanor was confused and distraught. O'Donnell had to repeat some of her questions several times until he answered them. Tatum found himself hoping O'Donnell would cut him loose. At some point Zoe came out of the house and stood by Tatum's side, listening.

"Can you think of anyone who'd want to hurt Catherine?" O'Donnell asked.

"No! Everyone loved her."

"Anyone she had an argument with? Anything out of the ordinary?"

A fragment of hesitation before he said, "No."

O'Donnell tilted her head slightly. "You mentioned Catherine had been sick this past week."

"Yes, she missed work."

"Where does she work?"

"She works as the administrator in my church."

"In *your* church? Are you a pastor?"

"That's right, at Riverside Baptist Church."

O'Donnell paused for a second to jot that down, and, Tatum guessed, to adjust her view of the case accordingly. He wasn't particularly attuned to Chicago's internal politics, but he assumed that a murdered pastor's daughter, who herself worked in the church, would be a high-profile case, in the eyes of both the media and of officials.

"So she called in sick recently," O'Donnell said. "How many times?"

"Two . . . no, three times in the past week. But . . . she missed some workdays before that."

"Did she say what was wrong?"

"No."

"Did she seem sick to you?"

"Yes. She was tired all the time. Cathy is such an energetic and happy woman, and in the past month . . ." His voice dissipated. The present tense hung in the air, invisible but razor sharp. After a second he cleared his throat. "She missed some of her volunteer work as well."

"Mr. Lamb," O'Donnell said. "You mentioned she seemed tired. Did she look sick? Complain about any pains? About a fever? Did she have a runny nose? Anything at all?"

"No, nothing like that. She said she had lady problems."

"Is it possible that something troubled her? That her problems were personal and not physical?"

"She would never skip work, not for something like that." His eyes shimmered, wet and desperate. "The church and her volunteer work were everything to her."

"Where did she volunteer?"

"In the church. As a religious counselor. Our church has two religious counselors, and she was one of them."

"A religious counselor to whom?"

"Anyone in need."

"Who did she advise regularly, Mr. Lamb?"

"All sorts. Troubled youths, poor families, people who were losing their way or their faith . . ." His speech slowed down, sounding like a man who was suddenly trying to think faster than he spoke. "Just people in need."

O'Donnell's eyes narrowed. She probably noticed Lamb's behavior as well.

"Troubled people," she said. "Women. And men."

27

"Yes," Mr. Lamb answered.

"People who were trying to mend their ways?" Tatum suggested.

"Yes, exactly."

"Ex-convicts?" Tatum asked.

A long silence.

"Was Catherine a counselor to former convicts?" O'Donnell asked, exchanging a quick look with Tatum.

"Some. You need to understand. These people would do anything for Catherine. They would never . . . not this."

"I understand," O'Donnell said.

She moved away from the topic, as if it no longer interested her, but the rest of her questions were just fluff, stuff that would lower the pastor's guard. When, by the end of the interview, she asked for a few contacts, he gave her the details easily. Including the second religious counselor.

Finally, O'Donnell had gotten all she needed, and the pastor left, his body stooped, drained by the worst day in his life.

"Well, you said the person who killed Catherine knew her," O'Donnell said.

"That's what I think," Zoe said.

"If he's a former convict from her church, he's not your guy, right?"

"Rod Glover has never been incarcerated."

"Fine." Finality entered her tone. "I'll keep you posted."

"The autopsy," Tatum said. "When will it be?"

"Probably first thing tomorrow morning."

"Can we be present? Once we have the autopsy report, we'll be out of your hair."

There was that frown and head tilt again, but she finally nodded. "Fine. Give me your number. I'll update you once I know the time."

CHAPTER 5

Sunday, October 16, 2016

Zoe and Tatum waited outside the morgue. The medical examiner, a middle-aged woman named Dr. Terrel, wasn't thrilled to perform the autopsy with three people watching her. "It's crowded enough here," she'd said, gesturing at the rows of body coolers behind her. Zoe had a feeling it wasn't the first time she'd used that joke. They'd used the time to grab some breakfast in a nearby café, reading the sparsely detailed news articles about the murder. They returned two hours later only to find out the autopsy wasn't over yet.

Zoe had already lost interest in the case. The homicide of Catherine Lamb in Glover's previous neighborhood began to feel like a coincidence and nothing more. There was too much deviance from Glover's usual MO and signature.

Glover attacked women outdoors, usually near a body of water, in relatively remote locations, where witnesses weren't likely. The last time Glover had attacked someone indoors was a month before, when he'd assaulted Andrea, Zoe's sister. The consequences for him had been nearly fatal, and Zoe found it unlikely that he would do it again.

The covering of the victim's body was also not typical of him. In all of his assaults, Glover showed a complete lack of interest in the victim's body once he was done. She saw no reason for this case to be any different.

No. Zoe's estimate was that Catherine Lamb had been attacked by someone she knew. The gloves the murderer used indicated the death probably wasn't accidental—he had planned to rape and kill her. But after the murder he'd had a moment of regret. He'd been confused, stepping in the blood, leaving his footprints behind. He'd covered the body to alleviate the guilt. Zoe wasn't sure regarding the necklace—perhaps O'Donnell was right, and it had been there from the start, ignored by the killer.

Then why take the woman's underwear? That niggled at her. Taking a trophy didn't feel like an act of guilt.

It didn't matter. Maybe he'd shoved the underwear into his pocket after tearing them. Every murder had its little anomalies.

She checked her watch impatiently. They were wasting precious time. This investigation couldn't be indefinite. Mancuso, the unit chief, had agreed to give Zoe and Tatum ten days in Chicago, tracing Rod Glover's steps, and their time was almost up. They had two more days, and there were still a few leads Zoe wanted to follow up on before they gave up. Every minute they waited here to hear the results of an unrelated autopsy was a minute they could—

The morgue door opened. Detective O'Donnell stood in the doorway, beckoning them in. She seemed pale, though perhaps that could be attributed to the white fluorescent light.

Zoe entered the room, her breathing already shallow, anticipating the typical stench of death intermingled with chemicals. Catherine Lamb's body lay on the table, a large Y-shaped scar over her torso. It was the first time Zoe had actually seen Catherine's body with her own eyes. Now that she could examine the lacerations on the neck up close, a chill ran up her spine. Glover's victims all had marks just like these.

"I've concluded the autopsy, and I have a few findings that I already shared with Detective O'Donnell," Dr. Terrel said. "The preliminary report will be ready tomorrow, but O'Donnell wanted me to tell you what I found."

"Thank you—we appreciate it," Tatum said.

Terrel nodded curtly. "The body was in full rigor mortis when I first checked it. Typically that means the victim died between twelve and twenty-four hours before, but it could be less than that in certain cases, especially if the victim's muscle activity was severe before death."

"For instance, if the victim struggled," Tatum said.

"Exactly. However, I did find something interesting when examining the lividity marks."

Lividity was the dark bruises that appeared on the body's skin after death. This was caused by the stagnant blood settling in the body, following the only force that kept working on it even after the victim's death—gravity.

"There are pronounced lividity marks on the victim's left side." Terrel pointed at dark bruises on Catherine's left arm and thigh. "But if you look carefully at the victim's right side, you'll see the faint lividity marks there as well."

"The body was moved after death," Zoe said. "Someone turned it to the other side."

"It was found lying on its right side," O'Donnell said. "I'm assuming that means it was moved a significant amount of time after death, when lividity was almost complete."

"So you think it was the father who moved it," Tatum said.

Zoe nodded. It made sense. Albert Lamb had found Catherine. According to his own statement, he'd shaken her, trying to wake her up, not realizing he'd turned her around in the process. If that was really what had happened, it gave them a likely timeline of death, since they knew when Albert Lamb had found the body.

It was interesting. The most basic instruction at a crime scene was to disturb nothing until the police processed it. But in this case, because of the manner in which Albert had moved his daughter's body, they had a more accurate timeline than before.

"It's impossible for me to know if it was first on the left side or on the right side," Terrel said. "And it's possible she was on the right side, turned to the left after a few hours, then turned back to the right when lividity was complete."

"Can you estimate how long she was lying on her left side?" Tatum asked.

"I estimate eight to ten hours."

In that case, if the scenario O'Donnell suggested was correct, Catherine Lamb was murdered between eleven p.m. and one a.m.

"I found signs of very recent sexual intercourse and abrasions on the labia minora. While that doesn't necessarily mean the victim was raped, these injuries aren't likely with consensual intercourse."

Neither were torn and shredded clothing and missing underpants. Dr. Terrel's job was to be as accurate as possible, but Zoe had no doubt regarding Catherine's rape.

"There are bruises on the face, the arms, the knees, and the left breast. None broke the skin. The cause of death is asphyxia. The marks on her throat correspond with ligature strangulation. The horizontal angle makes it clear that the strangulation wasn't caused by hanging, which makes it most likely the death was a homicide. The ligature marks are wide and shallow and left no abrasions or bruises. This makes me think that a wide and smooth device, such as a belt, was used."

Or a tie. Zoe couldn't suppress the thought any more than she could stop her heart from pounding. Rod Glover had used ties to murder his victims. The ligature marks they left were exactly the same as Terrel had described.

"I found no grooves or scratches on her neck corresponding to the necklace that was on the body when it got here." Terrel raised her eyes from the body. "I can't be sure, but I don't think she wore the necklace when she was murdered."

O'Donnell's eyes met Zoe's for a fraction of a second.

"What can you tell us about the knife wound?" Tatum asked.

"For one, I can tell you it wasn't a knife wound at all." Terrel circled the body and gestured at the wound on the arm. "If you look closely, you'll see three wounds, not one. Two small puncture wounds and a third, larger wound. These wounds were caused by a needle. There's bruising on her wrist, here, indicating that it was gripped hard. This is probably because he gripped her while inserting the needle."

"The victim was injected with something?" Tatum asked.

"I can't know for sure until I get the toxicology reports, but it's likely. However, this was a thick needle. The diameter is between 0.06 and 0.07 inches. That means it was a sixteen- or fifteen-gauge needle. Usually, when administering injections, thinner needles are used. This needle size is more typical for blood donations. Also, I don't understand why he kept jabbing the needle into her."

Tatum frowned. "It's possible that he simply doesn't know anything about needles."

Terrel nodded. "That's true. Look here—do you see this bruise?" She pointed at an extensive purple bruise around the largest wound. "This was probably caused by blood vessels rupturing during the injection."

Zoe bent to look at it. The shape and size of the bruise made her think of something else entirely. "Isn't the bruise too big to be caused by the needle?" she asked.

"It really depends. The large wound indicates the needle moved quite roughly," Terrel said, but Zoe thought she could hear the slight hesitation in the doctor's voice.

"What if the bruise was caused by suction?" Zoe asked.

Terrel scrutinized the bruise. "I suppose it's possible."

Detective O'Donnell seemed to catch on. "You think this is a hickey?"

"The needle mark was irregularly wide for an injection, like the doctor said," Zoe pointed out. "He might have been trying to draw blood from her for personal consumption. And when he saw it spilling, he couldn't help himself."

Tatum, O'Donnell, and Terrel all looked at her with varying degrees of disgust and astonishment. Zoe ignored their incredulity. Blood drinking was not unheard of and had happened multiple times with sexual predators and serial killers in the past.

"If that's what happened, it explains the wounds," Terrel said. "The first two puncture wounds sank into her muscles. He couldn't get to her vein. The third time, he hit the basilic vein, but he accidentally tore it. Perhaps the victim struggled with him, wrenched her arm away, and this was the result. The blood loss that occurred was the result of this tear. And to make this bruise, he would have sucked at it quite vigorously."

"Any way we can test this?" O'Donnell asked.

Terrel thought about it for a moment. "I can test for saliva remnants with fluorescent spectroscopy."

"Do you think he was experienced at what he did?" Zoe asked. "Or was he just jabbing the needle wherever he saw a vein?"

"It's hard to say, since it looks like she resisted. Even a professional nurse would have found it hard to use a needle in that situation. But a professional would have probably targeted the median cubital vein. This looks like the job of someone who *saw* how to do it, perhaps online, but never tried it himself and was never guided professionally."

Dr. Terrel pointed out some additional minor details, but Zoe was only half listening. In all his murders, Glover had never demonstrated any interest in the victims' blood, never mind consuming it. Like all the previous leads they'd investigated in the past week, this one led to a dead end.

CHAPTER 6

"You were right about the necklace," O'Donnell said as soon as they left the morgue. "He probably *did* put it there after he killed her."

Zoe didn't seem to be particularly thrilled about it. The profiler seemed much more tired than the day before. Well, that made two of them. O'Donnell was exhausted. Part of it was the autopsy. Those always made her feel like she just ran an unpleasant, foul-smelling marathon. But the last day had taken its toll as well.

Door-to-door questioning of the neighbors had resulted in nothing. No one on the street seemed to have heard or seen anything out of the ordinary, and none of them knew Catherine Lamb particularly well. O'Donnell spent a few hours talking to two of Catherine's closest friends. In the past few months they'd been seeing less and less of Catherine. She told them she was busy with her church work. They both said that whenever they met with her, she seemed unusually tired. One of them thought she might have been depressed.

O'Donnell didn't interview Catherine's father again. Her mother, it turned out, had died three years earlier. She'd been the church administrator, and when she'd died, Catherine had taken over, first unofficially, and it had later been made official.

She had a quick conversation with the other religious counselor in the church, a man named Patrick Carpenter. He was still shocked by the news when she talked to him, but he had a crisis of his own—his wife had been hospitalized due to a sudden scare with her pregnancy a week before. He hadn't seen Catherine for a few days but had talked to her briefly on the phone on Friday, several hours before she died. When O'Donnell asked him if Catherine seemed sick or tired lately, he answered that he hadn't noticed anything unusual. O'Donnell asked him for a list of the people they'd counseled, at which point the conversation became chilly. He refused to give her any names outright and finally agreed, quite reluctantly, to talk about it on the following day.

"Let me buy you two a drink," O'Donnell now offered.

"Thanks," Tatum said. "But we should really—"

"It will only take a moment." O'Donnell walked over to the vending machine across the hall. She swiped her card and bought a Coke for herself. She pulled the tab, the satisfying hiss already promising sugary goodness. She took a long swig that helped settle her nausea and headache. Then she turned to Zoe and Tatum, who were looking at her, bemused. "What's your poison? I need some sugar after an autopsy."

They both asked for Cokes as well. For a few seconds, the three of them sipped silently from the cans outside the morgue. This was great advertising material. "Coca-Cola, a fresh taste after seeing a brain being scooped out of a skull."

Maybe it needed a copywriter for a better catchphrase.

Her phone rang. It was Kyle.

"Yeah." She answered the phone in a tone meant to clarify to her husband that now was not the time to talk.

"Mommy?"

O'Donnell immediately softened. "Hey, baby," she said. "I can't really talk right now. Is everything okay?"

"No." Nellie sounded close to tears. "It's an emergency."

Nellie was five years old, but she already knew what an emergency was. Because she was only allowed to call her mother in case of an emergency. So an emergency meant any situation that warranted calling Mom.

O'Donnell sighed. "What is it, baby?"

"Daddy can't find my purple pants. And I need those pants for Anna's tea party, I *told* you I need them, and *you* said that you will wash them and that I could wear them, so Daddy said I have to wear my black pants, but I *can't*."

In the background, Kyle, her husband, shouted, "Nellie, don't bother Mommy—those are perfectly good pants. Come here. Nellie, don't . . ." His voice suddenly disappeared.

"Nellie?" O'Donnell said. "Are you there?"

"Yes. I locked myself in the bathroom."

O'Donnell sighed. "Tell Daddy they're on the laundry couch." The laundry couch was just a regular couch in the living room, but since it was constantly covered in laundry, no one actually sat on it, ever.

"Daddy already looked on the laundry couch. He made a mess." Nellie sounded pleased at the opportunity to snitch on her dad.

"It's in the third pile from the left, under the white shirts."

"Daddy!" Nellie screeched, presumably through the locked bathroom door. "The purple pants are on the laundry couch under the white shirts in the third pile."

Even though it wasn't perfect timing, O'Donnell still felt a strange joy at hearing Nellie say *purple*. She always said it a bit slow, as if struggling to get the syllables right. It was the sweetest thing.

"I already searched there." Kyle's voice was muffled and frustrated.

"Look again!" Nellie screamed.

O'Donnell glanced at Tatum and Zoe. "One more second," she told them.

"He found it," Nellie reported. "Thanks, Mommy."

"Bye, baby. Have fun."

Nellie hung up, and O'Donnell pocketed her phone.

"I talked to Martinez yesterday," she told the two feds. "Well, yelled at him, really. He had no place telling you about the murder without talking to me first."

"We didn't mean to overstep any boundaries," Tatum said.

"You didn't care about overstepping them either," O'Donnell retorted. "Never mind. Martinez said you're both a pain in the ass."

"We have a complicated relationship," Tatum explained.

"But he also said you two know what you're doing. And I could really use your opinion on this one. I've investigated two sexual homicides before. One was the ex-boyfriend; one was a rape that got out of hand. These are cases I can wrap my head around. But I never had a case where the murderer drank the victim's blood. Or took the time to put some nice jewelry on her before leaving. Martinez said if you could profile this murder for me—"

"We're currently on a different case," Zoe said.

"Your Rod Glover case—you told me. What if it's the same guy?"

"That's not likely."

"Why not?"

"This murder seems to diverge significantly from Glover's—"

O'Donnell's phone rang again. "Hold that thought." She pulled out her phone in annoyance. But it was Larsen, from Forensics. He was the one in charge of Catherine Lamb's murder scene. She answered the call. "O'Donnell."

"I've got something for you," Larsen said.

O'Donnell waited. Larsen waited too. He was the kind of guy who wanted you to play second fiddle to his tune. She sighed. "What did you find?"

"We went over the shoe prints that we got from the scene." Yesterday he'd told her they'd gotten both the left and right shoe prints of the murderer—a size 9. Larsen had told her he could easily match the shoe to the print, if she ever managed to find the shoe. It would be a good thing to have in court. "We took a bunch of them, in the different rooms. So I was filing them today, and one seemed different. It was only a partial print that we got in the bathroom. But it looked like a different shoe. One that definitely didn't belong to the victim. And since you made sure everyone put their shoe condoms on, it wasn't ours either."

"The father entered the scene before us," O'Donnell pointed out. "Maybe he went to the bathroom." She could imagine him running to the bathroom to throw up. It wouldn't be unusual for him not to mention it.

"The father is a size 7.5. The print we got is an 8.5. So we went through everything we had again, and guess what?"

Did she really have to guess? She decided not to. "What?"

"Those bloody finger smudges we found everywhere at the scene? Definitely belong to two different pairs of hands. I sent them over to an expert in fingerprinting, and he verified it. Even though the hands were gloved, there's a list of characteristics that can identify hands beyond fingerprints, and there were some key differences."

"So we have *two* unknown people in the victim's house after the murder. Both male?"

"Almost definitely male, according to shoe size and hand structure. And that's not all . . ."

There was that pause again. "What else?" O'Donnell asked.

"I got the idea to look outside more carefully, you know? If two men were at the door, maybe there'd be some indication. We found another footprint that matches the 8.5 shoe outside in the yard. And we have another handprint on the doorframe. Don't get excited, no fingerprints, but the handprint matches the same characteristics of the *second* individual."

"Got it. Anything else?"

"That's all."

"Keep me posted," she said, and knowing he expected it, she added, "Fantastic work, Larsen." Hanging up, she turned to face the feds.

Zoe had morphed. Instead of the tired, dejected person who had been there before, she was now tense and eager. "There were two men at the scene?" she asked.

"Looks like it," O'Donnell said carefully.

"That would explain the inconsistencies." Zoe glanced at Tatum. "If Glover paired up with someone else—"

"Someone less experienced," Tatum said. "Maybe easily manipulated."

"Subject to certain fantasies that Glover could accommodate," Zoe said. "This guy probably already fantasized about Catherine. That's why they targeted her specifically. It's someone who knows her."

"And he probably got her to open the door," Tatum said.

"He acts first—they agreed about it beforehand. Maybe he didn't even know Glover would kill her, but Glover knew."

"Then Glover kills her. His partner in crime feels guilty about it. He covers her. Finds her necklace and puts it on her."

"And Glover keeps his trophy."

O'Donnell watched them, caught in their own private dynamic, and felt a spark of jealousy. She'd been there before, with her first partner. She and Jim had been paired when she'd become a homicide detective. They'd been partners for fourteen months. She hadn't known how lucky she was. She assumed the relationship they had—this seamlessness—was something that always happened, a part of the job. But then Jim was promoted and transferred, and she was paired with Manny Shea. And what a mess that was. With Manny, she either had to become dirty or turn a blind eye. And when Manny's shady dealings finally collapsed, she paid the price. And of course, now she had no one.

Watching Tatum and Zoe complete each other's sentences, exchanging looks that held messages she couldn't read, was like being a child again, seeing the other kids playing in the schoolyard while she stood alone.

"I don't want to rain on your parade," O'Donnell said, though she did. "But there's no evidence your guy Glover is involved in this. And I don't want you getting any preconceived notions about the case and messing it up."

40

"You're right," Tatum said quickly. "But we would be glad to help."

"I don't need you to profile this murderer and tell me it definitely sounds like your guy," O'Donnell said skeptically. She'd wanted their help, but their agenda was glaringly obvious.

"We can start by profiling the second one," Zoe said. "The man who consumed the victim's blood. He's probably the same one who covered her."

"You can't be sure of that," O'Donnell said.

Zoe caught O'Donnell's gaze, the profiler's eyes reminding O'Donnell of a cat's stare just before it pounced. "We can help."

And frankly, O'Donnell was happy for all the help she could get.

CHAPTER 7

The man in control didn't like to sleep. Not lately, anyway, not ever since he'd stopped taking his medication.

Before that, it wasn't even a question he could contemplate. The various pills he took would knock him out for ten, twelve, sometimes fourteen hours a day, easy. A deep sleep that felt like he was submerged in wet cement. Dreamless, as far as he was concerned. He knew everyone dreamed, but what did it matter, if he couldn't remember it?

But now, off his medication for almost a week, he slept less and less.

He could remember his dreams now. It was like standing in a tempest of fear, anger, and lust. He'd wake up, his blankets twisted into strange shapes, sometimes crushed between his fists as if he'd throttled the bedsheet in his sleep.

When he slept, he lost control. And he knew it was the most important thing right now. Control. He'd lost control before in his life, and it had always ended terribly. Never again.

Control, he knew, wasn't an actual *thing* that you had. It was more like an outfit, something you put on. A disguise for other people to see. As long as you acted as if you were in control, you *were* in control. They said *a wolf in sheep's clothing* as if it was a bad thing. But wasn't it what everyone wanted? For you to be one of the sheep?

He got out of bed—short naps during the day were mostly dreamless and helped him stay awake at night. He glanced at his reflection in the mirror. There was a stain on his shirt. People in control didn't wear dirty clothes. He changed shirts, combed his hair. Smiled at the reflection politely, and the reflection smiled back.

Less teeth next time. A man in control didn't bare his teeth like that. He smiled with his lips.

He imagined himself buttoning the buttons of his control suit, took a deep breath, and got out of the bedroom. The guest room's door was shut. He hesitated, almost knocked, then decided to go to the kitchen instead.

He made himself a cup of coffee—coffee was his new friend, now that he'd left sleep behind. Maybe he should make himself a sandwich. He opened the fridge and scanned the shelves for the cream cheese he'd bought last Friday.

The five vials, full of crimson blood, immediately caught his eye. He'd managed to collect them from *her* before Daniel took her. His mouth watered, just seeing the vials. He remembered the metallic salty taste, so invigorating, so different from animal blood, so full of life. Couldn't he afford to drink just one? Not even the entire vial. Just a small sip to feel better.

Control. Those vials weren't for him.

He found the cream cheese and shut the fridge. A good sandwich and some more coffee could make him feel just fine. It wasn't like he even needed the blood. He was much better now.

It had been different just three days ago. He was sick as a dog back then. Headaches, sore throat, nausea, rapid heartbeats. The doctor said he was fine, but Google had told him different. Sepsis or a heart disease, he was almost certain. Not that the doctors cared. Like Daniel said, in this country, if you didn't have a million-dollar health insurance plan, no one gave a shit about you.

It was fine. He'd found out the truth long before. They didn't want anyone to know, of course. But it made total sense when you thought about it. Just a bit of blood from someone else could help almost any malady. It was a way to enrich your own white blood cells, bolster the immunity system. And if the blood was pure, really pure, it was even better.

If only it could have been someone else. But like Daniel had said, you wanted the purest blood possible, right?

Besides, it wasn't just himself he had to worry about.

And it had worked. Ever since that night he'd been feeling fine. Better than fine, really. He was Healthy with a capital *H*. He had to sleep a bit less, the dreams became worse, but that was to be expected. And it wasn't like he had a choice.

He realized he was standing by the open fridge, one of the small vials already in his hand. Funny, he was so lost in thought he'd done it without thinking. He uncorked it, just to smell the contents. Nothing more.

It smelled like Life.

He tipped it gently between his lips. It tasted different cold. Not necessarily worse, but different. And it was fine; he still had four more.

He washed the vial and then went over to the guest room's door, knocking on it.

"Yeah?" Daniel's voice was distracted.

He opened the door. The room was dark, the blinds pulled down. Daniel sat by the desk, the laptop in front of him. The monitor's white ethereal light reflected on Daniel's face, making his sunken features and pale skin look even sicklier than usual.

"I wondered if you wanted anything to eat or drink."

"Nah, thanks, man." Daniel glanced at him and smiled, tired. "You're looking much better."

"I'm feeling better."

"The treatment did the trick, huh?"

That was what Daniel always called it. The treatment. He was the one person who understood.

He licked his lips. "Yeah, it definitely did the trick. Are you sure you don't want—"

"Thanks, there's no need," Daniel said. "You know I can't."

"You'll feel so much better if you try."

"Well, that's not going to happen."

"Okay," the man in control said after a short silence. "Let me know if you change your mind."

"How are you feeling about what we did?" Daniel asked. "Better?"

He swallowed. "We did what we had to, right?"

"It's not our fault," Daniel said. "It's those damn insurance companies, right? If they'd just fund proper health care for people like us."

"Right, right."

"You sure you're all right? Because yesterday you were crying, and you said we should turn ourselves in. You freaked me out, man."

"It was just a momentary loss of control. I'm fine now."

"Uh-huh." Daniel met his eyes.

"I'll, uh, talk to you later." He shut the door and tried to calm his beating heart. If control was a disguise, Daniel was the only one who could see past it.

He suddenly felt exhausted. Forgoing sleep altogether wasn't such a good idea. Maybe he should get a good night's sleep. Just once. Once he slept, he'd have more control. Then he wouldn't give Daniel such a scare like he did the day before.

He went to the bathroom and opened the medicine cabinet. The pills all waited for him there, in little containers, with the days' labels on them. He'd skipped almost a week. Maybe he should take only today's pills and quit the pills after that. He opened the container marked Sunday and pried out one of the pills from the container.

"What are you doing?" The voice startled him, and he nearly dropped it.

He turned around. Daniel stood behind him in the bathroom's entrance.

"I thought I'd take today's pills, get a good night's sleep," he said. "I think yesterday I was just tired, you know?"

"Sure, sure." Daniel nodded. "Maybe that's not such a bad idea."

"You think so?"

"Could be. Sleep's important. You sure, though? Because you told me you hated how those pills made you feel."

"But just one day couldn't hurt."

"And you don't like the feeling in your throat, right? It feels like the pill is scraping the insides of your throat."

That was true. He'd forgotten, but now that Daniel said it, he recalled the ghastly sensation. And he had six pills to take. *Six.*

"I thought you looked better. Like you're in control now," Daniel said. "But maybe it's a good idea to take the pills today. Just to maintain control."

"I *am* in control." He saw the skeptical look on Daniel's face. Acting on a sudden urge, he emptied the entire container into the toilet and flushed it.

Daniel let out a short laugh, and the man in control smiled. It was nice to see his friend laugh.

"You're something else, you know that?" Daniel slapped him on the shoulder and turned away.

He watched Daniel return to his room and nodded to himself. He really didn't need the pills. He was in control.

CHAPTER 8

Zoe stared through the window at the far end of the large room. It was a rainy day, giving the street view a somewhat depressing ambience. Then again, the window faced the Cook County Juvenile Center, and that place wasn't cheerful even when the sun shone and birds twittered in the trees.

She and Tatum had been allocated two desks on the fourth floor of the FBI's Chicago field office as soon as they'd landed in the city. When they'd first arrived, they'd been two outsiders, treated with courtesy and suspicion. There were private jokes she and Tatum weren't privy to. Some of the agents had cryptic nicknames whose origins she didn't care about. On their second day in Chicago, one of the agents had a birthday. She was about to ignore the whole thing when Tatum dragged her along to join the tedious cake-and-greeting-card formality. She found herself standing there, listening to the agent, whose name she had already forgotten, thanking everyone for a gift she hadn't participated in paying for. Twenty precious minutes gone. The cake had been mediocre.

Now, a week later, she was still an outsider. But Tatum wasn't. He knew all the nicknames. Agents joked with him. He seemed to understand a lot of their discussions. One of the analysts was definitely flirting with him.

Obviously none of it mattered. They were going to leave in a few days. And she didn't want to waste her time small-talking about politics, or the weather, or the Chicago Cubs.

But somehow it was a relief that the room was mostly empty on weekends. That for a couple of days, it was just Tatum and her.

She turned back to her work, already annoyed that she'd let her mind wander. Finally, they had a lead. A scent they could chase. She couldn't afford to waste any more time.

First things first, she could use some music. She hesitated, looking at her music library. Taylor, Katy, and Beyoncé all waited for her choice. In a sudden moment of carpe diem, she selected albums from all three. A moment later she added Lizzo's *Big GRRRL Small World* and Adele's *25* to the mix, feeling almost giddy. She set it to shuffle. The first song began playing through her earphones, Katy Perry's "Peacock." She let her head bob with the beat, forcing herself not to sing with the chorus. Tatum was within earshot.

Photos were taped to the low wall of her small cubicle, and she removed them one by one. They were all crime scene photos from Glover's previous murders, and Zoe wanted her improvised office to be free from Glover's influence. O'Donnell had been right when she'd said they had to avoid any preconceived notions about the case. The evidence suggested that two men were involved in Catherine Lamb's murder. Nothing conclusive had been found about their identities yet.

After taking down all the photos, she collected the papers that were strewn on the desk. Most were transcripts—they'd spent a lot of time interviewing people who'd known Glover, most of them coworkers. There were also various documents that pinpointed his whereabouts— three apartment rental contracts, a speeding ticket for Daniel Moore, bank account records under Daniel Moore's name. Zoe kept wondering how Glover had managed to stitch up such a solid fake identity. Someone must have helped him.

But now was not the time to think about it. Fresh case, no assumptions.

Her phone blipped, a notification from her Instagram app. Aside from a brief two-week foray into Facebook and a barely maintained LinkedIn profile, Zoe never bothered with social media before. She did now. Andrea had an Instagram account, and since she'd moved away, Zoe had created her own account just to follow her sister. She never posted anything, had no profile picture, and her profile name was _____ ZBentley. And she followed only Andrea.

Her sister told her it was creepy, though Zoe didn't really understand why.

She tapped the notification, and the app opened, showing Andrea's new post. She'd taken a selfie and captioned it remembering the old days of sleeping in big-sis room. Zoe blinked, recognizing the poster in the background, a close-up of Winona Ryder's face from one of her favorite movies, *Girl, Interrupted*. She'd bought the poster a day after watching the movie, hanging it above her bed. Now the rest of the furniture in the room fell into focus—the familiar desk, the old bed light, the small night table. Andrea smiled in the picture, but her eyes were sad, and she seemed younger, almost a child again. Zoe felt a sudden tug of homesickness.

She almost responded with a bitter comment, mentioning that Andrea could have been sleeping in "big-sis's" apartment right now. But she didn't. Instead, she wrote, Missing you, and added a heart emoji for good measure.

They had hardly talked in the past two weeks. Zoe wasn't sure why. Their few phone calls were stunted and slow, with Andrea trying to find topics for conversation and Zoe struggling not to drop the ball of the conversation completely. Was this because of Glover's attack on Andrea? Did talking to Zoe remind her sister of that night? Or did those conversations actually remind Zoe of how Andrea had almost been raped and murdered because of her?

Maybe a bit of both.

She put down her phone and opened her case folder.

O'Donnell had sent them a digital copy of the current case file, and Zoe had printed the initial report and eight of the crime scene photos. She set them next to each other, two rows of four pictures each. Pictures of Catherine Lamb, covered and uncovered with the blanket. A picture of the bloody footprints. One picture of the bedroom, one of the bathroom, bloodstains on the sink.

It was a savage act, two men breaking into a woman's apartment, raping and murdering her. At first glance, that was all it was, a torrent of violence. Surely that was how Catherine had experienced it.

But looking carefully, she saw it wasn't one act; it was a series of smaller acts. And each of them had been initiated by *one* of the men.

Who chose the victim? Who planned the assault? Who jabbed her with a needle? Each of the acts said something about the attacker. Usually the details of the crime interlocked to create an image of one man. But here, she first had to painstakingly separate the acts into two different groups.

As a child, she'd had a jigsaw puzzle box she loved. The box contained two different puzzles of Mickey Mouse, each a hundred pieces. Golfing Mickey and Skiing Mickey. But the pieces inevitably mixed together in the box. When she began assembling the jigsaw, she always had to sort them into two separate piles before she could really get to work. The pieces had marks on the back so she could tell them apart. *X*s for Skiing Mickey, circles for Golfing Mickey.

In a way, it was similar here. She couldn't profile the killers without knowing each one's role in Catherine's murder. She had to sort them. Unfortunately, there were no marks to tell them apart.

She grabbed her notebook and began to make a list.

Familiarity with victim

Victim choice

Plan

Needle wounds
Rape
Murder by strangulation
Covering victim
Bloody footsteps
Trophy
Necklace

She looked at the list and thought about the two killers and their relationship. There were several cases of murderers working in pairs. Some were romantically involved, working as equals, but she doubted this was the case. There was too much disparity in the actions. No, in this case, one killer was dominant, and the other was a follower. This was a common rapport between violent criminals who worked together. She named the unknown subjects unsub alpha and unsub beta.

The plan had been hatched by alpha. Probably not just the plan, but the whole idea. He was the one in charge. He chose the victim, as well. It didn't necessarily mean he was the one who *knew* the victim. Maybe the other one, beta, was the one who was familiar with the victim, and alpha chose her to convince his partner or manipulate him.

Despite her resolve to set her assumptions about Glover aside, she couldn't avoid noticing the body's posture and ligature marks were identical to ones she'd seen in Glover's murder victims. Women who were strangled while being raped. The murder and the rape went together. That was an act that spoke of obsessiveness with power and domination. This was the work of the alpha as well.

Biting her lip, she circled each of the actions she assumed was committed by the alpha killer. In the background, Adele's soft voice asked someone to let her down gently. Someone tapped on her shoulder, invoking a flash of irritation. She hated being interrupted midsong. She paused it and turned to look at Tatum. "What?"

He grinned, raising an eyebrow at her sharp tone. "O'Donnell just called me. The medical examiner did the thingy with the microscope."

"The thingy?" Zoe clicked her pen repeatedly, following the unheard rhythm of the now-paused song.

"You know what I'm talking about. To check for saliva."

"Fluorescent spectroscopy."

"That's it."

"There's no microscope involved."

"Are you interested to hear what she found? Or do you want to keep mocking my ignorance?"

"What did she find?" Click-click-click, her thumb kept abusing her pen.

"Traces of human saliva around the large puncture wound. You were right."

Zoe nodded, her thumb pausing. "He sucked her blood."

"That's what it looks like. She said they're still waiting for the toxicology report, can't know for sure he didn't use the needle to inject her with something."

"Uh-huh." Zoe turned to her list and scratched out the words *Needle wounds*, writing next to them *Blood consumption.*

"Listen, I'm getting hungry. Do you feel like grabbing dinner?"

"In a bit," she muttered distractedly. "I'm in the middle of something."

"Don't wait too long. I might eat my keyboard."

A second after Tatum walked away, Adele resumed singing, but Zoe didn't join her, not even in the chorus. Blood consumption. One of the killers had sucked the victim's blood. Perhaps extracted some for later use.

Contrary to what people understandably thought, merely consuming human blood wasn't a definite sign of insanity. It indicated a very extreme, unconventional fantasy. But there were cases of people who turned to cannibalism or drinking blood but weren't, medically speaking, insane. And not all of them were killers.

Depending on who you talked to in psychological circles, clinical vampirism, or Renfield's syndrome, was either a myth or a real condition. There were definitely several cases of people drinking blood, but many psychologists claimed it was nothing more than a symptom of something else, like schizophrenia, and not an actual separate condition. Though Zoe wasn't sure where the debate stood and how extensive the documentations of Renfield's syndrome cases were, she knew a researcher in Atlanta who had studied the phenomenon for the past seven years.

She found his email address online and drafted a quick message. She explained that she might have run into a case of clinical vampirism in one of her investigations and asked if he was aware of any people who suffered from it in Chicago.

She returned to her list. So far, she'd attributed all the aggressive acts to unsub alpha. It was possible unsub beta had simply been a spectator, that everything had been done by the alpha, but Zoe doubted it. The man who covered the body, who put the necklace on her, wasn't the same one who took the trophy. It was someone who felt guilty. And that meant he did more than watch. He participated in the attack. Which probably meant he was the one who drank the blood.

Albert had told them that Catherine almost always wore the silver necklace. That indicated the person who put the necklace on her was the one familiar with the victim. He'd seen it was missing, went to look for it, and put it on her.

She kept sorting the list, occasionally glancing at the photos, trying to see any indications to support her deductions. Finally she had two smaller lists.

Alpha—Victim choice, plan, rape and murder, trophy

Beta—Familiarity with victim, blood consumption, covering victim, necklace

What about the bloody footprints? Checking the case report, she found there were multiple size 9 bloody footprints in the bedroom, from which beta had probably taken the necklace. Okay, the majority of the bloody footprints belonged to beta as well. He was the one who blundered into the bloodstain, who paced around the body multiple times.

One partial print of the other shoe size had been found in the entire apartment. Alpha had noticed that he'd stepped in the victim's blood and wiped his shoe sole. Careful, calm, mindful of the traces he left behind. Alpha had probably done this before. Beta was a first timer.

Her stomach rumbled noisily. She was starving. She paused the music and took off her earphones.

"Hey," she called to the adjacent cubicle. "Are you still hungry?"

"Must . . . eat," Tatum rasped, sounding like a parched man in the desert.

Zoe rolled her eyes. "Okay, okay. But let's find somewhere nice. I need a change of scenery."

CHAPTER 9

The belly of a man was a fickle thing.

There was quite a long culinary negotiation, and Tatum had to admit it was mostly his fault. He had a sudden craving for a burger joint and shot down several of Zoe's suggestions, none of which included burgers. Then, annoyed, she demanded that he decide, and suddenly he didn't want a burger anymore.

They ended up in a place named Niko's Taverna, which got a nice rating on Yelp, including one five-star review that said, Got engaged here to my sweet Tony, who is the love of my life!!!!!!! The souvlaki was good.

The place was crowded, but they had a free table for two at the far corner, and the window faced the bustling street. It was noisy inside, the sound of dozens of people talking, clanking kitchen utensils, and the background music of a cheerful bouzouki-played tune from overhead speakers.

Their waiter was a chubby man with gray hair, a thick mustache, and a wide grin. He suggested they try the "Niko couple special," which was an assortment of small dishes, enough for two people. Despite not being a couple, they quickly agreed it sounded perfect and ordered it. Tatum also ordered a glass of ouzo for himself.

"The music is driving me insane," Zoe said.

"I think it's nice." Tatum grinned. "Very atmospheric."

Zoe shook her head. They remained silent for a while. The music played on. At a nearby table, a woman laughed, way too loud, sounding a bit like a hyena. On the other side of the restaurant, a group sang "Happy Birthday," the song clashing with the music. Tatum hoped the food would be worth it.

"How's Marvin?" Zoe asked.

Tatum sighed. His grandfather had sent him a cryptic text an hour before. Do we have a hacksaw? Though Tatum did have one, he responded reflexively that they didn't, only to get a second text—Liar, I found it. Feeling that mild panic that always accompanied interactions with his grandfather, he asked carefully what Marvin was doing with a hacksaw. His grandfather didn't reply, nor did he answer Tatum's three phone calls. Tatum still debated with himself whether to ask the neighbor to make sure Marvin hadn't sawed off his own hand by mistake.

"He's fine," he said. "Keeping himself busy. He has a smutty book club that meets twice a week, mostly in my apartment. Him and about a dozen women. He's also trying to learn to play the harmonica, which I suspect he's doing to scare the cat. Oh, and he's practicing tai chi."

"Tai chi is a good idea," Zoe said. "It's really good exercise, and it's very meditative."

"Not the way he does it," Tatum muttered. Marvin did tai chi as if he were Bruce Lee fighting a hoard of nunchaku-wielding villains. "Did you ever do tai chi?"

"No, but Andrea had a phase. She did it every morning for a whole year."

"How's she doing?"

"She's fine. My mom is probably driving her insane."

Tatum nodded. That pretty much covered their non-work-related life.

He knew that Zoe would eventually use the lull in conversation to start talking about the case. He preferred to nudge the conversation away from the topic. For one, Zoe's preoccupation with Rod Glover had been bordering on obsession in the past week. She spent nearly every waking hour thinking about the killer, analyzing his past behavior, trying to anticipate his actions. She was getting more frantic every day, as the deadline of their return to Quantico loomed closer. And besides, talking about murders tended to mess up his appetite.

"So what do you think of Detective O'Donnell?" he asked.

"She seems capable. But she doesn't like me," Zoe said.

"Why do you say that? She seemed interested in your opinions."

"She is very impatient when I talk to her. She interrupted me several times and sounded really annoyed whenever I expressed an opinion."

"I think that's just her style. She did the same with me."

"Well, her style makes me think she doesn't like me." Zoe shrugged.

Tatum was about to ask another question, when their waiter showed up, balancing a dozen plates on his arms with no tray, a stunt that seemed dangerous in the crowded restaurant. Just one wrong move, and an innocent diner would end up with a bowl of tzatziki upturned on his head. Their table was small, and it took a certain amount of Tetris-related knowledge to get all the plates onto it. While he did it, the waiter announced the dishes he was putting down. "Taramosalata, it's fish roe. These here are artichokes with potato and lemon. Stuffed grape leaves with yogurt . . ." On and on the list went until the table was completely covered, and the waiter left.

Zoe seemed overwhelmed. She always gave a lot of thought to the way she ate her food, what to eat first, and which portions to combine together in a single bite. It seemed like the amount of possibilities momentarily short-circuited her brain functions.

Tatum stuck his fork in one of the stuffed grape leaves and took a bite.

They said smells could trigger memories, but Tatum didn't know tastes could do the same. All of a sudden he was back in Wickenburg, sitting at the table, his mother trying to teach him yet again how to hold a knife, her tone exasperated, while his dad told her to "leave the kid alone."

"My mom made stuffed grape leaves just like these," he said, his mouth half-full.

Zoe had managed to compute herself out of her dilemma and now dipped a piece of roasted cauliflower in the bowl of tzatziki. "I didn't know your mother was Greek."

"She wasn't, but she liked trying new recipes. She had a shelf in the kitchen with dozens of cookbooks." Tatum smiled. "They had these amazing pictures, and I used to look through them, imagining what they'd taste like."

"That was probably nice."

Tatum snorted. "Not to a kid. Most of my friends would have steak and fries for dinner. We'd have Peking duck or falafel. I used to *beg* my mom to make something normal for a change."

Zoe combined a sliced tomato and a piece of artichoke on her fork with the concentration of a nuclear physicist handling uranium. "Kids have almost three times as many taste buds as adults, so they experience taste differently and prefer simpler tastes."

Tatum smiled. "Whatever. I just wanted some fries."

Zoe closed her eyes as she took the bite, breathing through her nose. Tatum sipped from his ouzo and looked at her, for a moment unable to pull his gaze away. When her eyes were open, Zoe always seemed like a deadly predator, poised to pounce. But when she shut them, her entire face suddenly became so delicate, almost like a porcelain doll.

"How was the food at your grandparents' home?" she asked.

Tatum's smile wavered. "Well, it should have made me happy. Mashed potatoes, roast beef, hamburger, fries. My grandma bought vanilla ice cream for me every weekend because she knew it was my favorite. Of course, being a little asshole, I responded by telling her she cooked like shit and that my mom used to cook much better."

"Well, you lost your parents. You were probably struggling."

"That's no excuse."

She shrugged. "I didn't say it's an excuse. But you shouldn't feel guilty about it."

"Who says I'm feeling guilty?" Tatum asked, his tone becoming raw, angry. "And what if I am?" He picked up his fork, noticed that his hand trembled, and put it down. Then he flattened his palm on the table in embarrassment.

She gawked at him in surprise. Then she put her own hand on his. Her skin was warm and dry, and its touch made the trembling subside. "You should eat the artichokes. They're really good."

Tatum blinked and stared at the plate. One single artichoke piece lay on the plate, the rest already eaten by Zoe, apparently. "I'm not really hungry, thanks."

"You should try them," Zoe said, her voice tense. "It'll make you feel better."

"Okay." He picked up his fork and stuck it in the remaining artichoke.

"With the tzatziki. It's the best with the tzatziki." She pointed at the bowl, as if she doubted his ability to discern what she was talking about. "Just dip it."

He dipped the artichoke in the tzatziki and put it in his mouth obediently. "It's good."

She seemed to relax as he chewed. He had to smile. He swallowed the artichoke, which really was very nice.

"I used to say horrible things to my mom when I was a teenager," Zoe said after a moment. She speared a roasted eggplant. "Never to my dad. Just my mom. We used to get into these long screaming arguments. My dad would work, and Andrea would hide in her room, and we would just . . ." She shook her head.

"What did you argue about?" Tatum asked. He dipped a piece of bread in the tzatziki distractedly. Zoe almost never talked about her parents.

"Oh, everything. My choices of clothes, the books I read, the shows I watched, why I didn't go out more . . . she'd start every discussion in this really delicate tone of voice." Zoe clutched her fork hard, eyes narrowing. "Ugh, just thinking of it now . . . 'Zoe, why won't you put that book down and go meet a friend?'" She said the last sentence in a sweet, high, tilted tone.

"Most parents like it when kids read books."

"I think it was my taste that she wasn't happy with. Serial killer biographies, books about forensics . . ." Zoe had a distant look in her eyes. "Some steamy romance books too."

"Really?"

She ate the eggplant. "I was still a teenager, you know. Then I'd say something nasty, just to get her to stop talking to me as if I was a moron. And she'd get angry and scream . . ." She twirled the fork in the air. "It all went downhill from there. She made me so furious."

"I guess most teenagers get pissed at their parents."

"It was more than that. I blamed them. For Glover. For not believing me. For leaving Andrea and me alone that night."

When Glover had been Zoe's neighbor, she'd figured out he was the Maynard serial killer. She told the cops and her parents, and no one believed her. And then, soon after, he came for her. She locked herself with her sister in her room while Glover ranted and screamed through the door, trying to break in. Finally, another neighbor had called the cops, and he'd fled. Tatum couldn't even guess how that trauma had affected Zoe as she'd grown up.

Zoe's voice became silent, almost a whisper, and Tatum leaned in to hear her over the music. "And I blamed them for later."

"What happened later?"

She smiled ruefully. "Nothing. Glover disappeared. And despite what I'd told the cops, no one thought he was the murderer. They had a solid suspect. They figured I just spooked Glover, and he ran. Word got around. It was a small town. I was the crazy girl who chased her neighbor away. Kids started avoiding me at school. I mean, I still had one good friend. But I think her parents told her to stay away from me or something."

She bit her lip, her eyes far away. Tatum's heart squeezed.

"So anyway, I blamed my parents for all that," Zoe said, her voice much louder. She shook her head. "Teenagers, right?"

"Yeah," Tatum said softly. "Teenagers."

"You know what I think?" Zoe said.

"What?"

"I think I could go for dessert."

CHAPTER 10

The problem with maintaining control was that the pressure kept rising. He'd always known that. The term *out of control* was misleading. You didn't run out of control as if it were milk or fuel. Instead, the control you maintained so carefully might shatter under the immense pressure building inside you. People were just walking pressure cookers, and if they didn't let out some steam occasionally, they exploded.

Ordinarily, the man in control vented steam while sleeping. But that didn't happen lately. And he had to admit that some of the pressure had been regulated by those drugs he used to take. And while those things were harmful, and even poisonous, flushing them down the toilet might have been a bit hasty.

He felt the pressure building. When he talked to people, his skin prickled, and it sometimes seemed like he was seconds away from screaming, or bursting into tears, or even tearing his hair out in clumps. Could people see it building up inside him? Perhaps he gritted his teeth too hard? Or was his skin flushed?

He couldn't let this go on. He needed some way to reduce the pressure. And the answer was right there. The calmest he'd ever been was when he'd drunk Catherine's blood. And didn't he still have some vials in the fridge?

They weren't supposed to be for his *own* use, but this was an emergency.

Hurrying to the kitchen, he darted past the guest room. He couldn't talk to Daniel, not now, not so close to an imminent explosion. First the blood.

He nearly tore the fridge door open and paused, blinking in the light emanating from it. Only one vial left. How?

Hazy memories came back to him. Throughout the day, he'd drunk four himself. He recalled the sensation: his hand trembling, unscrewing the cap, and drinking it all in three hurried swallows, the salty metal taste feeling sublime. How had he forgotten?

He reached for the last vial, then froze. This vial was not for him.

Should he talk to Daniel and tell him they needed more? He could already imagine his friend's disappointed expression. Daniel would ask him if he finished all the vials already. And what could he say in response?

He'd have to go get some more on his own. He put on his coat and silently slipped out of the house. Daniel wouldn't notice anyway; he was used to his frequent trips out.

Being outside made him feel even worse. Inside, it was his home turf. Out in the street, he was exposed. The lit windows of houses down the street watched him, square yellow eyes in the darkness. His neighbors could be standing behind those windows. They would know something was off with him; they must have seen things that made them wonder. He resisted the impulse to hurry back inside and instead strode down the street, as fast as he could without looking strange. There was a fine line between man-in-a-hurry and man-in-a-panic. He didn't want to give the people looking at him any reason for suspicion.

At first, he saw only one person, walking his large menacing dog. But as he got closer to the mall, the streets filled with people. His nostrils flared. He could smell it.

Blood.

Every one of those people had, on average, nine to twelve pints of blood. The quantity made him feel dizzy. He imagined fifteen beer bottles in his fridge, all brimming with blood. Of course, that wasn't practical. He couldn't really empty a body efficiently. He just needed enough blood to make it a few more days.

A woman walked past him, reeking of perfume. She tried to mask the scent of blood, like prey had been doing for millions of years. But he wasn't fooled; he could still easily sniff it underneath. Once you knew how blood smelled, you couldn't ignore it. It was everywhere. He carefully turned around and began following her. She was walking in high heels, tap-tap-tapping on the sidewalk.

He tracked her for about five minutes, keeping a distance, his mouth salivating. She glanced back. Her footsteps quickened. Had she noticed him? He panicked and froze in his spot, and she was gone.

Angry, he whirled around, thinking of returning home, then caught his breath.

Two teenage girls, no older than fourteen, strolled on the other side of the street. They were chatting, laughing, and he could smell them over the traffic's stench.

It smelled better, fresher, purer.

With a blood so pure, all he'd need would be a few drops a day.

Katy regretted the chocolate cake she'd had. Sure, Mel had a piece of cake, too, but the way Mel looked, she could afford to eat cake every day. Katy knew she wasn't that lucky. When she ate cake, it stayed there.

Besides, it wasn't even the good kind of chocolate cake. It was too sweet and a little dry, and now she felt nauseated.

Mel kept talking about the cute waiter at the café. Katy nodded and laughed at the right moments and tried not to throw up.

"Let's see if anyone commented on our picture." Mel took out her phone. They'd posted a selfie of themselves on Mel's Instagram account, the cakes in the background. In the selfie, the cakes looked good, especially after Mel had applied the Ludwig filter. Mel used the Ludwig filter on everything. She used it as a verb—"I just Ludwiged it," or "Let's do some Ludwiging."

"Twenty-seven likes," Mel said, satisfied. "And Pat says she's jealous, but I told her we're going, and *she* said it's too cold."

Katy peered over Mel's shoulder, already sorry she'd posed for the picture. Taking a selfie with Mel was just another way to underline all of her faults—her weird ears, her chubby cheeks, her big front teeth. Mel was always perfect in photos, Ludwiged or not. And all the Ludwigs in the world couldn't make Katy as pretty.

Mel tapped a response, and Katy's attention wandered. The street was nearly empty, except for someone walking behind them. Hadn't he been following them for a while? She tried to remember when she'd first heard his footsteps. She glanced furtively backward. It was a man, and as soon as she turned her head, their eyes locked.

She quickly turned away, heart thumping. The guy seemed . . . weird. Something was wrong with the way he lumbered, with his posture, with his face.

"Oh, look." Mel laughed. "Now she's saying—"

"I think the guy back there is stalking us," Katy whispered. He was about ten yards away. Could he hear her?

Mel glanced back abruptly.

"Don't!" Katy hissed at her.

"He's just walking," Mel said casually. "It's the street, Katy. People are allowed to walk."

But now they were both quiet as they strode, tense. There was hardly any traffic. Was he walking faster? He was definitely walking faster. He was gaining on them. There really was no one else on the street. How could that be? Was it *that* late?

Mel grabbed Katy's hand. She tried to smile, but her eyes were wide, lips trembling. Without saying a word, they both began marching faster, breathing hard. She didn't dare look back, but she heard his foot-steps and even his breathing. Deep, raspy, *wrong*.

They were running now, and Mel glanced back and let out a shriek, and Katy felt as if her heart were lodged in her throat. The night's air was cold, and she swallowed it in fast gulps, burning in her lungs.

And then she saw Buddy's Drugstore on the other side of the street, and she yanked Mel's hand, dragging her friend across the road, through the parking lot, and past the glass door, which thankfully was unlocked. Once they were inside, Katy slammed the door and stared outside through the glass. It instantly fogged with her breath, obscuring the dark street.

"Hey, what the hell is wrong with you?" Buddy asked from behind the counter, face twisted in anger. "You tryin' to break the door?"

Mel sobbed, a faint stain on her crotch. Katy wiped the glass and peered outside. There was no one there.

He lowered his head, walking back home, heart pounding in his ears. His mind was in turmoil, and he had difficulty concentrating. He kept imagining those two girls as he came closer and closer. His fists clenched and unclenched. The need gnawed in his guts, clouding his thoughts, making his movements erratic, lurching. He needed to go back home, get himself under con—

And there was a woman, a baby in her arms, walking toward him. He could smell the baby. Its scent was as sweet as nectar. He didn't remember where he was going anymore. Because a baby couldn't fight back, couldn't run. And all he needed to do was grab the baby when he was close enough and run with it somewhere safe. A few minutes alone with the baby, and he'd be better, he knew.

The woman walked past him, a few feet away, and he almost made a grab for it.

Almost.

But he managed to stop himself in time, think it through. The woman would fight. She knew how he looked. He didn't live far away. The police would find him.

He turned around and watched her melt into the darkness. What was wrong with him? He was supposed to be in control.

He would go back home and talk to Daniel. He'd know what to do.

But which way was home? He was momentarily lost, his surroundings looking strange and unfamiliar. He panicked, his breathing fast and shallow, dizziness assailing him. Opening his mouth, he was about to scream, when a car drove past him, honking. He blinked, startled, and the street swam into focus. Of course he knew where he was. He lived just a short walk away.

But just across the street was a shop he recognized all too well. He'd stopped in front of the display window endless times before, mesmerized.

On the right side was a huge aquarium, full of glimmering fish, the aquarium's blue light rippling in the water. It illuminated several cages to its left. A pair of white rabbits in one, several hamsters in another, and a very large cage with four Labrador puppies.

He'd entered the store once, thinking of buying two or three puppies, but had lost his nerve when the girl behind the counter had asked if she could help him. No girl behind the counter now. The store was dark, aside from the aquarium's blue light.

The store stood in the corner of an alley, and it had a small window on the alley's side. But it was still large enough for a grown man to crawl through.

And it could be broken with a brick, the shattering glass hardly heard over the sound of the traffic.

He had just begun cleaning up his room when Daniel opened the door. Daniel's eyes widened.

"What the hell happened here?" Daniel asked.

The man in control raised his hands in a reassuring gesture. "It's just hamsters," he said.

Daniel's face twisted in disgust. "Hamsters?" His eyes scanned the bucket of soapy water, the bloodstains on the floor, the messy cleaver and cutting board, the pieces of bone and skin. "What did you do?"

"I just needed some blood, for my condition. It's no big deal."

"Where did you get hamsters in the middle of the night? Is there an all-night delivery for hamsters?"

"I broke into a pet shop." His voice was matter of fact. He had everything under control again. "Their cage was small. It was easy to take."

"Where?" Daniel's face suddenly went pale. "Where did you do this?"

"There's a pet shop not far from here."

Daniel slammed his palm on the door, and the sound made the man in control flinch. It was the first time he'd ever seen Daniel lose his temper. He was always so nice and cheerful. That was one of the best things about him. Without saying a word, Daniel turned away and left the room.

He decided to give Daniel some space. He focused on cleaning the bloodstains. When he was done, the water in the bucket had dirty pink tufts of fur floating on the surface. He took the cleaver and board to the kitchen and began to wash them in the sink. He felt Daniel step into the room and watch him as he did it.

"Listen," Daniel said. His voice was soft, gentle. "You can't do shit like that. The police are looking for us. You can't break into a damn pet shop near your home, okay?"

"I had to," he began to say. "I needed—"

"I know what you need. I understand. You don't act alone, okay? You come to *me*. We're in this together—you know that."

"Sure, but I needed some blood, fast. And they're just a few hamsters. It's not a big deal."

Daniel seemed to mull it over, then lowered his head. "This whole thing with Catherine put too much stress on you. I . . . I'm sorry. You shouldn't risk yourself on my account. I should turn myself in."

"No! Absolutely not!" He was aghast. "You can't do that. I'm fine . . . I'm really fine."

"You're obviously not. I can understand what you're going through. You're under a lot of pressure with the police investigation. It's no wonder you're getting these uncontrollable urges."

"It won't happen again, I swear! I'm back in control."

"Yeah?"

"It was a one-time thing, and it was stupid. I'll come to you immediately if I have any urges again."

For a moment they were both silent. He finished washing the cleaver, his hands trembling, and put it aside to dry.

"We'll go hunting again," Daniel said suddenly. "I need to as much as you do."

"When?" He felt the wave of relief washing over him. No more talk about Daniel turning himself in.

"Soon. I need you to pick up some stuff tomorrow, on your way home."

"What kind of stuff?"

"White paint and a knife. Maybe some candles."

"What is it for?" the man in control asked, feeling confused. They'd never discussed it.

"We'll need it for the next time," Daniel said. "Can you do that?"

"Yes, but—"

"Good." Daniel looked at him closely and then seemed to reach a decision. "Get the stuff, and we'll go hunting tomorrow night."

CHAPTER 11

Monday, October 17, 2016

O'Donnell decided to avoid the station that morning. It'd been forty-eight hours since the body of Catherine Lamb had been discovered, and her captain, Royce Bright, ascribed an almost mystical significance to that number. When a murder wasn't resolved within forty-eight hours, he called the assigned detectives to a meeting. The dreaded forty-eight-hours meeting could take up to two hours, thus morphing the already terrible forty-eight to fifty. It was typically a mess of suggestions, threats, and the occasional story about the old days.

She could do without it. She wouldn't be able to avoid him forever, but she hoped to have a tangible lead before he cornered her. And it seemed likely that Patrick Carpenter held that lead.

Marching into Mount Sinai Hospital, she saw that Agent Gray and Zoe Bentley were already waiting for her in the lobby. She checked the time—five minutes past nine. Gotta hand it to the feds: they were punctual.

"Sorry I'm late." She walked over. "Traffic."

"No worries," Tatum said. "You said on the phone that Patrick Carpenter wanted to meet us here?"

"His wife is here." O'Donnell led them to the elevators. "He asked if we could meet him here so she wouldn't be alone for long. I thought it might make him more cooperative."

It was more than likely that he hadn't told his wife about Catherine's murder to avoid unsettling her. If that were the case, he'd want to get rid of them as soon as possible, and the best way to do that would be to answer their questions. Hopefully giving them some names in the process.

"Wasn't he cooperative when you talked to him before?" Zoe asked.

"He was, until I began asking about congregation members." O'Donnell entered the elevator, the others following her. "Then he began talking about invasion of privacy and breach of trust. I hoped your fancy federal badges would make him a bit more helpful."

The elevator door opened into a long hallway, a nurse's station just to their right. A plump nurse with a large mole on her chin stapled multiple pages with zeal.

O'Donnell approached the nurse. "Excuse me, we're looking for Mrs. Carpenter's room?"

The nurse didn't raise her eyes. She stacked half a dozen pages, positioned them under the stapler, and slammed her hand on it, as if smashing a bug. She examined the result and nodded to herself approvingly. "Are you family?"

"We need to talk to her husband." O'Donnell flashed her badge.

The nurse didn't seem impressed. She got another stack of pages and put them on the counter. O'Donnell found herself flinching as the nurse's meaty hand came down on the stapler. This was a clear case of stationery abuse, but that was outside the Chicago Police Department's jurisdiction.

"Room 309." The nurse began to prepare her next stack.

O'Donnell hurried away, another slam echoing in her wake.

The door to room 309 was open, but O'Donnell knocked on it politely.

"Yes?" A cheerful feminine voice came from inside.

"Mrs. Carpenter?" O'Donnell peeked into the room. "Hi. We were hoping to talk to your husband, Patrick."

"Oh, Patrick will be here in a few minutes," the woman said. "Please come in."

"We can wait for him in the hall," O'Donnell said, uncomfortable.

"Nonsense. There are no chairs in the hall, and I have some cookies here. Please, come in—I insist."

The three of them shuffled into the room and sat down on chairs by Mrs. Carpenter's bed.

Mrs. Carpenter was a rosy-cheeked woman with long smooth chestnut hair. Despite being in a hospital bed, she was dressed in a bright-green shirt, which bulged over her pregnant belly. The hospital's blanket was draped over her feet. When they came in, she put down her book, *Praying for Your Unborn Child*, and smiled warmly at them.

"Do you work with the church?" she asked.

O'Donnell fumbled for an answer. "Not on a regular basis, but we have an interest in some of the congregation members."

"I think that's wonderful," Mrs. Carpenter said, who obviously misinterpreted the "interest" the three of them had. It was equally obvious that O'Donnell's earlier hunch was correct. Patrick hadn't told his wife about Catherine.

"My name is Leonor."

"I'm Holly," O'Donnell said hesitantly. "And this is Zoe and . . . Tatum. Nice to meet you. Any idea how long until Patrick returns?"

"He's on his way, but I delayed him because I needed some things from home," Leonor said. "I've been here for almost a week now, and you can imagine how many back-and-forth trips Patrick had to do for me. And it's not just to our house. I send him to my parents to do the laundry. Patrick is an incredible husband, but doing laundry, not to mention folding it, is beyond his capabilities."

"That's very nice of him," Tatum contributed.

"It really is. And he does so much for me. I've been driving him insane with my long lists. But can you imagine staying a whole week in a hospital bed, hardly able to even stand up without a nurse watching you? I need my own clothing just to feel normal. I would have gone home, but Patrick insisted that I stay here, monitored. You know how men can worry. At least I have books. If I didn't have those, I'd count the floor tiles." She mimed whispering. "There are fifty-two."

Leonor obviously loved to talk, and O'Donnell could imagine being stuck in that room for a week by herself made her desperate for company. No wonder she was so adamant they sit inside. Still, O'Donnell couldn't help but wonder what the woman needed actual people for. The conversation was entirely one sided, and the three of them could have been replaced by potted plants without significantly altering the dialogue. She was now talking about her pregnancy. O'Donnell only half listened.

" . . . our fourth pregnancy. The first three were early miscarriages." Her voice trembled slightly. "But then this one came, and it seemed to be going so well! God rewards pure and selfless souls, and we've been trying so hard. Last week, when the bleeding started, I was so terrified— I was sure I'd lost the baby. But then when we got here, I felt him kick. I was so relieved. And they said I have to stay here for a while. I thought they meant a few hours, at first—"

Someone coughed politely behind O'Donnell, and she turned around. A man stood at the door, a duffel bag slung on his shoulder, a large plastic cup in his hand. He was dressed in a white shirt and black pants, his cheeks clean shaven. But his dark hair was disheveled, and his eyes were swollen and bloodshot.

"Hello." He clenched his jaw.

"I told your associates they can wait here with me," Leonor said.

His shoulders slackened as Leonor said *associates*. He'd probably been worried they'd told her who they were or, even worse, told her about Catherine.

"Good." He tried to smile. "I brought you the books you asked for and a new tube of toothpaste. And I hope I got all the clothes right."

"I'm sure you did." She leaned to the side, as if to get up.

He was by her side in a second, gently pushing her back. He kissed her forehead and handed her the plastic cup. "Here," he said. "Fresh shake."

She let out a small laugh. "You and your fruit shakes. Every day it's the same." She took a sip from the straw and cringed slightly. "This pregnancy makes everything taste a bit strange, you know?" She smiled at O'Donnell.

"I remember," O'Donnell said. "I couldn't stomach red peppers. And I used to love them before."

Patrick turned to look at them again. "Would you like to talk outside?"

"Of course," O'Donnell said. "It was really nice to meet you," she told Leonor.

They stepped into the corridor and made their way to a secluded corner. Patrick turned around, glancing at each of them in turn.

"Is there any progress with finding who . . ." He blinked and looked away. "Who did this to Catherine?"

"We have some leads," O'Donnell said. "Mr. Carpenter, this is Agent Gray and his partner, Bentley, from the FBI."

"The FBI?" Patrick gawked, confused. "What does the FBI have to do with Catherine?"

"We wanted to ask a few more questions," O'Donnell said, ignoring his inquiry.

"What do you need?"

"Can we go over the last time you talked to Catherine again?" O'Donnell asked. They'd discussed it before, on the phone, but she wanted to see his face when they talked about it.

"Sure. Uh . . . it was three days ago, around noon. Catherine called me to say she was sick and wasn't going to church. She wanted to know if I could cover for her and meet some of the members who wanted to talk."

This matched the call records from Catherine's phone. "Do you often cover for each other?" she asked.

"It happens. Not too often, but sometimes there are urgent counseling sessions, and one of us is indisposed."

"And was there an urgent session that day?"

"I don't think so. She just wanted me to take over for her."

"And did you?"

"I told her I would, but then my wife began bleeding again." Patrick glanced down the hall. "And I forgot. I remembered later, and I called Catherine to tell her, but she never answered."

"And did you stay here?"

"Most of the evening, yes. I went out to get some stuff for my wife at one point. And I left when she fell asleep."

"When was that?"

"I don't remember. Probably around midnight."

"Can you tell us the names of the people Catherine was supposed to meet that day?"

"No. That's confidential."

O'Donnell raised an eyebrow. "Any of the members you and Catherine consult have a criminal past?"

Patrick's jaw tightened. "I'm not about to talk about the congregation members here. I won't break their trust by divulging their secrets to you."

"I don't necessarily need the secrets. A list of names will do."

"Absolutely not."

"This is a murder investigation, Mr. Carpenter."

"Exactly. And none of the people we helped hurt Catherine. I can vouch for each and every one of them. Instead of wasting your time chasing and harassing men who are doing their best to leave their past behind them, why don't you find the man who actually did this?"

Zoe cleared her throat. "How exactly can you vouch for them?"

Patrick frowned. "I know these people very well. I've spent hours talking to them, praying with them. These people are doing their best to change."

"Change how?"

"They've embraced God. They want to be better people. They—"

"Any of them ever convicted of sexual assault?" Zoe asked.

Patrick blinked in surprise. "*If* any of them were, they've paid their dues to society. They've confessed and begged forgiveness. They—"

"Catherine Lamb was raped before she was killed," Zoe said. "Whoever killed her has done it before. If you have rapists in your congregation, we need to know. They may have confessed and apologized and all that, but repeat sexual offenders don't change."

"Everyone can change," Patrick said.

"They can develop fear of getting caught." Zoe shrugged. "But they'll still want to rape."

Patrick folded his arms. "I'm done talking about this."

"Mr. Carpenter," Tatum said. "It's a common misconception that the police's job is just finding the guilty person."

Patrick glanced at Tatum. "Well, isn't it?"

"Of course. But they also need to make sure he's found guilty in court," Tatum said. "You tell us you vouch for each and every man in your church. Let's say I believe you. But when we catch the guy and get him in front of a judge and jury, what do you think will be the first thing his lawyer will say?"

Patrick remained silent.

Tatum answered his own question after a second had passed. "He'll say, 'My client isn't guilty, and I know who is. It's one of those ex-cons that Catherine Lamb worked with. The police didn't even bother talking to them. They just went straight after my client.'"

"He would build his whole case around it," O'Donnell added. "And the killer would walk."

Patrick hesitated, then said, "I will talk to Pastor Lamb. We will decide together what I can divulge."

O'Donnell nodded. "Fine." It was a start.

"One more thing." Zoe handed Patrick her phone. "Do you know this man?"

He stared at the phone, and his eyes widened slightly. O'Donnell glanced at the screen. It was a picture of a man, his arm over a woman's shoulder. O'Donnell could easily see a resemblance between the woman in the photo and Zoe.

"*Do* you know this man, Mr. Carpenter?" O'Donnell asked when he didn't reply. She already knew he did; it had been obvious the moment he'd laid his eyes on the image.

"Yes," he said. "That's Daniel Moore."

O'Donnell could almost feel the sudden jolt of energy that sparked among the three of them.

"Is he a member of your congregation?" Tatum asked.

"He was," Patrick said. "He left a few months ago."

"Do you have a phone number? Any way you can reach him? We would really like to talk to him."

"No. He never gave me his number."

"Was there anyone in the congregation he was close to? Any friends?"

"I don't know. What's this about?"

"Daniel Moore's real name is Rod Glover." Zoe took her phone from Patrick's hand. "He's wanted for the rape and murder of five women. Did he confess and beg forgiveness, Mr. Carpenter? Did he embrace God?"

"You're wrong. Daniel is a good man—"

"No, he isn't. He's a sadistic killer. But he's a very good liar."

CHAPTER 12

Zoe was hardly aware of her surroundings. The world around her shimmered, hazy and insubstantial, people's voices muffled.

Her brain felt on fire. Thoughts, ideas, and theories sparked through her mind at breakneck speed. Her focus was on the mental blizzard in her head, and she ignored Tatum and Detective O'Donnell completely, even when they talked to her. After a while she distractedly noticed that the three of them were walking, with her following Tatum, more out of reflex than anything else.

Rod Glover, she was now convinced, was *here*. In Chicago. He was one of the two men who had murdered Catherine Lamb. He was the murderer she had earlier nicknamed alpha.

It could be just a huge coincidence, but Zoe disregarded that option. The MO and the signature already pointed to him. The fact that he had definitely known the victim clinched it.

As she stared out the car window, vaguely wondering where they were driving, a bitter taste filled her mouth. Her heart beat wildly. Was it fear? Or excitement? Maybe a bit of both. She'd been searching for the Maynard serial killer for so long, and now she'd come face to face with his handiwork. She could catch him. Andrea would be safe, and he would stop killing.

The car engine died, and Tatum got out. Zoe stayed in the car, staring at the windshield, consumed by thoughts. After a few seconds, a sharp knock broke her concentration. Tatum, rapping on the window, looking exasperated. She opened the door and tried to get out, only to be yanked in. Oh, right, seat belt. She unbuckled it, got out, and followed Tatum into somewhere named . . . the Jackalope?

"Where are we?" she asked.

"Oh, you're back," Tatum said. "This is the Jackalope café. I told you we were going here. Twice."

"Why are we here?" Zoe followed Tatum inside. The Jackalope's interior was an explosion of bright colors, pop art paintings covering the walls from side to side. A few mounted heads of rabbits with deer antlers hung on the walls—probably the mythological jackalope.

"O'Donnell said it's a nice place, close to the police station, where we could talk, remember? We asked if you had any objections, and you stared at us with drool running down your chin."

"There was no drool."

"I literally told you to wipe it."

"You're just making that up."

O'Donnell sat at one of the tables, waiting for them. Tatum went over to the barista and asked for a cup of coffee.

"What do you want?" he asked Zoe.

"I don't know," Zoe said impatiently. "Sure, coffee sounds good."

Tatum paid the barista, and they sat down next to O'Donnell.

"Okay," O'Donnell said. "So your guy Rod Glover definitely knew Catherine Lamb. It's likely that he was one of the murderers."

"It's more than likely—it's a certainty," Zoe said. "He knew her. He must have developed an obsession about her, or maybe the obsession was from the other guy, and Glover reacted to it. I need to think it through, the other guy knew her as well, I think he did—no, he definitely did, because of the necklace, Glover wouldn't have cared about it, and he actually collected jewelry as trophies, I've seen it at least once, so he wouldn't have left it there, the other guy, unsub beta, he did that, and—"

"Zoe," Tatum said. "We need this to be an actual conversation."

"This *is* a conversation."

"No. This is you spewing your thoughts at us."

O'Donnell watched them both with apparent amusement. Then the barista said, "O'Donnell? Your order is ready."

While O'Donnell went to get her order, Zoe tried to frame her thoughts into concrete sentences. Glover's accomplice went to the same church. Did Glover meet him there? Was Glover even religious? She recalled meeting him at church once or twice as a child, but she had never gotten the impression that—

"Your coffee is getting cold," Tatum said.

"Oh!" She was surprised to see a cup of coffee in front of her. She sipped from it. It was fine.

"I just told O'Donnell about your sister."

"What about my sister?"

"She was in the photograph with Glover," O'Donnell pointed out. "I thought it was weird."

Zoe nodded. "Yes. That's what Glover . . . what are you drinking?"

"Hot chocolate," O'Donnell said and sipped from it.

Zoe followed the mug's movement intently. It was topped with whipped cream, cocoa powder sprinkled on top. Suddenly, Zoe's own coffee seemed tasteless. She noticed O'Donnell had a sandwich as well. God, she was starving.

"Hang on a minute," she blurted and went over to the barista. She asked for hot chocolate and a sandwich named the Centaur. She waited by the counter, trying to marshal her thoughts, occasionally glancing over at Tatum and O'Donnell. They were leaning toward each other, Tatum talking in a low voice. Filling her in on Glover's past, probably. That and his connection with Zoe.

After a few minutes, the barista handed Zoe her hot chocolate and sandwich. Zoe carried them back to the table, sat down, and took a tentative sip from the hot chocolate. The sudden creamy sweetness filled her mouth and nose, sharpening the world around her, focusing the chaos in her head more than anything else. She let the chocolaty liquid run down her throat, warming her up.

"I think both murderers knew Catherine Lamb," she said. "We know Glover did, but he wasn't the one who consumed her blood, or covered her body, or put the necklace on her throat. *That* was the other one. We can call him beta."

"That's assuming Glover really killed Catherine Lamb," O'Donnell said.

Zoe took a bite from the sandwich. Either centaur meat tasted like turkey, or this was a turkey sandwich. "Detective, at some point you need to narrow your focus down to an actual suspect. I'm not telling you how to do your—"

"I'm just saying nothing is final yet." O'Donnell frowned, tilting her head slightly.

Zoe glanced at Tatum, raising her eyebrows to make sure he saw that. He ignored the gesture.

"Presumably Glover met beta in the church," Zoe said.

"Either that, or Glover knew beta before, and beta introduced him to the church," Tatum suggested.

O'Donnell finished her hot chocolate. "So Rod Glover returned to Chicago from Dale City a few weeks ago. From what I understand, he was wounded, and terminally ill, and needed a place to stay."

"And he had at least one friend who could help him," Tatum said.

"He might actually be staying *with* him." Zoe spooned some foam off her hot chocolate. "It makes perfect sense that Glover would return to Chicago. This is where he feels safest. For the past decade he's been building a life here. Now that he is ill and has no job, he came back to get help from his friends." She licked the spoon but stopped when O'Donnell looked at her with a bemused frown.

"He's probably getting cancer treatment," O'Donnell said. "We can get a warrant, check the hospitals for a patient named Rod Glover or Daniel Moore."

"We already did that," Tatum said. "Got the warrants and had them look for him in hospital records. Nothing. We also showed his picture around, but there are over ten thousand cancer patients in Chicago, so it's looking for a needle in a haystack. Not to mention that hospitals aren't wild about divulging patient information. We have an analyst in Quantico still following up on that paper trail."

O'Donnell nodded thoughtfully. "If he's been living here for a decade, that's good for us. We can use the press, get his picture out there. Maybe someone saw him recently. And it might make his so-called friends come forward."

Zoe considered this. "I think that's a good idea," she said slowly. "Even if no one comes forward, it'll increase the pressure on him and might cause him to make a mistake."

"What if media interest prods him to kill again?" Tatum asked.

"That's not likely. Glover never showed any inclination of responding to the press in that manner," Zoe said. "He isn't interested in fame."

"I'll make sure the press get his photo," O'Donnell said. "I'll also talk to Patrick Carpenter and Albert Lamb again, see what more they can tell me about Daniel Moore, and check if I can get any names. What about the other man? This beta dude?"

"It's likely that he has a criminal record that starts with theft or harassment," Zoe said. "The theft might include strange objects like women's underwear, or shoes, or makeup."

"It's called fetish burglaries," Tatum said.

"Glover wouldn't partner with someone who would put him in serious risk, someone who'd attract suspicion, so this killer isn't a gibbering madman or a serious drug addict. It's likely he has some source of income Glover could leech."

O'Donnell raised her eyebrow. "I hoped for a more specific profile. On TV, you guys say stuff like, 'The subject is twenty-five years old, white, thin, has a limp, and probably stutters.'"

Zoe gave it some thought. "I don't see why *any* of that would be particularly likely."

"We'll try to create a more accurate profile of the other killer," Tatum said. "We need to move fast, before they both act again."

"*Again?*" O'Donnell said. "You think they might attack another victim?"

"Glover is dying," Zoe said. "He knows he doesn't have a lot of time left, and that diminishes his fear of being caught. As long as he is healthy enough, he *will* do this again. As for his partner, it's too early to say. But he was there to drink the victim's blood. That indicates a powerful obsession with blood consumption, and it is likely he'd want to repeat it."

"No pressure or anything," O'Donnell said.

Zoe blinked. Hadn't the detective listened to what they just said? "There's a lot of pressure," she stressed.

O'Donnell rolled her eyes. "I got that."

Zoe glanced at Tatum. "We need to update Mancuso. We can't leave yet."

Tatum sighed deeply, doing his martyr impression. "Fine. I'll talk to her."

"We'll check ViCAP, see if there are any other similar crimes where blood was consumed or taken," Zoe said.

O'Donnell snorted as she stood up. "Good luck with that. No one in our department bothers with your ViCAP system."

Zoe gritted her teeth in annoyance. "If you would invest the time to enter your cases into the ViCAP system, it would make solving murders like this significantly easier."

"Well," O'Donnell countered, "maybe if your fed buddies made the system easier to use, and I didn't have to answer more than a hundred damn questions every time I tried to enter one of my cases, I would start doing that. You know, in this city, I have a very limited amount of time to investigate a murder before the next one lands on my desk."

Zoe sipped from her hot chocolate, watching O'Donnell as she left. "She doesn't like me."

"She's just very intense." Tatum smiled at her. "Ready to leave?"

"I'm thinking of getting another hot chocolate to go."

"Well, don't rush into a decision you'll regret later."

"It's really good."

"I'm sure it is. Go get your hot chocolate. We have serial killers to catch."

CHAPTER 13

Harry Barry was in a gloating mood that afternoon. There had been a huge cocaine bust in South Chicago. Everyone was talking about it—it was front-page material. And who had the story? Was it Nick Johnson, the *Chicago Daily Gazette*'s senior crime journalist? Nope! Guess again. It was Harry Barry. He was the one with the source in the team that made the bust. He was the one with the witness account. He was the one scheduled to talk to a suspect's defense attorney. And Nick Johnson and his mediocre somber articles would have to watch while Harry basked in the glory.

Harry's mom had often told him as a child that gloating and bragging were things that "lesser men" did. But Harry quickly concluded that it seemed lesser men had all the fun. And besides, his mom would brag endlessly about her silver cutlery set and about that one time she met Richard Gere in person. Even as a child, Harry was quick to spot hypocrisy.

Just yesterday, Nick had sauntered over to Harry's desk to tell him the Catherine Lamb story, which Nick had written, had been quoted in an online *New York Post* article. But now Catherine Lamb was old news, a two-day-old case with no solid leads. All Nick had today was an interview with Lamb's dad. Harry had overheard that they'd told Nick to shorten the interview by three hundred words. He considered going over to Nick's desk to ask him how it was going along.

It definitely sounded like something a lesser man would do. And no man was lesser than Harry.

His desk phone rang. He picked it up. "Harry here."

"This is Detective O'Donnell from Area Central," the woman on the other side said. "I wanted to talk to the reporter covering the Lamb case."

"Oh yeah?" Harry said distractedly. "You got the wrong—"

"We're looking for someone who might be related to the case, a man named Rod Glover, and I hoped—"

"You got the wrong guy," Harry said, talking over her. "Here, I'll transfer you." He punched Nick's extension and hung up.

For some reason, his good mood had evaporated. The phone call had interrupted his internal gloating mechanism, and he was left with a sort of hollow sensation he couldn't quite place. He shook his head, about to return to work, when it sank in.

Rod Glover.

How had he missed it? Was his head so far up his own ass? Rod Glover was Zoe Bentley's childhood serial killer. He knew that; he was in the process of writing a damn book about it. And he'd just forwarded the call to Nick Johnson like a bumbling amateur.

Rod Glover was related to the Lamb case?

Harry stared at the half-written story of the cocaine bust. It suddenly seemed boring and trite. He'd quoted his source saying it was "another successful law enforcement success targeting major drug cartel activity." *Successful* law enforcement *success*. Who was this Neanderthal? Now that he looked at it, he realized half of what his source had said was badly phrased drivel.

The real story was the Lamb case. Deep in his heart, he'd known it even before this phone call. And now he *needed* it. But if he just offered to trade stories, Nick would sniff Harry's desperation.

Instead, he strode into their editor's office, closing the door behind him.

Daniel McGrath sat behind his desk, frowning at his monitor. He glanced at Harry briefly, then turned back to whatever he was reading. "What, Harry? I'm busy."

"I figured the cocaine bust could use a journalist with a bit more experience in the drug cartels."

Daniel blinked in surprise, turning his full attention to Harry. "What are you talking about? You were positively thrilled to write about it just an hour ago."

"I was willing to do it, sure. But—"

"You stood here and repeatedly said, 'Who da man.'"

"No I didn't."

"You said it four times. I counted."

"I think Nick should do it."

"Just last week you told me Nick's style was . . . let me see if I can quote you accurately: 'The boring drone of a fourth-grade history teacher.'"

"I may have been a bit harsh. Nick's great. He should definitely get this important story."

"What's your angle, Harry?"

"No angle."

"Nick is working on the Lamb story. Do you want the Lamb story?"

"The Lamb story is old news. *This* is the big item of tomorrow."

Daniel leaned back in his chair. "So you want the Lamb story."

"I want what's best for the team. Remember the email from our wise and generous boss, about teamwork?"

"Vaguely. Is it the one where he said we won't be getting raises this year?"

"I care about teamwork. I scrub your back, you scrub mine."

"That phrase isn't about teamwork. It's about exchanging favors. Not the same thing."

"Fine! Sometimes I scrub both our backs. It's a team—why not all of us scrub each other's backs? Me, you, Nick. Get some lather on our hands, scrub each other real hard."

"I'm getting uncomfortable with this metaphor."

"Teamwork! It includes everyone. We can invite Albert, from accounting, scrub his back too."

"Oh god."

"Not just the backs. There are other parts it's hard to reach in the shower. We can scrub each other's—"

"Fine! If Nick wants to exchange stories, I don't have a problem with it, okay? Just shut up about this communal shower we're all having. I have a very graphic imagination. I feel like I need to bleach my brain."

Harry grinned at him. "Thanks, Daniel, you're the best."

"You've ruined showers forever. Get out of my office."

Harry left Daniel's office, took a long breath, and wiped the smile from his face. Then he walked over to Nick Johnson's desk, muttering curses to himself, loud enough that anyone could hear.

"Something wrong, Harry-Barry-Garry?" Nick asked. This was the man's notion of wit. Adding additional rhymes to Harry's name. Rhymes that literally made no sense. Kids at Harry's kindergarten had come up with better taunts.

"I just had a talk with Daniel," Harry spat. "He said I should give you the cocaine-bust story. I'm supposed to tie up the leftovers of the Lamb story."

Really? Nick swiveled his chair, grinning. "Did he say why?"

"He thinks you have more *experience*." Harry made a double quotes gesture with his fingers. "We'll see what he thinks tomorrow when you make a mess of it."

Nick snorted. "Whatever. Forward what you have so far. Maybe some of it is barely usable."

"Yeah, yeah. And where are we at with the Lamb story?"

"I have the interview with the father, but it's done. I already gave it to Daniel. And the detective in charge just sent me a picture of someone they're looking for. You know the drill: the police are looking for this man, if anyone has information about him, yada yada yada. I'll forward you the details. There's a template somewhere. Even you can't mess this up, Harry-Barry-Larry."

"Send me the detective's contact number too. I might have some follow-up questions."

Nick had already turned his back, ignoring him. Harry returned to his seat, his earlier gloating mood replaced with something much better.

Excitement and anticipation.

CHAPTER 14

Tatum sat by the desk at the FBI field office, logged into ViCAP from his laptop, and began reviewing cases that involved blood consumption or any unusual interaction with blood.

Violent cases with actual blood consumption were few and far between. Tatum first checked the closed cases, reviewing the perpetrators' identities and the locations of the crimes. He followed up on any case that seemed to be even remotely connected, making calls to the detectives in charge of the case. Several of the apprehended criminals were still incarcerated. Two were dead. But he ended up with four names, though none of them had a last known address in Illinois. He made a note to check the current address of each of those men and see if they would fit as suspects.

He expanded the search of cases in Chicago, using looser search terms. There were two open cases in Chicago in which the killer wrote messages with the victim's blood. The cases weren't linked—the DNA samples and fingerprints definitely pointed to two different men. Tatum rolled his chair out of his own cubicle and drove it Flintstones-style into Zoe's cubicle.

Her earphones were plugged in her ears, and he heard the vague sounds of pop music from them. How loud was Zoe playing her abysmal music? His grandma had always warned him that if he listened to his music too loud, it would rip his eardrums to shreds, and her vivid descriptions had managed to instill a slight anxiety in him.

Zoe chewed her pen, her notebook in front of her. She had kicked her shoes off under her desk and sat cross-legged, her left foot jiggling with the music. She almost looked like a bored teenager, trying to think of her next diary entry. Aside from the horrific photos spread around her, of course. Still, it made Tatum smile.

She must've felt his eyes on her, because she turned her head, her eyes catching his, the teenager look gone in an instant. She removed her earphones. "What?"

"I talked to Mancuso earlier. She gave us a few more days, and we need to send her daily reports."

"Good." She turned back to the computer, already replacing her earphones.

Tatum cleared his throat. "I wondered about two cases here. Messages written in the victims' blood on the wall. What do you think? Is it relevant?"

She removed the earphones again. "It depends. Unsub beta consumed the victim's blood. The medical examiner said it had to be done quite vigorously to leave that mark. The question is why."

"Because he's batshit crazy." He said that mostly to poke the bear. Zoe hated when investigators reduced the actions of murderers to "crazy."

She didn't rise to the bait. "Well, one option is some sort of psychotic disorder that would lead to a temporary loss of control. In that case, *anything* is possible, not just writing with blood on the wall. His actions would be spurred by hallucinations or delusions that we'd have no way of foretelling."

"But you said Glover wouldn't work with a gibbering madman."

"That's true, but there's a spectrum, and many people with psychotic disorders function reasonably well in society. We can't rule it out. *But* if that's the case, like I said, there's no point in looking closely at any particular case, because there might not be any pattern. Previous cases could have involved blood, or cannibalism, or nothing of the sort."

"What are the other options?"

"Paraphilia, focusing on blood."

Paraphilia. That was Zoe's professional way of saying *people who get off on really weird kinky shit*. Tatum mulled it over. "If it's paraphilia, it would probably be focused on blood consumption, not messages in blood."

"I'd say it depends on the message," Zoe said. "Writing with the victim's blood could be an earlier fantasy, which had since mutated to blood consumption. But then I'd expect the messages to be sexual, and there would probably be semen at the scene."

"Not the case," Tatum said. "In one instance, the murderer wrote *bitch* on the wall. In the other, part of a verse from the Bible. And they found no semen in either scene."

"Right." Zoe counted the options on her fingers. She raised a third one. "The third option is named Renfield's syndrome."

"Renfield? He's the freaky dude from *Dracula*, right?"

Zoe's eyebrows shot up, and Tatum let out a short laugh. "What?" he asked. "Surprised that I read books?"

"I . . . no, I mean . . ."

She seemed so flustered that he laughed again. "Don't worry about it. Okay, so what's Renfield's syndrome?"

"Renfield's syndrome, or clinical vampirism, is a condition in which the person suffering from it is obsessed with drinking blood, for no other reason than blood consumption. There's no sexual aspect and no hallucinations or delusions."

"So we're talking about people who just feel like drinking blood. Like what, a culinary choice?"

"I'm not entirely sure," Zoe admitted. "It's not entirely clear if that's even a *thing*. I actually wrote an acquaintance of mine who's researching it. Hang on, I'll check to see if he responded." She opened her email.

"But if that's the case, then the messages on the wall aren't relevant either, right? Because as far as we know, blood wasn't consumed."

She turned her eyes from the screen. "That's true. There's no reason for someone suffering from Renfield's syndrome to write messages on walls with blood. It makes no sense."

"So that's out."

"Then those cases probably aren't related, since those are the possible reasons." She frowned at the screen, reading an email. "Looks like I have a meeting with a vampire."

Tatum was caught off guard. "Wait, what?"

"A clinical vampire. My acquaintance answered my email. Like I said, he specializes in clinical vampirism. He asked around, and it turns out there's a community of supposed vampires in Chicago. He organized a meeting with one."

"Today?"

"He said she'd be there until six. Not a lot of time left."

"You're not going alone," Tatum said, incredulous.

"She specifically asked I come alone. It's a public place."

"No way. I am not letting you meet a vampire by yourself. That's seriously horror movie material. What next? Are you going to say we need to split up to cover more ground?"

"You're being ridiculous. She's not *really* a vampire."

"Does she drink human blood?"

"That's what he said."

"Yeah, you're definitely not going alone."

CHAPTER 15

"Are you sure this is the place?" Tatum asked, his voice hushed.

"That's what my acquaintance said. Richard J. Daley Branch, Chicago Public Library," Zoe said.

"Why meet in a library?"

"I wanted a public place. She suggested meeting here."

"What's wrong with a café?"

"You know, you weren't even supposed to come, so I don't know why you think you can complain about this." Zoe's whispers were becoming louder, and an irate reader glanced at them and frowned.

"Okay, fine. How do we find her here?"

Zoe shrugged. "There aren't a lot of people. I'm assuming she would stand out."

Tatum shook his head. "We should have brought a wooden stake, like I said," he whispered as they began walking across the room, between tall shelves full of books.

He'd had lots of fun on the way, suggesting they stop next to a church to get some holy water, then repeatedly pointing out they were literally going to interview a vampire. Zoe had mostly ignored him.

Tatum inhaled, enjoying the smell. Libraries had a scent that nothing else did. Was it simply the intermingling smells of old pages, dust, adhesive, and ink? Or did the stories have a scent of their own? If you took papers and book glue and ink and mixed them together, would it smell the same? He was sure it wouldn't. He turned to ask Zoe what she thought, but she'd drifted away to another aisle.

He was at the far end of the library when he saw the woman. She stood in an aisle full of particularly old, thick books, thumbing through an enormous tome. She was thin and so pale she was nearly white, her lips as red as . . . well, blood. Her long jet-black hair seemed to shine strangely in the shadowy light. Tatum found himself pausing, hesitant. Though the library was public, this area was as quiet as a tomb, and though he was obviously larger and armed, there was something otherworldly about her.

He approached her slowly. She gave him a brief glance as he got closer, then returned to her book.

"Excuse me," he said.

She raised her eyes but said nothing.

"Are you Carmela Von Hagen?"

She frowned. "No."

"Oh, right." Zoe had told him the woman had a weird nickname. What was it? "Um . . . Night Temptress?"

The woman's eyes widened in outrage. She marched out of the aisle, half pushing him out of her way. As she left, she muttered, "Can't go anywhere without a pervert harassing me."

Tatum blinked and followed her out of the aisle. He was about to chase after her when Zoe said, "Tatum."

He glanced at her. She stood by the librarian's desk and waved him over. He joined her.

"I think she just left," he said.

"This is her." Zoe gestured at the librarian behind the desk. Tatum frowned at the woman. She was short, wearing a pair of square eyeglasses, her hair a curly brown. She wore a yellow flower-patterned dress. She pursed her lips, looking at him disapprovingly.

"You're Carmela Von Hagen?" he said.

"Yes," the librarian piped, her voice a tad high.

"The Night Temptress?"

"That's just my online nickname. I don't go around calling myself that." She sniffed and glanced at Zoe. "You were supposed to come alone."

"He insisted on coming," Zoe said. "I think he was worried for my well-being."

"What did you think?" the librarian asked him, her voice shrill. "That I would swoop down in the form of a bat and lunge at her throat?"

"I'm not sure," Tatum said weakly.

"Right." Carmela turned back to Zoe. "Never mind that. Are we doing this?"

"Doing what?" Tatum asked.

"Your girlfriend agreed to be my donor," Carmela said.

"I'm not his girlfriend," Zoe hurriedly corrected.

"Fine, whatever. Sign this." Carmela put a form in front of Zoe. "This says you are a willing donor."

"Hang on, what the hell is going on?" Tatum skimmed the form, incredulous. "You agreed to let this woman drink your blood?"

"I wouldn't meet you otherwise," Carmela said. "Do you think I'd be outing myself to any stranger who comes my way?"

"You can't be serious," Tatum said.

Zoe read the form, forehead crinkled in concentration, as if she were signing a simple bank statement. "This isn't a big deal, Tatum. Stop fretting. I want to see how she does it."

"Absolutely not!"

"Your boyfriend is a pain in the ass," Carmela said.

"I'm not her boyfriend, and she's not your damn food," Tatum snapped.

"It's safe." Zoe looked at him in exasperation. "My acquaintance vouched for her."

"I can drink *your* blood, if you prefer." Carmela scrutinized him as if she were inspecting meat in a butcher's shop. "Frankly, I'd prefer it."

"No one is drinking my blood."

Zoe signed the form. "Okay, I'm ready," she said.

"Let's go to the science fiction aisle," Carmela suggested. "It's usually empty around this time of the day."

Tatum followed the two women, feeling lost in a surreal dream. The science fiction aisle smelled different than the rest of the library, almost sweaty. The visible book covers displayed spaceships, planets, a red-eyed robot.

"Are you left handed or right handed?" Carmela asked Zoe.

"Right handed."

"Give me your left hand." Carmela fished in her purse, retrieving a box of disposable scalpels. She took one out, tearing the sterile wrapping.

Zoe hesitated for just a fraction, and Tatum immediately stepped forward, putting his hand on her shoulder. "Let's go."

She shot him a furious glance and gave Carmela her hand. Carmela took it and carefully pricked Zoe's thumb, making a small incision, about half an inch long. A large drop of blood materialized. Carmela pressed the skin by the thumb, and more blood emerged, starting to trickle. She then bent forward and licked the blood from Zoe's finger.

Tatum held his breath, his entire body tense. His right hand was just above his hidden holster, as if he was about to pull the gun and shoot the librarian vampiress. He forced himself to relax, breathing deeply. This weirdo was creepy as hell, but she wasn't dangerous.

She pulled away, smacked her lips, and watched Zoe's thumb as blood emerged a second time. She licked it again, then nodded, satisfied. "Not bad."

"The food is to your liking?" Tatum asked derisively.

"You'd be surprised—some people's blood tastes like shit," Carmela said. She retrieved a Band-Aid box and a small bottle of disinfectant from her purse and handed them to Zoe.

Zoe dabbed the cut with the disinfectant, then pried a single Band-Aid from the box. Her fingers shook as she put it on her thumb. As much as she tried to hide it, she'd been rattled by the eerie experience.

"Come on," Carmela said. "I've got a job to do."

She walked back to the counter, and Tatum followed her, eyeing Zoe worriedly. She was frowning, biting her lip, probably still processing the strange ordeal. Carmela grabbed a pile of books and began scanning them, one at a time.

"So," she said. "Nate said you have some questions. Are you two journalists?"

"I'm a psychologist," Zoe said.

Tatum leaned on the counter, deciding to let Zoe run the show.

"Okay. What is this? Are you writing some sort of academic paper?" Carmela asked.

"Something like that. We're interested in a specific case. A person in Chicago."

"Uh-huh. What do you want from me?"

"Did you hear about other people with your . . . condition in Chicago?"

Carmela raised an eyebrow. "Other vampires, you mean?"

Zoe hesitated for just a moment. "Yes."

"Sure. There's a whole community here." She said it matter-of-factly, and Tatum wasn't sure if she was being ironic or serious.

"A community of vampires?"

"Yeah. Ninety-six, last time I checked."

"Seriously?" Tatum blurted.

She shrugged. "Why would I lie? You think vampires are so rare? There are over five thousand self-proclaimed vampires in the entire world. And those are just the ones we know about."

"All drinking blood?" Zoe asked.

"Nah. Some are psychic vampires."

Tatum tried not to roll his eyes. "Psychic vampires?"

"You know, that tone you have right now? Not cool. Yeah, psychic vampires. They drain psychic energy." She shrugged. "Or that's what they say. I don't go around knocking down people's beliefs. Stones in a glass house and all that."

"But you feed on human blood, right?" Zoe asked.

"Well, duh."

"And you believe you *need* it to survive?" Tatum asked.

"I need it to stay healthy," she said. "I get headaches and dizzy spells. Sometimes all my joints ache. A little blood, and it's all gone."

Tatum's and Zoe's eyes met.

"Oh, yeah, I see what you're thinking," Carmela said. "Placebo effect, right? You think I have some made-up psychological illness, and when I drink blood, I get better because I believe it's helping me."

"What do you think?" Zoe asked.

"I wish that was the case," Carmela said. "Hell, I'd love to find out I don't need blood. It's not like they sell it in the supermarket. Sometimes it's a real pain in the ass to get some. But I didn't find anything else that helps."

"What first made you think that blood helps?" Zoe asked.

"I always had headaches and dizzy spells, even as a kid," Carmela said. "Then, when I was thirteen, I drank some of my friend's blood on a dare. And guess what? Poof—no more headache."

"Back to the case at hand," Tatum said. He suspected Zoe could spend all day talking to Carmela about vampirism. He wasn't particularly interested. "Can you give us a list of all, uh . . . self-proclaimed vampires in Chicago?"

"Hell, no." Carmela screwed up her nose. "You think I'd go and out all the community like that? The majority of them are totally in the coffin, won't even tell their parents, not to mention two randos."

In the coffin. Tatum had to smile.

"This is very important," Zoe said.

"Yeah? So's our secrecy. What do you think happens if people around us figure out we drink people's blood? Do you think they'd care it's all voluntary? They'd lynch us."

"We won't tell anyone," Tatum said.

"Dude, no offense, but I just met you guys, and it's pretty clear both of you are freaked out by my identity."

Well, you do drink people's blood. Tatum kept his mouth shut, but judging by the way Carmela eyed him, he didn't do a great job at hiding the way he felt.

"We can get a warrant for that list," Tatum said.

She stared at him. "Didn't you say you're psychologists?"

"She's a forensic psychologist," Tatum said, leaning over the counter, fishing his badge from his pocket. "*I* am a federal agent."

Well, at least now all three of them were freaked. Carmela looked as if he'd just announced he was Van Helsing or Buffy the Vampire Slayer.

"You two should leave," she blurted, taking a step back.

"One of your friends killed a woman a couple of days ago," Tatum said. "We need to know who."

"I don't know anyone who killed . . . everything we do is voluntary. We use donors!"

"Until one of you flips out, kills someone for her blood."

"I'm telling you, no one in the community would ever kill anyone."

"You know them all that well? All ninety-six?"

A flicker of hesitation. Both of them leaned over the counter, eyes intent on Carmela.

"Look," Carmela said, her voice trembling, eyes wet. "I don't even know them that well? I don't go to the parties or the events? And I'm not a lifestyler or anything—I don't have a cape at home?" Her tone shifted, each sentence ending in a question. "I just need a drop of blood every now and then to feel okay? It's not like I have a list of crypts in my pocket, or whatever?"

"But you have contacts," Tatum said. "Emails, probably some sort of Twitter users. Hashtag Chicago-vampires-for-the-win? Do you really want us to get a search warrant for your computer and phone?"

They couldn't; he knew that. No judge would sign it. And if she had two brain cells, she must have known it too. But there's knowing, and there's *really* knowing. And when you were afraid, even the things you usually took for granted were suddenly examined again. He watched her frantic tear-filled eyes, imagining what was going on in her mind. *Could they really do that? What if I'm a suspect? What if they took me to an interrogation room, like on TV?* And all the news articles about police brutality, and unconventional investigation techniques, and dirty cops who didn't follow the rules, were playing into their hands, inflating her fear.

"I know this guy," she finally blurted. "He's also a vampire, but he knows *everyone* here. Like, totally everyone. He'd be able to help you two for sure."

"Give us his name."

She shook her head. "No. I'll talk to him first. No way am I outing him to you two without making sure it's fine with him first."

The slightest pressure would get them the guy's name, phone, address, and favorite color. But they also wanted cooperation. And it wasn't like this woman was going anywhere.

"Fine," he said. "Set up a meeting with him. But if we don't hear from you soon—"

"You will," she exclaimed. "I promise you will."

CHAPTER 16

Zoe fished another pizza slice from the box, her eyes intent on the screen, poring through a long document in fascination.

She'd been half-sure Carmela was deluded when she had talked about the number of self-proclaimed vampires. As soon as they returned to the office, she began researching it online and quickly found something named the Atlanta Vampire Alliance. The alliance published the results of some surveys filled out by over a thousand individuals from the vampire community. The amount of data was immense, and Zoe was pleasantly surprised by its quality. Data and graphs were her drug of choice, and she was happy to see at least one vampire seemed to share her affection for them. She read off her findings to Tatum.

"There's a high correlation between self-identified vampires to self-identified Goths." She took a bite from her pizza.

"Not much surprise there." Tatum grunted.

"Yeah." Zoe had to agree. She scrolled down a couple of graphs. Her bandaged finger prickled slightly. She half regretted her decision to let the librarian drink her blood. It was a bit creepy, and she kept remembering the sensation of the woman's mouth around her finger. A shiver ran down her spine. Yuck.

When she was a teen, she loved shows and books about vampires. They had an inherent sexiness to them. But whatever the allure was, Carmela the librarian didn't have it.

Tatum rolled his chair over to her cubicle and took the last slice of pizza from the box. "I have a few leads from ViCAP, but nothing that really clicks," he said. "And none of the cases are in Chicago. I'll do some phone calls tomorrow, follow up on the names, see if I can locate them."

"Okay." Zoe closed the document. As much as she was interested in the vampire community, she doubted these statistics could help them tighten their killer's profile. "There's a Chicago PD database for local crimes. I used it in the Alston case."

Tatum groaned. "Fine, I'll talk to O'Donnell tomorrow about it."

"Why don't we do it together right now?" she asked. "We could finish up with it in a few hours."

"Seriously?"

She glanced at him. He seemed weary, his eyes bloodshot, his shirt rumpled. They'd been working nonstop on this case for more than a week, trying to squeeze every minute from their time in Chicago. But it took its toll. She opened her mouth to tell him never mind, it really was late, when someone cleared his throat behind her. It was one of the agents, a guy named John. Or was it Jerry? She was almost sure it was John.

"Hey," John-or-Jerry said. He stretched it out, saying it throatily, like Fonzie from *Happy Days*. "How are you two doing?"

"Fine," Zoe answered.

"You leaving for the day, John?" Tatum asked.

She was right—it *was* John. Zoe felt an inkling of satisfaction.

"Yeah, I wanted to tell you a few of us are going to head out for a drink. We were wondering if you want to come."

He spoke to them both but looked solely at Tatum.

"That sounds nice," Tatum said. He glanced at her, giving her a smile. "What do you say? I could use a break."

She was surprised to realize that a small voice in her head wanted to go. Not because she needed a drink or because she was tired. But because it sounded nice to go out with a group of people.

But it was a very small voice. Drowned by the fact that it would be a waste of time. That Glover was out there. That they wouldn't have invited her if it wasn't for Tatum. That she'd have to make small talk, and the music would be loud.

"You go ahead," she said to Tatum. "I might join you in a little while. I want to wrap up some stuff."

"You sure?"

She nodded. "Leave me the car. I'll call you once I'm done."

Tatum left with John. She heard him say something unintelligible, John laughing heartily. She considered getting up and following them.

Instead, she called O'Donnell.

The detective answered almost immediately. "Hello?"

"It's Zoe Bentley. I wanted to ask—you have some sort of database of local criminal activity, right?"

"Yeah," O'Donnell replied. "The CLEAR system."

"That's right," Zoe said, recalling the acronym. "Can I log into CLEAR?"

"You'll need a username and password, but it's no big deal; federal agents can get them. You need to submit a security form signed by your chief."

"I hoped to log in today." Zoe bit her lower lip. "Can you give me your username and password?"

"Forget it. I'm not giving you my user. I can't even imagine the shit I'd go through if anyone found out I gave my user and password to someone unauthorized."

Zoe expected as much. "Can you run a few searches for me yourself?"

"Listen, Bentley, it might surprise you, but I have my own leads to pursue." She sounded edgy, exhausted. "If you want, you can drop by here. The office is almost empty—we'd practically have it for ourselves. I'll let you use the system from my computer. How's that?"

"Drop by the station?" Zoe asked.

"You're in the FBI office, right? It's just a ten-minute drive. Call me once you get here."

Zoe had already put her coat on. "See you soon."

O'Donnell wasn't kidding when she'd said they'd have the office to themselves. Zoe found the silence almost eerie.

The Violent Crimes Section in the station was a large open space with three rows of L-shaped desks, each one with its own tidbit of personality. One had a bunch of potted flowers, the next was covered in Post-its with brisk unintelligible scrawls, a third lined with family photos. But they were all empty, their occupants long gone for the night. When Zoe had arrived, one other detective still worked in the corner of the room, but he hardly bothered glancing at Zoe as she followed O'Donnell to her desk. When the detective left, he grunted something that could have been *good night*, and O'Donnell answered in kind. And then it was just the two of them. The desk was just wide enough so they could sit side by side, their shoulders inches apart.

O'Donnell was going through a thick stack of printed papers—Catherine Lamb's phone call activity—matching calls to contacts, marking numbers that appeared repeatedly. Zoe sat by her side in front of the computer, the CLEAR system open. She carefully went through murder cases or violent cases that involved bite marks, needles, or strange cuts. She made a note of any case that seemed worth investigating further, noting the location, the date, the detectives in charge. Zoe usually accompanied this kind of methodical work with music. But in the thunderous silence that encapsulated them, she suspected it would bother O'Donnell, even if she wore earphones.

The problem with her search was that needle marks appeared frequently in the case files when the crimes were drug related. That added a lot of noise to the results, making the search for patterns almost impossible. She wondered if she should ignore the cases that involved needles altogether. After all, the medical examiner had mentioned that the needle marks on Catherine's arm indicated inexperience. Even if unsub beta had attacked someone before, it was more likely he'd bite them or cut them to drink their blood. On the other hand, she didn't want to miss anything important. She bit her lip as she contemplated her dilemma.

"I need the computer for a sec," O'Donnell muttered.

"Sure." Zoe tried to move away, but she couldn't back her chair more than a few inches without ramming into the desk behind her. She was about to stand up and do the shuffling dance—squeeze behind O'Donnell to let her through—when O'Donnell simply leaned over Zoe, grabbing the computer mouse. Zoe awkwardly pushed her chair to the corner to give O'Donnell access to the keyboard. The detective smelled of lavender. She wore a different shirt than she had that morning. She must have showered in the station. That made Zoe think of her own odor after a very long day.

O'Donnell was intent on the screen, a strand of blonde hair draped on her cheek. She had very long eyelashes. It was a weird thing to notice—Zoe never paid much attention to eyelashes.

"Just two more," O'Donnell said. She was checking some names to see if they had a police record.

"Sure, no problem," Zoe said.

Both names returned blank results. O'Donnell pulled away. "Thanks."

"It's your computer."

O'Donnell nodded distractedly. She marked a line on the page. "Where's Agent Gray?"

"I think he went out for a drink."

O'Donnell raised an eyebrow. "Really? Leaving you to do all the dirty work?"

Her tone was teasing, casual, but Zoe frowned in annoyance. Tatum had worked his ass off on this case, had in fact volunteered to work on it. They'd worked weekends and deep into the nights. The mere thought that O'Donnell would suggest Tatum was slacking off raised Zoe's hackles. "We've been working really hard on this case for a very long time."

"It's okay, I was only—"

"I don't see your own partner sitting here, contributing anything to the investigation."

It was as if a layer of frost instantly coated the air between them. The tiny smile that had been hovering on O'Donnell's lip dissipated. "Right." Her voice was sharp, angry. She turned back to her papers.

Zoe turned back to her search queries, feeling that jolt of indignation that came when masking guilt.

The next twenty minutes stretched as she did search after search. She'd decided to keep looking for cases with needle marks. If it made this evening longer, it couldn't be helped.

Her stomach grumbled. They'd been there for a couple of hours, and she hadn't really eaten a proper dinner—just two slices of pizza. But seeing as there was hardly any noise in the room, her stomach's growling filled the space, almost sounding like the rumble of distant thunder. She shifted uncomfortably. Cleared her throat. Another growl. O'Donnell's lips quirked slightly. She opened a drawer, got a jar out of it, placed it between them. It was full of assorted nuts.

"Help yourself." She opened it and took a handful. "It's my night snack."

"Thanks." Zoe took a few nuts, ate one, enjoying the saltiness. "These are good."

"Only the best for my guests." Her tone was still cold.

"Your partner probably has a good reason for not being here," Zoe suggested as a peace offering.

"I don't have a partner."

"Oh. Isn't it mandatory for detectives in your department to work in pairs?"

"There are exceptions."

"Are you one of the exceptions?"

O'Donnell didn't answer, flipping a page in the call records. Zoe waited it out, but it seemed like their discussion was done. She sighed, turning back to the computer. Conversations seemed so easy when other people had them. But for Zoe, a conversation was a delicate butterfly she invariably managed to squash.

After ten minutes, O'Donnell placed the stack of papers on the desk with a loud thump. "Well, Catherine Lamb sure talked on the phone a lot, and with a bunch of different people."

"Anything stand out?" Zoe asked, glancing at the pages. The top sheet had some rows marked with a bright-green marker.

"A few repeat numbers. The most frequent number is her father's, both ingoing and outgoing calls. She has two female friends who talk to her occasionally, though lately they initiated all the calls, and the conversations were short. She talked with Patrick Carpenter every three or four days, and there are a few other repeat numbers here. She was both the church's administrator and a religious counselor, so I guess the variety of phone calls is no surprise."

"So you're done for tonight?" Zoe asked. She was only through about half of the cases. She wondered if O'Donnell would let her stay.

"Nope. Still got her bank and credit statements. I have about an hour to go." O'Donnell looked exhausted. She glanced at the time. "Aw, crap. It's after eleven. I forgot to call my daughter."

"You have a daughter?"

O'Donnell nodded, picking up her phone. "Nellie. She's five."

"Oh. That's nice." Zoe wasn't in fact sure it was nice, but she couldn't think of anything else to say.

O'Donnell nodded, phone to her ear. Then she said, "Hey, hon. Sorry. I didn't notice the time. When did she go to sleep? Oh. No, that's okay. I'm sorry. I should have . . . yeah."

Zoe tried to concentrate on the screen, but she couldn't focus. O'Donnell's tone was so different, so much softer, when she talked on the phone; it was distracting.

"How was her school today?" O'Donnell asked. She listened for a few seconds, her face getting rigid. "They *what*? And what did she do?"

A long pause, in which Zoe quickly skimmed another case of a drug addict found shot, multiple needle holes in both arms. She didn't even bother noting it. Irrelevant.

O'Donnell sighed. "I'll talk to her tomorrow. Thanks. Good night, hon." She hung up and promptly exploded. "Those *bitches!*"

Zoe blinked. "Is everything okay?"

"Nellie has a friend . . . had a friend. Winona. And now Winona became friends with this group of girls, and they don't want to include Nellie in their sticker-collection group. It's like . . . Smurf stickers or something. So today Winona told Nellie she's not talking to her anymore." O'Donnell's voice trembled with rage. "And Nellie just spent the evening crying. It's the third time this month she ends up crying at home."

"It'll pass. Kids fight," Zoe said.

"*Nellie* doesn't fight. She's always so sweet. And last year, Winona didn't have *any* friends. She was so happy Nellie would be her friend."

"It's probably a phase." Zoe just wanted the discussion over. O'Donnell was overreacting.

"You know what I'd like to do? March in there, waving my gun around, maybe fire a few shots into the ceiling. Tell them I'm going to arrest them all. Put the fear of God into them."

Zoe wondered if she'd misjudged O'Donnell. The woman had seemed like a reasonable person at first, but now she sounded demented. "Maybe Nellie needs a different friend," she suggested weakly.

"Well, *yeah*, but she doesn't want a different friend. She wants Winona to be her friend. I should get her to start a different sticker-collection group. With *better* stickers. It'll be a sticker war."

"You should stay out of it. Let Nellie sort it out."

"Do you have kids?" O'Donnell eyed Zoe threateningly, her tone sharp.

"No. But research studies show that when parents start to involve themselves in their kids' lives more, it causes—"

"I don't care what researchers say, Bentley! My daughter cried herself to sleep today because of those . . . those . . ."

"Five-year-olds?"

"Those horrid . . . sticker-collecting gremlins."

Zoe decided to disengage from the crazy woman. She focused on the next murder case. Murderers she could understand.

O'Donnell flipped the pages of the bank statements violently, ripping one of the pages. Occasionally she'd mutter, "I'll give them stickers." Or, "Suddenly *she's* Miss Popular, and she doesn't want Nellie anymore." Then, after a while, she became silent.

Zoe was getting to the end of the case files. She had a handful of possible leads, but nothing more.

"Catherine emptied her bank account," O'Donnell suddenly said.

Zoe turned to look at her. "What?"

"She began to withdraw funds every week. The sums weren't particularly high—two hundred or three hundred a week, but she was consistently emptying her account."

"Did her father mention anything about it?"

"No, nothing."

"Drug habit? Gambling?"

"No drugs found in her home, but I'll make sure the toxicology tests include the widespread drugs she might have used. No online gambling in her browsing history, and no evidence of real-life gambling, either, so far, though it's possible. In any case, she was about to run out of cash. She has one hundred seventy-five dollars and change in her account. I'll ask the nearby bank for ATM security footage for her withdrawals."

"Why?"

"To see if anyone was with her when she withdrew the cash. And maybe get a glimpse of her state of mind when she did it. Was she crying? Was she getting the shakes?" O'Donnell shrugged. "I'll know it when I see it."

It sounded like a long shot, but Zoe supposed it couldn't hurt. "Good idea."

"I'm not actually going to arrest five-year-olds. Or start a sticker war."

"Glad to hear it."

"I'm just tired and frustrated. And kinda sick of nuts." O'Donnell pushed the nut jar away from her. "I accidentally skip meals, and then I end up eating those damn nuts."

"There's your real problem," Zoe said. "This is a clear case of chocolate withdrawal."

"I don't really like chocolate."

Zoe tried to adopt a playful tone, like Andrea did when she joked around. "Are you an alien? From planet Mars?"

O'Donnell frowned and tilted her head. "Um. No."

Joking wasn't Zoe's strong suit, but she tried again. "When I think about it, even an alien from Mars would like chocolate. Because of the um . . . planet name." She could feel her joke dying in her mouth. Maybe someone else could deliver that pun hilariously, but with Zoe it ended up as flat and stale as a year-old cracker.

"Oh, really?" O'Donnell folded her arms, letting a small smile show. "Well, I'm from planet Snickers, and we despise chocolate."

Zoe frowned, trying to figure out if O'Donnell was making fun of her. She finally decided that wasn't the case. "Here, let me show you." She got up.

"Where are you going?"

"To the snack dispenser in the hallway. Or as I like to call it, the emergency chocolate machine."

She quickly marched out to the dispenser, got two Kit Kat bars from it, and returned to O'Donnell's desk, handing her one.

O'Donnell unwrapped her Kit Kat and took a bite.

"What are you doing?" Zoe asked, aghast.

"Eating chocolate," O'Donnell said, her mouth full, a smudge of chocolate on her front teeth. "Why? What's the matter?"

"You don't eat Kit Kats like that! You break the fingers one by one." Zoe unwrapped her own chocolate and demonstrated by breaking a Kit Kat finger.

"It's unbelievable. You're patronizing even when it comes to chocolate." O'Donnell shook her head, still smiling.

Zoe shrugged and took a bite. She shut her eyes, the sweetness mixing with the leftover saltiness from the nuts. So good. She let the aftertaste linger and then ate two cashew nuts, followed by more chocolate. "These mix really well together."

"You're weird, Bentley."

"You can call me Zoe."

"Okay then." O'Donnell took another bite from her own chocolate. "You're really weird, Zoe. But you're right. I needed chocolate."

CHAPTER 17

The van's interior smelled of cigarettes and rotting food. The man in control breathed shallowly through his mouth, trying to ignore the stench. They'd cracked down the windows, despite the night's chill, to make the wait more bearable, but it would take a lot more than that faint breath of air to get rid of the smell.

He'd wanted to take a good rental, but Daniel had insisted they rent this used van for cash, leave as little trace as possible. And he trusted Daniel's intuition.

His friend sat in the passenger's seat, biting his nails. He'd been jittery all afternoon, had almost canceled the hunt. Daniel's photo had been circulated on some local news websites. They got his name wrong, calling him "Rod Glover," which should have been good news, but it just made Daniel angry. He'd even snapped once when they were getting ready, though he had quickly apologized.

The man in control understood. Everything was difficult when it became public.

The train station's parking lot was almost empty now; most of the vehicles had left during the early evening. They had been there for the past four hours because Daniel had said it was important to enter the parking lot during the busy hours to avoid any attention. When the eleven p.m. train had arrived, they'd both tensed, but all the passengers who had passed through the parking lot had walked in groups, except for two men. And besides, there were still too many people.

The midnight train was better. His heart thrummed when he watched the few figures crossing the parking lot. One was alone—a woman. But Daniel shook his head, not saying a word. She was the wrong kind of woman. Daniel had a way of knowing which was the right kind.

The man in control fidgeted. The one-thirty train was about to arrive. The seconds ticked slowly. Daniel didn't seem to mind; he sat in his seat, hardly blinking, his lips somewhere between a grimace and a grin.

He kept thinking about that baby. It would have been so easy to grab it. At the time, he'd lost his nerve, but would it have really been so risky? It had been dark; he would have grabbed it and dashed off before the woman could even react. And there was nothing purer than a baby. People shoved endless shit into their bodies as they grew up. Junk food, sugar, cigarettes, drugs. Their blood changed as a result, became tainted. But a baby would be different. It would—

He shifted in his seat, trying to break the train of thought. They weren't here for a baby. They were here for a woman.

"What if it's a bust?" he asked Daniel.

"Then we'll come again tomorrow," Daniel said. "This is a good place to wait. Trust me."

He did. Except he *needed* someone soon. He needed the blood. "Okay, but—"

"Just focus on the plan. Do you remember the plan?"

"Yes."

"You walk after her. Not too close. If she screams, it's over, you got that? If you see her calling someone, you get that phone before she has time to say a word."

"I remember." He did. He was in control. He remembered.

"I know you do." Daniel turned to him, gave him a smile. "You're as cool as ice, you know that?"

The man in control was glad for the darkness, as he felt his face getting warm.

The screech of the train behind them made him clench his jaw. He'd always been terrified of trains. As a kid, he'd throw a fit every time his mother tried to take him on one. As a grown-up, he'd avoided them completely. Until he met Daniel, he'd never thought trains had other uses. You didn't have to ride them. You could wait for them to come to you.

The train rumbled as it left. The man in control searched around for the passengers. Only one figure moved in the darkness. For a moment his body tightened, but then he saw it was a large fat man.

"Damn it," Daniel whispered.

Would they wait for the next train? It was *freezing* in the van, and he needed to pee, and it stank, and—

"Look." Daniel leaned forward in his seat, excitement in his eyes.

Another passenger. Walking slowly. Thin, petite, long curly hair. She had her eyes on the fat man in front of her. She must have waited on purpose because she didn't want this man walking behind her. She'd thought *he* was the risk.

The man in control grabbed the door handle. Daniel caught his arm.

"Wait," he said. "Not yet."

"But if she gets to her car—"

"She won't. That's her car, over there." Daniel pointed at one of the farthest vehicles. "See how she's looking at it? I bet she's regretting parking so far away now."

The man in control waited. Breath held, his heart racing, teeth almost chattering.

"Okay," Daniel said. "Go. Don't forget the bag. And remember, not too fast."

The man in control shouldered his bag and got out of the van without shutting the door behind him, just like they'd planned. He followed the woman, his steps long, hurried. He tried to make as little noise as he could, the sound of his feet on the paved parking lot thudding in his ears as if amplified. The woman hadn't noticed him yet. She strode briskly, probably both cold and afraid. Daniel was right: he could see how she focused on her car, her sanctuary. She rummaged in her bag, and he prepared to lunge as soon as he saw the shape of a phone. But all she took out were her car keys. She was completely intent on her one purpose—getting into her car.

And then she glanced backward. She saw him. *If she screams, it's over.*

But she didn't. Daniel had told him they almost never screamed at first. They walked away, mind churning with denial, hoping that the man following them was just a random guy. They were scared, but they didn't want to cause a scene.

She walked faster, getting away from him. He needed to keep pace. Daniel had told him not to give chase. That wasn't the plan. He had to stick to the plan, he was in control, and the plan was that he just follow her, get her away from the road and the station. He was in control, he was . . .

He ran now, his mouth full of saliva. He could smell her scent in the air, perfume, and shampoo, and sweat, and underneath it all, warm blood. He was almost upon her. She glanced back and screamed.

If she screams, it's over.

He didn't care. He kept running, chasing her—she was almost within his grasp. But she had reached her car, was about to unlock it, to drive away.

Daniel's figure unfolded into view. He'd circled the parking lot and had waited for her behind the car, and now he grabbed her, hand over her mouth before she could yell for help. She squirmed in his arms, struggling, her screaming muffled.

"I got her," Daniel hissed. "Damn it, why did you—"

He gasped as the woman elbowed his stomach. Daniel's hold over the woman became lax, and she clawed at his arms, raking them. Daniel let out a grunt of pain and pushed her, and she fell to the ground. The scent of blood filled the air.

She stumbled as she ran away from them, but in the wrong direction. She should have headed toward the road, toward help, and the train station's security. Instead, she ran the other way. She screamed now, but her voice was breathless, shuddering with fear. She was in a deserted parking lot, the few commercial buildings around them empty for the night.

The man in control ran after her, the thrill of the chase filling him with pure ecstasy. *This* was what he was born to do. As he ran, getting farther away from the road, the ground changed, gravel crunching under his soles, the moonlight shining on cracks crisscrossing the pavement. Ahead, the shadows of trees loomed. She saw them, swerved to the right, toward the structures, toward civilization.

Too late.

He crashed into her, and they both tumbled to the ground. He bit his tongue, a sharp blinding pain, and then he could taste his own blood, which only excited him more for what was to come. She struggled under him, trying to push him away, but her movements were sluggish. She looked dazed. Perhaps she'd hit her head; it didn't really matter.

He had a syringe in his bag. But he didn't need it. He was a predator. She was prey. Slamming her head to the ground, he ripped the scarf off her neck. Bent down, her scent enveloping him, intoxicating.

He bit hard.

She screamed so loud that his ears rang, but he was beyond caring about screams, about getting caught. Her taste filled his mouth, salty and wonderful. He grunted as he slurped the bleeding wound, the world fading away around him. Only this mattered.

And then he was shoved away. He blinked in confusion, raised his eyes. Daniel stood above him, looking furious.

"Jesus!" Daniel spat. "What's the matter with you?"

The words made no sense. Wasn't this what they were there to do? He licked his lips, the tangy taste of the woman divine. He wanted more.

"No!" Daniel pushed him away. He lunged, punched Daniel in the face. Daniel stumbled back, blinking in shock. For a few seconds neither of them moved.

Then the woman groaned.

"We'll take her to the trees," Daniel said, his voice clear and forceful. There was no arguing with that voice.

The man in control nodded, feeling drunk.

They dragged the woman to the trees, and he glimpsed the dark shape of the channel beyond them, the moonlight gleaming on the brackish water.

"Here's good," Daniel said, and the man in control heard an echo of his own intoxication in his friend's voice.

"Remember your job," Daniel said.

For a second he didn't. What was his job? But then he recalled the plan, the details. Why they were doing it all. He checked his bag and nodded at Daniel.

Daniel pushed the woman to her knees, wrapped a tie around her throat. The man in control had seen his friend do this before at Catherine's home. Back there, it had been shocking; he'd nearly lost his nerve. But now he was ready. Didn't even flinch when Daniel cut the woman's pants.

Something was wrong. His friend muttered to himself, sounding furious. The woman gagged, trying to breathe, and Daniel prodded at her, hit her, sounding more and more enraged.

It took the man in control a second to understand what the problem was. Daniel was struggling to get an erection. The man in control looked away, embarrassed, but then recalled his own job. He had an important part to play. He unslung his bag and opened it, began performing his task. The woman's eyes bulged, no sound coming from her now, her fingers clawing at the tie around her throat. Daniel yanked it hard, cursing, voice hoarse.

And then she was lying in the mud.

"Damn it!" Daniel snarled. "Fucking bitch!" He kicked her.

"Daniel," the man in control said.

"It's your fault!" Daniel shouted at him. "With your fucked-up biting, and snarling, and hitting me, like a damn animal!"

Daniel was right. He lowered his eyes.

"Shit," Daniel said. "Never mind. We still have work to do. Stay with her. I'll get the van."

The man in control nodded, not daring to argue.

Daniel left, still muttering curses.

The man in control knelt by the battered woman and took out the syringe. He had work to do—he knew that—but he wanted to try to get some blood first. If it was only him, he could just drink his fill now, but he wasn't the only one who needed the blood.

CHAPTER 18

Tuesday, October 18, 2016

Bill Fishburne woke up in the middle of the night, his mouth dry. He shifted in the bed and tried to sink back into sleep, knowing that if he got up to get a drink, it'd take him ages to fall asleep.

But the thirst nagged at him, and eventually he relented and sat up gently, not to wake up Hen.

It was then that he realized she wasn't in bed.

She'd called him in the evening, telling him she'd have to work until after midnight. Wasn't it midnight yet? It felt like much later. He sighed, fumbled for his phone, and lit its screen.

It was seven minutes past four.

The jolt of worry woke him instantly. His brain scrambled for an explanation and immediately found one—Hen must have returned home and then kept working on the computer. She did that every once in a while. When there was an important case. To reassure himself, he got up, slid his feet into his slippers, and padded to the bedroom window. They had a view out to the street, and their parking spots could easily be seen from the window.

Hen's car wasn't there.

He checked the rest of the rooms in the house, even peeking into Chelsey's room. He verified with the clock in the kitchen that it really was after four in the morning, feeling the anxiety blossoming in his gut.

Finally he grabbed his phone and called Hen.

Her phone was offline.

He could think of a simple explanation for all of this. Hen had stayed to work way beyond midnight and hadn't noticed that her phone had run out of battery power. It had never happened before, but she did occasionally mention that other paralegals in the firm stayed all night working. He called her office number and waited as it rang, counting the seconds. When he reached thirty, he disconnected the call.

He was annoyed with her firm—and with her. She should have texted him. He poured himself a glass of water. His hand trembled as he drank.

He wasn't really annoyed. He was scared. Hen would never have stayed at work so late without calling or texting him. She would have noticed that her battery had run out.

Something was very, very wrong.

He tried her office and her personal phone again. Nothing.

He found Gina's number in his contacts. He hesitated, knowing that calling anyone at four a.m. was a breach of every possible protocol. But his heart was thumping so hard it threatened to blow up in his rib cage. He hit send and waited for her to pick up.

She answered after ten seconds. "Hello?" Her voice was sleepy, confused.

"Gina, it's Bill. I'm sorry to wake you up so late but—"

"Bill Fishburne?"

"Yeah. I'm sorry, but I just woke up, and Henrietta isn't home. She hasn't returned from the office yet." Gina worked in the same office as Hen. In fact, Hen had gotten her the job.

"What time is it? She had to work late."

"It's after four in the morning."

A long pause followed. "Did you try her phone?"

"It's offline. And she's not answering in the office either. Do you think she stayed there all night?"

"No! When I left, she said she'd be finishing up in about an hour. And that was at ten thirty." Gina sounded wide awake as well, and her voice mirrored Bill's fear. "Hang on. She worked with another paralegal . . . Jeff. I'll call him, see if he knows what's going on."

"Okay, thanks."

She hung up, and Bill paced the kitchen. The seconds ticked by as he waited for Gina's call, occasionally picking up the phone, then putting it down again.

A tiny figure padded into the kitchen. Chelsey, blinking in confusion. "Daddy?"

"Hey, pumpkin, it's the middle of the night—go back to bed." It took all of his self-control to hide the trembling in his voice, to speak softly.

"I heard voices."

"I was just talking to myself. Come on—let's get you back to bed." He approached her and put an arm around her shoulder, gently turning her around. She obediently shuffled back with him, and he helped her into bed, tucking her in. Her dark curly hair spread on the pillow as she snuggled, hugging her unicorn doll. Bill bent down, kissed her forehead, and stepped out of the room. He returned to the kitchen, setting his phone to vibrate so that its ring wouldn't wake her up again.

It'd been thirteen minutes since Gina had hung up. What was she—

The phone lit up, vibrating. He slid his finger on the screen, had to do it three times because it trembled so badly.

"Hello?" he whispered.

"Bill, listen, I just talked to Jeff. He said they were both done by twelve thirty. They left the office together. He dropped Henrietta off at the train station and then drove home." Gina's voice cracked. She was on the verge of crying. "Are you sure she's not home? Maybe she was so tired she fell asleep in Chelsey's room? Or the bathroom? Or . . . or . . ."

"Her car isn't here," he said hollowly. His gut had become a heavy, freezing slab of ice.

"Maybe she went somewhere else? Or maybe . . ."

"I have to go, Gina. I'll call you once I find out where she is." He hung up the phone.

He wanted to lunge out of the house and look for her. See if her car was in the train station's parking lot. But of course he couldn't leave Chelsey alone. He contemplated calling Hen's mother, telling her to come over and watch over Chelsey while he looked, but he didn't want to scare her. And she'd wake up Chelsey by mistake, which would only make things much, much worse.

He did the only thing he could think of. He punched in a number he knew by heart and had always hoped he wouldn't need to dial.

They picked up immediately. "Nine-one-one, what's your emergency?"

After calling the police, Bill had a while to wait by his own, in the dark house. He spent it mostly imagining endless reasons for Hen's disappearance.

He was hard pressed to recall a time he had been more terrified in his life.

Chelsey had undergone a medical operation as a toddler, and that had been scary. But he had had Hen and Chelsey to comfort, and a doctor who'd kept telling him it was a routine operation, and nurses who kept coddling her.

Now, all he had was fear and no one to talk to.

Perhaps there'd been a train crash. Perhaps Hen had had an accident when driving back from the train station. Perhaps she'd recalled she'd forgotten something in the office, run back, and gotten hit on the way by a drunk driver and was now bleeding in a ditch somewhere.

One of the theories he concocted was that she'd managed to lock herself in the train station's bathroom. He clung to that possibility like a drowning man in a stormy sea, imagining her crying in the bathroom stall, waiting for morning so someone could get her out. Because the beauty of that theory was that at any moment, she would step into their home, traumatized but safe. And beyond an anecdote they could laugh about in a few years, there would be no impact on their life. Chelsey would wake up in the morning, not even knowing her mother had been missing for the entire night.

When the police finally showed up, he opened the door before they knocked.

"Thanks for coming," he said in a low voice to the officer in the doorway. "Please try to be quiet. My five-year-old daughter is sleeping."

They were two cops in uniform. The young one was black, making Bill feel slightly more at ease. He was taller than his partner, his face serious, his eyes alert. His partner was white, chubby, and short, and seemed at least ten years older.

"Are you Mr. Fishburne?" the young cop asked.

"That's right. Please, come in. But be quiet." If Chelsey woke up when the cops were there, she'd be terrified.

They both stepped inside, and Bill closed the door behind them, keeping the night's chill outside.

"I'm Officer Ellis," the young cop said. "This is my partner, Officer Woodrow. I understand that your wife hasn't returned home from work yet?"

"Yes," Bill said. He blurted the entire story, doing his best to impress upon them that this was a real emergency, not a case of a silly woman who forgot to call her husband. He mentioned several times that she was a paralegal, that her phone was offline, that her associate dropped her at a train station—

"And you said his name is Jeff?" Ellis asked.

"Yeah, he's another paralegal—"

"How well do you know him?"

"Not too well. I saw him once at a party. But he seemed like a good guy."

"Does your wife ever mention him? Does she talk to him on the phone?"

"Uh . . . no, not that I recall."

"Does she often stay at work late?"

It dawned on Bill that the cops were concocting theories of their own, based on their own experience. A woman who had a fling and fell asleep in her lover's bed, not noticing the time. Or maybe a woman who went out drinking and just hadn't returned from her late night of partying. This was probably what they mostly saw. Didn't they always say on TV that the police didn't investigate a missing person report until twenty-four hours had passed?

Bill felt a desperate need to convince the cops that this was not the case. Henrietta would *never* do any of those things. It was so out of the realm of possibility that he never entertained those thoughts.

"Henrietta would *never* just . . . not return, okay? She didn't leave me. She's not with another man. She's not drunk in a holding cell. There's something wrong."

"Mr. Fishburne," Ellis said. "I understand. We will look for your wife."

"Maybe she locked herself in the bathroom in the train station," Bill said helplessly. "And her battery ran out."

"We'll check it out," Ellis said. "Can you give us the names and phone numbers of your wife's associates? The ones you talked to? And the address of her firm, please."

He did. He showed them a picture of her. He watched them leave, the red and blue lights flickering as they drove away.

It was after five in the morning. He would need to wake up Chelsey in an hour, and Hen still wasn't home. And he'd have to explain somehow why there were no Mommy snuggles this morning and why he was the one combing Chelsey's hair.

CHAPTER 19

The early-morning chill had a bite to it, but Zoe didn't really mind. Once she started jogging, she'd mostly stop feeling the cold. She had a hat covering her ears and slim gloves for her fingers. Her nose would still feel like an icicle by the time she was done, but it was a small price to pay.

She used to hate jogging.

Andrea had dragged her a few times, when they lived in Boston, and Zoe had found the experience dreadful. Part of it, she had to admit, was that Andrea kept talking throughout their jogs, while all Zoe could do was grunt the occasional "Uh-huh" in between one labored breath and the next, her lungs feeling as if they were about to collapse into a black hole.

But ever since her ordeal in Texas the month before, she needed fresh air, and lots of it. She went for long walks at first, but that didn't do enough to curb the bursts of claustrophobic panic that hit her randomly throughout the day. Those dissipated almost completely once she ran.

Andrea had explained over and over that she needed to stretch. Her sister had a list of what seemed like hundreds of stretching techniques, some so complicated they reminded Zoe of illustrations in the Kama Sutra. Zoe's patience was just enough for a twenty-second stretch routine. Andrea had threatened her with terrible sports injuries, but Zoe decided, with zero evidence to support it, that her body wasn't the kind that got injured while running.

So she did her three stretching exercises and began running. When they'd gotten to Chicago a week before, she'd quickly discovered one of the city's best assets, as far as she was concerned—the Lakefront Trail. Better than any jogging route in Dale City.

It was still dark when she started, with a hint of blue dawn above the lake, the shoreline almost impossible to discern. A thin layer of clouds stood between the lake and the sky, a vista of ever-changing fluffy mountains.

Her mind worked differently when she ran.

Throughout the day, her brain churned and bubbled, a frothing soup of ideas and theories and unanswered questions. But when she ran, her thoughts quieted down, and she could focus on one thread, carefully reviewing it, thinking it through to the end.

She thought of Catherine Lamb's gruesome murder. But this time, instead of focusing on the actual act, she considered the moments before. The two men, approaching Catherine's house. Did they approach on foot, or did they drive there? Did they talk on the way? When they approached the door, did they walk side by side, or was one of them leading, the other behind?

It was difficult to imagine. The whole notion of Glover collaborating with another man was strange. Glover was a man who stalked and murdered alone. He hid under a carefully maintained facade of a nice, friendly man, someone you could have a drink with. And when he shed that facade, he didn't allow people to see it. Obviously, he didn't want to be caught. But there was more than that. Glover wanted to be *liked*.

When he was their neighbor, all those years ago, he'd gone out of his way to be friendly with her entire family. He would talk with her parents about politics, his opinions always matching her father's. But if her parents argued about politics, he would quickly find merit in both sides and make them both feel pleased with themselves. He would ask for neighborly favors, cunningly figuring out that when someone did you a favor, they often began to like you more. And he'd been absolutely charming with Zoe, giving her what teenagers most wanted, a nonjudgmental listening ear. He wanted to be liked in the way a psychopath did. Not because he was remotely interested in anyone else, but because when someone liked him, it affirmed his positive opinion about himself. He watched people's reactions to him like a man checking a mirror, verifying that he looked good.

And also because he judged human connections to be useful. And he was right. After all, didn't the police and her own parents prefer to take his word over Zoe's?

But he'd shown his true face to someone, an accomplice. What made him do it? And how had that worked?

The sun had emerged between the clouds, instantly painting the sky in a bright orange, the light giving the waves in the lake a shimmer. Zoe took out her phone, took a wobbly picture. She made a mental note to send it to Andrea.

She ran past Ohio Street Beach. Her eyes glanced at the smooth sand, where three months before, Krista Barker had been found dead, her body embalmed. She and Tatum had arrived at the crime scene bickering and arguing and hating each other's guts. It was a lifetime ago.

Turning around, she started making her way back while nudging her mind gently back on track.

Glover didn't show his true self, not even to his partner in crime, she decided. Glover wanted to be adored by everyone, and the only people who saw his true self were his victims. And aside from her and Andrea, none of the women who saw that side survived. Perhaps the main reason he was so obsessed with her was that unlike others, she had *really* seen him for who he was, all those years ago.

No, whatever Glover showed his partner was another disguise. He'd be friendly and accommodating and fun to be around, just like with everyone else. And when he finally broached the subject of his need, he would do it very carefully, in a way that made it seem like it wasn't his fault at all. He would be the *victim* in his narrative. Who would he blame? Women? Society? His own parents? Whoever it was, it would be the thing that would get him the most sympathy from his partner. Sympathy and collaboration.

And he'd have to find the right partner. Someone he knew for sure wouldn't be horrified or disturbed by what Glover told him. How had he found him? Had he searched online for like-minded people and, by a stroke of luck, found one who lived nearby? It felt wrong. As much as she hated to admit it, a large part of Glover's charm was face to face. His easy smile, his disarming build, his easygoing body language. All a disguise, sure, but one he wore well. And he would use it when he sought someone he could trust.

She could see the parking lot in the distance and slowed her jog to a walk, breathing hard. Cupping both hands in front of her face, she breathed on them softly, thawing her nose.

Glover had met his accomplice face to face. Like Tatum had said, he had either met him at church, or he had met him somewhere else, and then his newly found friend had introduced him to the church. But what would Glover do in a church? Repent of his sins? Pray?

Something was missing. She needed to learn more about Riverside Baptist Church.

CHAPTER 20

Riverside Baptist wasn't much to look at on first sight. A redbrick structure with a single tower, the entrance a simple arched crimson door. But as Tatum parked the car, Zoe noticed the little things. The blooming flower beds lining the external walls. The clearly tended lawn in the churchyard, three freshly colored wooden benches on its edge. Unlike the rest of the street, the area surrounding the church was clean of dry leaves. This place was tended with care.

Her phone rang just as Tatum switched off the engine. It was O'Donnell.

She motioned Tatum to give her a second and hit answer. "This is Zoe."

"Bentley." O'Donnell's voice was sharp and icy. "Why did you tell the press that you were helping us with the case?"

Zoe frowned in confusion. "I didn't tell anyone."

"Well, it certainly wasn't me. There's a detailed article here outlining your involvement. Hang on . . ." A short pause followed, and then O'Donnell read aloud. "Sources close to the investigation report that the renowned profiler Zoe Bentley and the FBI were consulted regarding the case. Bentley helped the Chicago Police Department before, in the Strangling Undertaker case, and played a crucial part in his—"

"I didn't tell anyone about this. What about the guy who saw me at the station yesterday? Maybe he leaked it?"

"He didn't even know who you were and didn't care. Besides, I had a journalist ask me about you yesterday afternoon. Told me he knew you."

Zoe's heart sank. "What was his name?"

"It was something stupid. Like . . . Nick Brick. No . . . it was Jimmy Kimmy—"

"Harry Barry?"

"That's the guy. He wanted to know what Zoe Bentley said about the case, and I said I couldn't divulge any information and asked how he knew you were involved. And he said that he knew you. You shouldn't have told him anything; I don't care if you're buddies. We agreed—"

"He's not my buddy, and I didn't talk to him. You got played." Zoe wanted to punch something. She'd forgotten that among the two and a half million people in Chicago, there was one Harry Barry. To her chagrin, he was writing a book about her. She'd even given him a lot of the material herself. And now he'd tricked Detective O'Donnell into admitting Zoe was involved in this investigation as well. Damn it, that meant Glover knew as well. He'd be more careful, possibly more dangerous.

"What do you mean, I got played?" O'Donnell's voice shifted. The anger was still there, but it lacked a target.

"He was fishing. He had no idea I was involved until *you* told him."

"Shit. But how did he—"

"Harry Barry is a pain in the ass," Zoe said, annoyed. "Listen, I'll call you back later—we'll decide how to handle this."

"Okay."

Zoe hung up and checked the *Chicago Daily Gazette*'s website on her phone. She found the article easily enough; it was a classic H. Barry headline: *Renowned Profiler Advises Police in Pastor's Daughter's Murder.* Trust Harry to mention Zoe, the church, and the murder in one sentence. She tapped the link and skimmed the contents, irritated to see her picture above Glover's. The least he could do was put Glover first. That was the important part.

"Mancuso won't be pleased," Tatum said, looking over her shoulder at the phone. "And O'Donnell's boss probably won't be thrilled either."

"Well, it's done," Zoe muttered. "I'm more worried about Glover's reaction. This might make him more erratic."

"Well, he might end up making a mistake."

"Yeah." Zoe didn't feel convinced. She scrolled the article up and down, alternating between her own picture and Glover's.

Tatum plucked the phone from her hand. "Come on," he said. "No point in worrying about this. Let's go check out the church."

The air wasn't much warmer inside the empty church. To the right of the entrance was a bulletin board, a large portrait photo of Catherine Lamb pinned in the middle. Above it was the inscription *In Loving Memory*, in a curly delicate font, and below the picture, in the same font, *Catherine Lamb 1991–2016*. Dozens of pictures were pinned around it, the details hard to make out in the dim light. Against the wall under the bulletin board was a table holding a large wreath. Around it lay numerous bouquets, lit candles, and handwritten notes.

Zoe examined the photos on the board. All of them were of Catherine with other people, presumably belonging to the congregation. In some they were standing together, smiling at the camera, while in others, the photographer had caught them in various activities. Painting a wall, Catherine holding a large brush, specks of white paint on her face. Tending to a weedy garden, Catherine on her hands and knees, dirt up to her elbows, talking to a young teenager who worked by her side. In a large kitchen, Catherine smiling at a woman who was tending to a large pot. The photos had obviously been chosen because Catherine looked attractive in them, and whoever had chosen them had paid little attention to the other subjects. In many photos, the people around her were blurry, or blinking, or occasionally just captured with a weird face conversing in midsentence. It didn't matter, because this was about Catherine. But it gave the entire collage a strange effect. As if Catherine was sharper, more real, more *alive* than the others.

"Church looks empty now, but the candles have been lit recently," Tatum said, looking at the table. "Maybe they did some sort of memorial for her earlier this morning, before people went to work."

He was right. The flowers were fresh too. White lilies and carnations dominated the table, and Zoe got the sense that the majority had been supplied by the same shop. Maybe one of the congregation members was a florist.

Another board, which had a monthly schedule and a few other notices, hung next to Catherine's shrine. A list of handwritten names was posted on it, and inspecting it more closely, Zoe realized they were volunteers who listed themselves to cook for Pastor Lamb in the difficult days ahead. There was a notice about a picnic that had been canceled because of Catherine's death and another notice about a postponed collection for the homeless. Scanning the monthly schedule, Zoe saw a weekly "senior street painting" event every Tuesday and an event for donating clothes for a women's shelter.

She could feel a deep sense of community in this church.

"Glover would have been drawn to this place like a moth to a porch light," she said.

"What do you mean?" Tatum asked, looking around him.

"Well . . . he lived in Maynard for years. A small town." She thought back to her childhood. "Everyone on our street knew each other by name, and you couldn't step out of the house without meeting someone you knew. I used to love it. And then, as a teenager, I *hated* it." She smiled despite herself.

"It was the same in Wickenburg, I guess," Tatum said.

She remembered that there had always been random pieces of light gossip flying around. She could almost hear her mother's conversations with their neighbors. *So-and-so's daughter came from Alaska to visit— why did she move there in the first place? It's so cold. Did you hear about the thing at the barbershop last week? They're still cleaning up the foam. Mrs. Godfry, the third-grade teacher, is sick again; those poor kids should have a proper teacher.* Tidbits of familiarity and kinship.

"It was a real community," she said. "Everyone was part of the Maynard tribe. And Glover *loved* it. He was always superfriendly with everyone. Happy to chat, to pass along things he'd heard."

"What, like gossip?"

"Or national news. And sometimes he'd make up lies, thread them into the truth, to make the conversation more interesting. To make *himself* more interesting." As a child, she'd just accepted it as who he was. Now she knew better. Psychopaths were often great at imitation, watching the people around them, figuring out what worked and what didn't. What made people like you more.

Tatum saw where she was going with this. "And then he gets to Chicago. And it's not the same."

"Right. A fast city, with too many people. At first, maybe that's what he was looking for. A place to hide, to blend in with the crowd. But after a while he began missing the casual talks, the chummy hellos."

"He didn't get it at work either," Tatum said.

"No, he didn't." They'd been to the office he'd worked at. People working in separate cubicles, a huge tech company, everyone in his department constantly on the phone with angry customers. "And then he sees this place. This church's community, brimming with a sense of kinship. He probably passed by them once or twice—a congregation picnic or a group of them standing outside the church, talking. And that was it. He saw his prey."

Zoe stepped away from the board, paced between the pews, looking around her. Glover would have come here on Sundays, when it was fullest—more people to meet. More people to see him there, the pious Christian. First just showing his face, then maybe joining their conversations, their activities, volunteering here and there. Becoming the "good man" Patrick Carpenter had mentioned.

People would crowd this space, listening to the pastor, and Glover would be there as well, watching around him, passing the time by checking out the younger women, fantasizing. Where would Catherine be sitting? In plain sight? How many times had he leisurely spent his morning glancing at her, imagining her naked, a tie wrapped around her throat?

And there was someone else here. Unsub beta. Zoe chewed her lip. Someone else who'd developed an obsession with Catherine. Maybe wondering how her blood tasted.

Churches and crosses didn't keep you safe from vampires in the real world. At least not from this one.

How had he and Glover met? What made them see that they shared a common dark interest? This wasn't a normal church community chat. *I thought the sermon today was powerful. What about you? I wasn't really listening; I was fantasizing about killing the woman sitting in front of me. Oh, same here.*

Somehow, Glover had found him. She needed to know how.

"Zoe," Tatum said. "Check this out."

He pointed at one of the photos. Zoe returned and studied it.

One face, blurry, out of focus, hardly noticeable.

Glover.

He was talking to someone who stood just outside the frame of the photo. Zoe leaned forward, frowning, trying to glean info from the photo, but found nothing. A picture of Catherine and others from the congregation at a picnic, all of them laughing and talking, ignoring the camera. Catherine held both hands up, demonstrating something to a man she was conversing with. Albert Lamb sat by her side, listening to her, his face serene. Glover at the corner.

She was reaching for the photo when the church door opened. She turned around to see a man looking at them, holding a bouquet of red roses. He had curly brown hair and thick lips.

"Hello," he said, his voice light and easygoing.

"Hello," Tatum said back.

"Are you two searching for someone?"

"We were just looking around."

He stepped closer and frowned. He cleared his throat. "We've had a few people just looking around lately. Are you two detectives as well?"

Tatum glanced at Zoe, and she shrugged.

Turning back to the man, he took out his badge. "Special Agent Gray."

"Oh. I'm Allen Swenson," he said. "Is this about Catherine?"

"Yes. Did you know her well?"

"Well, I've been going to this church for twelve years, so I talked to her several times. We ran a charity event together once. She was a sweet woman."

"Are those flowers for her shrine?" Zoe asked.

He licked his lips, seeming confused, then glanced down at the rose bouquet in his hand, as if just remembering them. "Yes. I missed the memorial this morning, but I figured I'd drop by and put these here."

He went over to the table and gently placed the bouquet beside another. Then he turned to look at Zoe. "What's *your* name?"

"Mr. Swenson," Tatum interjected. "Would you mind if we asked you a few questions?"

There was a slight pause. "No, go ahead; I'll be glad to help."

"When did you hear about Catherine's death?"

"On Sunday morning. I came over for the service and met a few of the congregation members. They told me."

"Was there a service on Sunday?"

"No. The pastor wasn't here, and neither was Patrick."

"Patrick?"

"Patrick Carpenter. He sometimes does the service, if Pastor Lamb can't make it." Swenson cleared his throat again. "Is there any progress in the investigation?"

"We're not at liberty to say," Tatum answered. "Did you notice anything out of the ordinary in the week leading up to Catherine Lamb's death?"

"I wasn't really around. I mostly come to the Sunday services."

"When was the last time you saw Catherine?"

"Well . . . she wasn't at church on the previous Sunday. I guess that *is* pretty unusual. I did spot her on the street when I drove by the church about a week and a half ago."

"How did she seem?"

"Okay, I guess. I was talking with a friend, so I didn't really pay attention, but I waved, and she saw me and waved back."

"Anything else?"

"No, like I said, I was driving. I didn't stop to chat."

"Can you think of anyone in the congregation who was particularly close to Catherine?"

"A lot of people. She organized a lot of the church's activities."

"Anyone *particularly* close?" Zoe asked.

He seemed to hesitate for a moment. "Well, she and Patrick were a bit close. But I guess it was because they were both really invested in the community. Last few weeks they weren't as close, though. I thought maybe they had a falling-out."

"What gave you that idea?"

"Just small stuff. They used to sit next to each other during the service, but the last two times I noticed they sat apart. And they didn't talk too much."

Zoe and Tatum waited for more, letting the silence stretch. Swenson's eyes kept darting around, but he didn't say anything else.

"Do you know this man?" Zoe tapped the photo, pointing at Glover.

He frowned, looking closely. "Oh, yes, I saw him around. Uh . . . Moore, right?"

"He called himself Daniel Moore," Tatum said.

Swenson nodded slowly. "Uh-huh. Yeah. I've seen him."

"Ever talk to him?"

"Maybe once or twice. Just casual talk."

"Did you notice him talking to anyone else?"

He frowned. "Is he the guy who did it?"

"We just want to talk to him," Tatum said. "Notice him talking to anyone in particular?"

He thought about it. "No. Just seen him around. He was a regular."

"Since when?"

"I'm not sure." Swenson took a step back. "Listen, I'd love to help, but I need to go to work. Do you have a business card or something?"

Tatum handed him his card. Swenson pocketed it and gave Zoe a long look. Then he turned and left.

"He knew Glover," Zoe said. "It wasn't just a familiar face."

"Definitely not," Tatum said.

Zoe took another close look at the photos, searching for Glover. Catherine's father, the pastor, was in a few of course, always wearing a somber expression. Patrick Carpenter appeared in seven of the pictures; his wife, Leonor, in five. Leonor was talking or smiling at someone in all of the pictures. Always interacting. Patrick, on the other hand, seemed more still. Thoughtful. Swenson was in two pictures as well. In one of them, it was just him and Catherine, outside the church, sitting on one of the wooden benches, talking.

Tatum took out his phone and snapped a couple of photos of the entire setup and a close-up of the picture with Rod Glover. "Let's go talk to Albert Lamb and hear what he has to say about Daniel Moore."

CHAPTER 21

Bill managed to get Chelsey ready for school and drive her there through a fog of turmoil and panic. He didn't think she'd noticed, but it was impossible to know for sure. She could be frighteningly perceptive. He'd told her Mommy had to go to work early that morning, a lie that instantly injected guilt into the hurricane of emotions roiling inside him. When she got out of the car and waved, he waved back, a smile plastered on his face. She turned around, and he drove off, stopped a block later, stepped out of the car, and threw up.

Now, he sat back in the car and breathed, trying to get a grip. He couldn't drive like this. The fact that he'd driven Chelsey to school in this condition suddenly seemed irresponsible and downright stupid.

He tried Hen's phone again, like he'd been doing the entire morning, and it was still offline. He had three missed calls from Gina and a text from her asking him to update her as soon as he knew something.

The police were looking for her right now. Whatever had happened, they'd figure it out.

Unless the police were somehow responsible.

It was a sudden, reflexive thought. As soon as it emerged, he began thinking about wrongful shootings, cooked-up charges, police brutality. Maybe Officer Ellis and his partner already knew where Hen was when they'd shown up. Maybe they were just going through the motions.

He was helpless, unsure how to continue. He googled on his phone, What to do with missing person.

The first result was actually helpful. He could do quite a lot. He could give more information to the police. He could call all the hospitals in Chicago. He could visit local jails. Call all of his wife's friends. Post on social media. He could print flyers. He found out there was something named the National Missing and Unidentified Persons System.

Now he felt even worse. He had so much to do, and he didn't know where to start. And he had to be home by noon to make lunch for Chelsey.

He could start by driving to the train station. See if Hen's car was there. It would help him figure out when she'd gone missing. It would help the police.

It was difficult to perform simple acts like driving. He forced himself because of Chelsey, but he was standing at the edge of a precipice, a dark chasm just inches away. And everything he did could make him stumble and fall. It took him much longer than it should have to reach the station's parking lot.

But now that he was there, things became easier. All he had to do was drive between the rows of parked vehicles, looking for Hen's car. He found something relaxing in giving himself away to this one easy task that required his full concentration. He was methodical, starting at the southwest side of the parking lot, zigzagging his way through the lanes slowly.

He'd gone through four lanes when something caught his eye at the far side of the parking lot. A squad car, its lights still flickering. He changed course, driving toward it, and saw something that chilled him to the core. A yellow tape, cordoning off a section of the parking lot. And beyond the tape, Hen's car.

He hit the brake and got out of the driver's seat, sprinting toward the yellow tape. A cop stepped in his way. He recognized him immediately. It was Ellis.

"What happened?" he asked, his voice loud, wavering. "What happened to Hen?"

"Mr. Fishburne," Ellis said. "You can't go in there."

"Is she there? Did she have an accident? Is she hurt?"

"We haven't found Henrietta yet," Ellis said. "She isn't here."

A jolt of relief. Then confusion. If Hen wasn't here, why had they cordoned off her car? What was going on?

Details swam into focus. A man wearing gloves scraped the ground near Hen's car, placing the result in a small plastic bag. Another man was dusting one of the car's door handles with a small dark brush.

And then he saw three men at the far side of the parking lot, moving through the trees carefully, their eyes on the ground.

"What happened?" he whispered.

"I don't have an answer for you yet. We're looking into it."

"But something made you call those people, right? You found something."

Ellis hesitated. "I don't know anything for sure, but there are some indications that a violent altercation took place here."

"And those men over there . . . are they looking for my wife?"

"Mr. Fishburne, I promise I will give you an update as soon as we know more. But you can't be here."

Ellis gently pushed him away from the yellow tape. Bill complied, realizing that the way Ellis escorted him back to his car wasn't very different from the way he had helped Chelsey go back to bed, just hours earlier.

CHAPTER 22

Albert Lamb's home was a small white house on a quiet street. The wooden stairs drummed hollowly as Tatum climbed them, Zoe following close behind. Instead of buzzing the bell, Tatum knocked, as if the ringing of the doorbell would somehow sully the atmosphere of grief in the house.

A series of loud barks erupted beyond the door. A few seconds later Albert's voice called, "Just a second." A longer wait followed until Albert Lamb opened the door. He was dressed in a suit, but it was rumpled, his thin hair in disarray. Eyes puffy from sleeplessness, or tears, or both. A large golden retriever pushed past him, wagging his tail, and sniffed Tatum's legs.

Albert looked at them blankly. It took a moment until the sliver of recognition shimmered in his eyes. "Oh. You're working with Detective O'Donnell, right? Tatum Gray?"

"That's right," Tatum said. "Can we come in?"

Albert motioned them inside. The house was dark and still. Even the dust motes seemed to hover in space, unwavering, frozen by grief. Albert led them to the living room, shuffling strangely, and Tatum suspected that he might be intoxicated. The dog followed them, his own head lowered, tail drooping. He clearly wasn't impervious to the heavy blanket of sadness that hung in the air.

The living room was surprisingly colorful—the rug round and blue, the couch off white, a couple of matching chairs. A glass coffee table sat in the middle of the room. A potted plant stood in the corner, identical to the one in Catherine Lamb's home. Tatum guessed that she'd bought two of them, one for herself, one for her father. Albert Lamb's plant showed no signs of neglect. Yet.

"Sit down." Albert motioned at the couch. "I'll be just a second."

Tatum sat down; Zoe remained standing. Albert stepped out of the room, and Tatum decided he'd been wrong: the man wasn't drunk—he was simply an inch away from breaking. Every movement seemed to take a toll.

Zoe immediately began pacing the room, examining a bookshelf, a picture of Catherine hanging on the wall, the window. Tatum had no idea if she was trying to build some sort of profile for the old man or just nervously reacting to the sadness that weighed the room down. The dog followed Zoe everywhere, looking up at her, expectant. Tatum counted the seconds until Albert returned with a small tray, holding three glasses of water and a bowl of crackers. He laid the tray on the coffee table and sat down on one of the chairs. Zoe joined Tatum on the couch.

"How can I help you?" Albert asked. His voice was tired, uninterested. He didn't ask for news about the case. People handled grief in different ways. Many of them wanted the guilty party to be found, hoping it would give them some sense of justice or an inkling of closure. Albert Lamb didn't seem the type.

"Mr. Lamb, we were hoping you could tell us about one of the people in your congregation."

Albert sighed. "Patrick told me you were focusing the investigation on our church members."

"Not all of them. Just one man. You know him as Daniel Moore."

Albert picked up one of the glasses and sipped from it. "Does he have a different name?" he asked.

"His real name is Rod Glover."

Albert nodded thoughtfully. "So *that* was his name."

"You knew he'd changed his name?" Zoe asked abruptly. "How did you know?"

"Because he told me."

For a moment, no one said anything. Tatum blinked, trying to get his thoughts in order. "What else did he tell you?"

"Not much. He said he wanted a fresh start. He had a disturbed childhood and a violent past. He said there were people after him and that he came to Chicago to leave his past behind. He wanted to change. He wanted to do some good."

"Did you, perhaps, ask him to elaborate about his violent past?" Zoe said, her voice sharp.

"He said he wasn't ready to talk about it, and I respected his privacy."

Zoe opened her mouth to answer back. Tatum shot her a warning glance. She shut her mouth, her jaw clenched tight.

"Do you know where to find him? Do you have a phone number for him?" Tatum asked.

"No."

There was a loud squawk, and the three of them turned around. Albert's dog stood at the corner of the room with a large rubber ball in his mouth. He shifted the thing in his mouth, and the ball squawked again. He approached Albert expectantly, but the pastor didn't move.

"Can you tell us who he was friends with?" Tatum asked.

"He was friendly with everyone."

"Anyone in particular?"

"Not that I know of, but I wasn't keeping track."

The dog dropped the ball at Albert's feet and whined. Both Albert and the dog stared at the ball for a few seconds without moving. Tatum fought the urge to pick it up and toss it for the dog to catch.

"So you just let this man into your congregation? Into your community?" Zoe asked abruptly. "A man you *knew* had a shady past? And you didn't even bother to keep track of him?"

Tatum cleared his throat, raising an eyebrow at her. Whatever went on in Zoe's mind clouded her judgment. He hoped she would shut up and let him carry on with the interview.

Albert glanced at Zoe. "I am not running a business or a school. I run a church. If I shut the door when the people who needed it most came—"

"Rod Glover was not one of those people."

"You think he had anything to do with Catherine's death?"

"We can't divulge any information about the investigation," Tatum said.

"Well, if you think so, you are mistaken."

"How do you know?" Tatum asked.

"I've talked to him several times. I've seen him help the needy, play with children, support people in the community. This man would *never* do what was done to my daughter."

Zoe opened her mouth again, and Tatum raised his finger and glared her into silence. He waited a few seconds, looking at the dog, who faced Albert with wide glum eyes, his tail between his legs. Finally the dog padded away to the corner of the room and slumped on the floor, his ears drooped.

"If he's innocent, he has nothing to worry about from us," Tatum said. "We just want to ask him some questions. If you know where we can find him—"

"Like I said, I don't," Albert said wearily. "He left two months ago. A family emergency. He said he didn't know when he'd be back."

"We have reason to believe he had a good friend in your community," Tatum said. "Any idea who?"

"Not that I can think of."

"What about this picture?" Tatum asked, taking out his phone, finding the photo with Glover's blurry face in the corner. "Do you remember who he's talking to?"

Albert took the phone from him as if it were a delicate porcelain doll. Tatum doubted he could even see anyone else in the image, with Catherine sitting in the center. "I remember that day," he said. "Catherine organized this picnic with Leonor. I wasn't enthusiastic about the idea. It was supposed to rain, and it sounded like a hassle. But those two could make *anything* happen. It turned out to be a perfect day. Catherine made apple pie that kept attracting bees."

"Who else was at that picnic?" Zoe asked.

Albert shook his head. "I don't know. Dozens of congregation members. Where did you see this picture?"

"It's on the memorial wall in your church," Zoe said. "Haven't you seen it?"

"Oh. No, I haven't. I've been meaning to go, but . . ." He put the phone down. "I've been tired."

"You don't remember who he spoke to? You seem to recall that day so vividly, and he sat just a few feet away from you."

"I remember Catherine." Albert shook his head, as if the presence of Catherine at the picnic dimmed any other detail of that day in his memory.

There was something eerie about the man, something fragmented. Tatum got the feeling that Albert Lamb was a man used to giving big speeches, full of booming, colorful phrases and powerful body language. A man who spoke in the vast space of his church and made sure everyone could hear his words, his conviction. But now, struck by grief, he spoke in short, tired sentences, his voice almost monotone. Tatum could still glimpse a shadow of what the man used to be. A dramatic movement with his arm. A word spoken with sudden emphasis. But it was all jittery, spastic reflexes. Pastor Lamb was gone, perhaps forever. This was Albert Lamb, a widower who'd lost his only child.

"Do you know who made the memorial board?" Tatum asked. Whoever made it probably had other photos from that picnic. Maybe they could see who Glover was talking to. Maybe there would be another photo of Glover. Anything that could shed light on the time Glover spent in that community would help them pinpoint his partner.

"A congregation member. Terrence."

"Can you give us his phone number?"

Albert picked up his phone from the table, tapped the screen a few times, and handed it to Tatum, who copied Terrence's phone number.

Zoe persisted. "Can't you think of anyone Glover was close to? Did you maybe see him sit next to the same person at church? Maybe he'd show up with someone? Leave with someone? Any person at all?"

Albert shrugged. "Like I said, he helped a lot of people."

"What sort of people?"

"People who could use his experience. People with a similar background who wanted to turn a new leaf."

Tatum felt nauseous. He glanced at Zoe, saw her eyes widening as she began to understand as well. "People with violence in their life?" he asked.

"Yes. Soon after he joined the community, he told me he would be glad to shepherd others like him. People who grew up with violence and had *been* violent. People who might feel uncomfortable coming to me or Patrick."

"Or Catherine?" Tatum suggested.

"Well, Catherine was still young back then. She didn't really offer counseling yet. So I told everyone that if they had violence in their life, and they wanted support they couldn't get from me, they could approach Daniel. That he could help them become better men."

The pastor had let the killer of his daughter into his church and might have even introduced him to his accomplice. "We'll need a list of all the people who approached Daniel."

"I don't have one. The whole point was that this was confidential, that they could approach Daniel without talking to me or anyone else first."

147

They stayed in Albert's living room for ten more minutes, Zoe rigidly silent, Tatum asking questions, the pastor answering them quietly, almost distractedly. And if he knew anything about Catherine's murder or about Rod Glover, it was hidden behind the impenetrable wall of his grief.

Eventually, they showed themselves out. Zoe walked to the car, her footsteps brisk, as if she needed to get away from Albert Lamb's house as fast as possible, and Tatum kept pace. He knew her well enough to easily see her rage in the twist of her lips, the narrowing of her eyes.

He should have been used to her anger by now; Zoe was always impatient, quick to flare up. She was easily annoyed by stupidity or by someone disagreeing with her or, even worse, ignoring her opinion. But something in her demeanor right now set his teeth on edge. This wasn't Zoe's usual temper, like a fire in a dry field, burning fast, gone in minutes. This was a slow simmering emotion that could stay boiling hot for long.

"If we knew who Glover was talking to that day, it would be *something*," she said.

"Why that day in particular?" Tatum asked.

"I don't care about that day. But this was one time when there's an actual shot of him, something we can trust. The camera doesn't lie."

"You think Albert lied to us?"

"I think Glover lied to him, and he's passing on the lie, which is the same thing. And every single person in that community has been told some version of the same lie. No matter who we talk to, it'll be vague stories. But the photo tells the truth. It can show us facts. I want to see how Glover interacted with those congregation members, who he talked to, the kind of people he was attracted to."

"Okay," Tatum said, pulling out his phone and finding Terrence's number. It was time to see if there were any more photos.

CHAPTER 23

Terrence Finch was a professional photographer, and he told Tatum that he would be in his studio until evening. The studio was in South Ashland Avenue, a quick drive from Albert's home. Zoe seemed so electric and volatile that Tatum actively wished he had a Katy Perry album, or one of the other musical horrors she listened to, just so she'd calm down a bit.

The studio was located between a car wash facility and a sad-looking hamburger joint. Someone had sprayed a heart in black spray paint on the studio's wall and then tried to write names inside it. However, the heart was too small, and it ended up being the love declaration of *blob + unreadable scrawl*. Tatum wondered if Blob and Scrawl were still together and whether they had kids, perhaps named Smudge, Blot, and Splotch.

Zoe pressed the buzzer for much too long, resulting in a sharp, angry drone that made Tatum wince. They waited for ten seconds, and Zoe hit the buzzer again.

The door swung open, an irate man with a goatee standing in the doorway.

"Terrence Finch?" Tatum asked.

"Shhhhh!" The man put his finger on his lips and motioned them inside. They followed him, and the door closed behind them.

The studio was a very large room, tall lights in the corner, all aimed at the center. A large white fabric was stretched over the rear wall and the floor, littered with toys. A baby crawled on the fabric, chasing an orange ball. A photographer circled the set, taking photos of the toddler, who was utterly mesmerized by the ball.

The man who had opened the door ignored them, walking over to a woman who stood in the corner of the room. Both of them were staring at the baby with pure adoration. Tatum surmised that the man with the goatee wasn't Terrence Finch; he was the child's father. There was no real resemblance, but maybe the baby used to have a goatee, too, and they'd simply shaved it off for the photo shoot.

The photographer paused for a second to glance at Tatum and Zoe. "I'm Terrence. I'll be with you in a moment," he said, already turning back to the baby, who screamed in frustration as the ball rolled away.

Tatum watched as Terrence shifted around the setting, his camera repeatedly clicking. He was about forty, brown hair, his scalp peeking through in patches. He had a gangly body, his arms twisted in uncomfortable angles as he tried to get a good shot of the baby's face.

The baby picked up a cube, put it on top of another cube, then added a third. But they weren't aligned properly, and the tiny tower tumbled down. He let out a screech of outrage at the audacity of gravity.

"Try again, Leo," the mother said encouragingly. Leo's father looked frustrated, poised to move, as if at any moment he might step in, take over, and show Leo how you *really* build a tower with three cubes.

The session kept going for a few more minutes. The mother wanted Terrence to photograph Leo hugging the big teddy bear. Except Leo wasn't in the mood. Whenever someone waved the teddy bear at the baby, he'd hurriedly crawl to the other side of the set, eyes wide in terror. The kid had good reflexes. Tatum approved. He would never let himself be mauled by a ferocious teddy bear.

Finally, confused by his parents' instructions, Leo sat in the middle of the set and burst into tears. Terrence stopped photographing, probably realizing this was not a moment that Leo's parents would want to frame and put on their mantel. The mother picked Leo up, and the family left, with Terrence promising to send them the pictures.

Once they were gone, Terrence nervously approached Tatum and Zoe. "Hi, sorry. You're the special agent I talked to on the phone, right?"

Tatum nodded, showing his badge. "Agent Gray. This is my partner, Zoe Bentley."

"This is about Catherine." His eyes were wide and sad. His voice broke as he said her name, ending in a hoarse whisper.

"How well did you know Catherine?" Tatum asked.

"Pretty well. I've been going to the church for the past ten years," Terrence said. "Everyone in our congregation knew her. I don't know what will happen to the church now that she's gone."

"What about him?" Zoe asked, showing Terrence her phone. It was the image of Glover with Andrea. "Do you know him?"

Terrence glanced at it. "He's in the church too. His name is Daniel."

"How well do you know him?"

"I talked to him a few times. Seemed like a nice guy."

"Did you see him talking to anyone in particular? Did he have any close friends?"

"Not that I noticed."

"We were at the church this morning and saw the memorial," Tatum said, taking out his phone and finding the photo of the picnic, Glover's blurry head in the corner. "Did you take this photo?"

Terrence glanced at it for a second. "Yes," he said. "I took all the photos on the memorial board."

"Any idea who Daniel is talking to in this picture?"

"No. I didn't even notice he was there. This picture is about Catherine."

"Do you have the rest of the pictures from that picnic?" Tatum asked. "And other activities of the church?"

Terrence shrugged. "Sure. What other activities?"

"There were more pictures on the memorial board," Tatum said, swiping his screen. "Gardening, sorting clothes, cooking for the home-less . . . anything you have."

"That would be thousands of images," Terrence said. "Can you be more specific?"

Tatum and Zoe glanced at each other. Excitement sparkled in Zoe's eyes. "Anything you have," he said. "We'll be happy to have a copy."

Terrence frowned. Tatum was about to mention that it was crucial to finding Catherine's killer, when the photographer said, "Sure. It'll take me a while to get it all sorted. It's stored on backups in the back room."

"We can wait," Zoe said. "Any way we can start looking over some of the pictures while you get us copies of the rest?"

"Sure," Terrence said, his tone far from thrilled. "I have some other pictures I printed of Catherine that didn't end up on the memorial board. You can go over those for now."

He walked over to a plastic drawer stand in the corner of the room and opened the top drawer. It was full of paper envelopes, and he thumbed through them, finally taking one out.

"If you need anything, just holler," he said, handing the envelope to Zoe. "I'll be in the back room."

He left, and Zoe took out a thick stack of photos from the envelope. She started flipping through them, Tatum leaning over to see, their heads nearly touching.

The first time Glover showed up in a photo, both of them stared at it for a long minute, taking in the details. In that picture, they could see the man he was talking to, a burly African American. A few photos later Glover appeared again, this time talking to a pair of women, one of them laughing with her palm over her lips. And then he appeared again. And again.

"Shit," Zoe muttered.

Tatum shared the sentiment. He'd had a vague hope that the person Glover was talking to at the picnic was his partner, his close friend. It now became clear that Glover didn't have just one person he was close to in the congregation. He'd slithered into the community, spreading his fake charm, making sure he was known and liked by everyone he'd talked to.

His partner could be anyone in the congregation. Anyone at all.

CHAPTER 24

Zoe's mind crackled with static. Her body was clenched, as if ready to strike. Somewhere on the street, a car honked twice, and she gritted her teeth, the shrill sound infuriating her.

They'd gone back to their motel, Tatum driving, Zoe glaring out her window. Tatum had tried to talk a few times, but Zoe's monosyllabic responses had driven him to silence. She'd known that any conversation right then would end badly.

Now, in her room, she paced back and forth on the faded rug. It felt like ants were crawling under her skin, or something was wrong with her fingernails, or her clothes were too tight. She didn't know if she was too warm or too cold, maybe a bit of both. There was a constant grating noise, like the dragging of something heavy on an asphalt road, and she knew it was her teeth, grinding against each other.

She sat on the bed and forced herself to focus, trying to profile the type of men who'd approach Glover. Men with violent lives who wanted someone to help them get better. And at least one of them made Glover think *him*. See a potential ally. Someone to corrupt even further. If she concentrated, she could figure out that person's characteristics, make him much easier to identify.

She grabbed her notebook, a pen. Tapped the pen on the paper a few times, inflicting a series of angry ink dots on the empty page. Pushed the notebook away, turned on her laptop, scrolled through some of the pictures Terrence had given them. Thousands of pictures of events indoors and outdoors, some with just a few participants, some with dozens of people. And Glover was everywhere. He'd morphed the documentation of a wholesome church community into a twisted Where's Waldo? game.

She began sorting the pictures. Terrence was organized—the folders had a date and a short description of the occasion. She created a copy of the folders, keeping only the images Glover appeared in. She put on a Katy Perry album as she did it, but the music only irritated her, and she shut it off.

A knock on the door. She opened it. Tatum stood in the doorway, hands in his pockets.

"I figured we could talk about what we know and brainstorm about going forward," he said.

"Sure." Zoe moved aside, letting him through the door. Tatum walked inside, grabbed the one chair in the room, sat on it. Zoe paced back and forth, biting her lip, not knowing how to start.

"There's a good chance that more than one man approached Glover for advice like the pastor suggested," Tatum said. "Do you think Glover really assisted any of them?"

Zoe let out a bark of forced laughter. "Oh, I'm sure he made it seem like it. Talked to them, got them to open up, confess their dirty little secrets to him. Made it feel like there was someone in their corner."

"Why?"

"Maybe he found it amusing. Or he wanted to know about their vulnerabilities. It's possible he was looking for an accomplice all along." Zoe tried to think it through. "He joined this Christian community. But he might have felt uncomfortable, going there Sunday after Sunday, listening to sermons about sin. Maybe he wanted to see there were others in that church who were like him. It would have made him more relaxed."

"Are you telling me Glover had impostor syndrome?"

Zoe clenched her fists. "He was literally an impostor. It's not a syndrome if it's true. Glover tried to worm himself into the community, but all he saw around him were people praying, talking about good deeds and good intentions, and he *knew* who he was. Even if he pretended to be a stand-up guy, he'd killed several women before, had constant fantasies about killing again. Some part of him must've found this dissonance uncomfortable. So he went to that idiot pastor—"

"Don't call him that."

"Fine! That gullible pastor, gave him a sob story about his violent past. This gets him two things. First—it's a confession of a sort, so now he doesn't feel like he's hiding. *And* he gets a queue of ex-cons, wife beaters, violent criminals, all happy to talk to him and get their *own* guilt off their chest. Lucky for Glover, Baptists don't have confession, or this ploy probably wouldn't have worked. Now he can sit every Sunday, listen to the sermon, comfortable in the knowledge that he's surrounded by violent men. And that moron Albert Lamb believes that he—"

"Stop saying that!" Tatum's voice had a bite to it, and Zoe paused, bewildered.

"What?"

"Stop calling Albert Lamb an idiot."

"Why?"

"Because it bothers me." Tatum raised his voice. "There's no need to talk trash about—"

"Tatum, he *let* that man into his community and introduced him to other potential killers."

"Albert Lamb is a good person. He saw a man who was trying to change his ways and decided to help him."

"That man raped and killed five women!"

"But he didn't exactly hand his résumé to Albert Lamb, did he? How could Albert have known that—"

"He couldn't! But he could've been more careful. A stranger comes to you, telling you he has a violent past, you don't give him a welcome party. Especially not if you have a whole community that trusts you."

"What do you want? Everyone in the world to be suspicious of every single person they meet? How on earth do you expect people to function like that?"

Zoe clenched her fists in frustration. "A little suspicion could go a long way!"

Tatum's eyes widened, his eyebrows rising. "Who are you angry with here?" he asked.

Zoe's fists tingled. "What?"

"This isn't about Albert. He had no way of knowing who Glover is. You realize that. Because you did the same thing, right? Didn't you tell me you once invited Rod Glover to your *room?*"

"I was a kid!" Tatum was being obtuse. The difference was obvious. "I didn't know better. Albert Lamb had a responsibility."

"Like your parents did?"

"No, that's not—"

"You told me Rod Glover ate at your house plenty of times, right? In fact, he had the key to your front door. Because he was such a nice neighbor."

"Tatum, shut up, you have no idea—"

"And what about the police in Maynard? Ignoring the truth, even when you laid out the facts in front of them?"

Zoe's ears hummed; she was about to scream. Just screech wordlessly until Tatum shut up. Her jaw clenched tightly to stop that scream from emerging.

"All the people who later thought you just scared an innocent man away?" Tatum softened his voice. "So *you* grew up feeling lonely, while Rod Glover found himself a nice new community to love him."

Zoe realized she was leaning against the corner of the room. Her body tried to shy away from Tatum's words.

"Albert Lamb, Glover's coworkers and boss, the police, your parents, *you*." Tatum counted on his fingers. "It's no one's fault. You can't prepare for someone like Glover. People who don't have our training can't even imagine ever *meeting* someone like him. And thank god for that, or no one would ever go outside their home."

"You're talking about him like an earthquake or a flood. Glover's just a man."

"A twisted, perverse man in a perfect disguise of a nice, honest, chummy kind of guy. There's no way to know what's inside him. Not unless you're us."

Zoe felt exhausted, could hardly stay upright. Tatum looked tired as well.

"Look," he said softly. "It's been a long day. I need a rest. I don't think I can handle another long night."

"I want to work." She didn't feel like she could. But she didn't feel like she could rest either.

He stood up and sighed. "Of course you do. But I can't. Not tonight."

At the door he paused and turned to face her. For a moment, Zoe wanted him to step toward her, gather her into his arms. Maybe that way, she could rest for just a bit.

But he didn't. "Good night, Zoe."

"Night."

The door shut behind him. Zoe wavered on the edge of crying.

She returned to sort the photos instead.

CHAPTER 25

Tatum's weariness felt beyond sleep. In fact, he wasn't sure he'd be able to fall asleep at all. He sat on his bed, took off his shoes and his pants, then paused to reflect.

Back in LA, he'd had a partner, Bobby O'Leary, who claimed that he did his best thinking in the bathroom, sitting on the toilet. Because pants, Bobby said, got in the way of any major thought process. So Tatum and he would be talking about a case, reviewing it, thinking it through, when Bobby would suddenly say, "This is a tricky one. Gonna take a dump, think it through." He'd go for twenty minutes and return with clever insights and ideas. Tatum often suspected that if the bureau let Bobby simply work in his underpants, he'd be promoted to chief in no time.

Tatum wanted this to work for him. He wanted an epiphany that would either crack the case or figure out a way to get Zoe to chill. But the only thing that happened, as he sat on the bed in his underpants and socks, was that he felt chilly.

His phone rang from the pocket in his discarded pants. He struggled with the pocket, wondering why it was always more difficult to get things out of pockets of unworn clothes. Yet another unsolved mystery. It was Marvin on the phone.

"Hey, Marvin, how are you doing?"

"I'm fine, Tatum. How's Chicago?"

"Pretty much the same. Cold."

"Yeah? Buy yourself some warm socks. That's the best way to get warm, Tatum. Socks."

Sage advice from a wise old man. "I'll remember that."

"You do that, Tatum. How's your partner?"

Tatum frowned. Was the old man telepathic? Did he feel a disturbance in the force? "She's preoccupied. This case is wearing her a bit thin. But she'll be fine."

"Her sister is saying differently."

"You talk to Andrea?"

"Why are you so surprised, Tatum? People find me nice to talk to. You know why? I listen. You could try that once in a while."

Tatum sighed. "We were questioning someone today, and she just got so angry . . ." He paused, trying to figure out how to explain it. "When we get a case, we need to be able to keep it at arm's length. We need to stay objective. It shouldn't be personal."

"But this case *is* personal for her, Tatum. So what are you going to do about it?"

"What do you want me to do? Drag her back to Quantico, kicking and screaming?"

The old man grunted. "That's not such a bad idea."

"Look, Zoe is under a lot of stress, but she's handling it. You can tell that to your new best friend, Andrea, next time you talk."

"Sure, she's handling it just fine, Tatum. Your partner was buried alive a month ago, and she's now chasing a killer who lived next door when she was a kid. I'm sure she's just dandy."

"Did you call just to lecture me?"

"I want you to look after your partner—that's all I'm asking. Her sister is worried about her, and you should know that. Don't shoot the messenger, Tatum."

"I'm looking after her. You have my word."

"Fine." Marvin grunted. "Listen, I wanted to ask, where are the cat snacks?"

"The what?"

"The cat snacks. Can you hear me? Hello? Cat snacks, Tatum, where are the cat snacks?"

"I heard you, I heard you. Why do you want cat snacks?"

"I think Chicago made you slow, Tatum. I want cat snacks for the cat. What did you think I want them for?"

"The cat? Freckle?"

"Of course Freckle. Do you think I got another cat while you were gone? Did I give you the impression that I crave the company of *additional* cats?"

"Then . . . why do you want to give it a snack? You hate Freckle."

"Damn it, Tatum, I ask you a simple question, I expect a simple answer. Not this federal investigation. Is that what you're doing over there? Harassing your suspects over cat snacks? No wonder it's taking you so long to get your guy. The ladies from the book club are here. They think the cat's cute. They want to give him snacks. Is that okay with you, Tatum? Can you please tell me where the cat snacks are? Or do I need to go buy some myself?"

"Settle down, Marvin. Don't get your blood pressure up. The cat snacks are in the top left cupboard."

"It's not there. I looked. The only thing there are those weird salty crackers."

Tatum frowned. "We don't have any crackers."

There was a moment of silence. "Top left cupboard?" Marvin said. "Yeah, okay."

"Marvin, did you eat the cat snacks?"

"I . . . listen, I'm pretty sure these were crackers. They don't taste so good, but I've had worse."

"There's a picture of a cat on the package. They're supposed to taste like chicken. Didn't you find that strange?"

"You know what, Tatum? When you were younger, you didn't use that tone with me. You had a lot more respect."

"That's because I didn't know you ate cat food."

"You're hilarious, Tatum. I'm going back to my guests. It's a lot nicer than talking to my wiseass grandson."

"Bye, Marvin."

"Yeah, yeah."

Tatum put the phone on the night table, grinning. The image of Marvin sitting in the kitchen, drinking tea, and distractedly munching cat snacks was one he intended to treasure. Then, he thought of Zoe. Marvin, annoyingly, was right. Zoe wasn't okay; Tatum knew that. It wasn't just today, with her constant short temper and her fury over Albert Lamb. He'd seen glimpses of it the whole week. Moments when she seemed adrift. Losing her focus for long periods of time. Sudden moments when she clenched, her eyes wide in fear, which seemed to fade the moment he asked what was wrong.

He almost decided to go knock on her motel door again. He slid one leg into his pants, then stopped. The thought of walking into her room, the electric sharp atmosphere everywhere, drained his resolve. He would do no good to Zoe in his current state. He needed one evening of rest.

CHAPTER 26

The man in control came home early, unable to wear his facade for long. He kept feeling as if anyone who looked at him knew. They could somehow see through him, perceive the sickness and the guilt. He'd checked his face in the mirror every few minutes, examining it from every angle, making sure that he was the same. And he was, unless the mirror lied. Which was an uncomfortable thought in itself, not an actual fear, not yet, but the hint of a future anxiety. *What if the mirror was lying to him?*

He'd thought he would feel better, like last time. And he had, for a few hours. After they'd finished the night's work, they'd gone home; his sleep had been deep and dreamless.

But when he'd woken up in the morning, he could already feel the nervousness clawing inside him. It had been amplified when he'd seen Daniel, felt the simmering rage under his friend's chilly behavior. A volcano trapped within a glacier. He'd drunk one of the vials then—he'd collected eight this time. But it had given him almost no reprieve.

Now, back home after a torturous day, he paced his room like a trapped animal, an ugly feeling in the pit of his stomach. Daniel was angry with him. He didn't even bother hiding it. He was angry at the loss of control the night before.

It was like being a child again, lying in his bed after being caught, after his mother cried her eyes out, and he'd promised he'd never ever ever do it again. He'd lie in bed and hear her talk to his dad through the thin walls. Telling him that the teacher called again, that they caught him cutting himself with a pair of dull scissors, or that he'd drawn that painting again, the black and red shapes. His mother would sob, and his dad would try to reassure her, tell her that they'd find a different doctor. Someone who would figure out what the problem was.

He'd spend the following week knowing his parents were angry with him, walking around the house as quiet as a mouse, sitting silently at school, doing his best not to attract any attention. And the unpleasant guilt and worry gnawed at his gut like a voracious intestinal parasite.

And now, there it was again. He kept holding his breath and listening. Perhaps he'd hear Daniel talking silently with his father. "Last night he bit that woman like some sort of animal. I don't know what to do with him."

But his father was dead, he reminded himself. And Daniel was his friend.

In fact, in all the years they'd known each other, Daniel had never been angry at him. He'd always been so understanding, so gentle. Daniel was the only one who was *always* there for him, happy to talk to him when he was stressed, reassuring him that his thoughts and desires were normal, that everyone had them.

His friend was changing. It was the tumor. The tumor was changing him.

He suddenly recalled how angry Daniel had been when he'd seen the name Rod Glover on the news. As if it meant something. Perhaps it did.

Perhaps that was the tumor's name.

No wonder Daniel was acting so differently. Something was devouring him. A ravenous, corrupt tumor. Rod Glover. He imagined the cancer spreading into the brain, destroying it, until all that was left of Daniel was an empty shell, piloted by the tumor.

And as Daniel's friend, he had to help in that fight. Help Daniel retain himself.

He checked the mirror again, took a deep breath, put his mental costume on, his face slackening, a small casual smile on his lips. He entered the kitchen, opened the fridge, took one of the vials. Perhaps something was wrong with the last one. He shook it, then drank it in a quick, hungry gulp.

Nothing. No momentary relief, no exhilaration.

Behind him, he heard Daniel step into the kitchen. His friend leaned past him into the fridge, took a beer.

"I'm sorry for last night," he told Daniel.

"Will you stop apologizing about it already?" Daniel growled. "You said you're sorry ten times."

Had he? Maybe he had. "I just don't want you to be angry at me."

"Not everything is about you," Daniel said, taking a swig from his beer.

"Then what are you angry about?"

Daniel shook his head. "Nothing, don't worry about it. It's not about *you*, okay? I'm not angry at all. Everything is just great."

"Okay." He knew better. He knew about Rod Glover. But he didn't say anything. It might make Daniel feel ashamed.

"I'm getting worse," Daniel said. "I thought I'd get better by now, but the pains are worse, and yesterday . . ." He tightened his grip on the beer bottle, and for one fleeting moment it seemed as if he was about to smash it on the counter. But he didn't. "Never mind."

"There are some vials in the fridge."

"Thanks, I'll pass." Daniel took another swig. "They still haven't found the body. There was nothing in the evening news. Nothing on any of the usual websites either."

"Maybe they found it but haven't told the press yet."

Daniel grunted, unconvinced. "Well, I don't have the time to wait for them. We need to make the call."

The man in control felt a stab of fear. "Do you want me to do it?"

"No. Someone might recognize your voice. I'll do it tomorrow, early morning. They already know I'm involved."

"Okay."

A tiny grim smile stretched Daniel's lips. "And we'll have to go hunting again in a few days. Are you ready for that?"

The man in control nodded. He was more than ready. He *needed* it. They both did.

CHAPTER 27

Wednesday, October 19, 2016

"Oh, shit," Zoe muttered as Tatum maneuvered the car into the parking lot of the Kickapoo Woods.

She counted eleven news vans parked in a row. The gaggle of onlookers surrounding the yellow crime scene tape looked like the crowd at a rock concert, all shoving and jostling each other to get to the front row.

This crime scene was very far from the relatively private murder of Catherine Lamb.

The tape was stretched across the paved trail that led down to the river, and it cordoned off a large stretch of the woody area that surrounded the water. Beyond it, Tatum saw uniformed police officers moving slowly through the brush.

"There's O'Donnell." Zoe pointed at the detective, who was getting out of her car.

O'Donnell motioned them over. There was a section of parking designated for the officers, EMTs, and crime technicians. Tatum parked the car by an ambulance.

Zoe got out and hunched her shoulders against the morning chill. The air smelled of wet earth and wood, but another odor intermingled with it. A stench of death and rot.

"Glad you could make it," O'Donnell said.

Zoe nodded. "Thanks for calling us."

"What do we have?" Tatum asked.

"Got a call from Officer Ellis, from Chicago South," O'Donnell said. "A woman named Henrietta Fishburne went missing on Monday night. A patrol officer found her body this morning when he followed up on a call to dispatch about suspicious individuals entering the woods here."

"Why did they call you?"

"The ME saw a similarity between this and the Lamb case and suggested contacting me."

"So this Ellis is the detective in charge?" Tatum asked as they reached the crowd surrounding the crime scene tape.

O'Donnell took point, jostling through the gaggle of onlookers toward the yellow tape. "No, he was the officer who got the missing person report. He kept at it after his shift, found her car in the 147th Street train station's parking lot, about a mile from here. There were bloodstains near the vehicle, but nothing conclusive. He was on shift again when the body was found and drove straight to the crime scene. There's a detective from Chicago South in charge here, but it's up to the brass to figure out who's leading the investigation." She shrugged. "For now everyone's playing nice."

Zoe followed O'Donnell and Tatum to the cop who stood by the tape. O'Donnell flashed her badge, which didn't seem to impress him. She explained who they were, and it turned out he hadn't been told to expect them. He had to check it out with the detective in charge.

Zoe scrutinized her surroundings, waiting for the officer to let them enter the crime scene. It seemed like a good place to dump a body. Anyone could drive a few hundred yards into the park, and the foliage was wild, creating a dense hideaway from prying eyes. A killer could just pick his spot, walk ten yards through the bushes and trees, and hide the body. She glimpsed patches of the river between the trees.

"What river is that?" she asked.

"It's the Little Calumet River," a familiar voice said by her ear. "Fancy that."

She turned around and saw the waggling thick eyebrows, and her gut sank.

"Harry Barry," she said dryly.

"Zoe Bentley! What an amazing coincidence. We keep meeting in the strangest places."

"It's not a coincidence. You're following me everywhere."

He widened his eyes, his face twisting in a wounded expression. "Me? I'm not following you anywhere. I *live* here."

"You live in the Kickapoo Woods?"

"Well, no," he conceded. "But when I heard a young woman was killed, so soon after the Lamb murder, it made me wonder. After all, with you here, it could mean only one thing." He mimed with his lips, *Serial killer.*

Zoe's expression remained wooden. "I'm just here as a professional courtesy. As far as I know, this case has no connection to what I'm investigating."

"I was just wondering about that. Wasn't there another murder some years ago by the Little Calumet River?"

She felt sick. She'd known he'd bring it up. One of the two murders they believed Glover was responsible for in Chicago occurred by the Little Calumet River. She'd told Harry this when he'd written his long article about her, months before. And the obnoxious man forgot nothing.

"Zoe," Tatum said. "We can go through."

"Don't write anything without talking to me first," Zoe said, her teeth clenched. Then, before he could respond, she turned away and crouched under the crime scene tape.

She signed the crime scene logbook and took a pair of latex gloves that O'Donnell handed to her, sliding them on. Then she followed the detective down the paved trail.

A young uniformed officer approached them, wearing latex gloves as well. "Are you O'Donnell?" he asked.

O'Donnell nodded. "That's right. Ellis, right? Thanks for contacting us." She introduced them, and Ellis motioned them to follow as he turned toward the trees.

"You have a positive ID on the victim?" O'Donnell asked as they stepped off the trail and into the brush, leaves and twigs crackling under their feet.

"We took her fingerprints to verify, but it's Henrietta Fishburne. She matches the photographs we have of her, and there are two small scars on the left ankle, which match scars that Fishburne got in a bicycle accident as a kid. We didn't find her bag. No phone either." He paused and glanced at them. "They told me this might be related to another case. Was there anything in that case that pointed to devil worship?"

"*Devil worship?*" Zoe asked, bewildered.

"Better see for yourselves," he said grimly and resumed walking.

A few people were milling around by the trees, all wearing gloves. The river was now in full view in front of them, its green water shimmering in the sunlight, tiny eddies upon its surface. Both banks were lined with trees. A crime scene technician crouched by the muddy bank, placing another evidence marker. There were officers on the opposite bank, too, spread to keep away an enterprising media crew and curious bystanders who were trying to catch a glimpse of the proceedings. The stench of death was much worse as they got closer, and Zoe took short shallow breaths.

As Zoe moved forward, she got her first glimpse of the body, a dark foot. She took a few more steps, eyes widening in disbelief.

It was a graphic account of the woman's last moments, told in violence. She lay naked on her back. Curly hair, spattered in mud and filth. Black bruises on ribs, face, thighs, scraped knees. A knife, stuck deep in her belly. Flies buzzed around the body, and Zoe did her best to avoid looking at the eyes, where she'd glimpsed maggots crawling.

The body was framed within a large uneven white circle, splotched on the ground, lines crisscrossing it inside. It took Zoe a few moments to realize what it was. A pentagram, drawn in paint on the rough earth.

She could already feel the toll she would pay later for this glimpse of pain. A dark churn in the back of her mind, trying to get free. She mentally boxed it, shoving it away, and stepped toward the body, focusing. The medical examiner, Dr. Terrel, was crouching by the victim, placing a paper bag over one of her hands, her movements slow and careful, almost gentle.

Zoe knelt by Terrel, carefully avoiding the white paint on the ground, and scrutinized the body. The killer hadn't been concerned about covering this one. On the contrary. He'd taken effort in posing her after her death. This didn't align with the Lamb case. What did?

The woman's skin was dark, which made it hard to see the bruises, but they were there. Ligature strangulation, same angle, same width. But was that enough to connect the two cases?

O'Donnell cleared her throat behind Zoe. "What do we have so far?"

Terrel didn't slow down to glance at either of them. "Lividity completely set, but there's almost no rigor mortis left, so the time of death was probably between twenty-four and thirty-six hours ago. I'll be able to give you a better estimate once I conclude the autopsy. Lividity patterns indicate the body was moved shortly after death."

"Cause of death?" O'Donnell asked.

Terrel glanced at her, raising a single eyebrow.

"I won't quote you on it," O'Donnell said in a low voice. "Just a hunch."

"No way to be sure yet, but I'm guessing the knife was thrust into her belly postmortem," Terrel said. "Or they did a hell of a cleaning job. You can see the bruising on the neck, indicating ligature strangulation."

Zoe checked the knife again. The entry wound was clean, hardly any blood around it. If the victim had been alive when stabbed, the blood would have gushed out. And cleaning it thoroughly during the night would have been difficult. Which meant, like Terrel had said, this wound hadn't killed the victim.

She'd probably been strangled to death, just like Catherine.

"Is that why you called me?" O'Donnell asked. "Because she'd been strangled?"

Terrel pointed to the victim's arm, and Zoe leaned to look closely. Two tiny holes punctured the skin. "The other arm has them too," Terrel said. "Looks like syringe marks. I can't say for sure it's the same size; I'll verify it during the autopsy."

Zoe frowned, getting up to look at the other side of the victim's neck. The skin was ravaged and torn, and a thick trickle of dried blood ran down it. "Any idea what that wound is?" she asked, pointing.

"From what I could see, it's a bite mark," Terrel said. "I'll get saliva samples from it, compare it to the ones from the previous murder."

"Sounds like a form of escalation," Tatum said. "At first he only used syringes. Now he bites the victim."

Zoe frowned. She wasn't sure about that. "But he still used syringes."

"Maybe he stores some of the blood, and that's what he uses the syringe for," Tatum suggested. "But the fantasy evolved. He wanted to bite her. Like a predator."

Zoe thought about the spattered blood next to the victim's car, which O'Donnell had mentioned. The body had only two visible deep wounds—the knife and the bite. And the knife was postmortem. "He probably bit her by the car," she said slowly. "That's where he attacked her. But that wasn't the plan."

"Who said there was a plan?" O'Donnell asked.

Zoe gestured at the image on the ground. "This wasn't easy to draw, and there's a lot of paint here. They brought it with them. Took the time to do it for some reason. There was a plan here, an agenda. But something went wrong." She straightened. "One of them lost control. Bit her."

"I can see another loss of control here," Tatum said darkly, gesturing at the victim's bruised ribs. "I've seen marks like these before. Someone kicked her when she was down."

Zoe nodded. "That's a clear sign of anger."

"Or domination," O'Donnell suggested. "A show of force."

"No," Tatum and Zoe said at once. Zoe glanced at Tatum and nodded at him. *You go.*

Tatum cleared his throat. "Offenders who rape and murder for power or domination are called power-assertive offenders. They typically plan to rape the victim, and the actual murder is an accident. *This* murder was definitely planned. They brought the paint and the syringe. And then they . . ." He frowned. "Hang on. We assume they attacked her in the train station's parking lot Monday night, right?"

"That sounds like a logical assumption," O'Donnell said.

"They probably killed her and drove here to dump the body."

"Most likely so they could pose her like this, without the train station's security seeing them," Zoe said.

"Then who are the suspicious individuals that our caller saw?" Tatum asked. "The person who called dispatch to tell them about suspicious individuals called this morning, not last night."

"Maybe it's just a coincidence," O'Donnell suggested. "He saw a bunch of teenagers going into the park to party and decided to do his civic duty and ruin their fun."

"Uh-huh." Tatum peered at her dubiously. "Let's check." He stepped away, pulling out his phone.

"Having paint in their car doesn't mean they planned all this. It doesn't mean they had an agenda," O'Donnell told Zoe. "I once had a can of paint in my trunk for two months. But I had no nefarious agenda except painting my living room."

Zoe felt frustrated. The smell of the body, strong even in the open air, made her sick, and the constant pounding in her skull was impossible to ignore. She bit down a sharp response and turned to look at the river's murky water until she was calm enough to answer. "Anything is possible," she said. "Our job, as profilers, is to point out what's *likely*. Like Dr. Terrel astutely noticed, there is a lot of similarity between this murder and Catherine Lamb's murder. I think this murder was planned, but they deviated from the original plan. And I think Glover and his partner from the previous murder killed this woman as well."

"Fine," O'Donnell said. "Then what's with the pentagram and the knife? From what you told me, it doesn't fit in anywhere."

It was true. She'd called it a plan, but a plan for what? This fit with neither of the men's profiles. She shook her head. "I don't know. There's something we're still missing."

"Zoe." Tatum walked over and handed her his phone. "I just got dispatch to send me the recording of the phone call. Listen to it."

Zoe hit play on the screen. The voice of the dispatcher emanated from the phone's speaker. "Nine-one-one, what's your emergency?"

And then another voice—gritty, low, and chillingly familiar—said, "I want to report a suspicious activity at Kickapoo Woods. I just saw two guys going in there, carrying something heavy. I think they had guns. They looked like terrorists."

The dispatcher asked for an exact location, and the caller began to explain it in specific detail, but Zoe couldn't focus on the words anymore. Just the voice and the nausea that spread through her stomach as she listened to it.

She gaped at Tatum. "That's Rod Glover."

CHAPTER 28

Bill sat in front of his computer, staring blankly at the screen. He'd meant to prepare a flyer that he'd print and tape around the neighborhood. But he needed to select a photo first. And scrolling down the photos, he found the one he'd taken that perfect afternoon at the beach. Henrietta and Chelsey hugging, their cheeks flattened against each other, grains of sand scattered on their faces and hair. Both grinning at him, that same impish glee reflected in their identical eyes.

It was the wrong photo for the flyer, but he couldn't pull his eyes away from it.

Chelsey had been difficult that morning. He found it harder and harder to explain where Mom was, and when he'd claimed she was at work, she'd demanded they call her. He'd had to go shut himself in the bathroom before he either lost his temper or started sobbing uncontrollably.

The loud knock startled him. He got up and trudged heavily to the door, opening it without checking who it was.

Officer Ellis stood at the door, and behind him was an unfamiliar blonde woman in a gray suit. Their expressions were somber, the faces of bad news.

"Mr. Fishburne, this is Detective O'Donnell," Ellis said. "Can we come in?"

"Sure," Bill croaked, moving aside. Perhaps he should have asked if there was any news. But as long as he didn't ask, he could stretch the moment, live in the realm of possibilities.

They came inside, and O'Donnell shut the door behind her.

"Mr. Fishburne," she said. "Your wife is dead. Her body was found this morning. I'm sorry for your loss."

He walked over to the living room and sat down on the couch. "What happened?" he whispered.

"She was killed on Monday night, in the train station's parking lot," O'Donnell said.

"Murdered?"

"Yes."

"Do . . . do you know who . . ." He couldn't finish the sentence.

"Not yet. But I assure you we're doing everything we can to find the person who did this."

"How did she . . ." He was about to ask the question but realized he didn't want to know. Not yet. "Did she suffer?"

"We believe her death was very fast."

Had there been a slight pause there? He didn't dwell on it. He glanced at the clock. Chelsey would be home in less than four hours. He would have to tell her. He had no idea how. Mommy is gone? Mommy is in heaven? They weren't religious, had never discussed heaven at length, but now he wished they had. It would have been so much easier to tell Chelsey that her mother was somewhere lovely, watching them from above.

And then, randomly, he recalled that Hen was supposed to organize Chelsey's birthday in two months. He'd have to do it now.

He'd have to learn to braid her hair.

What did that say about him? That his first thoughts after learning his wife was dead were centered on things *he* needed to do? Instead of thinking of their shared memories and moments?

"Should I . . . do you need me to identify her body?"

"No," O'Donnell said softly. "We don't do that anymore. Your wife had to provide her fingerprints when she started working in her last job. We identified her using those fingerprints."

"Oh." He didn't know what else to say.

O'Donnell talked a bit about the autopsy, explaining the schedule, the process. He took it all in. He would need to get his wife's remains. She wanted to be cremated; he knew that much. He had to take care of the funeral.

He had to tell Chelsey, somehow. It seemed like an impossible task.

"Mr. Fishburne, do you mind if I ask you some questions?"

"No, go ahead."

Did his wife have any enemies. Did she act strangely lately. How did she sound on the phone when she talked to him. He answered her hollowly, numbly. Reducing Hen's existence to a series of dry facts. He wanted to tell O'Donnell what a wonderful mother Hen was. And what a wonderful friend she was. How it felt to be hugged by her. Of the conversations they had. About the miscarriage before Chelsey was born and how Hen couldn't stop crying for days after. How happy she was when Chelsey was born. How she liked cherries. That she was infuriated by the smell of sweaty socks.

But all that didn't interest O'Donnell. It wouldn't help her do her job and find Hen's killer. The person who'd taken Hen from him and his daughter, turning them from a family of three to a broken two.

CHAPTER 29

Zoe stepped into the precinct conference room, a large Starbucks cup of hot chocolate in her hand. She wasn't sure how long this meeting would be, but she had a hunch it might take hours. Most of the participants were already seated. There was an empty spot between Tatum and a police captain.

She sat down and took a sip from her hot chocolate, letting its sugary goodness linger on her tongue. She thought about Glover's phone call. At first, she'd received a jolt of trepidation and excitement each time she'd listened to the audio of Glover's voice reporting the suspicious activity. Only after listening to it dozens of times could she analyze it objectively, already knowing the words and the inflections by heart. He'd sounded tense in the recording, and she didn't think it was an act. Glover was unsettled. And underneath the tension she could hear an undercurrent that she knew well. Rage.

"Everyone here?" the police captain by her side asked. "Let's start. A quick introduction—I'm Captain Royce Bright from Area Central Violent Crimes."

He then introduced the rest of the participants. Officer Ellis sat next to O'Donnell. Agent Valentine represented the FBI's Chicago field office, and Zoe recognized him as one of the agents who'd befriended Tatum. Detectives Koch and Sykes from Chicago South . . . Zoe almost didn't catch the last name because a strange smell was distracting her.

For a moment it almost reminded her of livestock, but an industrial undertone accompanied the scent, like burnt plastic. It took her a few seconds to realize the odor came from Captain Royce Bright, who sat next to her. Now she realized why the chair on his other side was empty as well.

Zoe put her cup next to her nose, sniffing the hot chocolate. It did a reasonable job of masking Bright's odor.

"Most of you know Dr. Terrel, the medical examiner," Bright said. "And finally, Agent Tatum Gray and Dr. Zoe Bentley from the FBI's Behavioral Analysis Unit in Quantico."

He let the introductions sink in and then asked O'Donnell to summarize the initial investigation of Henrietta Fishburne's murder.

O'Donnell cleared her throat. "Yesterday at four thirty-two a.m., Bill Fishburne called the Chicago PD to report that his wife, Henrietta Fishburne, hadn't returned home from work. Officers Ellis and Woodrow showed up to take his statement. They forwarded all the pertinent information to Missing Persons and resumed their shift. When it was over, Officer Ellis decided to check if Henrietta Fishburne's car was in the train station. He found it on the far side of the parking lot and spotted several bloodstains on the pavement nearby. He called it in, and Koch and Sykes were assigned to the case. The crime scene technicians found additional bloodstains leading away from the car toward the trees in the northern part of the parking lot. There were some signs of a possible struggle, but they found nothing else."

She kept talking as she hooked up her laptop to the room's projector. "This morning at six and three minutes, dispatch got an anonymous phone call informing them about a suspicious activity in the Kickapoo Woods forest preserve. Patrol investigated and found the dead body of a woman in her late twenties." She paused for a moment as an image materialized on the large screen, and everyone turned their heads to look at the victim lying in the center of the white pentagram.

"There were no possessions by the body, so there was no quick way to identify her. However, dispatch correctly assumed it was Henrietta Fishburne. Officers Ellis and Woodrow were on shift and were sent to the location. Ellis made the informal identification with the assistance of Dr. Terrel, and we later verified it with fingerprints."

O'Donnell then flipped through several shots of the train station's parking lot, of Fishburne's car, and of the trail of blood leading toward the trees. Zoe felt momentarily dizzy, images flickering in her mind. A glimpse of darkness. Henrietta running away from her attacker, stumbling on the uneven pavement, her neck pulsing with pain—Zoe forced the thoughts down. *Later.*

"Livor mortis indicates the body was moved about two hours after death," O'Donnell said. "We found thirteen different bloodstains in the train station's parking lot and no bloodstains in the forest preserve where the body was found. Traces of color were found on the body's back and limbs, indicating the paint was still wet when the body was dragged over it. This leads to the assumption that she was killed in the northern part of the train station's parking lot, then taken in a vehicle to the forest preserve. The perpetrators parked their cars, located a good spot, and drew the pentagram on the ground. Then they carried the body to the location, posed it, and left."

As she spoke, the photos on the screen kept changing, giving them close-ups of the details she talked about, as well as multiple shots of footprints in the muddy ground of the forest.

"We think the victim's possessions were thrown into the river. A team of divers is searching the area. We checked the security camera footage and have a total of four cars leaving the train station's parking lot at the estimated time of death, and one of them is a van. We are trying to trace those vehicles, and particularly the van, but unfortunately, the camera's resolution isn't good enough to give us a license plate, and the drivers and passengers aren't visible in the darkness. There is no security camera footage of the northern part of the parking lot, in which the victim was attacked, but we have footage of her leaving the one-thirty train." A blurry photo appeared on-screen of a single woman walking through an empty train station. Henrietta's last moments alive.

"The lab took samples of the paint used to draw the pentagram," O'Donnell continued. "It's water-based, run-of-the-mill stuff. They're trying to figure out the brand. The knife is a simple chef's knife, usually used to cut meat. No fingerprints on the handle, and it hasn't seen much use. There are remnants of a sticky substance on the handle that might be the glue of a price tag. They're looking into that as well."

She clicked her mouse, and the image on the screen changed again to something that looked like a Coke can. "This was found ten yards from the scene of the crime. It's a makeshift crack pipe. The technician who found it thinks it was left there recently. If it was, we might have a witness."

Bright perked up. "Any prints?"

"Smeared, but they'll see what they can do," O'Donnell said.

Ellis cleared his throat. "We might be able to trace the person who left it there. There's a crack addict who often sleeps under the bridge on South Halsted Street, very close to that location."

O'Donnell nodded at him and moved on. "The anonymous phone call that alerted security was made by a mobile number that is now offline. We're in the process of pulling records for the number."

It was almost certainly a burner phone, but even then, they'd be able to know where he'd called from.

"The voice was identified by Dr. Zoe Bentley as probably belonging to Rod Glover, a man on the FBI's Most Wanted list for the rape and murder of five women. We have solid reasons to assume Rod Glover was involved in the murder of both Henrietta Fishburne and Catherine Lamb."

"Before we continue, I would like a quick summary of who this Rod Glover is," Bright said.

Zoe cleared her throat when, to her surprise, Agent Valentine said, "I believe I can do that."

"I am in a better position to summarize Glover's background," Zoe said dryly.

Agent Valentine smiled at her. "Well, I reviewed the file thoroughly. But thanks."

She knew the tone all too well; she'd been hearing it nonstop for the past five years. The reasons for the condescension varied—maybe Valentine had issues with the BAU sticking their nose where they didn't belong. Or maybe it was because she was a civilian, not a bona fide agent. Or because she was a woman. Probably a little of each. She was already on edge by the darkness churning in her mind, and the smell of Captain Bright didn't improve things. Blood rushed to her face.

A brief touch on her palm. Tatum. He lifted a single eyebrow at her, eyes widening slightly. She'd been about to lash out, probably getting them both kicked off the case.

Instead, she took a slow sip from her hot chocolate and smiled at Valentine, baring her teeth. "Absolutely, go right ahead."

Valentine nodded and glanced at the file in front of him. "In 1997, three women were raped and murdered in Maynard, Massachusetts. No one was charged with the murders—"

"Actually, someone was charged," Zoe said. "A teenager named Manny Anderson. He committed suicide in prison and was never tried."

"Uh . . . right," Agent Valentine said, glancing at his papers. "Anyway, it is now believed that the actual murderer of the three women was Rod Glover, who had lived there at that time and left town immediately after the third murder—"

"It wasn't immediate," Zoe said sweetly. "It happened four days later."

Valentine blinked. Across the table, O'Donnell grinned at Zoe, seemingly enjoying the spectacle.

"All three women were in their early twenties—"

"Only Beth Hartley was in her early twenties. Twenty-one, to be exact. Jackie Teller and Clara Smith were both eighteen."

"Dr. Bentley, perhaps it would be best if we let Agent Valentine summarize," Captain Bright said. "If you have anything you want to add, you can say it once he's done."

Zoe seethed. Agent Valentine let his lip curl and continued. "All three women were found near sources of water. They'd been raped and strangled to death."

"What were they strangled with?" O'Donnell asked.

"Um . . ." The agent scanned his papers. "Some sort of cloth noose."

"They were strangled with gray ties," Zoe said.

"Thank you, Dr. Bentley," O'Donnell told her.

"Right," Valentine said. "Anyway, after leaving Maynard, Glover's whereabouts were unknown, until—"

"Why did he leave Maynard?" O'Donnell asked, blinking innocently. "Didn't the police have another suspect in custody?"

"He was probably concerned he was under suspicion."

"He actually wasn't," Zoe said. "But the police were tipped off that he was seen lingering at one of the crime scenes and that he had a boxful of trophies from the murders under his bed. He ran before they could arrest him for questioning."

"Thank you, Dr. Bentley."

"You're welcome, Detective O'Donnell."

"Detective." Bright's voice was tight. "Please let Agent Valentine finish his summary. Any question you may have can wait until he's done."

Valentine's face was flushed. "Glover's whereabouts after that are unknown until he showed up in Chicago in 2008, killing two women—"

"I'm sorry," Zoe said apologetically. "I really have to interrupt. We have solid evidence that he was in Chicago ever since 2006."

Agent Valentine laid the papers on the desk. "Dr. Bentley. Would you like to take over this summary?"

183

"Thank you, that would be great," Zoe said brightly. She quickly outlined their investigation into Glover's past, his last workplace and apartment. She detailed the two murders they suspected he'd committed in Chicago. Then she summarized his attack on Andrea the month before.

"During the time Glover spent in Dale City, he went to see a doctor because of frequent headaches and repeated vomiting," she said. "He was diagnosed with anaplastic astrocytoma. That's a grade-three glioma brain tumor. We've interviewed the doctor and consulted a specialist. Their opinion was that Glover had no more than a year to live, and in six months he would probably need constant medical supervision and nursing."

Captain Bright leaned forward. "Did this guy Glover ever leave pentagrams in the crime scene? Or do anything else with satanic ramifications?"

"No," Zoe answered promptly. "We haven't seen anything like this in his previous murders."

"So we're assuming the pentagram and the knife are his accomplice's idea?"

Zoe hesitated. "It's possible. We don't know enough about the psyche of the unsub to be sure."

"What do we have linking the two crimes other than the phone call?" Bright asked.

"Footprints match for one of the murderers," O'Donnell said. "The techs said there's no doubt about it. We didn't have a good enough footprint of the second man in the Lamb crime scene to get a definite match, but the shoe size fits. In both cases, the murderers wore gloves, so we have no fingerprints. I think we have DNA . . . Dr. Terrel?"

"I took DNA samples from the bite on the woman's neck," Dr. Terrel said. "In addition, there's dry blood under her fingernails, which might belong to one of her attackers. Both samples are being compared to the saliva sample from the Lamb murder. Since the FBI had agreed to make this case a priority in their lab, we'll have a result within a day."

O'Donnell nodded. "In addition, both women were strangled to death, and both had syringe marks on their arms. We believe the syringe in Catherine Lamb's murder was used to extract blood from the victim."

"Was Henrietta Fishburne raped?" Bright asked.

"Not as far as I can tell," Terrel said.

Zoe blinked, startled. Up until now, she'd assumed it was a foregone conclusion. "Are you sure?"

"The victim's knees and palms are bruised in a manner that seems to indicate she was forced to her knees," Terrel said. "However, I found no indications of recent penetration."

She'd been stripped, forced to her knees, and strangled from behind . . . but not raped. And then there was the pentagram and the knife in the woman's stomach. And that damn phone call. Zoe tried to turn those things in her mind, find some explanation for them. It didn't fit with Glover's profile, nor with his partner's.

"Any progress on the Lamb case?" Bright asked.

"So far we have no definite suspect, but we are quite certain he belongs to a church in McKinley Park," O'Donnell said.

She summarized what they had so far, mentioning Zoe and Tatum's involvement at profiling the suspect. "We already have several statements that confirm that Rod Glover was part of the congregation, and considering the choice of Catherine Lamb as the first victim, we think it's probable that Glover's accomplice, unsub beta, belonged to that congregation as well."

"That's quite a leap, isn't it?" Valentine asked. "Since we know Rod Glover was familiar with the victim, the unsub could be anyone at all."

"There are indications that the unsub knew Catherine Lamb as well," Zoe said.

"Like what?"

Zoe explained about the necklace and mentioned the covering of the body.

"But Rod Glover could have done that as well, right?" Valentine pointed out.

"It doesn't fit his profile."

"Killers can be unpredictable. We can't base the investigation on a theory that has nothing solid to support it."

Was Valentine only arguing because she'd made him look like an idiot? Well, for one, he could blame only himself. "I'm not saying we limit our work to investigating the congregation members, but this is a highly likely theory."

"We have limited resources," Valentine said. "We have to decide how to allocate them."

"Okay, okay." Bright raised his hands. "How many parishioners in that church?"

"We couldn't get a definite number, but over the last few years, there have been hundreds," O'Donnell answered.

"Hmm. For now I agree with Agent Valentine," Bright said. "There's nothing concrete that ties the second murderer—the unsub—to the church's congregation, and interviewing hundreds of parishioners is something we can't spare any time on."

"We're already working on the list," O'Donnell said. "And we can start by checking the ones with a criminal record."

"Fine. Start by making a list, and then we'll see." Bright checked his watch. "It's been nine hours since Henrietta Fishburne was found and about thirty-eight hours since she was killed. I want both these cases investigated together. I've discussed it with Captain Miller from South, and with the chief of the bureau's Chicago field office, and we've agreed to form a task force, led by me."

Zoe saw O'Donnell's eyes narrow. She had been the one to catch the first murder case. Zoe intuited that O'Donnell had expected to lead the investigation herself. Instead, Bright had just taken over.

"We can use this room as a situation room," Bright continued. "We will assign additional manpower to the task force later. Let's get going. We need to get these monsters off the streets of Chicago."

CHAPTER 30

Three glowing monitors flickered in the dark room. Each monitor displayed angry Twitter arguments, vicious forum debates, toxic comments, violent images. The room was lit not by lamps or by ceiling lights, but by hate.

Laughing_Irukandji leaned back in his chair, slurping ramen noodles, occasionally putting the bowl down to click a link or type a quick angry comment.

He had an actual name, but he didn't call himself by that name anymore. That name belonged to his physical body, which he no longer cared about. His real life was beyond those monitors, traveling at light speed through cables that spanned the world. And there, he was Laughing_Irukandji.

He opened Twitter feeds on two of his monitors, watching raging arguments bloom, dozens of furious Twitter users screaming in revulsion, a new comment appearing every second. He smiled, reading through choice comments as they shouted about racism and misogyny. They assumed they were arguing with actual people. They were actually engaged in a shouting match with five bots. Bits of brainless scripts, just vomiting whatever Laughing_Irukandji told them to. He got that tingle of satisfaction, imagining all those people gnashing their teeth as they hammered responses, arguing with nothing.

He had at any given moment a few hundred bots, his small army of chaos, masquerading as men and women, Democrats, Republicans, teenagers, middle-aged men and women. His favorite at the moment were three bots pretending to be celebrities. Just that morning, thousands of Instagram users were shocked to see one of their favorite fashion models announce that Hitler was right about many things.

He slurped another glob of noodles and winced as he accidentally chewed with his aching tooth. It'd been bothering him for a few days now, but he wasn't about to go to the dentist and check it out. Last time he went, the dentist actually showed him how to brush his teeth, as if he were a child. He came back home furious and sent his bot army to troll the bitch's Facebook page, sending her threats and sexual propositions until she shut down her profile.

That'd teach her.

Aside from his bots, he had viruses and Trojan horses that did his bidding, replicating through the net with a speed that astounded even him. He had access to computers in China, Russia, France, England, Israel, Australia . . . the list went on. Here, sitting in his chair, his throne, he wasn't just a man. He was a god.

He browsed to his favorite troll forum. One of the users had cracked the password of his neighbor's phone and found nude photos on it. Laughing_Irukandji took a few choice photos, entered the girl's Facebook account, and, through it, sent the pictures to all of her friends. Another glimmer of satisfaction. But just a glimmer. It wasn't a rush like it used to be.

These days, he needed more.

He checked his finances. He had three strains of ransomware running, and they each provided him with a few hundred dollars a day. He kept them low scale, no need to get greedy. Getting greedy was how people got caught. And Laughing_Irukandji had no intention of getting caught.

He then browsed his preferred websites. Everyday Feminism, ChicagoPride, ThinkProgress . . . he read the articles carefully, feeling the fury rising in him. He cultivated his emotions with care. A gardener, watering and tending his anger, and hate, and venom. Sometimes it was hard to care. But he did his best to keep the fire going.

An alert popped up, and he tensed. A message from *him*. He felt the rush of anticipation and excitement as he clicked it.

The Twitter comments kept materializing on one of the monitors, unnoticed. He read the message from Jack_the_Ripper over and over again, and in the darkness, he smiled.

CHAPTER 31

Tatum stretched in his seat and rubbed his eyes. For the past hour he'd been studying the two murder case files, trying to outline the similarities and the differences, trying to understand the progression in the minds of the murderers.

Serial killers changed and adapted. They constantly obsessed about their last murder, the things they could do differently next time. They often changed their behavior because their confidence grew. Sometimes they just shifted their behavior as their fantasies and desires became more intricate. If he could figure out why they did things differently this time, perhaps they could predict the changes *next* time, as well.

But as difficult as it was to do with one murderer, it became infinitely harder with two. For example—Catherine Lamb had been covered, while Henrietta Fishburne had been left on display, posed grotesquely. Was it because Glover didn't want this victim covered? Was it because neither of the men knew this woman, so they didn't care? Or maybe it was because the unsub's fantasy somehow included this abhorrent spectacle? He'd actually listed all the possible reasons as they occurred to him, stopping when he reached ten. This was the opposite of useful. A profiler's job was to tighten the killer's characteristics, narrow the pool of suspects. If he explained all the various ways things *might* have transpired, it would only serve to muddy the waters.

He looked around the situation room. Zoe sat alone at the far end of the large table, looking at crime scene photos, biting her lip. Agent Valentine sat a few feet away from her, typing on his laptop. Koch was working one of the murder boards, painstakingly drawing a timeline of the Henrietta Fishburne murder.

The crime scene photos dominated the murder board. One shot of the entire battered body, framed in the circular pentagram. Then close-ups of the ligature marks, another shot of the bite mark, and a third shot of the knife in the victim's body.

Above was a photo of Fishburne taken from her Instagram account. She was smiling, leaning back on the railing of a bridge. The scenery seemed European. He hoped it had been taken on a long vacation and that Henrietta had had the time of her life. The contrast between the smiling woman and the mutilated corpse was difficult to stomach.

"What do we know about her?" Tatum asked Koch.

Koch took a moment to collect his thoughts. "Henrietta Fishburne was a paralegal working in a large law firm located in the Chicago Loop. She lived with her husband and daughter in Riverdale—that's a neighborhood in South Chicago. She was a dedicated employee, worked hard."

"Was it customary for her to leave so late at night?" Tatum asked.

Koch shrugged. "According to her husband, in the past three weeks, Henrietta always worked late, but she usually left the office by eight in the evening. However, Monday night she was asked to stay with one of the firm's lawyers, working on an important case. So she left at half past midnight. Which meant she was on the train that stopped at 147th Street at one thirty-five in the morning."

"Did anyone know she was going to stay late? Did she tell someone?"

"Some coworkers and her husband."

Tatum nodded, satisfied, and sat down next to Zoe. "Fishburne didn't usually leave the office so late," he said. "It was a one-time thing."

Zoe raised her eyes from the photos on the table. "So even if the killers had followed her around or had watched the parking lot for a few nights, they couldn't have expected her to leave work so late."

"The attack was probably random. The killers had been waiting in the parking lot for someone, anyone who fit, to show up when there were no nearby witnesses. Henrietta Fishburne just happened to fit the bill."

"That matches Glover's usual MO," Zoe said. "Lurk in a remote location, nearby a water source, patiently waiting for a victim to show up."

"But it doesn't match the murder of Catherine Lamb."

She nodded. "That parking lot at the train station must have been one of Glover's spots."

"His spots?"

She raised her eyes to him. "There were no murders between 2009 and 2016."

He guessed he was somehow supposed to link the two sentences together, but as often happened when talking to Zoe, he felt at a loss. "So?"

"Glover lived here for at least ten years. But he only killed two women, both in 2008. What did he do the rest of the time?"

"Indulged in fantasies. Masturbated to keep his sexual needs in check."

"That's right. But to keep them exciting, he'd need to freshen them up a bit every once in a while."

"Why? How do you know he didn't just relive his earlier murders over and over?"

"If that had been the case, the entire porn industry would have collapsed long ago," Zoe said, a bit impatiently. "Sexual fantasies need variety. Especially with obsessive sexual predators, like Glover. And we *know* he responds to certain locations. That's why he almost always goes nearby water. So he'd probably get a buzz when fantasizing at his special locations. I assume he'd go to spots that fit his MO and fantasize. He'd wait, just like last night, for a woman to walk by, alone, and he'd concoct a fantasy in his mind about how he would grab her, rape her, and strangle her to death."

"So you're thinking he simply returned to somewhere he used to frequent before?"

"I'm almost sure of it. I'm betting he knew the train schedules by heart."

"But he didn't actually rape Henrietta Fishburne. Why?"

Zoe tapped one of the pictures. Tatum studied it closely. It was Henrietta's ribs, blooming with bruises.

"They confirmed this bruise is a result of a kick," Zoe said. "He kicked her when she was down."

"Or his partner did."

"I don't think so. His partner wants blood. Whatever the reason, this was his focus. And he got the blood he needed. But Glover desired something and *didn't* get it. So he got angry, and he kicked her."

Tatum thought about it. "You think he couldn't function?"

"Yes. Maybe it's the cancer. He must have been infuriated." To Tatum's surprise, she sounded worried.

"So?"

"It might significantly shorten the time until the next murder."

They both let the silence stretch. Tatum was the first to break it. "Why the pentagram, the knife, and the phone call?"

"Well, like you already figured out, he *wanted* us to find her like that. And he wanted it to happen as soon as possible, probably before the body could decompose significantly."

"But why?"

"He could be trying to throw us off," Zoe said, doubt in her voice.

"Or he could be doing it to send you a message," Tatum suggested. "Maybe he wanted *you* to see the body."

"Why a pentagram, then? That makes no sense. There's no significance to a pentagram for me *or* Glover."

"It could be about publicity. Now that his time is running out, he's trying to leave his mark."

"That's possible," Zoe conceded. "Glover never showed any interest in publicity before, but his circumstances changed significantly."

Agent Valentine sighed audibly from his seat. "You're obviously missing the point."

Tatum glanced at the man. During their time in the Chicago field office, he'd gotten to know Valentine a bit. He was a nice enough guy, with a good sense of humor. But Valentine's patronizing manner toward Zoe set him on edge. "Which is?"

"There's a religious aspect to these murders. First murder, they place the necklace of a cross on the victim's neck, right on the marks of the noose that killed her. In the second murder, they draw a pentagram and then pose the victim like a sacrifice to the devil, a knife in her stomach. I bet *that's* why he called to brag about it. Maybe he thinks he's the next prophet or something."

"Rod Glover isn't a religious fanatic," Zoe said. "He couldn't care less about it."

"Maybe. People change when they face death. Like you said, his time is running out."

"That's absurd. It doesn't align with his profile at all."

"The man has brain cancer. Who knows what's going on in his head right now? He might be completely deranged. Besides, it might be his partner's idea. The guy's already drinking blood. You think devil worship is beyond him? Hell, maybe that's what the blood drinking is all about."

"Fine," Zoe said curtly. "Your suggestion is noted. Thank you."

Valentine shrugged, returning to his work.

"Here's something else that's bothering me." Zoe pointed at a pair of photographs. One was from the Lamb crime scene—the markings of bloody footprints pacing around the body. The other was from the recent scene—indentations of footprints in the mud circling a part of the pentagram. "We assumed he was out of control in the first scene, which was why he was pacing around the body over and over again. But he seems to be doing the same thing here."

"Here they've been drawing the pentagram, posing the body," Tatum pointed out. "They'd have to walk around it repeatedly."

"But it almost seems to be in a sort of pattern. See? Three paces, and he stops, turns to face the body. Then he steps sideways twice, and then here . . . three paces, and he turns to face the body. In the other scene it's similar. I checked with O'Donnell. In both cases it's the unsub's footsteps, not Glover's. It looks like some sort of obsessive ritual that follows the murder. Something that might not be related to the blood."

"What does it tell us?"

She shook her head. "Nothing yet. But we need to look for other patterns. Perhaps this man has a set of obsessive-compulsive rituals he does. If that's the case, it would be visible when talking to him."

"We'll keep an eye out for that."

"Where's O'Donnell gone?" Zoe asked, glancing around.

"She went with Ellis to look for that crack addict and get another look at both crime scenes."

"We should go and have a look at the parking lot too," Zoe said.

"Tomorrow morning?" Tatum suggested hopefully.

"I want to see it tonight, when it's dark. That's how *they* saw it."

Tatum sighed. "Of course you do. Let me finish up, and we'll go there together."

CHAPTER 32

Zoe stepped into her motel room, letting the door click shut behind her. After visiting the train station's parking lot, she'd meant to go back with Tatum to the police station and keep working. But a chill had crawled up her spine. She had to take a break. So she'd asked Tatum to drop her off at the motel.

The dark presence of Henrietta Fishburne's death festered in her mind. She could feel it like a physical presence, straining against her skull. She had to let it out.

She took off her shoes and socks and slipped under the bedcover, letting its weight settle over her, a secure cocoon. She forced her body to relax. The day had taken a toll, especially after the little sleep of the past week, and lying down was a relief.

Shutting her eyes, she thought of the parking lot. Henrietta's car was gone when they got there, but it was easy to imagine it, surrounded by empty parking spaces in the dark. Henrietta's heart must have pounded in her ears, even before anything happened. Just crossing that parking lot in the dark, alone.

High heels tapping on the pavement, a brisk pace. It was cold. Zoe's own breathing quickened, and despite the blanket on top of her, she shivered.

She reached the car, was already about to unlock it. A sudden movement in the shadows. A hand grabbing her, pulling her. A blazing pain in her neck. A struggle.

Zoe's fingers tightened, grasping the bedsheet. She thought of the bloodstains on the pavement and envisioned what they meant: Henrietta, consumed by terror, fleeing from her attacker, not even realizing that she was getting farther from safety. Trees looming ahead, the darkness consuming her surroundings as she left the parking lot's spotlights behind her. Someone grabbing her, hissing threats. The fabric tightening around her throat. Zoe still remembered how that felt, would never forget: Glover behind her, his grunts as he tightened the noose, a desperate need to breathe, clawing at her own neck. His rough fingers touching her skin, prodding, scraping.

She trembled, her memories merging with what Henrietta must have gone through. She'd waded into a stream, only to have her feet plunge deep, tumbling, realizing it wasn't a stream at all. It was a turbulent river, the current pulling her down.

She gasped, fought her way out of her waking nightmare, pulling herself back with the sensation of the fabric between her fingers. She was in the motel's bed, gasping for breath. It wasn't the first time she'd imagined a victim's last moments. But knowing Glover had been there, the memory of her own encounter with him still vivid, had turned this into something much worse.

She threw the blanket off her. Her body was clammy with sweat, and she still felt the phantom touch of his hands on her skin. She took off her clothes and hurried to the shower, turning the water boiling hot. The water felt sublime, and the tension that gripped her body slowly diminished. Her mind wandered.

Running in the dark, stumbling, someone gripping her, turning her around, Glover's leering face close to hers.

Zoe stifled a scream, shutting off the water. Her mind drew her back.

She knew from experience that not letting the imaginary sequence run its course would only result in horrific nightmares. She toweled herself, then returned to bed.

Despite the fact that Zoe had been dogging Glover's murders for twenty years, Henrietta Fishburne's body was the first victim she'd actually seen lying at the scene of the crime. Seeing that body must have jarred her mind, awakening all the memories and traumas connected to him. His attack on Andrea. The murders of Beth, Jackie, and Clara. Her own encounter with him, just months before. Barricading herself and Andrea in the room as he pounded on the door.

She could rationalize what she was going through, but it did little to help the trembling that took over her body again.

And it couldn't stop the images of Henrietta, running in the dark, Glover close on her heels.

CHAPTER 33

The door to the situation room opened abruptly. Tatum raised his gaze from his laptop, meeting O'Donnell's tired eyes as she stepped into the room.

She looked around, taking in the empty seats and discarded coffee cups. "Where *is* everyone?"

"Koch and his partner are interviewing Henrietta Fishburne's parents and close friends," Tatum said. "I dropped Zoe back at the motel after we went to take a look at the parking lot. Agent Valentine is at the forensic lab. Ellis was with you. Some uniformed cops are still doing door to door in the vicinity of the train station."

She shut her eyes and massaged the bridge of her nose tiredly.

"Any luck finding the mysterious witness?" Tatum asked.

"No luck so far. Ellis thinks it's a guy named Good Boy Tony, but he wasn't in his usual haunts. We'll try again tomorrow. Any news here?"

Tatum got up from his chair and walked over to the Fishburne murder board. "Diver team found some of the victim's clothing and purse." He pointed at the picture of the muddy items in clear evidence bags. "We have a shirt and a single shoe. The purse had her car keys and phone. The car keys match her silver FIAT, in case we had any doubt. The phone was sent to the lab."

"They made sure we'd find the body but threw her stuff into the river," O'Donnell said thoughtfully. "Maybe there's something incriminating in her phone?"

"It's possible, but I doubt it. She was a random victim. I think they just did their best to cover their tracks. Waste our time." Tatum frowned, a glimmer of an idea in his mind. "They're buying time. Maybe because Glover just knows he'll die soon? But it seems almost as if it's more than that. They're working fast . . ." It was frustrating, feeling that idea flutter just out of sight.

"Any luck with the van?" O'Donnell asked, pointing at two grainy pictures of a banged-up Chevrolet van.

"Managed to get a better shot of the license plate," Tatum said. "But it's splashed with mud to a point where it's almost certainly deliberate. However, Koch managed to find the moment they entered the parking lot. The van showed up at seventeen minutes past nine p.m. Parked somewhere in the western part of the parking lot, far from prying eyes, close to the train tracks. Left at two thirty-seven a.m."

"They'd been waiting for a while," O'Donnell said.

"Just over four hours." Tatum nodded. "Glover is patient. Koch sent police patrols looking for that van in the area of McKinley Park and in the vicinity of Kickapoo Woods; maybe we'll get lucky."

"Yeah." O'Donnell's eyes were glazed over. He doubted she'd heard anything he'd just said.

"Anything wrong?"

"It's a decent picture of her." O'Donnell pointed at Fishburne's picture on the murder board. "But when I went to notify the husband today, there was an image on the computer, of Henrietta, with her daughter, on the beach. And she almost looked like a different person. Do you know what I'm talking about?"

"No."

"My daughter is about the same age."

"As Fishburne's daughter?"

"Yeah." She sighed. "He asked me if Henrietta . . . if his wife suffered when she died."

"They always ask that."

"I told him she didn't."

"Good."

"Her death was horrifying, Tatum. She was terrified and hurt. She couldn't breathe—"

"But you don't tell that to the family."

"No," she whispered. "You don't tell that to the family. Never tell that to the family."

"Are you okay?"

She blinked. "I need to call my daughter, say good night." She took out her phone and glanced at it. "Shit! It's ten forty. She's asleep by now."

"You'll see her in the morning."

"Right," she said, slipping the phone in her pocket.

He eyed her, concerned. "Listen—"

"Any news about the phone used to report the murder?" Her voice was blank, the fragility he'd spotted before gone.

"Uh . . . yeah. The phone is a burner and was never used before that call. It was turned off after use. The call came from an area in the Loop."

"That's where Henrietta used to work."

"You think it was somehow intentional?" Tatum asked.

"Could be . . . but it's an area that's easily accessible by the 'L,'" O'Donnell said. "Glover might have gotten on a train, rode a few stations, got off, made the phone call, probably trashed the phone somewhere nearby, and hopped on a train back home."

"Sounds plausible."

"If that's true, we can pull security footage from likely stations and see where he got off," O'Donnell said. "Though it'll be a nightmare to look through."

"You can talk to Valentine; he might be able to help there," Tatum suggested. The FBI had image-recognition software and enough CPU to go through all the footage, searching for Glover.

"That's a good idea," O'Donnell said. "I'll suggest that to Bright tomorrow."

A bitter tone accompanied her last sentence. He sympathized. When it was just the Catherine Lamb case, she'd been in charge. Now the whole investigation was managed by Bright, despite her catching the first murder. Even though he wasn't an expert in police politics, it sounded like she was being pushed aside. He knew what that felt like.

"Any progress with the congregation members?" He changed the subject.

"I got an email with a list of names from Patrick Carpenter," O'Donnell said. "Three hundred and twelve names, out of which one hundred and seventy-one are male. There's no mention of age, so I'm not sure which are relevant. It's far from a complete list; those are just the people he remembers. He doesn't have phone numbers or addresses for most of them. I'm trying to get a similar list from Albert Lamb, but it sounds like he can barely get out of bed. It's like pulling teeth. And with Valentine telling Bright that it's a waste of time, it's hell to actually get the damn thing—"

"Okay." Tatum raised his hands as her tone rose. "I get it. It sucks being you."

That gave her pause. "That's a succinct way of putting it," she finally said. "Though not very useful."

"Look," he said. "It's late. You've been awake since six in the morning—"

"Five. I woke up early and couldn't go back to sleep."

"And when did you last eat?"

"I . . . it's been a while."

"There's leftover pizza," Tatum said, gesturing at the box on the table.

She lunged at it like a puma catching a stray deer. She flipped the lid, and her predator's eyes stared at the metaphorical deer with disappointment. "There's pineapple on the pizza."

This puma was quite picky. "So?"

"Who orders pineapple on their pizza?"

"I do," Tatum said defensively.

"And here I was starting to like you." She picked up a slice and bit it, chewing morosely. "And it's cold. Ice-cold pizza with pineapple. This is what my life has become."

"I like that whole self-pity thing you've got going there." Tatum grinned at her. "Want to go grab something else?"

She shrugged. "I guess both my daughter *and* my husband are asleep by now, so I might as well go eat with you."

"Thank you for making me feel so special."

His phone rang. It was Zoe. He motioned O'Donnell to wait for a second and answered the call.

"Tatum?" Zoe's voice sounded strange, fragmented.

"What's up?"

"I'm in the motel room . . . ?" The sentence stretched, almost as if she wasn't sure she really was in the room.

"I'm here with O'Donnell. Is it important?"

"Oh." A long pause. "No, it isn't important. It can wait. It's nothing, really."

"Zoe, is something wrong?"

No answer. Just breathing.

"Zoe?"

"What?" She sounded startled. Then, a second later she said, "No. Nothing's wrong. I'll see you tomorrow." She hung up.

Tatum frowned at the phone.

"So," O'Donnell said. "Are we going to grab that bite?"

CHAPTER 34

The man in control spent the entire day away from home, feeling like a bad theater actor acting out a script of his own life. It was as if he kept forgetting his next line or what his mood was supposed to be. All of his movements felt mechanical and exaggerated. His entire body was a cumbersome suit that he was desperate to remove. He wanted to give it all up and storm off the stage. But there was no stage and no script. And he knew Daniel would be aghast if he did anything to draw more attention to himself. So he held it together.

But by the time he got home, his jaw was clenched so tightly that his head began to pound. And when he closed the door behind him, he could already sense that Daniel was having a bad day. When you lived with a sick person, you developed a sensitivity to his pain. Maybe it was something in the odors produced by his breath and his sweat. Or maybe he heard Daniel groan faintly through the guest room's closed door. It didn't matter. Sickness lingered in the house.

He stumbled to the fridge and yanked the door open. He still had five vials remaining. Perhaps the blood was somehow diluted. He needed to consume more. Grabbing three vials, he went over to the cupboard and removed a large coffee mug. He emptied all the vials one by one into the mug, filling it almost to the top. A bubble materialized on the thick crimson surface and then popped.

He put the mug to his lips and drank greedily, feeling the viscous liquid sliding down his throat, coating his tongue, and gums, and teeth, salty and metallic.

It worked. Sudden tranquility flooded his body. This was what he'd needed all along. How could he forget—

A sudden lurch in his gut, and he scrambled to the bathroom, bile rising at the back of his throat. He made it just in time, grasping the toilet with both hands as he heaved and vomited. He coughed and gagged, his eyes tearing up. Wiping his face, he watched the toilet, the water bubbling with red vomit, the previously white porcelain spattered with pink and brown stains.

The blood of that woman was tainted. That was why it hardly helped, and that was why he couldn't stomach it.

He moved to the sink and turned on the water, splashing it on his face. He gargled some of it and spat reddish leftovers in the sink, watched them circling and disappearing into the drain.

Putting his coat back on, he stepped outside, still coughing and spitting, trying to get rid of the taste and smell of his own vomit. The street tilted, or maybe he did, as he lurched, one step at a time, following the noise of traffic.

He wasn't sure what he was looking for; he just wanted to get *away*. But after walking for a while, hugging himself, trembling, he saw her.

The woman with the baby. It was the same one he'd seen a few days before.

This time, he wouldn't lose his nerve. He needed something pure.

Everyone kept giving Joanne advice about raising her son. She'd expected it from her mother, who assumed she always knew better, and from her sister-in-law, who had three kids and appointed herself the guru of child raising. But it turned out her neighbors had opinions, and the clerk at the supermarket, and her husband's bachelor friends. It seemed everyone knew how to raise babies better than Joanne and felt the need to share. Their favorite tips concerned sleep. Specifically, how the baby should be put to sleep, what should be done when he woke up, and the numerous ways Joanne was doing it wrong.

At first she'd resisted. She'd tried to explain that not all babies were the same. Some of them didn't sleep as well. Some had teething problems, and the pain woke them up. And no, just leaving her son to cry in his crib for hours wasn't something she was willing to do. But after endless eye rolls and sighs and condescending do-what-you-feel-is-right comments, she now just nodded. That seemed to make everyone happy. They gave advice; she nodded and kept doing what she knew was right.

Her son fell asleep easily when she took him for a walk. And it really wasn't such a big deal to go for a walk once after lunch and once in the evening.

He slept right now, and she smiled at his angelic face. As she raised her eyes, her step faltered.

A man walked toward her, a strange grimace on his face. He was disheveled, and his movements were strange, jerky. And what made her breath hitch were his eyes, which were wide and fervent, and staring directly at her son's stroller.

Instinctively, she swerved the stroller, quickly checking the road for oncoming traffic. There was none, and she crossed, walking faster. She wanted to call her husband, but he was, as usual, working late. And he never answered her calls at work.

Anyway, what would she say? *I saw a weird guy on the street?* He'd laugh his ass off. And she wasn't about to—

The man followed her. She saw him crossing the street from the corner of her eye, and now he was walking after her. He'd *turned around* just to follow her.

She hastened her pace, her home just a few yards away now. Crossing the street again, she heard him closing in. She pushed the stroller with one hand now, the other trembling hand in her coat pocket, fishing for her house keys. He was close. Too close. She would never unlock the door and get inside in time.

She whirled around and said, "If you come any closer, I'll scream." Her voice trembled, but she spoke loudly, fiercely.

He slowed down and said something, but he wasn't really talking to her. He muttered to himself, his mumbling incoherent. His chin had a strange gleaming sheen, and she realized with disgust and horror that it was coated with drool.

She turned around and sprinted to her home, the jostling waking up her son, who began to scream. She thrust the keys into the lock, turned them, opened the door, and they were inside, door slamming behind her. She jammed the dead bolt shut and took a deep gasping breath.

The baby cried.

"Shhhhh," she said, tears in her throat. "Shhhhhh." She searched in the stroller bag for her phone. Usually she loved the bag, which seemed to be able to contain everything she needed—bottle, pacifier, diapers, baby wipes—but now she hated the messy thing, with its clutter. Where was her damn phone?

There! She quickly dialed her husband. She waited for eight rings before hanging up, frustrated. She glanced out the window.

The man was there, walking back and forth on her doorstep, still talking to himself. His voice was louder now, and she caught a few words. *Control . . . baby . . . door . . .*

She dialed 911.

"Nine-one-one, what's your emergency?"

"There's a man outside my house," she whispered. Her son screamed in the background, and she wanted to pick him up. But her palms were so clammy and slippery; she would drop the phone if she did that. "He chased me to the door."

"Is the door locked?"

"Y . . . yes."

"Is he still at the door?"

"Yes, I can see him through the window. He's talking to himself. Please send someone—I'm scared."

"Can you tell me your address?"

For a moment she almost couldn't recall it, but then she did, blurting it in panic.

"Okay, miss, what's your name?"

"Joanne."

"Joanne, I need you to stay calm. I just sent a patrol car over. Can you still see the man at the door?"

Joanne glanced through the window. The street was empty. "N . . . no, I think he left."

"The officer will come over, look around, and make sure you're fine, okay? Joanne?"

But Joanne couldn't answer; her voice was gone. She'd just seen a shadow flit across the window of the kitchen. Just by the back door. The same door she constantly forgot to lock, one more task slipping due to the sleep deprivation that clouded her life.

Had she locked the back door this time?

She distinctly remembered opening it that morning to water the plants in the backyard. But she couldn't remember locking it.

The doorknob turned while the voice on the phone said, "Joanne? Are you there?"

CHAPTER 35

The door was locked. He rattled the doorknob several times, only half remembering what he was doing there. The baby wailed from inside, and he blinked, startled. He'd been standing in that strange backyard for several minutes, just staring at the door. Had he tried to open it? He rattled the doorknob. It appeared to be locked. Oh yeah, he'd tried it already.

Someone was talking, and he paused to listen, but the voice became quiet, and only the baby kept wailing. Then he realized it was *him*. He was the one who had been talking, talking to himself.

He tried to piece together the events of the evening. Had he really intended to snatch a baby out of its carriage?

He was letting his control slip.

That scared him more than anything. It had happened before, long ago, and since then he did his best, but tonight, no one drove the train, and it had gone off the rails.

He turned and fled, not to the street—he was afraid someone would see him. Instead, he fled over backyard fences, running through private yards, stomping flower beds, knocking down patio chairs, his pants ripped by a thorny rose patch. He saw the blue light of a police car passing by from the corner of his eye. Were they looking for him? For a moment he got confused, thought he was running away from

Catherine's home after they had left her dead. But then he recalled a day had passed, or maybe two days? Four?

He reached a fence he couldn't climb over and decided instead to return to the street. It was dark, no sign of the police car, no passersby. Just him and the shadows.

He forced himself to breathe deeply, the cold air clearing his mind. The nights were the worst. During the day, he did fine. Talking to people, doing his job, going through the motions. He was almost certain no one suspected a thing. But at night, it all became so much harder. It had always been that way.

He found his way back home, locked the door, and barred it behind him. Evidence of his control slip was all over the place. Two of the vials discarded on the kitchen tabletop. One had rolled and fallen to the floor, shattering, leaking some leftover blood drops on the floor. The mug he'd used to drink the blood had been left on the counter, and the residue had coagulated. Glancing at the bathroom, he could see the toilet still spattered with his vomit.

He cleaned it all up, then took a long shower, breathing heavily as he did so, trying to clear his head. He was in control. He was in control. He was in control.

CHAPTER 36

Zoe's breaths were fast and shallow. The walls of the room closed in on her, the space around her shrinking with every heartbeat. She'd tried taking a long walk when she felt the creeping effect of claustrophobia, but as soon as she stepped outside, into the night's darkness, she could feel the phantom presence of Glover somewhere nearby. Behind her.

And who was to say that he wasn't? He'd followed her before. What would prevent him from doing it again? Walking alone at night, with him lurking in the shadows, would be foolish.

She backtracked into the room, locked the door, tried to calm down.

But it was impossible to withstand the tidal waves of panic that kept hitting her.

Even in her current state, a detached part of her kept analyzing. She could understand what was happening. The little sleep she'd had lately, combined with her PTSD, had triggered a full-blown panic attack. Her imagination, fueled by emotion, battered her with vivid scenarios that served to fuel the inferno of fear in her mind.

Understanding it didn't help. If anything, it made it worse.

When she'd called Tatum, she'd hoped for help. But he'd said he was with O'Donnell, his tone slightly impatient. And suddenly she couldn't figure out why she'd called him. What could he do to help her?

Only she could help herself. She knew that, had always known that.

She was shivering in her bed again, clinging to the sensation of the sheets around her. She wasn't outside, chased by Glover. She wasn't buried in a coffin underground. She was in a motel room. She was *fine.*

She didn't feel fine. She needed to throw up.

She lunged, trying to untangle herself from the blanket. The sheet clung to her, and she struggled, the vomit rising up her throat. She retched several times as she threw up, gasping, clawing at the pillow. For a while she just coughed and gagged, acid in her mouth. Then she was shaking, spent, her heart pounding.

Something else was pounding. The door.

"Zoe?" Tatum called through the door. "Are you okay?"

"I'm . . . fine." Her voice was shaky. Choked.

Pause. "Open the door."

"No. I'll see you in the morning."

"Open the door, Zoe."

She shut her eyes in desperation, then squirmed out of the sheets, heart still racing. She stumbled to the door, unlocked it, wiping the vomit from her chin quickly. She pulled the door open.

Tatum's eyes widened as he saw her. She must have looked just as shitty as she felt.

"Just some nightmares," she croaked. "I'm fine now. Really." She began shutting the door.

He blocked it with his foot. "Like hell you are." He pushed the door open, slowly so it wouldn't hit her. Then he brushed past her and entered the room.

She followed his eyes as he took in the bed, the messy sheets, her own stained shirt, her trembling hands.

He grabbed her and pulled her close, his large arms engulfing her. She struggled, not wanting to get vomit on his clothes, but he just held her tight until she stopped squirming in his hug, becoming limp. The fear was gone, though she could still feel it lingering, waiting. Now, she was mainly mortified.

"I think I ate something that didn't agree with me," she mumbled.

"Maybe it was all that hot chocolate," he suggested, still holding her.

"Yeah. But I'm feeling better now."

"Go take a shower."

She did, stumbling to the bathroom, taking off her foul shirt in disgust. The hot water made her feel better. Tatum had probably left. She'd apologize tomorrow for being such a mess. She took the time to brush her teeth, getting rid of the acrid taste of vomit.

He was still there when she got out of the bathroom, wrapped in the motel's towel. He must have called for clean sheets and was now carefully making the bed, the old sheets crumpled in the corner of the room.

"I can do that," she said.

"I'm almost done."

She quickly grabbed underwear, a sweatshirt, and yoga pants from her suitcase and dressed in the bathroom. She could hear Tatum moving around in the other room. She wanted him to leave. But the very idea of him leaving her alone in the room resulted in a stab of icy fear in her gut.

She took a deep breath, and it was so easy to do now that she found it strange she couldn't possibly do it before. Then she opened the door again. Tatum sat in the chair by her bed.

"Thanks for the help," she said. "I think I'll be better once I sleep."

"I'm sure you will."

She shuffled to bed, sat on the mattress, suddenly relieved that the sheets were crisp and clean. Tatum had spread them tightly, almost as if someone from the motel's room service had done it.

"Good night," she told him.

He didn't budge. Didn't say anything.

"I had a panic attack," she finally said. "I've been working too hard. But it's over now. I'll go easy for a few days."

He raised one eyebrow. "Uh-huh."

"I will!"

"No, you won't. I'm calling Mancuso tomorrow. I'll tell her she needs to pull you from the case."

"No!" She was horrified. Mancuso wouldn't be able to make Zoe leave Chicago. But she could cut her off. Make sure she wasn't involved in the investigation. "If you do that . . ." She searched for a threat, some way to intimidate him. She had nothing.

"I need to know what happened to you tonight," he said. "I'm your partner. I'm worried sick. But if you won't talk to me—"

"It was *just* a panic attack."

"It wasn't. You've been acting strange for days now. I mean, you're always a bit strange, but you've been acting . . . unlike you."

She shut her eyes and chewed her bottom lip. She wondered if maybe he was bluffing. Would he really get her pulled off the case? He knew what it would do to her. Opening her eyes, she glanced at him, saw his face.

He wasn't bluffing.

"It's something that happens to me," she finally said guardedly. "I have these moments when I imagine what the victim went through."

"We all do that. It's part of the job."

She shook her head, frustrated. "No. Not like that. It's . . . more vivid. I lie in bed, and I can see it and feel it all happening. Almost like I'm her . . . the victim."

"Like a hallucination?"

"No!" That would get her off the BAU for good, not to mention this case. "I know where I am and who I am. I know it's just my imagination. But it's very vivid, and I can't stop it. Maybe that's why I'm so good at this. I can get into *everyone's* head. The victim and the killer. It's part of the package."

She huddled in the blanket. Now that she'd started talking, she couldn't stop. "I can almost feel the fear. And the pain. My body reacts to it all, so I have a bit of trouble breathing, fast pulse. It usually ends after half an hour."

"How many times did that happen?" Tatum asked.

"I don't know. Dozens."

"Jesus, Zoe."

"If you tell this to anyone, they won't understand. They'll kick me out of the BAU." She already regretted telling him about it. "It's really not a big deal. I've got it under control."

"You definitely looked under control when I showed up here."

"This time was different."

"Why?"

"Part of it is what happened in San Angelo. I still have moments of claustrophobia." She didn't go on.

"And part of it is this case?" Tatum said. "If you were putting yourself in Henrietta Fishburne's place, feeling what you believe she felt . . . you were reliving Glover's assault of her."

"Parts of it. Fragments. But I couldn't make it stop." She shivered, then forced herself still, clenching her teeth. "I never told anyone about this. You can't . . . please don't . . ."

"I won't tell anyone," he said heavily. "But you can't go on like this. You know that, right?"

"It won't happen again."

He didn't respond to that. She knew it was obvious that she couldn't back that up in any possible way.

"He's careless now. And he has an unstable partner who's spiraling out of control. It's a matter of days until he gets caught."

"Maybe."

"And once he's caught, I will never have to worry about him again. He's already dying! He has less than a year left. Andrea will be safe. *I* will be safe. It'll be over. But I need to see this through."

The silence stretched between them. Tatum kept looking at her, eyes soft and worried, until Zoe turned away, unable to take it any

215

longer. She should have kept her mouth shut. She should never have called him. She shouldn't have trusted him with this, it was too much, she should have known she could only trust herself, had always known it, should never have—

"Okay," Tatum said.

"You won't ask Mancuso to pull me from the case?"

"I won't."

She shut her eyes, blinking away a tear. "Thanks."

"Good night, Zoe."

He got up, walked to the door. And she could already feel the darkness, lurking, waiting.

"Do you want me to stay here awhile longer, just to make sure you're all right?" he asked.

She shrugged. "I don't care. If you want."

Tensing up, she listened, her back to him, waiting for the door to open, for him to leave, not sure what she preferred.

"I'll just stay a bit."

A wave of relief washed over her, and she winced in embarrassment at her own reaction. "You can lie down here," she said, shifting over.

The bed creaked as he lay by her side with a sigh.

She stayed awake for what felt like hours. Finally, certain that he wasn't about to get up and leave, she relaxed and slept.

CHAPTER 37

Thursday, October 20, 2016

The light woke up Tatum, accompanied by the fact that he still wore his socks. And his pants, for that matter. His mind was sluggishly figuring out the WWW of waking up. Not the World Wide Web, but the *What? When? Where?*

There was gentle snoring beside him. He glanced sideways and saw Zoe. She was curled facing him, her hair a messy veil on her cheek. She was so surprisingly peaceful and gentle in her current state that for a few seconds he just lay there, transfixed. His gaze ran down her curved nose, her small parted lips, her slender neck, and stopped just as he realized that in this pose, her shirt collar was loose, exposing quite a bit of her pale skin. He tore his eyes away.

He tried to get out of bed quietly, but the motel had a penchant for squeaking beds that almost seemed intentional. As he rose, the bed let out a startled squawk, as if it were offended by their unceremonious parting.

Zoe's eyes opened at once, and she blinked at him, already seeming much more focused and alert than he was. "What time is it?"

"Uh . . ." He searched around for his phone. He'd fallen asleep with it in his pocket, which explained the dull throb in his thigh. He took it out. "Quarter past eight." It was very late. They were usually on their way out by seven.

Zoe blinked. "I slept well," she said.

"Good."

"It's the first time in weeks I didn't have nightmares. At least I don't think I did."

Tatum thought back to his own dream. "I dreamed I was in the North Pole, doing the hundred-meter dash against a bunch of penguins. I was doing pretty well, since my legs were much longer than theirs, except I was naked, freezing my ass off. And I kept thinking that it was nationally televised, and everyone I knew was watching, which was pretty embarrassing."

"There are no penguins in the North Pole. Only in the South Pole."

"That's true. I should have told that to the penguins. Who's embarrassed now, right?" He needed to brush his teeth.

"I'm sorry about last night."

"You have nothing to be sorry for," he said. "But from now on, we need to slow down. You need more sleep."

"Okay." She fumbled at her nightstand. "Where's my phone?"

"It's right there, by your hand . . . and now you've dropped it on the floor."

Zoe bent down to pick it up, nearly toppling from the bed herself. Tatum looked away and searched for his shoes.

"Oh, shit," Zoe muttered. "He published the story."

"Who did?" He found his right shoe but not the left one, which was ridiculous. He'd taken them off together. Was there a shoe-thieving pixie in the motel, with a penchant for left shoes? Maybe it was the penguins from his dream, trying to hobble him so he'd lose the race.

"Harry Barry. He saw me at the crime scene yesterday and put two and two together. The man is a public menace."

"I think that's giving him too much credit. Public annoyance, maybe."

"Fishburne murder possibly related to the Lamb murder." She read the title of the article from the phone. "Oh, for god's sake, listen to this. 'An aura of mystery envelops the two murder cases, and the police are still refusing to comment on why the accomplished profiler Dr. Bentley is advising on the case.'"

Tatum sighed. "You need to get a leash for your pet reporter."

"He's not my pet reporter." Zoe put the phone down. "This might work in our favor. Both killers are under a lot of pressure. Keeping this story in the headlines might increase the pressure, and one of them will make a mistake. Especially the unsub, who is probably already losing it."

"Let's hope he doesn't go completely off the rails and start a killing spree," Tatum said darkly. He found the left shoe and put them both on.

"I'm really hoping he'll snap and approach the cops to confess," Zoe said. "It's happened several times before. Kemper, Wayne Adam Ford, Spahalski . . ."

"There was that guy from Britain," Tatum said. "Michael Copeland. And what's his name with the creepy smiley face drawings."

"Keith Jesperson. He was obsessed with the media."

"Oh, and Mack Rey Edwards." Tatum scrolled through his own messages on his phone.

"Edwards only confessed because some of his victims managed to escape. He knew he was about to get caught."

"Well, we're hoping our unsub feels the same. And there's an even bigger chance someone will spot Glover and recognize him from the picture or call in with pertinent information."

"I just wish Harry would stop using my name with those adjectives. Renowned, accomplished, famous."

"Guy's got a crush on you."

"Don't be ridiculous. He's just doing this because he's about to publish a book about me, and he wants to increase his sales."

"It can be both."

"I need to go talk to him." Zoe put her phone down. "Let's go grab a coffee, and I'll swing by the *Chicago Daily Gazette* afterward, before going to the station."

Tatum stared at a message from an unfamiliar number. I had a chat with Peter Damien. He's a clan elder. He wants to talk to you. He frowned at the nonsensical text. Then it clicked.

"We'll get the coffee to go," he told Zoe. "Our vampire librarian has a friend who wants to talk."

The door was painted black, with the store's name, Night Fangs, in red. The paint on the letters trickled down, as if it had been written in blood. Underneath, someone had written in Gothic letters, *Go out with a FANG*. Tatum rolled his eyes as he pushed the door open.

The interior of the store was in surprisingly good taste. Tatum had half expected a coffin or two, perhaps some fake skulls on shelves, and cobwebs everywhere. But instead, it was a small brightly lit room with a few pictures on the wall and a large wooden table. A lanky young man with long blond hair sat by the table, frowning at something in his hands. Tatum came closer and saw the man was carefully applying a sort of clay onto a mold of teeth.

"Welcome to Night Fangs," the man said, glancing at Tatum and then at Zoe. His eyes seemed to widen. "Oh, wow. I know you said you want the troll fangs, but can I suggest you reconsider?"

"What?" Zoe sounded incredulous.

"Your boyfriend, *he's* definitely troll material. But with you, what I'd aim for is a seductive vampiress. Trust me, with your eyes and small fangs, you'll be like the real-life Drusilla. I'd be willing to give you a discount if—"

"We're not clients." Tatum flipped his badge.

"Oh," the man said, startled. "You're the FBI people Carmela mentioned. I thought we'd talk on the phone."

"We figured talking in person would be better," Tatum said. He felt miffed about being tagged as *troll material*. "You're Peter?"

"Yeah, but you can call me Damien, whatever."

"I'll call you Peter." Tatum looked around him. "You sell fangs?"

"Custom-made fangs and claws. Vampires, trolls, orcs, werewolves. I just did some dragon teeth for a client in China."

Tatum walked over to the pictures on the wall. Each one displayed one of Peter's customers as they showed their fangs to the camera. A man snarling, a mouthful of razor-edged teeth. A girl in a black cloak smiling mysteriously, the hint of fangs at the edges of her grin. Another girl with two tusks curving over her bottom lip and chin. "You actually make a living doing this full time?" he asked, amazed.

"Yeah, I guess? I have orders from all over the world, and I have some famous clients. You know the Bloody Barnacles?"

"No."

"Did all of their fangs. Now every time they have a concert, I get a few orders. And by March I'm always totally booked for Comic-Con. I am the *fang* in *fangirl*, you know? Ha ha. Cosplayers are half my orders."

Tatum had a vague idea what the man was talking about at best, but he let him go on. Peter was clearly nervous, and Tatum wanted him to relax.

"So are you a vampire?" Tatum asked, trying to keep the snark from his voice.

"I'm like, a psychic vampire, so I don't actually drink blood, you know? But I'm like, the head of my clan. I mean, sort of. It's complicated." Peter ran his hand through his hair. "I feel weird telling this to like . . . law enforcement. You aren't here to arrest me, right?"

"As incredible as it may sound, vampirism is not a federal offense," Tatum said. "But Carmela said you had something you wanted to tell us, right?"

Peter shifted uncomfortably. "You guys are investigating that woman's murder from last weekend, right? And Carmela said you think one of us did it."

"She mentioned you knew all the vampires in Chicago," Zoe said.

"I mean, I guess. I'm one of the elders, right?"

Tatum's poker face was having a hard time staying straight as the pimpled twenty-five-year-old called himself an elder.

"We need a list of all the Chicago vampires."

"I can't give you that."

Tatum leaned over the table, got close to Peter's face. "Listen, *Damien*, a woman was killed. If you don't give us that list—"

"It wasn't one of us, I swear!" Peter's voice squawked. "But I think I might know who it was."

Tatum's eyes widened. "Who?"

"We have this forum, right? Where we all talk. But, like, some of the members aren't vampires. Some of them just want to learn more, so they lurk, or they ask a question. And some are donors. We're doing our best to cultivate a sense of equality between donors and vampires. Anyway, one of the users began asking a few questions a while ago. Wanted vampires to describe what blood tasted like. And he was talking about nonconsensual blood drinking, which we are *totally* against. I mean, this is the twenty-first century, not the nineteenth century in Transylvania, right?"

Tatum glanced at Zoe. She hardly even breathed as she listened to Peter talk.

"Anyway, some members bashed him, and he stopped posting. But I was, like, worried that he might do something weird? So I reached out with a personal message and explained what people had an issue with and suggested that he maybe find a donor who would role-play as if she was nonconsenting. Some donors are excited by that."

"And was he interested?" Zoe asked, tense.

"Nah, he wasn't interested at all. He said that it wouldn't work, whatever that means. Then I didn't hear from him for a while. Then, two weeks ago, he began talking to me again. He asked if I thought drinking blood could cure anything. I was like, um . . . no, it's good for some things, if you need it, right? But if you break your leg, or, I don't know, have diabetes, go to the doctor. And then he asked if I thought drinking blood could replace antipsychotics." Peter paused, shaking his head.

"What did you tell him?" Tatum asked.

"I told him no way! And he kept going on about what if the blood was really pure, like if the donor was purehearted or whatever, so I just straight-out told him he was being stupid. And he didn't answer. So I was, like, thank god, I got some sense into him, right? And then, two days ago, I got a short message from him."

"What did he say?"

"He said that I was wrong."

"What then?"

"Nothing. I answered, asked him what he was talking about, but he didn't reply. I sent him a few more messages, but I got absolutely nothing. And then when Carmela talked to me, I thought, shit, that could be your guy."

"We need the email he was using," Tatum said.

"The forum doesn't use emails, just usernames and passwords. His username is Dracula2."

"Fine. We'll need admin access to your forum and to talk to whoever is running it." Unless Mr. Dracula2 was a technological wiz, the bureau's analysts would be able to locate him in five minutes.

"It's a Tor-based forum," Peter said.

Tatum gritted his teeth. The Tor network, commonly known as the dark web, almost completely guaranteed digital anonymity. This was why it was often used by pedophiles or for black markets such as the Silk Road, which sold drugs and guns. And, apparently, it was also used by Chicago's vampire community.

"Peter, if this guy is the one we're looking for, he might kill more people," Tatum said, neglecting to mention the fact that he already had. "We need to find him as soon as possible."

"Listen, I'll give you what I can, okay? I'm just saying there's a reason we use this forum. Some vampires don't want to be found."

"Did this . . . Dracula2 ever mention the *purity* of blood before his last messages?" Zoe asked. "Any mention of that word at all in one of his earlier messages or his posts?"

Peter thought about it. "I don't think so. I mean, I'll check, but I feel like the first time was two weeks ago."

"Is it something you talk about routinely on the forum?"

"Nah, I don't remember anyone talking about blood purity. I mean, we talk about STDs a lot, so there's that."

Zoe caught Tatum's gaze, her eyes telling him that they were done.

"Can you find the posts by Dracula2 to show us?" Tatum asked. "And the forum's details too."

"Uh, sure, hang on. My laptop is in the back room. Don't touch the fangs on the table, okay?" He exited the room, leaving them alone.

"What do you think?" Tatum asked. He could see the spark in Zoe's eyes, the way she bit her lower lip. She thought it was their guy.

"It fits," she said. "The timeline works, and everything he told us fits the profile. The fact that he wasn't interested in role-playing clarifies his blood drinking isn't a result of paraphilia."

Tatum took a few seconds to catch up. When they'd analyzed the various possible reasons for consuming blood, Zoe had said that paraphilia was a possible reason. A sexual fetish. "Why does it mean that?"

"Well, if it was a sexual fantasy, I'd expect him to be interested in role-playing it. In fact, I'd think he'd be thrilled. But it didn't interest him at all. He said it wouldn't work."

He could see the logic in that. "So that leaves . . . a psychotic disorder or Renfield's syndrome, right?"

"I don't think it's Renfield's syndrome. I'm not even entirely convinced Renfield's syndrome is real," Zoe said. "But in any case, it doesn't sound like he's just after blood, right? He was talking about nonconsensual blood drinking. There's something more intricate, and violent, in his desires. And the fact that his username is Dracula2 is interesting."

"Because it's a dumb username?"

"Well . . . yes. It means he doesn't really care about vampire lore or vampire culture. These guys, most of them can recite all the vampire names from TV shows or Anne Rice's books without blinking. But he tries to get a username for the forum, chooses Dracula, and it's taken. Instead of picking Lestat, or Edward Cullen, or Spike, or anything else, he goes with Dracula2. Dracula is the only vampire he knows; he's not interested in being in a clan or adopting their lifestyle. So he doesn't want to be a part of the community, and just regular blood drinking doesn't interest him. Add that to the fact that he mentioned antipsychotics. I'd say he has a mental illness that results in delusions, possibly a form of schizophrenia."

"That would make him unpredictable," Tatum said.

"Unpredictable . . . and susceptible to pressure."

"Why did you ask Peter about the purity thing?"

"Two weeks ago, this guy starts asking around if pure blood can replace antipsychotics. He's never mentioned it before. Do you think there's a coincidence here?"

Tatum frowned. "You think Rod Glover gave him that idea."

"I'm *sure* he did."

CHAPTER 38

O'Donnell sat behind the steering wheel, eyes set ahead. Ellis sat by her side, drinking the remainder of his Starbucks coffee. Outside, the street was still, aside from the occasional vehicle that passed them by. They were waiting for Good Boy Tony to make his appearance.

"So why is he named Good Boy Tony?" O'Donnell asked.

"It's an old nickname," Ellis answered. "He used to live with his mother a few years ago. And whenever we ended up knocking on her door, looking for him, she'd tell us that he'd done nothing wrong and that he's a good boy. So it stuck."

"He doesn't live with her any longer?"

"She died last year." Ellis finished his coffee and looked around the car. "You don't have a place to throw trash here?"

"Nope."

"Why not?"

"Because if I do, the trash just sits there. And then it starts smelling. This way, I don't have trash in my car."

"But I have this cup in my hand now. It's trash. I want somewhere to put it."

"Later we can drive around, look for a trash can," O'Donnell said. "I don't think he's coming."

"Let's give him ten more minutes. It's a beautiful day. And it's Thursday."

Frannie's Scrap Shop was open on Mondays, Tuesdays, and Thursdays. According to Ellis, Frannie was one of Good Boy Tony's major income sources. And he almost never missed a Thursday, because missing Thursday meant he'd have to wait until Monday to sell her whatever he'd collected. And that meant a difficult weekend.

"As far as crackheads go, Tony's pretty reliable," Ellis said. "He'll show up—you'll see."

O'Donnell yawned, regretting her decision to go with Ellis on this stakeout. Her time would be better spent working on those "L" stations' security cams like she'd discussed with Tatum the day before. Ellis could have picked Tony up and taken him to the station to be questioned. But Ellis didn't think that Tony would be very cooperative that way.

Ellis placed the empty cup on the floor of the car.

"Don't forget it there," O'Donnell said.

"I won't."

"I don't want my car smelling like coffee."

"Yeah, I get it." Someone crossed the road ahead of them, pushing a shopping cart full of junk. Ellis pointed. "That's him. Told you. Reliable."

They got out of the car and approached the man. He was so thin O'Donnell had no idea how he managed to push that cart. He had on a grimy sweater and stained blue jeans. As they got closer, she could see one of the telltale signs of a crackhead—two ugly burn marks on his lips.

"Morning, Good Boy," Ellis said cheerfully. "How's the haul this morning?"

Tony's eyes darted around. "It's fine. I got twenty-three cans, mostly Coke cans. And I found some wire, I din't swipe it, I know it looks like I swiped it, but I din't, it was lying on the street. I think I might get a good price for the wire. Usually I don't find so many cans, but I think there was a conference or something by the school. Maybe they gave the people Coke, like for refreshments. I figured if I knew about conferences in advance, I could maybe always go afterward, collect the cans. That's a business opportunity, right?" He kept pushing the cart as he talked, the wheels squeaking, accompanying his monologue.

"That sounds like a good idea," Ellis said. "And I see you also have a long metal pole there. You didn't saw off one of the traffic signs, did you?"

"No, I jus' found it, I don' steal traffic signs. I know some people do, but I don', it isn't safe for the cars. I jus' collect what I find."

Ellis motioned at O'Donnell. "This here is Detective O'Donnell. She's investigating a homicide."

The man's eyes darted around. "Okay."

"Tony, I got a feeling you already know what this is about."

"Nobody I know died," Good Boy Tony said. "And I don' know anyone who killed anyone. I try to stay out of trouble, an' people mostly leave me alone. I have a friend who died two months ago, but it wasn't a murder or anything, he jus' died of the cold. It can get really cold at nights, and he slept outside that night, so he died of hypothermia. He was half-naked when they found him. Did you know that when people get hypothermia, they sometimes feel really hot? So they take off their clothes. That's what happened to Randy. Randy was my friend, the one who died."

"We're talking three nights ago. You were under the bridge at South Halsted, right, Tony?"

The man seemed to think this over. He breathed hard, the wheels squeaking. O'Donnell shuffled in half steps to keep his pace.

"Yeah," he finally said.

"Did you see someone while you were there?" O'Donnell asked.

He didn't answer.

"This is important," Ellis said. "I know you don't want to get in trouble, but we know you were there. If you don't tell us what happened, we'll have to take you to the station and talk."

"And my stuff?" Tony asked. "I need to sell my stuff. Frannie closes at four. If I don' get there by four, I'll have to wait until Monday. And people might steal my stuff. Back in the summer some of my stuff got stolen. They punched me and took my stuff, and the police din't do anything back then."

"Tell us what you saw, and we won't delay you any further."

"I won' have to go to the station and give a statement?"

"Not right now," O'Donnell said. "But we'll record this conversation." She took out her phone and started recording.

"And I won't have to testify in court?"

"We might need you to do that later," Ellis said. "But it'll be months from now, if we'll need you at all. And we don't care that you were smoking crack. This isn't about that at all."

He stopped walking, and O'Donnell exhaled in relief as the wheels stopped their squeaking.

"I was looking for a place to smoke," he said. "Usually I try to do it behind the mall, but the security guy spotted me, so I went to the bridge. Nobody cares if I do that under the bridge. So I finished, and I got out, stepped into the woods to take a piss. And when I got away from the bridge, I could hear two people talking. But, like, in hushed whispers." He stopped, staring at the cart's handlebar.

"What did they say?" O'Donnell prompted.

"Don' know at first. I was high, and it was good stuff. So I wasn't concentrating. And when one of them spoke, he was whispering, but he was angry, so he was kind of shout whispering? You know what I mean? So his words were all like a hiss, and that made me feel uncomfortable because it was an unpleasant sound, and I was high, so I shut my ears. And I lost track of time, kept seeing flashes of light, and I was nauseous . . . but when the high faded, they were talking about someone. They said to move her and dump her stuff. And I heard some splashing from the river."

"Did you see them?" O'Donnell asked.

"No, it was dark, and anyway, you don' go looking for company in the middle of the night in the woods, you know what I'm saying?"

"And then what?"

"One of them kept talking to himself. It sounded like he was praying or something. And then later he said that it wasn't good, that she was too dark."

O'Donnell and Ellis exchanged glances.

"Are you sure that's what he said?"

"Yeah, he kept saying, 'She's too dark. It's no good; she's too dark.' And then after a while they left."

"Can you describe their voices?"

"They were . . . I don't know. Regular. Like I said, they mostly whispered."

"Did you notice an accent? Anything at all?"

"No."

"Do you think if you'll hear one of them talking, you'll be able to identify him?"

"I doubt it."

O'Donnell sighed. "And what then?"

His eyes jumped around. "I don' . . . listen, I don' know. I was high. I'm sorry, I was high. I want to quit, I swear. Ellis knows. I'm gonna quit. Jus' after this weekend. After selling this stuff, I'll have enough for two rocks, but that's it. I don' want to be like this." A tear slid down his cheek. "I jus' need these two rocks because it was a really difficult week, and then I'll clean my act. I have a cousin who can get me a job at garbage disposal, and he can find me a place to stay. I've been planning to talk to him for a while, I told Ellis about it, right?"

"Right," Ellis said. "Your cousin at Pullman."

"That's right."

"What happened then, Tony?" O'Donnell asked. "I promise you you're not in trouble, okay?"

"I . . . I went over there. Just to see if they left something. And there was this woman. But she was dead, I'm sure she was dead. She had a knife stuck in her. Even if I called the police or got her to a hospital, they wouldn't be able to help her, right? Right?" His tone got more and more desperate.

"She was already dead, Tony," Ellis said. "There was nothing you could have done."

"I thought so. And I wanted to call the cops. But first I needed to go somewhere, get my shit together, you know? So I went to this place where I sometimes crash. And I got really scared, because sometimes after I smoke . . . I started thinking those guys were probably looking for me. Because I heard them. So I hid. And later I heard the police found the body, so there was, like, nothing else I could do, right?"

"No," Ellis said again. "There was nothing else you could do."

CHAPTER 39

The thing Harry never admitted to anyone and vowed to keep a secret even on his deathbed was that he was proud of everything he wrote.

Even the trashiest pieces, and sometimes *especially* the trashiest pieces, about celebrity infidelity, or errant nipples peeking from plunging necklines, or that one ridiculous article about the Chicago Cubs' coach stepping in dog shit. He wrote them knowing he did it better than any other reporter in America. Sure, Bob Woodward did an amazing job covering the Watergate scandal. But could Bob manage to write a five-hundred-word article about top model Tiffany Wu walking around an entire day with dry toothpaste on her chin? No, he could not.

But he was proudest of the articles he wrote about Zoe Bentley. Not because they were proper journalistic work, or because he wrote about something that mattered, or any of that rot.

It was because in a world of sordid stories about murderers and gory violence and heroic police work, he was the one reporter who understood that the real story was Zoe. And he made her shine.

His fingers were flying over the keyboard, pouring words onto the screen, an unlit cigarette sitting limply between his lips. He didn't want to take a smoke break outside, so he tried in vain to suck the nicotine out of the cigarette as if sucking a lollipop. The filter was getting soggier by the minute.

"Harry Barry."

For a moment he thought her imperious voice was just a figment of his imagination. After all, he'd spent the last few hours replaying in his mind their short conversation from the previous morning, milking it for what it was worth. But then he realized that no, Zoe was right behind him. He swiveled his chair, taking the wet cigarette out of his mouth.

"Dr. Bentley! What a pleasant surprise. I didn't expect to see you here."

Her blazing eyes met his. "You wrote about a possible connection between the murder of Catherine Lamb and Henrietta Fishburne. I told you *not* to write this story before you talk to me. It was irresponsible and misleading, and furthermore—"

"We've been through this before," Harry interjected. "Several times, in fact. You do not get to decide what I publish. My editor does. If you want a newspaper for which you can call the shots, why don't you get the FBI to start one? Call it the *Bureau Gazette*. I'm sure it'll be very popular. Federal agents are known for their creative flair."

"There's nothing that positively links those two cases, and—"

"Sure there is."

She blinked. "What?"

"*You're* linking those cases," he said. "And if you're involved in both of them, I can only assume they're related."

"I want to talk to your editor."

Harry's grin widened. "Please do. His door is over there. He's named McGrath."

Zoe looked at the door, hesitating.

"You should knock first. He gets grumpy when you just enter unannounced."

She bit her lip, then glanced over his shoulder at the screen. "Is that another article about the murder?"

"That?" He turned around and minimized it. "No, that's something else I'm working on."

"The headline said, 'McKinley Park Residents Outraged by Police Incompetence.'"

"Yup."

"The police are not incompetent. They are doing their very best to solve this murder case."

"Uh-huh. Sure they are. And what about the three other murders in the past five years? Only one was solved. And that weird drunk guy in the mall who keeps catcalling women? What about him? Why won't the police do anything about him?"

"What weird drunk guy?" Zoe asked, incredulous.

"If you lived in McKinley Park, you'd know. And the woman who almost got her baby snatched? And the graffiti epidemic? And the school break-in? The residents of McKinley Park feel unsafe."

"Where are you getting all that?"

"Mostly from comments on my other articles."

"And you're writing a news article about . . . reader comments on a different article?"

"I don't tell you how to do your job; don't tell me how to do mine."

Zoe shook her head in disbelief. "Whatever, I don't care. About your article linking the murders—"

"Tell me," Harry said. "Why are you even worried about this article?"

"Serial killers are often obsessed with news articles about themselves. Those articles make them accelerate their pace and sometimes change their pattern. Especially when those articles are cheap and loud."

"You flatter me. And in your opinion, is *this* killer the sort of killer affected by the press? I'm asking because the police are the ones who circulated Glover's photo with the media."

"Those pieces also taint jury pools. You spread hysteria—"

"Zoe, don't you get it?" Harry said, losing his patience. "You *need* me to run these articles."

She frowned, saying nothing.

"Do you want that picture of Rod Glover to keep circulating, or don't you?" Harry asked.

"I do," Zoe admitted after a second.

"Then you need to keep this story on the front page. People are losing interest in the Catherine Lamb murder. If I tie it to the Henrietta Fishburne story, it'll get more eyes. More people actively looking around for Glover to show his face. None of the other papers are giving the Lamb story even *half* the coverage that we are. But by tomorrow, after I run my next piece, half of Chicago will know what Glover looks like. We're going to use his photo again, as well as Catherine and Henrietta's photographs."

She paused, then said, "Okay. But I need you to use different pictures than the ones you've used so far."

Harry shrugged. "Give me whatever you want, and I'll see what I can do."

Zoe rummaged in her bag and took out a flash drive.

"There are pictures of Glover and Catherine Lamb here," she said. "Can you use those instead?"

Harry stuck the flash drive in his USB port. A folder opened containing two images. She'd come prepared. He briefly wondered if this had been her real intention all along. He double-clicked the first image. It was a close-up of Rod Glover talking to someone, smiling. The photo had caught him in a bad moment, his smile turned into a sneer, morphing his face into something sinister and cruel.

"This picture isn't as good as the other one," he said. "I think he's less recognizable here."

"Perhaps, but he's perceived differently."

It was true. In the previous image he was smiling at the camera cheerfully, looking like everyone's favorite uncle.

He checked the second image, of Catherine. "Oh, we're not going to use that."

"Why not?"

235

"Because we have a much better photo of her. Didn't you see it? Looking so happy, with the sun shining on her hair, that gorgeous view in the background. It's the perfect victim picture. A beautiful life snagged too soon and all that."

"But this one is haunting," Zoe insisted.

"Readers don't want the victims to be haunting."

"I don't care. *I* do."

Harry studied the image more carefully. Catherine was sitting outside in a garden, the shadow of a tree on her face. She was smiling slightly, but it was a sad smile, full of pain. And she looked at the camera in a cryptic way that seemed mysterious. Knowing.

"Why do you want the photo to be haunting?"

Zoe said nothing.

"I won't use it if you don't tell me."

"If I tell you, you'll quote me."

"I won't. It's off the record."

Zoe hesitated, then said, "There are indications that the murderer who killed Catherine cared about her. He felt guilty. I want *him* to see this picture."

Harry snorted. "You think he'll feel so guilty he'll confess?"

"Yes, or that he'll make a mistake," Zoe said. "It happens more often than you'd think. Murderers feel guilt. Not all of them, but some."

"And you think Glover feels guilty?"

She shrugged.

"I'll use this image," Harry said. He began to like the idea. "I'll use both of them."

CHAPTER 40

Rhea Deleon yawned in her patient's face for the third time. A wide, impolite yawn, a real-life imitation of Munch's *The Scream*.

"Oh, god, I'm sorry," she said, stifling yet another yawn.

Her patient, a pug puppy named Syrup, tilted his head, his brown bulging eyes seemingly fascinated. Syrup had been dropped off this morning by his owner, a woman who complained the "dog looked drunk all the time." She seemed more mortified than worried, as if her friends and family would shun her for having an alcoholic dog.

"You don't look drunk at all, do you?" Rhea asked Syrup affectionately as she scratched his neck.

He wagged his tail, tongue lolling. That was the issue—his tongue protruded slightly from his mouth, even when he shut it, giving him an adorable if mildly dumb look. It was called hanging tongue syndrome. Rhea wanted to make sure it wasn't due to a neurological problem.

"Well, maybe you look a bit drunk," Rhea conceded. "But a nice drunk."

Syrup wagged his spiraling tail.

She examined him slowly, everything feeling difficult. Being tired was the norm lately. She woke up tired, and it got worse throughout the day. Coffee hardly seemed to help. It'd been going on for a while, but it had taken her months until she'd finally gathered the courage to see a doctor.

It was the stupidest thing ever. A vet, literally a doctor, afraid of going to the doctor. If she'd had a tail, it would have been wedged between her legs as she stepped into her doctor's office.

"But people-doctors really *are* scary," she told Syrup. "They are impatient and angry, and they never give me a snack when they do a checkup. They don't even scratch behind my ear."

Syrup sneezed twice and turned around, trying to leave. As far as he was concerned, the examination was done. Rhea gently pulled him back.

It was probably just anxiety. Her clinic was on the verge of bankruptcy. Lately she found herself juggling the bills, trying to figure out which of them she could stretch a couple of weeks more. The week before, she'd burst into tears when she got the electricity bill. She spent hours every day calculating the ins and outs of her business, trying to figure out a way to do the impossible. Make more with less. She increased her online advertising, and maybe it worked, but it was really hard to tell. And she struggled with the yawning horror caused by constantly pouring money into the internet abyss like some sort of primitive sacrifice to a volatile god.

"You know what I need?" she said. "I need a rich cat lady. Someone with forty cats and a fat bank account. Maybe you know someone?"

Syrup sighed.

"You don't, huh?" She picked up her flashlight. "Let's look at those eyes."

For some reason, the flashlight made Syrup lose his shit, and he squirmed away from her hands and bolted underneath the desk, yelping.

Rhea was about to go after him when the clinic's phone rang. She picked it up. "Happy Paws Clinic, how can I help you?"

"This is Dr. Brooks. Is Rhea Deleon there?"

"Hi, that's me." She could already feel the stab of fear. What was it with her and doctors?

"I have your blood test results." Dr. Brooks sounded stern and displeased. "You have serious iron deficiency anemia."

"Oh. Okay." That wasn't so bad.

"I want you to come over as soon as possible, and we'll discuss treatment. Should we make an appointment now?"

"Now isn't a good time . . . can I call you back?" She already knew she wouldn't. She'd take some iron supplements and hope the problem would go away.

The doctor stressed that this problem couldn't be ignored, as if she could read Rhea's mind through the phone. Then they ended the call.

Rhea got a dog snack and lured Syrup from under the desk. As he munched on the snack happily, she yawned again and scratched his back.

"I'd settle for two cat ladies, with twenty cats each," she told the pug. "Get the word out."

CHAPTER 41

As time went by, the task force's status room underwent changes Tatum had seen happen in similar situations. The whiteboards filled up and then were erased and redrawn to accommodate new information, leaving leftovers of previous notes in the corners. The long table filled up with crumpled pieces of paper, empty cups, the occasional sandwich wrapper. The smell of the room changed as well, becoming a mixture of body odor, coffee, and the scent of whiteboard markers.

"What's your poison?" Sykes asked Tatum. "Chinese or pizza?"

Tatum raised his eyes from his laptop screen, the question making no sense whatsoever. "What?"

"Food," Sykes clarified. "I'm ordering us some food. What do you prefer?"

"Uh, Chinese, I guess."

"Noodles? Rice? Vegetarian? Are you allergic to peanuts?"

"Sykes, just order whatever you feel like. I don't care," Tatum said impatiently, then turned to Zoe, who was writing furiously in her notebook. "Zoe, Valentine just sent us the DNA report."

She glanced at him. "And?"

"There's a match between the DNA found underneath Fishburne's fingernails and Glover's DNA." They had Glover's DNA for comparison from his attack the previous month on Andrea, but Tatum didn't point that out.

Zoe exhaled slowly. "So that's it. Direct evidence."

"Yup."

"What about the sample from the bite?"

"No match to anything in the database, but it matches the DNA sample taken from Catherine's body."

"Zoe, do you want Chinese or pizza?" Sykes asked.

Zoe didn't miss a beat. "I want spring rolls, if they have any with meat, and chop suey, but I want that fried with noodles, not rice, and tell them to go easy on the coriander—that's important."

Sykes gave Tatum a look and ambled away.

"Does anyone have Valentine's personal phone?" O'Donnell called from the other side of the room. "I can't reach him on the office."

Tatum found the number and handed her his phone. On his way back, he noticed Koch was sifting between multiple images of pentagrams.

"What are you looking at there?" Tatum asked Koch.

"Well . . . I'm trying to figure out the reason for the pentagram. Originally we thought it might be a satanic ritual, right?" He shifted a few images and picked one up. It was an illustration of a man in some sort of clerical garb standing over a naked woman. The man was holding a carving knife. "This is an illustration from, uh . . . *Le Satanisme et la magie*. It's the Black Mass."

"No pentagram there," Tatum pointed out.

"No, but the pentagram crops up in different references. But there's another explanation." Koch spread some of the images on the table. They were photos of graffiti depicting various symbols. Each had a pentagram. "Those are gang tags. The five-pointed star is used by the People Nation alliance and particularly by the Latin Kings."

"So . . . you're thinking the murders are gang related?" Tatum asked, his voice strained.

"Not directly, but one of the killers could be a gang member, right?"

241

"Glover isn't in any gangs, and the unsub's DNA doesn't have any matches, meaning he wasn't incarcerated."

Koch shrugged. "It's worth checking."

Tatum nodded and walked over to Zoe. "How's it going?"

"I'm working on the initial profile of the unsub. I think I can give them something to work with."

Tatum sat down and leaned backward. "How do you figure it all happened?"

"What happened?"

"Glover and the unsub? How did they start working together?"

"Well . . . I assume the unsub was in the Riverside Baptist Church, like Glover was. Then, when Glover gave them his speech about wanting to help people with a violent life, the unsub approached him."

"Yeah, that's what I figured. This guy has some violent thoughts about blood drinking—"

"We don't know that was the nature of his delusion back then."

"But we can guess." Tatum waggled his eyebrows and grinned when Zoe gave him a frustrated look. Zoe hated the word *guess*.

"Glover can read people well," Zoe said. "He saw a man on the verge of violence, easily manipulated. And his fantasies aligned with Glover's. I doubt Glover thought about him as a partner back then. But he must have figured that he might be able to use this at some point."

"So Glover befriends him. Makes him trust him more." In the background, Tatum heard O'Donnell telling Sykes that she wanted no pineapple on the pizza.

"Maybe he even tried to push the unsub into action back then, see if he could make him act out his violence," Zoe suggested. "Testing the guy's boundaries."

"That sounds plausible. He can't get him to act, but Glover knows that the guy is medicated. And it might occur to him that he'd be easier to manipulate when off his meds." He enjoyed the discussion, feeling for once that he was keeping up with Zoe, that they were on the same wavelength.

"Then, last summer, Glover disappears for a while," Zoe said. "He goes to Dale City and, during that time, gets the prognosis that he's dying of cancer. He also gets shot."

"Courtesy of Marvin," Tatum said.

"He flees back to Chicago. He's hurt, low on funds, and he knows his time is short. He needs help."

"So he reaches out to someone he can trust, his weird psycho friend. Do you think Glover already figured they could become a serial killer duo?"

She bit her lip, thinking about it.

"Last chance to change your mind," Sykes said loudly. "I'm ordering the takeout now."

"He could have," Zoe finally answered. "I think that at first, Glover was just desperate for help. But when he got better, he began to plan his final months. And for whatever reason, he felt he needed an accomplice."

"He might be suffering symptoms. His tumor might be screwing him up. Blackouts, confusion, problems with his motor skills." Tatum shrugged.

"That makes sense. That's when Glover figured he should get his friend on board, and that meant getting him off his meds. He suggested blood could replace them. Pure blood." She frowned. "He already decided their first target would be Catherine Lamb at that point. Why?"

Tatum considered it. It could be the result of a sexual fantasy that Glover had concocted, but it seemed like a too-easy explanation. They took a big risk, attacking Catherine in her own home. There must have been a very good reason for it.

"She must have known something," Tatum suggested, just as Zoe said, "She knew something."

Tatum smiled. "Catherine saw them together, or maybe our unsub asked her if she knew good ole Daniel Moore was back in town."

"It could be something more serious," Zoe pointed out. "Her father had said that something had been bothering her. Maybe the unsub was actually asking for her opinion about blood drinking."

"Whatever the reason, Glover probably figured that once they began killing, Catherine would be a problem," Tatum said. "So they started with her. Glover told his friend they had to start with Catherine because only *her* blood would be good enough to replace the meds completely."

"They kill Catherine . . . ," Zoe said. "And then Henrietta Fishburne followed very fast afterward."

Tatum nodded. This was where their story faded. There were too many questions. Why so soon? What was the purpose of the pentagram and the knife? Why did Glover call the police?

"We need to figure out Glover's agenda," Tatum said.

"No arguments here. But first, let's give them what we have about the unsub." Zoe stood up and walked over to one of the whiteboards. She rapped on it loudly. Eyes turned to face her around the room.

Only Sykes kept talking on the phone. "That's right. Go easy on the coriander. And a large bottle of Coke."

Zoe shot him a withering look. He quickly left the room, still whispering into the phone.

"We have a general outline for our unsub," she said.

"Let's hear it," Bright said.

"Since we know Glover had chosen him as an accomplice, we can infer some of his characteristics. Glover is obsessed with control, and he would look for someone he could boss around. He would definitely avoid dominant people, and in all probability the unsub would be someone who's used to taking instructions from others. Glover would also choose someone who was useful. That means the unsub has a job, or some other source of income, probably an apartment and a car."

Tatum watched her, enjoying the way she dominated the room. Everyone's attention was focused on her, people hardly breathing as she talked. Zoe had a way of handling herself, her body language making it clear that everything she said was crucial. She was the same when she told Sykes to go easy on the coriander, or when she explained to Tatum why Taylor Swift was a genius, or when she profiled a killer with a handful of evidence. Sure, she was brusque, often even rude. But she left no possibility of disregarding her.

"According to the witness statement acquired by O'Donnell and Ellis, the unsub had said about Fishburne, 'It's no good; she's too dark.' This makes it likely that he has a racial preference. He's interested in white victims. There's also an indication of ritualistic behavior in the crime scene. The unsub keeps walking in circles around the victims, which indicates a possible obsessive-compulsive personality."

She locked glances with Tatum and continued. "This morning we might have located someone who chatted with our unsub online." She proceeded to outline their conversation with Peter, the fang designer.

"Then you think the murderer is . . . what exactly?" Koch asked.

"According to his own questions, he was on antipsychotics. We now know that his desire for blood is caused by delusions. He might have a bipolar disorder, or he might be suffering from schizophrenia."

Zoe continued. "Usually, a delusional murderer would be disorganized, go on a chaotic, unpredictable killing spree. And the age would be somewhere in the early twenties, since the onset of these conditions is around the age of twenty. But this case is different because he was medicated, which means he was already under treatment, so we can't assume his age. Also, since he is probably manipulated by Glover, his killings are more organized. They are, in fact, organized by someone else."

This, Tatum knew, was both good news and bad news for the task force. Disorganized killers were unpredictable and could potentially go on a killing spree. But they were also usually caught quite fast because they were careless and behaved bizarrely in public.

"We can also make some assumptions because we know Glover wouldn't have chosen a partner that would attract attention," she continued. "So our guy probably has a lot of control over his own behavior or at least can fake it really well. He won't necessarily be easy to spot in a short interview. But he'd crack during a long interview. The pressure would mount, and eventually he'd lash out or behave erratically. Especially if he's in an unfamiliar, hostile environment like a police interrogation room."

"So Rod Glover is effectively unleashing the unsub as some sort of trained beast?" Bright asked.

"That was the dynamic, but as time goes on, he'll lose his grip on him. The unsub's delusions will grow stronger, and he'll spiral out of control. We will . . ." She frowned. "Uh . . . we will . . ." She stopped.

"What is it?" Bright asked her.

"Nothing," she said after a moment. "This is what we have so far." She sat down and picked up her phone.

"What is it?" Tatum asked her in a low voice.

"It's something Harry told me. It's probably nothing . . . but I should check. Hang on." She put her phone to her ear. After a moment she said, "Harry."

Tatum noticed, bemused, how her expression became instantly annoyed, her tone brusque and hostile.

"That article you wrote about the police in McKinley Park," Zoe said. "A woman reported someone tried to snatch her baby? Do you have a name?"

She waited on the line for a minute and then said, "No last name? Just Joanne? Yes, I know, but I thought you *might* have actually done some investigative work and talked to her. Fine, did she call the cops? But we've checked the recent case files in the area, and there's no case file about . . . yes. Okay, thanks." She hung up.

"What was that about?" Tatum asked.

Zoe raised her eyes from the phone. "A woman named Joanne from McKinley Park called the police yesterday and said a man chased her while she was walking with her baby in the street. She thought he wanted to snatch the baby away. And he stalked around her house for ten minutes afterward. She said he seemed unhinged."

"That might be our guy."

"Could be," Zoe said. "It's the same neighborhood as Catherine Lamb's and likely close to where he lives. Harry said Joanne got the sense that the police didn't take her complaint seriously. No one came to interview her. They sent a squad car to drive around, but that was it."

"The call would be in the dispatch logs," Tatum said. "Let's check them out."

CHAPTER 42

Tatum sighed and rubbed his eyes. His head throbbed.

They'd found the relevant dispatch log easily enough. O'Donnell had called the woman to get additional information. She wasn't able to give a useful description about the person who had chased her, aside from the fact that he was Caucasian. It could be their guy, or not.

And then O'Donnell pointed out that if there was one incident, there might be more. They got the dispatch logs of the past week. They filtered out anything that wasn't in the vicinity of McKinley Park. Then they read the logs, searching for anything that might be relevant to their case.

"I have an interesting call here," Tatum said. "From a man who saw a strange object in the sky. The dispatcher asked if it might be an airplane, and he said, 'Oh yeah, that's probably it.'"

Zoe raised her eyes from her monitor. "That's irrelevant."

"You think?"

She turned back to her monitor. "I think I found something. There's an entry on the sixteenth. That's . . . Sunday. A drugstore owner called at ten fifty-one p.m. to say two girls ran into his store because someone chased them. He saw no one, but the girls wouldn't leave until their parents picked them up. It could be the unsub."

They kept going through the logs, finding two more instances of people reporting a man walking around the neighborhood, talking to himself, sometimes following passersby.

"You think this is all our guy?" Tatum asked Zoe.

"It's possible. He's probably spiraling out of control, and those could be moments when he snapped. All four instances are late in the evening. In each case it was a white male. Three out of four say he was talking to himself."

"Sounds like the same person was reported," O'Donnell said. "It's anyone's guess if this is the unsub or not."

"We should get those people to talk to a sketch artist, see if we can get a common description," Koch said.

"I'll increase patrol presence in the area," Bright said. "I'll brief dispatch to relay any weird calls they get from the area of McKinley Park to the task force." He got up and left the room.

"Hey, check this out," O'Donnell said, sounding excited. "This is an actual case file. Vandalism. A shop's window had been broken on Sunday night, not far from the location of that drugstore."

Tatum didn't see the connection. "It could be anything."

"Originally, this was reported as vandalism because nothing was stolen. Except when the uniformed cops talked to the shop owner, he told them he thought maybe he had a cage missing. He wasn't sure, because he said they might have been sold, and his assistant just forgot to list them—"

"Who's they?" Zoe asked.

"Hamsters. A cage of hamsters."

Tatum stared at her. "You think he might have stolen some hamsters?"

"I mean . . . he's obsessed with blood, right? And if he couldn't get human blood that night—"

"That works," Zoe said. O'Donnell grinned. "Do they have security cameras there?"

"Unfortunately not," O'Donnell said. "But we'll send some crime technicians over tomorrow. They might still get some fingerprints from the area of the windowsill."

"If we line up the reports of the sightings and this burglary, maybe we can get an idea of his route," Zoe said. "If they're all connected and it's really the unsub, we can use geographic profiling to get a better idea of where he lives."

"And we'll do that, first thing tomorrow," Tatum said.

"We have a breakthrough here," Zoe said.

"I've heard. You have a lead. It sounds like a good lead, but it can wait until tomorrow. It's already ten."

Zoe frowned at him. "This could potentially—"

"Zoe." He raised his eyebrows, hoping she'd get the message.

"Fine." She groaned. "We'll head back to the motel."

"It's late, and my kid's already asleep," O'Donnell said. "Do you want to grab a drink before heading back?"

Tatum frowned. "It's late. We should probably—"

"Yes," Zoe said to Tatum's astonishment. "I'd love a drink."

CHAPTER 43

Bernice's Tavern was just what Zoe needed. As if to contrast the dark moments from the night before, it was a cheerfully lit room, with tiny Christmas lights twinkling on the walls. Old-school bar paraphernalia covered every wall—beer posters, framed pictures of bands and celebrity bar patrons, a street sign. None of it was tacky or forced; it didn't feel like stuff that had been bought at a hipstery garage sale. The clutter was a tapestry of the place's history.

Zoe ordered her usual Guinness, Tatum ordered Honker's Ale, and O'Donnell had a beer named Daisy Cutter, which Zoe wasn't familiar with. There was an actual jukebox in the bar, and Zoe considered walking over and choosing a few songs. She hadn't done that in years.

"So is this a typical case for you?" O'Donnell asked, taking a long swig of her beer.

"No case is really typical," Zoe said. "Each one has unique characteristics."

"Serial killers are like snowflakes, huh?"

Zoe frowned. "I can't really see the comparison."

"No two are alike."

"Well, serial killers do have some common traits," Tatum said. "That's why we can do what we do. We don't just make up a profile. We base it on comparison to similar individuals."

"For example, the blood drinking isn't unique at all," Zoe said. "There were several well-known cases, even just in the United States. John Crutchley was one. And the Vampire of Sacramento, of course. And—"

"Okay!" O'Donnell raised her hand to stop her. "So you look at the common traits and derive the killer's psyche from that?"

"That's part of it," Tatum said. "But it's not just about creating a profile. We try and come up with a strategy to catch the killer, using methods that have been successful before."

"And how long have you been doing it?"

"Well . . . what year is it?" Tatum made a show of glancing at a calendar hanging on the wall. "It's 2016, huh? Then I've been doing it for about . . . three months now."

"Seriously? Three months?" O'Donnell sounded miffed. "I thought you two were serious hotshots, not the FBI's newbies."

Tatum grinned. "Oh, Zoe's the real thing. She's been doing it for a while now. I'm here mostly for my good looks and razor-sharp wit." His phone rang, and he took it out. "Hello? Yeah, Marvin, I . . . it's music. Yes, I know you know what music is . . . I'm in a bar. Yes, killers are still prowling the streets of Chicago. What? What do you mean the cat broke it? How did he get the remote? Hang on—I can hardly hear you." Tatum gave Zoe an apologetic look and stepped out of the bar.

"Who's Marvin?" O'Donnell asked Zoe.

Zoe ran her finger along her mug's rim. "He's Tatum's grandfather. They live together."

"Oh. Is Tatum taking care of him?"

"I'm not entirely sure." Zoe frowned. "His grandfather is quite capable. And from what I can tell, they mostly just argue. But I think Tatum is Marvin's only family, so they stick together."

"Hang on . . . Marvin is Marvin Gray?"

"You've heard of him?" Zoe asked in surprise.

"He appears in the case file of Glover's assault of your sister. He *shot* Glover."

"That's him. Like I said, he's very capable." Zoe felt weird about O'Donnell reading about Andrea's assault. It was relevant to the current investigation, and professionally she *should* be aware of Glover's past. But it somehow felt personal. As if O'Donnell had found out about a family secret.

"So it's just Tatum and his grandfather?"

"And a cat. And also a fish, I think."

"No girlfriend?"

For a confused second, Zoe thought she was referring to Marvin's girlfriend. Then she got it. "No. Uh . . . I don't think so. Tatum doesn't have a girlfriend." She took a sip from her beer, wishing Tatum would come back.

"And what about you? Do you have a husband? Or boyfriend?"

"No."

"Uh-huh." O'Donnell tilted her head.

"What?" Zoe asked, feeling annoyed.

"Nothing. Well . . . the way Tatum looks at you and talks about you. I just wondered."

"Wondered about what?"

"If you two ever hooked up."

"Of course not." Blood rushed to Zoe's face. Flustered, she turned away, gulping some beer.

"Why not?"

"We're working together. We're practically partners."

"So . . . what, you didn't hook up because it's against the bureau's regulations?"

"Yes. No! We didn't hook up because we're not interested in each other like that."

"Okay."

"You're doing that thing with your head again."

"What thing?" O'Donnell blinked innocently.

"This . . . thing." Zoe tilted her own head to demonstrate.

"I don't do that."

"You do that all the time."

"Look, I'm just saying: Tatum practically worships you. I think that's an attractive quality in a man. Plus, you know, he's actually attractive. Don't tell me you haven't thought about it."

Zoe thought about that morning. Waking up to see Tatum there. The feeling of being held in his arms. She shook her head violently. "That would be a terrible idea even if either of us were interested."

"No argument there. I'm just messing with you." O'Donnell winked at her and finished her mug. She motioned to the bartender and asked for another.

Zoe still felt unsettled by the entire idea. "No guy is worth throwing away your professional life for."

"Maybe that's true about *your* professional life. My job ain't that precious these days. Of course I'm already happily married." She waggled her fingers, showing her ring. But something dampened her smile. She seemed suddenly broody.

Zoe finished her own beer and decided to order another one as well. After doing so, she asked, "You aren't happy with your job?"

O'Donnell snorted. "I don't know if you've noticed, but I'm not everyone's favorite person in the department."

"I haven't noticed."

O'Donnell rolled her eyes. "Aren't you supposed to be more perceptive?"

"Why do you think people don't like you?"

"I'm on the division's shit list," O'Donnell said, her tone brimming with sharp edges. "O'Donnell the pariah."

"Why?"

"My last partner was dirty. He's under investigation by IA. Suspended." She pursed her lips, glanced at Zoe, narrowing her eyes. "I'm not dirty, in case you were wondering."

"Okay. Then what? People think you are?"

O'Donnell shook her head. "They think I ratted him out."

"Ah." It was a universal, ancient rule. One of the first things you learned as a kid. Snitches get stitches. People could forgive a lot, but it was hard to forgive a snitch because you never knew when he'd turn on *you*. Life was full of moments when you needed someone to turn a blind eye, instances when the rules clashed with reality, and nothing was black and white. And the last thing you wanted in a moment like that was to wonder if the person who had your back might stick a knife in it instead.

"They don't even care what he did," O'Donnell said vehemently. "It's all about what they imagine *I* did. The deals I made with Internal Affairs. How I sold him out. I'm paying for Manny's mess."

Zoe nodded. She wanted to say she was sorry but felt that if she did, O'Donnell would bite her head off. "It'll blow over," she finally suggested.

"Maybe. If I was a man, it definitely would have. But if a woman's a snitch, everyone thinks, *She's screwing the guy from Internal Affairs.* Or *She was screwing Manny, but he dumped her.* Or *She* was *screwing Manny and dumped him for the guy from Internal Affairs.*"

"You don't know that's what they think—"

O'Donnell whipped her head, grimacing, nostrils flaring. "Don't I? You think people here are subtle? Want to see the note someone left on my desk? Or one of the emails I got?"

Zoe bit her lip, saying nothing.

O'Donnell sighed. "Never mind. You couldn't possibly know."

Zoe chose her words carefully. "I know what it's like to be resented."

"Well, yeah, maybe, but I really tried, you know? I wanted to be liked." O'Donnell sipped from her mug and then, realizing what she'd said, hurriedly added, "Not that you didn't. I mean . . . ugh. I'm sorry—I shouldn't have said that."

Zoe raised an eyebrow. "It's fine." She emptied half of her glass.

"I sometimes feel sorry for myself," O'Donnell said. "It's not a fetching quality."

"I never really tried," Zoe admitted. "I wanted people to like and respect me for who I am. But I can be blunt and insensitive. And it pushes people away. Even people who are close to me."

O'Donnell fiddled with a beer coaster, slowly peeling it apart. "Tatum seems to get you."

"For now. But one day I'll say the wrong thing . . . or maybe it won't be one thing. Maybe I'll just erode him." She was surprised to feel the tremor in her voice. "Just one blunt comment after the other. I'll exhaust him."

O'Donnell leaned closer. "Zoe, seriously, the way he looks at you, there's no way—"

Zoe shook her head. "Forget it. I'm just being stupid." But she wasn't; she knew that. It had happened before, with other friends. Now with Andrea, who could hardly talk to her. She felt like she couldn't explain that feeling to anyone. Except O'Donnell kept looking at her, a tiny reassuring smile on her lips, and maybe she really could understand. Zoe took a long breath. "It's just that—"

"Speak of the devil," O'Donnell said, glancing over Zoe's shoulder.

Tatum walked over to them and plopped himself on the stool, looking very annoyed.

"Everything okay?"

"I probably need to fix the TV," Tatum said. "Someone broke it. Apparently the remote control ended up in the fish's bowl. Marvin claims it's part of a mind game between the cat and the fish. Aren't cats and fish known as self-sufficient animals?"

Zoe cleared her throat, getting her bearings. "Maybe they are, but grandfathers aren't."

"True. So what were we talking about?"

"Who even remembers?" O'Donnell said. "We got a second round."

Tatum emptied his mug in one long gulp. He put it on the bar and motioned to get the bartender's attention. "Then I need to catch up."

CHAPTER 44

This time, their vehicle didn't stink. He'd insisted on it. Daniel had complained that it ended up costing them double, but the man in control didn't care. They could afford it.

It was a different parking lot than last time, but after a while, sitting there, he couldn't even be sure of that anymore. It was more of the same—rows of cars, trains rattling, brakes screeching, passengers going back and forth.

And waiting. Endless waiting. He repeatedly shifted in his seat, opened and closed his window, tapped the steering wheel, one leg constantly jumping as if it had a mind of its own.

"What's the matter with you?" Daniel barked at him finally. "Can't you sit still?"

He couldn't—that was the thing. He nearly whimpered at the itch under his skin, at the tension in his gut. He needed this, needed it to be over.

The one o'clock train had already gone by, with five passengers, all men, walking past them. There was one more train. Daniel had said that if that train was a bust, they'd go home, try again the next night. But he couldn't. He *needed* the hunt, the prey, the blood.

And then the train stopped. The first passenger, walking in the shadows, was a man.

Then, the thin form of a woman.

"There we go," Daniel growled. "Are you ready?"

Was he ready? He was born for this. He was already poised to move, to stalk her, to pounce, to feed. His mouth salivated as he imagined the iron taste of blood . . .

"Ah, shit," Daniel said.

A man joined her side. They were a couple. But the man was small. They could easily take him out. He would tear the man's throat with his teeth, leave him to bleed to death. He opened his door, put one foot on the pavement.

Daniel caught his wrist. "What the hell are you doing?"

"I'll handle him," he hissed at Daniel. They had no time. The couple was getting away. He needed this!

"No!" Daniel pulled him. "Close the damn door."

For a moment he nearly punched Daniel's face. His fingers tightened into a fist as he clenched his teeth . . .

He didn't. He was in control. He relaxed.

"Tomorrow," Daniel said. "We'll find one tomorrow."

"Yeah." He shut the door and started the car, still vibrating with tension. "Tomorrow."

Rhea woke up with a start and looked around her, confused. She had fallen asleep in her clinic, by her desk. That was a new low, even for her. She remembered doing some paperwork, then thinking she'd just lean back in the chair for a minute, give her eyes a rest. Ugh, it was already dark outside; she must have slept for over an hour.

She got up and shut all the windows in the clinic, then went over to the alarm panel and switched on the alarm. The thing emitted its shrill beeping, and the display counted down from twenty. She grabbed her bag, shoved her phone inside, and blearily shuffled to the door. She slid outside, shut it, then locked it. Inside, she heard the alarm panel giving its final beep as it turned on.

She turned around, took a few steps down the street, then frowned.

It was way too quiet. The road was empty of traffic, and there was no one around. Sure, her clinic wasn't exactly in the busiest part of the city, but still. What time was it, anyway?

She checked her phone, blinking in shock.

Half past two in the morning?

She'd slept over six hours in her chair. No wonder her body felt so stiff, her neck like a rusty hinge.

Her house was only fifteen minutes away on foot. She walked to her clinic and back home every day. But she'd never done it so late at night.

For a second she considered going back inside, calling an Uber. But she'd already locked the clinic and turned on the alarm, and besides, taking an Uber for less than a mile drive?

This was one of the safer neighborhoods of Chicago. Didn't she always tell her parents that when they fretted? Her dad practically thought she lived in a war zone. But in all her years in Chicago, she'd never been a victim of a crime, unless she counted spam mail.

She began walking home.

There was something creepy in striding down the empty dark street. And it was so freaking cold. She shivered, told herself it was because she was freezing, not because she was afraid. She would get home, take a nice long hot shower, and sleep in her bed, like people actually did. And in the morning she'd definitely book an appointment with Dr. Brooks, because falling asleep for six hours in her clinic wasn't normal. It wasn't a problem that would go away by itself.

But first she'd go home and get some sleep.

"Don't be disappointed," Daniel told him, his voice loud over the engine. "We'll go again tomorrow."

"I'm not disappointed," he answered, fists clenching on the steering wheel. He wanted to explain to Daniel that you couldn't be *disappointed* by the complete lack of air. You couldn't be *disappointed* when your throat was parched and the oasis you thought you'd spotted in the distance was nothing but dry sand. *Disappointed* didn't even begin to describe it.

But he didn't say anything. It dawned on him that even Daniel didn't really understand him.

They were waiting at a red light when he spotted the movement. A thin silhouette walking in the shadows. A woman.

"Light's green," Daniel said.

She was walking alone. The street was empty, not another car in sight. He couldn't believe it.

"Hey, are you paying attention? The damn light is green. Drive!"

He drove. Swerved to the left, van screeching. His foot flooring the gas pedal.

"Where the hell are you going?" Daniel shouted.

The woman looked back, alarmed. The van's lights shone on her face. She was beautiful.

Daniel was still shouting. "What the . . . no. No!"

Yes.

The driver was clearly drunk. Rhea moved farther from the road, waiting for him to drive past. But he didn't.

Instead, the van swerved toward the sidewalk, its brakes squealing as it hit the curb with a bump, just a few feet away from her. She froze in shock, staring incredulously at the bright lights. The asshole could have run her over!

The driver's door opened, and she was about to shout at him, when she caught a glimpse of his face.

She'd seen that expression before, when she'd had to put down a dog with rabies. The snarl, the glistening eyes, the drool.

Reflexes kicked in. She turned and ran. Heard a growl behind her. She ran faster, giving it all she had, fumbling in her purse for her keys. She could key his eyes.

"Help!" she screamed. "Someone help me!"

A sudden burst of pain flared through her scalp. He'd grabbed her hair, pulled her back. She let out another scream. He clamped his fingers on her mouth, her nose. She couldn't breathe.

Something metal in her fingers. Her keys! She thrust the keys in the direction of his face, felt the scrape as she hit something, then an angry grunt. She bit hard on his fingers, tasting sweat and blood, but she kept biting, shaking her head, gnawing at it.

He shoved her, and her body exploded in shock and pain as it hit something metal. A lamppost. Her vision blurred, and now there were two figures, not just one, and they were dragging her, and she lost her keys and couldn't scream, or talk, or even move. The lips of one of them brushed her cheek, wet and slimy. The street dimmed, her thoughts fogging.

Then her vision focused, and she saw they were manhandling her toward a black maw, and she knew if she let them drag her there, it was all over. She struggled again, and one of them cuffed her across the face.

"Stop that, bitch," he snarled.

And then they tossed her into the blackness—the back of a van. She was about to scream again when they crammed something into her mouth. With blood running from her nose and the rag in her mouth, she could hardly breathe. One of them rolled her onto her stomach, pulled her arms back, a sudden pinch on her wrists as he somehow tied them together. She whimpered into her rag, tried to kick him, but it was feeble and useless.

"Get behind the wheel—let's get out of here!" one of them said to the other.

She was pushed onto her back, saw their vague shadows.

"Let's go! Someone probably already called the cops."

Please. Let the cops come. Please.

And then the second man bent down and, to her disgust and horror, licked her face.

"Damn it!"

Daniel wrenched him back, and for a moment he fought to get to her face, to taste her *again*.

Daniel shook him. "Get a grip!" he roared at him. "We need to go!"

He nodded, scrambled to the driver's seat, with Daniel still in the back with her. He turned the wheel, maneuvered them back to the road, floored it, the engine screaming, getting them away.

"You asshole, what did you do?" Daniel screamed at him. "Do you want to get us both arrested?"

He heard the words but didn't care. Her taste still lingered on his lips. It was sublime.

Now he knew that all the rest of his victims had been contaminated, even Catherine. He'd *known* Catherine wasn't pure, had known it for some time. He had actually told Daniel about it.

And it turned out he was right.

This woman, she was the real thing. Completely pure, her blood touched by the divine. A mere taste of it could perform miracles. Not just for him. He wasn't the only one who needed help, after all.

"Drive east, to the lake," Daniel said. "We'll find an abandoned beach, handle her there."

"No," he said, his voice thick with certainty. "We're taking her home."

CHAPTER 45

Friday, October 21, 2016

Logan Square's streets were dark and silent, sunrise still a few hours away, the residents enviably asleep. But as O'Donnell turned onto North Spaulding Avenue, the atmosphere changed. Flickering red and blue patrol car lights, multiple silhouettes of cops moving briskly throughout the street. Many houses had their lights on, figures standing behind windows, watching a true crime show that none of them had asked for.

O'Donnell parked her car and stepped out, hunching her shoulders against the night's chill, her breath expelling a cloud of mist. She flipped her badge at a cop who approached her and brushed past him. She'd already spotted Lieutenant Samuel Martinez.

He talked on the radio, looking sharply around him. He saw her and motioned her over, still talking on the radio.

"The tech crew is still not here," he was saying.

The radio crackled. "Bravo twelve, this is dispatch. They're on their way. They'll be there in ten minutes."

"Copy. Get them on the phone, and tell them to turn on their damn radio."

"Bravo twelve, copy."

Martinez glanced at O'Donnell, the squad car lights reflecting on his spectacles. "O'Donnell, thanks for coming."

"What's going on?"

"It's an abduction case," he said. "Twenty-nine-year-old Rhea Deleon was snatched from the street. Several witnesses said she was dragged into a black van by two men wearing hoodies at a quarter to three."

O'Donnell glanced at the time. Ten past four. "Any descriptions?"

"Well, like I said, they wore hoodies, one black, one gray. People only got glimpses through their shades, so most of them didn't give us a lot more than that. Caucasian, average height. But we have one witness whose house is right across from where they grabbed her. She got a good look at one of them. That's why I called you."

O'Donnell tensed. She already knew what was coming. "What did she say?"

"She said he was very thin, and pale, and that he seemed a bit familiar. When I pressed her for details it came back to her. She said he was the guy she saw in the newspaper."

"Rod Glover."

"Listen, I don't know if it's him. At first she said she wasn't sure, he looked kinda different; then she said he had the same look in his eyes, which sounds like bullshit to me. But I thought you should have a word with her."

Both of them stopped talking as a uniformed cop strode over to them with an evidence bag in his hand. "Found this under one of the parked cars," he said.

Martinez took the bag from him and peered through the translucent plastic. He then showed it to O'Donnell. The bag contained a key chain with several keys.

"Maybe belonged to the victim," Martinez said. "We found her handbag; that's how we have a possible ID. But it had no keys in it."

O'Donnell studied the keys closely. One of the keys seemed speckled with reddish-brown dots. "Lieutenant, I think there's blood on one of the keys."

"You're right." Martinez turned to the cop. "Put those keys in a *paper* bag, or it might damage the DNA sample."

Another vehicle showed up, the headlights momentarily blinding O'Donnell.

"Finally," Martinez said, turning toward the van, which parked on the sidewalk. Crime scene technicians.

He was about to walk away, and O'Donnell quickly grabbed his arm. "Where's the witness?"

She was a middle-aged woman in a turquoise robe, her blonde hair tangled, eyes puffy and red. A white cat sat on her lap, its tail swishing, eyes narrow in pure feline rage. She was petting it distractedly as she talked to O'Donnell, words pouring in a torrent that only stopped for the occasional sob.

"Maybe I should have shouted at them to stop, but I was afraid. That poor woman—she's the local vet, you know? She does Dana's vaccines."

"Mrs. Weaver," O'Donnell said. "You said you saw one of the men."

"It was that man from the paper—I'm sure of it. They were so violent! Slamming her head like that, I thought they'd killed her. But they didn't; she was still struggling when they dragged her off."

"You weren't so sure it was the man from the paper before."

"But I'm sure now. I was just confused, you know? He was just a bit thinner and paler. But he had the same eyes. Cold and angry, like a killer's."

O'Donnell had to agree with Martinez. It didn't sound promising. "Did you get a glimpse of the vehicle? A license plate?"

"They took her to a black van. I ran for my phone to take a picture. I wish I would have thought of it faster. They took off by the time I got back."

"What about the other man? Did you see him?"

"He had his back to me, and he wore a hoodie, so I couldn't really see his face. But at one point, he . . . he forced himself on the poor woman, and I could see his cheek and his ear."

"What do you mean, he forced himself?"

Mrs. Weaver shifted uncomfortably, and her cat's eyes got even angrier. "He . . . I think he kissed her. It was so violent . . . it didn't even look like kissing. But I was confused, and it was so fast and violent; he was probably just kissing her."

There was something there. "What do you mean, it didn't look like kissing?"

"He forced himself on her. She was struggling."

"But you said it didn't look like kissing. What *did* it look like?"

The woman hesitated. "It looked like he was licking her."

O'Donnell leaned forward. "Was she bleeding when he licked her?"

A small pause. "Yes. She was. Blood ran down her face."

"Do you think he may have been licking her blood?"

Mrs. Weaver's eyes widened. "Yes," she whispered. "That's what I thought at first. But that can't be right. Why would he do that?"

O'Donnell didn't answer, feeling sick. If Glover and his partner really abducted Rhea Deleon, the chances that she was still alive were very slim.

CHAPTER 46

Everything hurt. Her ribs and legs were bruised after one of the men had kicked and punched her several times. Her throat was raw from screaming into the rag they'd crammed in her mouth. Plastic zip ties bit into her skin, scraping her wrists raw. Worst was her head, which felt as if someone were tightening it in a vise.

Sounds were warbled, accompanied by constant ringing, and spots danced in front of her eyes. A concussion, no doubt about it.

Breathing was a problem too. She couldn't use her mouth, and her right nostril was caked with blood. She breathed through the left nostril, inhaling softly. When she panicked and drew the air in fast, it sent a sharp stab of agony through her skull.

Everything was hazy; she had trouble recalling what had happened. They'd driven for a while, one of them shouting at the other, a barrage of ignored instructions. At one point, the man had grabbed her around the throat and started squeezing, and after a few seconds of pure terror, she'd drifted away. She could vaguely hear both men arguing through the haze.

She'd woken up as they'd dragged her out of the back into a dark garage. She'd tried to struggle, and that was when one of them had kicked her several times until she'd curled in a fetal position on the floor. Then they'd lifted her again. Took her *here*. Tied her to the sink's drainage pipe.

She was in a bathroom that smelled vaguely of piss. The floor was spotted by droplets, several of which had soaked into her pants.

They were still arguing outside.

"That bitch will end up getting us arrested, you idiot! We need to get rid of her. It's not too late."

"No. She's the real thing, Daniel. She is! She'll make everything better. Didn't you say it yourself? We needed someone pure. *She's* pure."

"Then we'll empty her into a damn bucket, and you can have a taste whenever you like."

"It doesn't work when it's not fresh. You said it yourself."

"Don't tell me what . . . I know what I fucking said, it's not . . ." The voice rose, the man losing his cool. "We'll find another one, okay? But we gotta get rid of this one."

Rhea didn't doubt what *getting rid of* meant. She struggled against the pipe. Maybe she could break it apart. Grab part of it. Hit them when they came in. She had to try. The pipe clunked as she struggled. *Come on, you bastard, come on . . .*

The door opened, and one of them stepped in. It was the thin sickly one. His face twisted in fury, spittle at the corner of his mouth. He kicked her in her gut, and she groaned, her breath gone.

Then the other guy strode inside, pulled the sickly man back.

"You make any more noise, I'll kill you," the sickly man snarled at her.

"Daniel, don't. She won't make any more noise. You see? She's silent now." The other man glanced at her. "You'll be quiet while my friend and I talk, right?"

She nodded, still trying to catch her breath, doing her best not to throw up into her gag.

They left, shutting the door behind them. Their voices were low now, or maybe she faded away; she couldn't be sure. She inhaled the fetid air and sobbed.

After a while she calmed down. Began to think. That guy, the one named Daniel, he wanted her dead. He was the violent one. The dangerous one. A psycho, a monster.

But his friend was different. He needed her alive, maybe for ransom. Isn't that what he said? That she'd make everything better? He was probably talking about money. Maybe they thought her parents were rich. What would happen when they found out that they weren't?

But then they said other things. *Empty her into a bucket. It doesn't work when it's not fresh.* What could it all mean?

The door opened again. The other guy stood in the doorway. He beamed at her.

"Don't worry—we won't hurt you. We need you alive. I'll get you some food and drink later, okay?"

She nodded.

"But you need to stay quiet. If you make any noise, we won't be able to keep you here. And we'll have to kill you." His voice was casual, straightforward. A man stating an unarguable fact.

Two psychos. Two monsters.

She tried to talk into her rag, and he shook his head. "Later. We can talk later."

Then he crouched by her side and raised his hand. To her horror, she saw he held a small disposable scalpel. She let out a muffled scream, and he instantly put the scalpel against her throat.

"Remember," he whispered. "You promised to be quiet. You'll be quiet, right?"

She nodded, trembling.

He sliced the fabric of her right pant leg, exposing her thigh.

"This will hurt just a bit," he said. "No screaming."

The scalpel plunged through her skin. She tensed, her eyes widening, as the blood ran down her leg.

And the man put his lips to the cut and sucked.

CHAPTER 47

"Rhea's office is that way," Tatum said, looking down the street. He held the photos from the crime scene, matching the sunlit, peaceful surroundings with the dark, ominous images of blood, tire markings, scattered possessions. "She was walking home from work."

"We don't know that," Zoe said, crouching to look at the tire markings on the sidewalk. "She might have been returning from a night out. Two in the morning is an unusual hour to return from work."

"Her office has an alarm system, and they checked the logs. The alarm system was turned on at two twenty-nine. Martinez is there now to see if he can figure out why she left so late at night."

Zoe stood up. "Look at all those windows," she said. "Snatching a grown woman here, even in the middle of the night, is . . ."

"Insane?"

"Or very desperate."

Tatum looked at her worriedly. She had that distant look on her again. Was she storing the details in her mind to relive the event at night?

It was after two o'clock. They'd gotten the lab report an hour before—the DNA retrieved from the blood on the keys matched the DNA taken from the saliva in the previous murders. It belonged to the unsub. The Rhea Deleon kidnapping case was officially part of their joint investigation.

"The van came from the direction of her office as well," Tatum said. "Do you think they were following her?"

"Maybe," Zoe said. "But I doubt it. She would have noticed a van driving slowly behind her. No, I think they were on their way somewhere, saw her, and decided to grab her. The unsub was probably driving. I don't know if Glover realized it was about to happen."

"That matches our theory that Glover's cognitive functions are impaired and that he can't drive."

"It makes sense." Zoe nodded. "Letting his accomplice take the wheel is a significant yield of control. Not typical for Glover, unless he had no other option."

Tatum's phone rang. He checked the screen, frowned at the number on the display. Not a number he recognized. "Hello?"

"Agent Gray? Uh . . . this is Damien."

"Who?"

"Peter? From Night Fangs."

Oh yeah, the guy who sold fangs. "What is it?"

"It's probably nothing, but I was just contacted by that guy I told you about. Dracula2. He's asking me stuff."

"What kind of stuff?" Tatum tuned out the noise of traffic, his entire focus on the phone call.

"It's really normal stuff, for vampires. That's why I thought it was nothing. I mean, there's no creepy shit about pure blood, or nonconsensual biting, or anything like that. He just wanted to know how much blood he can take from a donor every day. So that's good, right? I guess he found a willing donor."

Jesus Christ. "Did you answer him?"

"Not yet. I called you first. But he's still online. And he's kind of impatient."

"Okay, listen, I need you to buy us some time. Ask for details, like how much his donor weighs, what's her height . . . ask if it's a woman. Tell him you need to check charts—"

"There are no charts, dude."

"I know that! I don't care. Just tell him you're consulting with an expert and that you'll have an answer in an hour." He glanced at his watch. It was two thirty. "No! Forty-five minutes."

"Uh, okay, but—"

"It's important that you talk to him casually." If this was the unsub, and Tatum was sure it was, he was probably extremely paranoid right now. "Like you always chat online, okay? Don't ask him for any specific detail—not his name, not who his donor is, nothing."

"But what do I tell him in forty-five minutes?" Peter's voice cracked, sounding panicky.

"You won't tell him anything. By that time, we'll be taking over."

CHAPTER 48

Tatum had a vague idea of what he needed. They would get one of the Chicago field office tech geeks in front of a computer. Then, they would wait for the unsub to log in, at which point the tech geek would start some sort of cyberattack, muttering sentences like, "I'm hacking into the mainframe . . . now," and "I'll just reroute the encryptions. He won't see it coming." Finally, the tech geek would whirl in his chair and give them an address.

"It's not that simple," the tech geek said.

The tech geek, whose name was Barb Collier, was a woman in her midtwenties who chewed gum. She occasionally made a small bubble gum balloon and popped it with her sharp fingernail. The chewing and balloon popping were distracting.

"Listen, Barb," Tatum said, checking the time for the tenth time. "We have fifteen minutes. A woman's life depends on it. We need you to trace him."

"I can't do that. No one can do that," she said. "He's using a Tor-based browser. The whole point of Tor is that it can't be traced."

"But we're the FBI," Tatum said. "We have back doors, right? For emergencies?"

"No."

"What *do* we have?"

"Can you get him to open a file?" She made a small balloon and looked at him expectantly.

Tatum considered it. "What sort of file?"

She popped the balloon with her fingernail. "Any executable. Any Microsoft Office file. Get him to run a JavaScript or Flash. A PDF file—"

"I can get him to open a PDF file," Tatum interrupted.

"Good. PDF files have a ton of exploits I can use. I can hide a Trojan horse in the file . . . you know what a Trojan horse is, right? It's a hidden program inside another benign program. Like the Greeks did with the wooden—"

"I know what a Trojan horse is," Tatum said. "Vaguely."

"So I can hide a Trojan horse in the PDF file. If he opens the file, I'll gain complete control over his computer. I'll be able to give you his IP, look through his files, activate his webcam . . . basically, he'll be toast."

"Let's do it."

They browsed online, found a few charts that had to do with blood donations, and pasted them into a document.

"It doesn't have to make a lot of sense," Tatum told her. "But we need to make sure he doesn't suspect he's being duped."

"Is he technically savvy enough to know PDF files can hide Trojan horses?"

Tatum considered it. "I'm not sure. He's using Tor, so that shows some knowledge. But more to the point, it's likely that he's very paranoid. So if he feels like something isn't right, he might concoct a paranoid delusion that'll make him unpredictable."

"Hey, you're not paranoid if they're really chasing you, right?" Barb asked.

"Trust me, this guy probably *is* paranoid, no matter what."

She prepared what she called the "payload" while chew-chew-chewing her gum to oblivion. Meanwhile, Tatum phoned Peter-call-me-Damien to get his username and password for the forum. It took some very specific threats, which Tatum was totally willing to actually follow up on, before Peter relented. The username was Abchanchu. Tatum also instructed Peter to stay off the forum for the foreseeable future.

Logging in as Abchanchu, Tatum checked the list of members currently logged on to the forum. Dracula2 was offline. He opened the chat between Abchanchu and Dracula2, skimming it. Dracula2 had told Abchanchu that his donor was female, weighed about 125 pounds, and was five feet, six inches tall. Tatum forwarded this information to Martinez to make sure it matched with Rhea. Then he sent a message with the chart to Dracula2 and wrote, Hey, you can see the recommended amount of donated blood in the attached chart. He fought the urge to ask for details. *Who is your donor?* or *Where do you live? I know a good place to buy syringes.* Any unprompted question could spook Dracula2. And he needed him to open the file.

He checked the online members. Dracula2 was still offline.

Tatum glanced at the time at the bottom corner of the screen. It was twenty minutes past three. "Come on, you bastard," he muttered. "Where are you?"

CHAPTER 49

Zoe scrutinized the photos on the table. Shots of the street from different angles, a close-up image of a bloodstained lamppost. A handbag discarded on the sidewalk, its contents scattered. A picture of Rhea Deleon from her clinic's website, smiling at the camera, hugging a large dog.

She leaned back, her eyes glazing, hardly taking in the other occupants of the room. Martinez in one corner, talking to Captain Bright, both of them hunched over a stack of reports. Agent Valentine pacing the room, talking on the phone. O'Donnell, Koch, and Sykes arguing about their actions going forward. Status reports, instructions, questions. She lowered her eyes, filtered it all out, concentrated.

And the main question she had to address, before she could address any other, was who called the shots.

She was almost certain Glover had planned the first two murders. But this abduction didn't feel like Glover. It was too random, too dangerous, too far from his comfort zone. Grabbing a woman in the middle of the street?

He'd have to be desperate to do it.

Then again, he was dying, his time running out. Maybe he didn't care anymore. He was on his final crime spree, inflicting as much damage as he could. It was possible.

It felt wrong.

"We have the tech report on the tires," O'Donnell said, sitting down beside her.

"Anything interesting?"

"The tires are very worn, different from the previous one, meaning they switched vehicles. But it's a van. Possibly even the same make."

Zoe nodded distractedly.

"Any thoughts so far?" O'Donnell asked.

"This wasn't planned," Zoe said. "This was an impulsive act."

"I agree. This wasn't a street in which women typically walked around in the middle of the night. According to her parents, Rhea Deleon usually left her job early in the evening. They had no way of knowing she'd be there. Or anyone else for that matter."

"They drove by, saw her, and then they grabbed her."

"So . . . what? Is Glover becoming more unpredictable?"

Zoe frowned. "The murder of Henrietta Fishburne was carefully and diligently planned. The car, the location, the time, the gear they brought with them. They moved the body and spent an hour posing it for some reason. Everything followed an agenda. And then just four days later, *this* happens?" She looked at O'Donnell. "This wasn't Glover's doing. This is his accomplice. He's spiraling out of control. Out of *Glover's* control."

"He's cracking?"

"Exactly." Zoe thought for a moment. "We should interview some of the male congregation members from Riverside Baptist."

O'Donnell raised an eyebrow. "*Now?* Why?"

"Glover's accomplice is going through an intense psychotic episode, which led to this crime," Zoe explained. "That means that he'd be much easier to spot during an interview."

O'Donnell shook her head. "Maybe. But we don't have the people or the time to do it. As a matter of fact, we still don't even have a complete list of congregation members. And what if we do it and find nothing?"

"We can prioritize the list—"

"Valentine and Bright don't even believe the accomplice is necessarily from the congregation."

"But you do."

"I think it's probable. But that's not enough. We can't base our entire investigation on your hunch. Especially not now, when we have new leads. And Rhea's life might depend on our speed."

Zoe's face flushed. "It's not a hunch."

"It is." O'Donnell shook her head. "Don't give me that look—I'm not blowing you off. I'm telling you it can't be done. There are just too many of them."

"What if I narrow it down?" Zoe asked. "Give you a short list of ten names?"

O'Donnell hesitated. "You think a short interview will do? Fifteen minutes?"

"Yes."

O'Donnell nodded. "Do it."

Zoe's foot jerked repeatedly as she worked through the list that Patrick Carpenter had provided for the police. As O'Donnell had already pointed out, it was incomplete, in more ways than one. It seemed as if Patrick had sat down, with no reference aside from his imperfect memory, and jotted down names. Several names appeared on the list more than once. Some were only the first name, or the last name, and a few congregation member names were written in their short form. These issues also caused some conundrums. For example, both Josh Wilson and Joshua Wilson were listed as congregation members. Were they the same person, simply denoted differently? Or different people?

Some had a phone number or address, but most didn't. With enough time and patience, she could probably locate some of them, but she was running short on both.

She took out her phone and dialed Patrick Carpenter. The phone rang unanswered for twenty seconds, and Zoe hung up. She considered just driving over to meet him. But she couldn't be sure if he was at home, at the church, or with his wife in the hospital.

She dialed Albert Lamb instead. He picked up almost immediately.

"Hello?" He sounded weak, as if he'd been fading away since his daughter's murder and was now almost gone.

"Mr. Lamb, this is Zoe Bentley."

He sighed. "What can I do for you?"

"I need to go over the congregation members list with you."

"Mrs. Bentley, I'm tired. It's been a long . . ." His sentence stretched as if he tried to pinpoint the time frame. Long day? Long week?

"I understand. But a woman has been abducted. We have very good reason to believe the man who killed Catherine is responsible. He's from your congregation, Mr. Lamb—there's no doubt. And the woman's time is short."

A pause. "I'm at home, Bentley. Can you come over here?"

She stood up and grabbed her bag. "I'm on my way."

CHAPTER 50

"I don't know who half of these people are," Albert said, studying the list with bloodshot, puffy eyes.

He looked even worse than last time, but it was the smell that was really getting to Zoe. He smelled of sickness, and stale vomit, and anguish. She was almost sure he still wore the same clothes from a few days earlier. His dog watched them with big wet eyes from the corner of the room.

"This is a list we got from Patrick," she said. "They're members of your congregation."

"I know . . . I mean, the names are familiar. But I'm having a hard time connecting them to people. Catherine was the one who remembered everyone. If she were alive, she would give you a detailed list of each and every one of them, including their profession, their hobbies, and their favorite food. She was like that. I don't know how the church will function without her."

If they could talk to Catherine, she could just tell them who'd killed her, who Glover's accomplice was, and get it over with. The thought came unbidden, accompanied with a flash of impatience and followed by guilt. Albert was trying to help, and it wasn't his fault that every moment made him think of his dead daughter.

"What if you saw pictures?" Zoe suddenly asked. "Of the people? Would you be able to connect them to names?"

He nodded hesitantly. "I'm good with faces."

She took out her laptop and turned it on. She opened the most recent folder, double-clicking the topmost picture. The image popped up on the screen, and to Zoe's relief, Catherine wasn't in it. It was a picture in church, five members of the congregation sitting on a pew, smiling at the camera. Glover wasn't there, either, but there was one familiar man who Zoe had a hard time placing.

Albert made a hiccupping sound, and for a second, Zoe thought he was about to burst into tears. But he actually smiled, just slightly. "The woman on the left is Harriette. Next to her is John, her husband, and then—"

"John what?"

"Hobbs."

Zoe wrote the image number in her notebook and the name. Then she added *Caucasian, average height, married*. "Do you know what he does for a living?"

"Uh . . . road maintenance, I think. I remember he was once hurt in his job by one of the tools they use and couldn't work for almost two months."

Road maintenance. "Anything else you can think of?"

"They have two kids."

Two kids. "Okay. Next one?"

"That's Allen Swenson."

That was who he was. The guy she'd seen in the church. She jotted him down in the notebook. "Job?"

"Accountant."

"Married? Kids?"

"He was married. Divorced now."

"Anything else?"

"Not that I can think of."

"Next?"

"I don't remember their first names, but their last name is Wilson."

They didn't matter. The Wilson couple were African American. The witness who had seen the men take Rhea had said both men were Caucasian. "Okay. Next." She clicked for the next picture, taken in the church's entrance. Catherine was talking to a tall man.

Albert reached out as if to touch the screen. Then he drew back and said, "This is Leon. Last name, uh . . . Farrell."

Zoe tried not to look at the time. This was painstakingly slow, but she was getting somewhere. "Married?"

"No. He moved here from Nevada two years ago."

They developed a rhythm. As the images went by, Albert seemed to become more focused, perhaps reliving a happier time. Zoe listed the members, cross-matched them with Patrick's list. Did her best not to rush Albert. And hoped Rhea was still alive.

CHAPTER 51

They had only one bathroom in the house.

It hadn't occurred to him before, but keeping the woman in the bathroom posed some difficulties. Daniel didn't seem to care. If anything, he used the bathroom more now that the girl was in it.

But the man in control couldn't do it, not with the woman there. Even though she looked away, he just couldn't. For now, he peed in a jar inside his room, constantly eyeing the door. But he'd have to find a better solution soon.

The whole situation got to him. The tension between them was unbearable. And he worried about the girl; the gash in her forehead was inflamed. He suspected she needed to see a doctor, and that was out of the question, of course. But she couldn't die, not yet. He still needed her.

He prowled in the apartment, going to the kitchen, the bathroom to look at the woman, and back to his bedroom. Daniel kept his own door shut most of the day, probably asleep.

The man in control had drunk the girl's blood again, just a drop, from a small cut that he'd sliced into her right arm. He had to make sure he didn't drink too much of her. He'd tried to research how much he could drink earlier but had found nothing.

Oh, but he'd asked that guy on the vampire forum, hadn't he?

It frightened him, how hazy the past few hours had been, as if he was losing his hold on reality. He usually left home every day to live his other life. The life that now seemed remote and far away. He needed that life; it was what anchored him. Here, at home, with the woman, and Daniel, and the blood, he was floating away, like in a dream.

Tomorrow. Tomorrow he would go out again.

He sat down to check the forum. The admin, Abchanchu, was much nicer than he'd been last time they'd chatted. Now he saw Abchanchu had sent him a file. He wrote that the amount of blood could be found on those charts.

Clicking the file, he downloaded it to his own computer but didn't open it. He could hardly focus on reading the chat, not to mention understanding a complex chart.

He answered Abchanchu, trying his best to sound casual. Can you give me a tldr version of this? Charts make my brain hurt LOL.

Abchanchu answered after a few seconds. Haha. It's a really simple chart. It's best if you have a look at it, to make sure you aren't taking too much.

He gritted his teeth. Like, what would be a safe amount for the weight and height I told you earlier?

The chat window showed that Abchanchu had received the message, but he took his time answering. I wouldn't take too much. But if you really want to play it safe, check the chart. I don't want to be responsible for giving you the wrong info.

He sighed. He'd have to focus and read the chart.

A sudden sound drew his attention. At first he thought it was some sort of strange vermin. But it wasn't—it was the woman's muffled screams.

CHAPTER 52

"He must have opened it," Tatum said again, staring at the screen.

"He didn't open it," Barb answered, exasperated. "We would have seen an indication."

"Maybe you messed up the Trojan horse?"

"I didn't mess it up," Barb said between clenched teeth. "Tell him to open it."

"I can't tell him to open it, because Peter wouldn't have told him to open it. Peter wouldn't have known he *didn't* open it." He wanted to smash the laptop to pieces. "Damn it! We must have spooked him somehow."

"How?" Barb asked incredulously. "We hardly said anything."

"I told you, he's extremely paranoid right now—anything could set him off."

"But he's still online." Barb pointed at the screen. "Wouldn't he have logged off?"

Tatum had no idea. As far as he knew, the unsub could have curled into a fetal position, crying, in the corner of the room. Or fled out to the street. Or maybe the concept of opening a PDF file freaked him out so much that he decided to kill Rhea and himself. There was no way to tell.

"I'll prompt him. Maybe he's just confused," Tatum finally said.

It took him a while to formulate the sentence, avoiding anything that would make it sound like Abchanchu really cared one way or the other.

The chart is really simple. Do you see the column on the left, where it says "weight"?

That could make the unsub decide to open the damn file. Tatum had quit smoking a few years before, but he suddenly craved a cigarette. He watched the screen, hardly daring to blink, praying for the indication that the file had been opened.

CHAPTER 53

He rushed to the bathroom, turned the doorknob, the woman's screams dying away. The door didn't budge. He blinked, confused, for a second thinking the woman had somehow managed to free herself and lock herself inside.

But then, as her muffled voice completely stopped, he realized what was going on. Daniel had locked the door and was now taking care of the woman.

"Daniel!" he screamed. "Open the door."

Nothing. He shook the doorknob. "Daniel! Don't do it!"

One heartbeat. Two heartbeats. Three. No, not when he finally had a woman with truly pure blood. He'd never find someone like her again. He screamed and slammed into the door. Something cracked, and it flew open.

Daniel knelt by the woman, a noose tight around her throat. The woman's face was purple, eyes bulging as she struggled frantically against the zip ties that held her to the sink's pipe.

He pulled Daniel away, slammed him against the wall, screaming obscenities at him. Then he crouched by the woman, his fingers trembling as he tried to loosen the noose. It was too tight; he couldn't get a grip. The woman's eyes rolled back in their sockets. He let out a frustrated shout, dashed to his room, got one of his scalpels, ran back, and cut, slicing deeply through her skin. Blood ran freely down her neck to her shirt, soaking it. Her eyelashes fluttered as he tore the gag from her mouth, clearing the way for air.

She coughed and spat, her gaze focusing on the bloody scalpel.

"Don't scream," he said, waving the scalpel threateningly.

She let out a hoarse, fearful sob. Then she inhaled, wheezing, shutting her eyes.

He got up, whirled to face Daniel, who'd gone to the kitchen and was soaking a towel in the sink.

"You asshole!" he screamed at Daniel.

"Lower your voice," Daniel said in a measured tone. He applied the wet towel to the back of his head. "You nearly broke my skull."

"I'm sorry I didn't." His eyes were tearing up. Betrayal. He'd felt it before, but he never thought Daniel would do that to him. "After everything I did for you? This is how you—"

"What *you* did for me?" Daniel snarled. "What about what *I* did for you? Who set you free? Who helped you to drink real, fresh blood for the first time? And now you place *me* in danger? I can't leave this place. My face is plastered on every TV screen and newspaper in this city. I'm stuck here, with you and that damn bitch, waiting for the moment she'd manage to scream for help or free herself."

"She won't. She can't!" He shook his head. "Why would you even want to leave?"

"We had a deal, remember?" Daniel asked. "I help you heal, and you do the same for me. I'm sick! I'm dying. You know what I need to get better."

"But you don't have to do it like that. Try her blood. It's so pure—it'll cure you, I know it! Just try one sip—"

"Her blood won't cure my damn brain cancer!" Daniel trembled in rage now.

"Yes it will," the man in control whispered.

Daniel took a few long breaths. Then, he let a small reassuring smile show. "Listen, you know why I did that? I was trying to protect you too. Her blood is tainted. She told me."

"What? No, it isn't."

"She *told* me. She somehow managed to push the gag out. I went to the bathroom, and she was laughing. She said her blood is corrosive. She has HIV."

"No. You're lying!"

Daniel's eyes widened, filled with hurt, and the man in control felt a stab of guilt.

"Would I lie to you?" Daniel asked, his voice barely a whisper.

No, of course he wouldn't. Daniel had never lied to him. "I'm sorry."

"You can't drink her blood. It will kill you."

His world was coming apart. No! It couldn't be. He'd *tasted* her; she was so pure. "I need to make sure she doesn't scream again," he said weakly.

He went back to the bathroom, knelt by the wheezing woman. The blood still trickled from her neck, though not in copious amounts. He was about to place the gag in her mouth, when she croaked, her words impossible to understand.

"What?"

"I didn't tell him that," she rasped. "I don't have HIV."

Well, of course *she* would say that. She *wanted* him to get sick. But then . . . he'd tasted her. He'd know if . . .

It was the tumor. It was *Rod Glover*.

The tumor would have no problem lying to him. It wanted *him* dead as well. For a second he glanced back, scared he'd see the tumor behind him, a viscous blob of corrupted brain cells, slithering on the floor.

But all he could see was Daniel, still in the kitchen, pressing the towel to the back of his head.

"Can you get me some water?" the woman gasped.

He nodded and got a glass of water from the tap. He put down the bloody scalpel and helped her drink, holding the glass to her lips, tipping it slowly. She gulped some, and then, as the glass tipped too much, she coughed again. He took the glass away.

"More?" he asked when she stopped coughing.

She shook her head. Behind him, he heard a door slamming. He glanced back, saw Daniel had returned to his room, shutting the door behind him.

"You can't let him near me," she said. "He'll kill me."

"I won't let him. He knows that he shouldn't."

"Just don't let him near me."

He took the gag and placed it in her mouth. Then, unable to stop himself, he bent forward and licked the blood off her neck. It was *sublime*. How could he have thought the blood was corrupted? He licked it all, until her skin was clean; then he sucked the remnants of blood from her shirt collar. She groaned, tried to get away from him, but it was no use.

Her skin was hot. "You have a fever," he muttered.

There was nothing in the house to treat a fever. He'd have to buy something tomorrow.

But could he leave her alone with the tumor?

CHAPTER 54

Zoe was back in the motel, sitting on her bed. She read her notes, scrolling through the images on her laptop. She'd decided that Rhea's abduction was a good enough reason to break her promise to Tatum and work into the night.

It had taken her and Albert four hours to go through all the pictures. He hadn't recognized all the people in the photos, but he'd been familiar with the majority. He'd also managed to find phone numbers for thirteen of them. Catherine's phone would have many of them as contacts, and Zoe could work with that tomorrow.

Now she did what she could to find the rest of the members' names. The tall bald guy, who in two separate images was talking to Rod Glover, was unnamed. But he appeared in seven different images with a man named Donald Holcomb. After a quick search, she found Holcomb's profile on Facebook. And there was the unnamed tall guy, listed as one of Holcomb's 147 friends. His name, according to Facebook, was Bobby Cross. And she could glean a lot from both of Holcomb's and Cross's profiles. Age, other friends. Cross was single, Holcomb married with a fourteen-year-old daughter. She scribbled in her notebook, her mind already mapping the likelihood of any of those men being the killer. And Cross had another of the unnamed people as *his* friend.

She kept working, checking the images, the social media, adding notes to members, sometimes circling one of the names.

The photographer also had a knack for catching small hidden moments. A hissed argument between husband and wife. A man tearing up at church. A child outside picking flowers from a freshly planted flower bed, his mom running toward him, her face twisted in anger. These were invaluable for Zoe.

When she'd left Albert's home, that's all they had been. A list of names, with the occasional detail—profession or age. Now, these people started to grow in her mind. Jeremy Finn had started out as a thirty-year-old married man. But after two hours of seeing him over and over in the pictures and checking his social media account, he metamorphosed. His wife appeared in only two pictures with him; in the rest, he appeared talking or standing nearby a much younger, perky congregation member. In one of them, he was touching her shoulder. And on his Facebook profile, half his "friends" were women in underwear—probably bots.

Archie Mann was the man whose eyes in the pictures always seemed distant, even when he was talking to someone. And his hands were *always* in his pockets.

Kyle Raker kept checking out men, his wife apparently oblivious.

Vincent Greer had sweaty armpits.

They grew in her mind, people she'd never met, each becoming a character in a macabre years-long play that ended in a violent death.

And throughout those pictures, playing their parts, smiling, talking, sometimes aware of the camera, sometimes not, were Rod Glover and Catherine Lamb. In the earlier pictures Glover was missing, and Catherine was an angel-faced teenager, usually standing by her mother's side. But a bit later, Glover made his first appearance, and both he and Catherine started dominating the pictures as they became the focal point of the church's community. In the final couple of years, they both appeared more in the photos than either Albert Lamb or Patrick Carpenter. Catherine had taken her mother's place, so that made sense. But it was a testament to Glover's charisma that he'd managed to make himself such a crucial part of the church community's life.

CHAPTER 55

Rhea shivered in the darkness, the bathroom walls spinning. She had a high fever and was weak from hunger, thirst, and loss of blood. It was hard to concentrate. Maybe it wouldn't be the men who'd kill her after all. Maybe it would be the infection.

She could feel the prickle underneath her leg, her one tiny hope. It had been so easy to shift her leg slightly, hide the scalpel. The one who'd helped her drink had been so frantic, so confused, he hadn't even noticed the blade had gone missing. Now she had to force herself to wait. She could still hear movement outside the bathroom door. One of the men was still awake. And if they came in while the scalpel was visible . . .

No, she'd wait.

Her shoulders and back ached from the unnatural position she was tied in. And she was cold. So cold.

Was it late enough? She'd been in the darkness for hours, for days. Surely the two men had gone to sleep.

She moved her leg. It was hard to see the small scalpel on the floor. Impossible to reach with her hands, but she could do it with her feet. She kicked off her shoes, then carefully slid off one of her socks. She wiggled her toes, increasing the blood flow into them. Then she tried to grab the scalpel between her big toe and her index toe. It seemed to take ages. The angle was all wrong, the scalpel flat, and she kept trembling. *Come on, come on, come on.*

Finally, to her amazement, she managed it. The scalpel was held loosely in the air between her toes. Now, all she needed to do was get the scalpel to her hand. Once she did that, she could maybe cut the plastic zip ties. There were only two.

It turned out to be impossible.

She could *almost* get the scalpel to her hand. If she bent her knee and stretched against the plastic zip ties, her fingers were inches away from it. But it wasn't enough. And then the scalpel dropped, tumbled to the floor by her waist.

Footsteps. Someone was coming. Panicking, she twisted her body, throwing herself on the scalpel. Her shoulder exploded in pain as she twisted it.

The door opened. It was that guy Daniel. His eyes glimmered in the darkness. Now he'd kill her, when his friend was asleep. She whimpered.

"What are you doing, Daniel?" a voice asked in the dark.

Daniel turned around. "Nothing," he said, his voice casual. "I couldn't sleep. I need my pills. They're in the bathroom cabinet. Is that okay with you?"

"Yeah. Just making sure."

Daniel shook his head, going for the cabinet. "Fucking psycho," he muttered, taking something from the cabinet. Then he stepped over Rhea, ignoring her completely, opening the tap. She could hear the sound of running water and then a different sound as he filled a cup. Then she felt a sudden cold shock as water started dripping on her. The pipe she was tied to leaked.

He swallowed the pills, drank the water, and left the bathroom, not even glancing her way. She heard a door shut.

Then movement. The other man. He was dragging something. A mattress. He placed it in front of the bathroom door. He was going to sleep in the doorway.

To Rhea's relief, he shut the door. He groaned as he settled down to sleep.

She moved off the scalpel, her shoulder aching. She might have dislocated it. Her brain was flooded with pain and cold. This was what hell was like.

There was no way she could get the scalpel to her hands. And frankly, even if she could, she doubted she could cut the zip ties in this position.

New plan.

She examined the pipe she was shackled to. Back home, her sink had a plastic thing connected to the drain . . . was it called a trap? She'd actually taken it apart once when it was clogged. It had been easy. There was one plastic nut that twisted easily by hand, and once she unscrewed it, she could just twist the thing off. It had been messy, and she'd nearly ruined her shirt, but she'd gotten a sense of satisfaction in managing it by herself.

This drain had no plastic parts. The twisting part of the pipe was connected with two metal nuts—one to the sink and one to the wall. She could slide her tied hands up and down the pipe easily enough, reach both nuts with her fingers. Theoretically, if she unscrewed both, she could dismantle it easily.

But both the pipe and the nuts were corroded, and when she tried twisting them, nothing moved.

Maybe if she just unscrewed the part that connected to the sink, she would be able to twist the pipe off. That would mean she only had to unscrew *one* of those damn things.

She grasped it and twisted. It was wet, and her palm slipped. But she tried again and again.

Finally, it seemed to budge. Just a little.

She could get it unscrewed. And then she'd be free, with a scalpel for a weapon and the element of surprise. It wasn't a lot, she knew. But it was something.

CHAPTER 56

After a while, flipping through the images of the congregation felt like a saga. Zoe found small stories woven into the collection. For example, at first when the photographs began documenting the church's events, most of the events were picnics. But then, when Catherine became more dominant in the images, perhaps taking a more active role in the administration, there seemed to be more volunteer work, more events revolving around the neighborhood.

But there were other, banal stories in that tapestry. A married couple that for a few years were close seemed to drift apart as the years went by, and finally, the husband disappeared altogether, only the wife left. A sweetly smiling child growing up into a sullen teenager. A teenage girl becoming thinner in every picture, then disappearing completely for almost a year. And when she returned to appear in the photos, she seemed healthier, but distant, never smiling.

Some of it she probably imagined. As the hours went by, her tiredness grew, and she seemed to spot tenuous connections. Was Holcomb's marriage falling apart? Two pictures in which he and his wife were staring in opposite directions made Zoe think so. But maybe not. She couldn't make assumptions.

Something nagged at her. A connection she hadn't managed to pinpoint. A piece missing in the puzzle.

She was almost sure she had a list of likely candidates. Not even ten names. Eight. She sent the list to O'Donnell. Then she scrolled through them all again to verify her choices. Her eyes slowly shut, the photos still flickering on the screen.

In her dreams, she kept seeing the pictures, but they were moving, and she could hear the people talking. One of them, she knew, was a killer, Glover's accomplice. She kept trying to find him, but he moved, always remaining in her peripheral vision, and she couldn't get a good look at him. She whirled and whirled, the people around her becoming insubstantial, the one man she was trying to see staying one step ahead of her. And Rod Glover moved through the crowd as if it were made of mist, walking straight for her, his lips twisted in a malicious grin.

CHAPTER 57

Saturday, October 22, 2016

The door creaked open, and Rhea blearily raised her eyes. It was the blood drinker. He held a glass of water.

Her palm throbbed. She'd spent the night struggling against the pipe until finally she'd sunk into unconsciousness. Had she done it? She definitely remembered it budging a bit more. But she'd been too weak to keep going. It had been easier to give up.

He crouched by her side, removed the gag from her mouth, and put the glass to her lips. She drank greedily, doing her best not to spill anything. She emptied the entire thing.

He put his hand on her forehead and said, "Your fever is still high."

"Infection," she whispered. "I need some antibiotics."

"We don't have any here."

"I need to see a doctor. The infection and the fever could kill me."

He seemed to care if she lived or died. Perhaps he could be persuaded.

He didn't listen, staring at her neck. "What's that?"

"What?"

"That cut." He touched the place where *he'd* cut her the day before.

"You did this with the scalpel yesterday, remember?"

He frowned. "No, I didn't. I did the one on the leg."

"And the arm and the neck."

"I *didn't*. I would have remembered. I would definitely have remembered. I bled you only once. I remember. Once. And not on the neck, never on the neck, I wouldn't have . . ."

"No . . . you did those too," she said desperately. "You cut me several times."

"I . . . didn't. I'm not . . . it's impossible." He shook his head violently. "*You* did those. You're trying to bleed yourself to death to take the blood from me!"

Spit flew from his mouth, his eyes bulging. Fury twisted his face, turning him into a beast. He was going to kill her. Heart thrumming in her chest, she blurted, "It was the other guy. Daniel, he did this."

He paused, frowning. "Daniel?"

The man had clearly lost any connection with reality. Could she use it? "He came in at night. Stepped over you when you were sleeping," she said, voice trembling. "He cut me and drank my blood. He wants all the blood for himself. He wants to bleed me dry."

He seemed to struggle with the concept. "It wasn't Daniel."

"It was. I swear."

"No, it was the tumor. The tumor took control over him. Now he wants to infect *us*. It's the tumor. Rod Glover. The tumor."

"That's right," she babbled. "It's his tumor. It came here, it drank my blood. It was the tumor, I remember now. You have to help me. The tumor wants to steal your blood."

"Yes. You're right. I need to take care of it." His lips quivered. "I need to take it out."

"Exactly. Cut him up and take it out. It's the only way." She could do it. Get him to kill his partner.

He thought about it. "No. I'm going to buy you some antibiotics. I'll ask them if they have something for the tumor. I'll *ask* them."

If he left the house, his friend would kill her for sure. "Don't leave! He'll kill me. Take care of him first!"

"Don't worry." He took the rag, shoved it into her mouth. She struggled, tried to spit it out, and he tightened the knot, making sure the rag stayed in her mouth. "He took his pills last night. He sleeps until noon when he does that. I'll be back long before."

He got up. She screamed through the gag, tried to dislodge it with her tongue. It was no use.

"Just don't make too much noise. He'll sleep right through," he told her and shut the door.

She wasn't going to wait for this maniac to come back. One guy had left; the other one was sleeping, medicated. If she freed herself now, armed with the scalpel, she had more than just a slight hope. She had a real chance.

Invigorated by that thought, she twisted the nut connected to the sink's drainpipe with all her strength.

And with a rusty squeak, it turned.

CHAPTER 58

Zoe woke up with a start, nightmares lingering in the back of her mind, her breath short. She was on the brink of figuring something out, an important detail in the photos she hadn't noticed before. What was it? Perhaps a significant look exchanged between Glover and one of the other congregation members? Or someone who repeatedly appeared with Glover in the photos?

But she'd scrutinized the photos in which Glover appeared so many times that by now she knew them by heart. She could recite the names of all the people who appeared in those photos. In fact, she'd made a note in her list of how many times each person was photographed talking or engaging somehow with Glover. The person who seemed closest to him was a guy named Dennis Blake. He was one of Zoe's top eight. Unmarried, aged thirty-six, worked as a sales associate at Walmart. It was likely that he was used to being managed, that he was the type who would let Glover boss him around. And Glover would have noticed it immediately.

That was what niggled at her. He was significantly more likely to be their unsub. She picked up her phone, about to dial Tatum's number.

No.

She didn't sense the relief of putting her finger on what was bothering her. Whatever it was, it wasn't related to Dennis Blake at all.

What bothered her wasn't what she'd seen in the picture. It was something that was *missing*.

Someone who made a point of avoiding being photographed with Glover? There were thirteen men in the photos who didn't appear with Glover even *once*. She thought about each of them in turn. Nothing clicked.

The problem was, she was focused on *Glover*. How people related to him in the photos. If they talked to him, did he smile at them, or at their spouses, or their children? It was as if she couldn't profile the unsub without pointing out how every characteristic related to Glover. *The unsub is Caucasian like Glover, his height average like Glover. He has a mental illness, which Glover used to manipulate him. He is a follower, which is what Glover would look for in an accomplice.*

The unsub was a killer as well. Maybe Glover had pried the beast out, but it had been there before, lurking. And his characteristics weren't related to Glover at all. This was her own problem, the problem that hounded her. When Rod Glover appeared, she viewed the world differently. Through a warped lens.

After turning on her laptop, she scrolled through the entire photo collection, this time focusing on the photos in which Glover didn't appear. Searching them for anything. Anything at all.

She found it within twenty minutes.

A photo she'd seen on the church memorial board was missing from this collection. And she instantly knew who appeared in the photo alongside Catherine.

Allen Swenson.

She found the photos that Tatum had taken of the memorial board in the church and flipped through them. Allen Swenson appeared in two of them. In one, he and Catherine stood with a group of other people, smiling at the camera. That one also appeared in the photos she'd gotten from the photographer, Finch. But the second was a photo of Allen and Catherine on a bench in the garden, talking. And *that* photo was missing from Finch's photos. Why?

In fact, now that she thought about it, there were hardly *any* recent pictures of Allen at all. But he'd told them that he came to most Sunday services. She checked again. Swenson appeared only a handful of times, in large group shots.

She looked through the images yet again, this time focusing on the file names, making a note whenever the numbering jumped. Overall, the image numbers were consecutive. There would be a jump in the image numbers whenever the dates of the images changed, presumably because unrelated photos had been taken in between. Occasionally, one or two images would be missing, perhaps because they were blurry or unusable, deleted outright. But in the more recent folders, there were numerous missing pictures, the consecutive numbers suddenly leaping by four or five. A total of thirty-two photos were missing from the last two years.

Some photos had been removed. Was this done at Swenson's request?

He'd told them he'd seen Catherine when he had been driving by the church. She thought back to that conversation. He'd said he had been talking to a friend. They'd never followed through on that. Which friend? Glover?

Had Catherine seen them both together in the car? If Glover thought she'd recognized him, saw that he was with Swenson, that could be enough to prompt her murder.

He wasn't on her list because she'd based it on the pictures she had. Pictures he hardly appeared in. Since she assumed the unsub had met Glover in church, *and* saw Catherine there regularly, she focused on men who'd appeared frequently in the pictures, who were part of the congregation's community. It never occurred to her that pictures with specific people could be missing.

She searched for him on social media, found his profile on Facebook. She scrolled through the posts. He was divorced, no children. He'd taken several selfies with women considerably younger than him.

She dialed Tatum.

"Hey." He sounded exhausted.

She suddenly recalled the online trap Tatum had set for the killer the day before. "Any news with the virus thing?" she asked.

"It's not a virus—it's a Trojan horse." He yawned when he said *horse*, so it sounded like *hooooorse*. "No news. He hasn't logged off, but he didn't open the file either. No idea why. I tried asking him if he found what he was looking for in the file this morning. Still no response."

"Are you at the station?"

"Yeah, I slept here. We did a sleepover party. Agent Valentine has pink PJs."

"Really?"

"No. But I find it amusing that you thought it's remotely possible."

"Tatum, do you have the phone number of the photographer we talked to?"

"I think so. Finch, right? Hang on . . . okay, I sent it to you. Why?"

"I think there are some missing photos," Zoe answered vaguely, not sure if her hunch was strong enough to go into detail. "I'll keep you posted."

"Okay. I think there's a status meeting at—"

She hung up before he could give her the details. Self-preservation. Then she dialed Finch. It took him a long time to answer.

"Hello?"

"Mr. Finch, this is Zoe Bentley. We met a few days—"

"I remember. How can I help you?"

"It's about Catherine Lamb and Allen Swenson."

The long pause told her she'd gotten it right. She smiled grimly.

"What about them?" Finch finally asked.

"There was a photograph of both of them missing in the files you gave us. A photograph you used for the memorial board."

"That must have been a mistake. Maybe I missed a folder."

"From what I could see, you missed more than just a folder. There are missing photos throughout the last two years. Have you removed some of the photos, Mr. Finch?"

"Like I said, it was probably a mistake. I'll look through the photos on Monday morning, send you the missing files."

If he had a reason to hide them, he might delete them by then. "What if we send a patrol officer to your studio now? With a search warrant? Would you be able to find the photos faster?"

"There's no need for that."

"A woman has been murdered, Finch. If you're withholding evidence—"

"You can't tell him that I talked to you," Finch blurted.

"Tell who?"

"Allen."

"Allen Swenson?"

"Yeah. He came into my studio on Tuesday and told me to delete all photos of him from the past two years."

Tuesday. That was the day they'd met Swenson at the church. He'd seen them looking at the memorial board and had probably gone straight after to talk to Finch and get rid of something he didn't want them to know. "Did he tell you why?"

"He said I invaded his privacy. Threatened he'd sue me if I didn't do it."

"Did you delete the photos?"

"I removed them from the folders. But I have a backup."

"We need those photos right now."

"I can get to my studio in about twenty minutes and send them to you."

"Send them to my email." She gave him her email address. "Be quick about it."

The wait was interminable. She kept refreshing her email box, checking if he sent them yet. Just as she was about to call him again, she got the email. She scrolled through them.

One photo sometimes really *was* worth a thousand words, and there were thirty-two of them. Some were innocuous. But those weren't the ones Swenson was worried about. Finch had a knack for catching unique moments. And seventeen of those photos told a story.

Allen and Catherine talking with each other in the church, their bodies a bit too close for casual acquaintanceship. A few images of them kissing in a dark corner. Then another one, with Allen placing his hand on Catherine's waist, with her trying to move it away or hold it there. And then a few more pictures of them talking, Catherine distraught, Allen calm. A picture of Catherine in tears, with Allen staring at her stonily. And then another picture of a kiss. An aggressive kiss, Allen gripping Catherine, her own hands held to the side, rigid, as if she forced herself still.

Zoe phoned O'Donnell, her gaze still focused on Catherine's face in that final image. Catherine's eyes were shut tight, as if she was trying to unsee what was happening to her, perhaps make it disappear. But in the end, she hadn't shut her eyes tight enough.

CHAPTER 59

The pipe wouldn't twist. Rhea let out a muffled groan of despair. She pulled it with all her strength, not caring if it made any noise, not caring if the other guy, Daniel, woke up. *Come on . . .*

Nothing.

The mechanism wasn't the same as in her sink back home. Maybe it was similar, but not close enough. It just wouldn't twist off, despite the one nut she'd loosened completely.

She would have to do the other one. Once she unloosened *that* one, she'd be free for sure. Except no matter how much she tried, it wouldn't budge. Not even a fraction of an inch. Her angle was all wrong for that one. And she was getting tired. And she could see the rust. So much rust . . .

A thought occurred to her. She slid her bound hands so that the zip ties lay directly over the rusty connection and then lifted her body, placing all of her weight on the pipe.

It groaned. Flakes of rust dropped around her. She tried to pull it, but with almost no support, it was impossible.

Still, maybe it gave just a bit?

She lowered herself, took a few deep breaths, then tried again. And again. The pipe held fast.

She straightened, raised her hands, and with one swift move, pulled them down. The pipe clanged, the noise making her heart sink. But a lot more rust dropped around her. She tried it again.

Clang.

And again.

Clang.

Clang. Clang. Clang.

She stopped. Then lifted herself, dropping her weight on the pipe. Something gave. She was doing it! The entire connection was so rusty she could break it.

And the door opened.

She dropped at once, hiding the scalpel with her body.

Daniel shuffled in, blinking, yawning. He wore an open bathrobe, a pair of underwear, socks, and a greasy white shirt. He glanced at her, shook his head, then stepped to the toilet bowl. Rhea looked away. She could feel him leering at her as he peed.

He finished; didn't flush; trudged over to the sink, just above her; and washed his hands and face.

Water trickled from the two nuts that connected the drain, spattering on the floor, making a noise like rainfall. Rhea hurriedly shuffled sideways, letting the water trickle on her hair and shoulders instead. If he noticed the splashing water, he'd figure out what she was doing, and it'd be the end . . .

He didn't. He finished washing in the sink and turned the water off.

"Hey, did you make any breakfast?" he called out to his friend.

There was, of course, no response.

Daniel left the bathroom. She imagined him checking the rooms to see if his friend was there.

When he returned, there was a gleam in his eye.

"Well," he said, "looks like we were left alone. *Unchaperoned.*"

Rhea breathed fast through her nose, terrified.

"I could be done with you now." Daniel smiled. "Thirty seconds, and no more Rhea Deleon. That's your name, right? Rhea Deleon? The police are looking for you. Well, you and me, really. We were the stars of the evening news yesterday. Maybe I can take care of you, and the police will find the remains of Rhea Deleon, discarded in the river. What do you think of that?"

She shook her head, and his smile widened. He clearly enjoyed her reaction, enjoyed her fear. And she was terrified.

He tapped his lips thoughtfully. "No reason we can't have fun, right? I doubt my partner would begrudge me that."

He stepped out of the bathroom, leaving the door open behind him.

Where was the other guy? He'd said he was just going to the pharmacy. It'd been at least an hour since he'd left; he should have returned by now. It didn't matter. She had a few minutes at the most. She needed to make them count.

She strained against the pipe, lifting herself. The pipe groaned. Then with a sudden jolt, it broke, drenching her with sludge.

She was free. For a few seconds she just breathed heavily, not believing what had just happened. She fumbled at the gag, but it was tight, and her hands were still tied to each other. She picked up the scalpel and tried to wedge it between her hands and cut the zip ties.

The scalpel cut her wrist, blood seeping, making the zip ties sticky. She managed to get it between her wrists and tried to saw the plastic, but it was completely impossible. The blade wasn't serrated and kept sliding across the plastic. She was too weak, the angle too awkward.

"Be careful with that—you might hurt yourself."

He stood in the doorway, holding a long gray piece of cloth. She scrambled back, thrusting the scalpel in his direction.

He took a step inside the bathroom and kicked her in the face. The explosion of pain was worse than anything she'd ever experienced. She felt something *crunch*; the world blurred. The scalpel tumbled from her fingers, clattered to the floor.

He grabbed her wrist and yanked her toward him, dragging her across the floor, thrusting her on her stomach. Something tightened around her throat, *the cloth*, and she couldn't breathe. She squirmed, trying to pull free, kicking at nothing, trying to scream, nothing coming out.

He yanked her torn pants to her knees, and his fingers roughly pawed at her, *in* her. The noose on her throat relented, letting her breathe, and she screamed into her gag. She shut her eyes, prayed for it to be over fast. His breathing became heavy, guttural. And then suddenly, the rough hands drew away.

She opened her eyes. He stared at her, red faced, eyes wide. Furious.

"It's *your* fault! It's because you're so damn ugly!"

The noose tightened again. No air. She couldn't scream, couldn't whimper.

Her only consolation was that the pain wasn't as bad as before. In fact, she hardly even felt it anymore.

CHAPTER 60

O'Donnell watched Swenson on the monitor. He was losing his patience, pacing in circles around the interrogation room. She hoped this wouldn't be another dead end. She'd just finished interviewing the people from Zoe's list. Sure, they'd been nervous, like anyone would be, but none of them had stood out.

"Is that Swenson?" Tatum joined her side.

"Yeah," she said. "They picked him up just as he was leaving his house."

"Did he say where he was going?"

"He said he was on his way to meet a friend."

Tatum nodded. "Any luck with the search warrant?"

"Koch is working on it. I don't know if we have enough."

"Let's try to give Koch something bigger to persuade the judge with," Tatum suggested.

They stepped out to the hallway and began walking to the interrogation room. Then O'Donnell paused.

"Look who's here," she said.

Patrick Carpenter strode toward them, his face twisted in rage.

"Detective," he shouted, still a few yards away. "Isn't it enough that our congregation lost Catherine? People are still deep in mourning, and you keep harassing them, trying to pin this heinous crime on one of them?" His bulging eyes were bloodshot, his clothes disheveled. Was it because of Catherine's loss? Or was it related to his wife's pregnancy?

"We're not trying to pin anything on—"

"Mr. Swenson called me to tell me you were *interrogating* him."

O'Donnell raised an eyebrow. "I thought he called his lawyer."

"Oh, I did contact a lawyer on his behalf, I assure you. And apparently he's not the first person you've harassed this weekend? A few other members have sent me messages telling me they've been subjected to—"

"Mr. Carpenter, we are just trying to find the people responsible for Catherine's death. I assume all the members of your church want that?"

"We want her killer brought to justice. We don't want this . . . this . . . witch hunt. Picking up our members one by one, fishing for information—"

"As you already know," Tatum said, "Daniel Moore, a member of your congregation, was actually Rod Glover, a killer on the FBI's Most Wanted list. We believe—"

"You think *Allen* had anything to do with this? Did you even talk to the man? He's one of the most amicable people I know."

"Mr. Carpenter, please lower your voice, or I'll have to—"

"Not to mention that he's thin and quite frail. Do you really think he is capable of enacting those violent crimes alongside a dying man? Do you have anything to back those preposterous accusations with? Did you arrest Allen just because he and Daniel happened to be passing friends?"

O'Donnell's brain sparked into high gear. Swenson and Glover were friends? She needed to keep Carpenter talking. "We believe Mr. Swenson has critical information about his friend. Surely you agree he should tell us anything he has."

Patrick seemed to realize he'd given her too much. He suddenly paused, then, after a few seconds, hissed, "I can't stay for long. My wife is being released from the hospital today. Otherwise, I assure you, I would have insisted on being present in the questioning of Mr. Swenson. And you better not ask him a single question until his lawyer gets here."

"We won't," O'Donnell said. "I hope everything goes well with your wife."

He didn't deign to answer her, leaving without another word.

"That was interesting," Tatum said. "At least we have something to start with."

"Yup." O'Donnell took out her phone and called Koch.

"Hey." Koch picked up almost immediately.

"How's it going with the warrant?"

"There's some delay. It might take another hour before the judge reviews it."

"Okay, listen, we have something else for you. Patrick Carpenter just told us that Swenson and Glover were friends."

There was a pause. "Then we have enough for a warrant for sure," Koch finally said.

"We have Swenson here, and we'll do our best to keep him here, but we can't arrest him, not yet."

"I'll try to get them to hurry." Koch hung up.

O'Donnell slid the phone into her pocket and entered the interrogation room.

"Detective," Swenson said, his voice tight. "I've been waiting for almost an hour. I want to be helpful, but it's the weekend, and—"

"And we appreciate your help." She sat down. "We just wanted to ask a few questions. We've been talking to congregation members all morning—perhaps Mr. Carpenter told you that when you called him."

Swenson sat down, saying nothing. She noticed he had an ugly scratch on the lower side of his left cheek.

"How well did you know Catherine Lamb?" she asked, easing into it.

"I told the agent here I talked to her a few times. We ran a charity together once. That's it."

"What about Daniel Moore?"

"Just in passing. Again, I've already told—"

"Patrick Carpenter said that you and Moore are friends."

His eyes wavered nervously. "I wouldn't call us friends. I may have talked to him once or twice. He's a friendly kind of guy."

"When did you see him last?"

"I don't remember. A while ago. I think he's been gone for a few months."

"Do you know where?"

"Not really. Like I said, we weren't close."

Time to tighten the screws. "How did you get that scratch?"

He touched his cheek. "I cut myself shaving."

She thought of the specks of blood found on the keys. "That's careless of you. You said that you talked to Catherine just a few times. But in her phone records, we have you calling her ten or twenty times."

He tensed. "Like I said, we ran a charity together. We had to plan it out."

"Was that charity five months ago?"

"Uh . . . yeah, I guess so."

"We saw photographs from that event. Did you know you weren't in any of the photos we initially got?"

"I was busy doing some administration. I guess I didn't have time for a photo op. But I took some with my phone if you want proof—"

"Mr. Swenson, you misunderstood," O'Donnell interrupted. "We *initially* didn't get the photos. But when we asked the photographer, he told us you instructed him to delete all of the photos of you from the past two years. Luckily for us, he didn't delete them. So we got to see all of them after all."

She'd expected the widening in his eyes as he understood the implication. His gaze seemed to skitter around the room, as if searching for a way out. For a few seconds his body was frozen, tense.

And then a change came over him. His expression became blank, his posture lax. He leaned back and smiled, his teeth clenched tightly. "I think I'll wait for my lawyer now."

CHAPTER 61

One of O'Donnell's earliest memories was watching the movie *The NeverEnding Story*. Her dad had brought the video home one day, telling her that it was a great movie, full of adventure. "You'll love it," he'd said, and she actually remembered the exact words and his smile, because it had turned out to be the first time she'd felt betrayed by her father.

It had started really well, with the strange creatures and the ominous dark *Nothing*. And her dad promised her that later there would be a beautiful furry dragon. She was excited to see the dragon and to find out more about the Nothing. But first Atreyu, and his white horse Artax, had to drudge through the Swamps of Sadness. The swamps inflicted deep sorrow on anyone who entered them. And halfway through, Atreyu's horse suddenly stopped and let himself be swallowed by the swamp.

At first O'Donnell was tense, waiting to see how the horse would suddenly emerge, encouraged by his friend. But no. He was gone. She actually asked her father, disbelieving, "Is he dead?"

"Yes, but watch—the dragon is about to show up."

She never actually saw the dragon. She burst into hysterical tears, occasionally screaming at her dad that he *lied* to her, until her mother walked in and stopped the video. O'Donnell cried for hours that weekend, and days later she would start sobbing again for no apparent reason.

She'd bought the video as a teenager, planning to watch that scene again and laugh at her own childish naive tantrum, only to find herself blubbering as Atreyu screamed for Artax to move. She'd ejected the video and smashed it.

Now, as an adult, she would occasionally feel as if she herself was trying to make her way through the Swamps of Sadness. Each step more difficult than the last until just stopping and letting the swamp swallow her sounded almost peaceful.

That was her state of mind right now.

Koch had managed to procure the search warrant and had called from Swenson's house twenty minutes before. They'd entered the premises, and the house had been empty. There was no one else there. He said he'd call if they found something they could use.

Swenson's lawyer had shown up, and they were talking in the interrogation room. It was a safe bet that they wouldn't get another useful word from Swenson, and his lawyer would insist that they let his client go. He wasn't under arrest, not yet. They had nothing tangible on him.

She took out her phone, intent on calling Koch, but her finger wavered. She dialed her husband instead.

"Hey." A tinge of chilliness in his voice. No one else would have spotted it, but she could almost feel the phone's temperature dropping. They were supposed to go to the zoo that morning. Instead, she was here.

"Hi, hon. Sorry, I think it's going to be a long day again. Something happened . . ." She wanted to tell him about Rhea Deleon. A woman walking in her neighborhood, taken by killers who raped their victims after drinking their blood. But she didn't. She'd found out long ago that talking about work at home was a bad idea. "Anyway, I'll probably miss bedtime again."

"Okay."

"Can you put Nellie on the phone?"

A moment of silence, and then, "Mommy?"

"Hey, baby."

"Guess what I have in my hand."

"Daddy's phone."

"No, in my other hand."

"I don't know. What?"

"You have to guess."

"Is it one of your dolls?"

"No."

"Uh . . . a ball?"

"No." Nellie giggled.

O'Donnell smiled. "What, then?"

"I won't tell you," Nellie said teasingly.

Apparently, O'Donnell was a worse detective than she'd thought. Not only could she not get Swenson to talk; she couldn't even convince her five-year-old. "I bet it's dog poo."

"Ew! No it isn't."

"It's smelly dog poo."

"Ew, Mom!"

"I'll tell my cop friends that Nellie is holding dog poo."

"It's not poo—it's a lollipop."

"Ah! That was my next guess." She grinned idiotically. "Baby, I might not make it until bedtime. But I'll call to say good night."

"Promise you'll call?" There was a clear tone of accusation in her question.

"Yeah, cross my heart."

"Okay, Mommy."

"Bye, baby."

"Bye."

She stared at her phone after hanging up. After a few seconds it lit up and rang. It was Koch.

"Hey," she said. "I was just about to call you."

"I've got something," Koch said. "Swenson's computer is locked, and we were told not to mess with it until our techs get their hands on it. But we found a bunch of DVDs here, and I checked a few with my laptop. It's homemade porn. Swenson appears to be the main star."

He was dying to tell her something. "And?"

"Several of the videos are of him and Catherine Lamb."

Got you. "Do you think she was aware that he was filming?"

"We already found the camera. It was well hidden. And she showed no indication in the video that she was aware of its existence."

"Bastard."

"Also, I don't know if you can use it, but he's been keeping a lot of cash hidden under his mattress. There's over five thousand dollars here. My first thought was drugs, right? But I couldn't find any here. I spoke to the guys from K-9; they're sending a dog here just in case."

"That's a good idea." She doubted he'd find any. The money wasn't related to drugs.

"That's it so far. We'll keep looking."

"Send me some photos of the cash. And call me the moment you find anything else. Great job." She hung up. She wasn't stuck anymore. She knew how to get Swenson to talk.

Nellie wasn't holding dog poo, but Swenson sure was.

CHAPTER 62

She entered the bare, brightly lit interrogation room, Tatum a step behind her. Swenson tried to seem as if he was comfortable, but O'Donnell had watched him pace the room earlier. He was on edge.

They sat down, and O'Donnell said aloud, "Detective Holly O'Donnell and Special Agent Tatum Gray, initiating the interview of Allen Swenson."

"Is my client under arrest?" the lawyer, Garry Nelson, asked.

He was bald and had a large mole on his chin. His lower lip was much thicker than the top one, giving him a toad-like demeanor. His voice, which had a croaky undertone to it, made it worse.

"No, he's not," O'Donnell said. "He's just here for questioning."

"Then I would like—"

"But we found some things when we searched his house."

"You searched my house?" Swenson yelled, the calm facade evaporating.

She slapped the copy of the search warrant on the desk. "You going into the movie business, Swenson? Found some interesting footage on your DVDs."

Nelson snatched the warrant from the desk and skimmed it. "I can have this thrown out. You got my client here on false pretenses—"

"Go ahead and try," O'Donnell said dryly. "Everything we did is perfectly within the law."

Nelson ignored her, his eyes fixed on the warrant. "I would like to confer with my client."

O'Donnell sighed. "Again?"

She and Tatum stepped outside.

"You know what this guy reminds me of?" Tatum asked.

"A toad?"

"*You too?* I keep expecting him to catch flies with his tongue."

"It's really distracting," O'Donnell agreed. "Maybe that's his strategy. He gets us confused and then hops off with his client in tow."

They both smiled. It was a tense smile, fragile. O'Donnell's nerves were frayed, and she had a feeling Tatum wasn't much better, despite his cool facade.

"It's weird that lawyers always confer," O'Donnell said. "Why not just say *talk*, like a normal person? Does anyone other than lawyers confer?"

"No. And I don't think anyone objects, either. Regular people just say, 'You're wrong.'"

"I sometimes say 'I object.'"

"No you don't."

"No," O'Donnell admitted. "I don't. But my mom used to say she objects to my tone."

"That's different. Moms can say whatever they want."

Ten minutes later, the door opened, and Nelson said they were done "conferring."

"The DVDs in my client's possession are inadmissible," Nelson announced as soon as they sat down. "You won't be able to use them in court, and any line of questioning that stems from whatever you saw on those DVDs is inadmissible as well."

O'Donnell folded her arms, annoyed. "We've been through this. The warrant permits us to search the property for—"

"For any concealed person or weapons, or any writings or records identifying the locations of those people, specifically Rhea Deleon and Rod Glover, a.k.a. Daniel Moore," Nelson said, reading from the page.

"That's right."

"And those DVDs?"

"We found them while looking for those writings and records."

"I have no issue with *that*. But I fail to see why you viewed their content."

"They could have something to do with the locations of Rod Glover and Rhea Deleon."

"How exactly?"

"Well, they could hold files pertaining to that," O'Donnell said. "Or security footage from wherever Rhea Deleon is being held."

"You're reaching, Detective. If you wanted to look through my client's electronic media and computer files, the search warrant should have stated it."

It should have; he was right. O'Donnell wanted to step outside and repeatedly kick Koch. He should have made sure the warrant contained that. But then, every second they delayed could be the last second of Rhea Deleon's life. Could she fault Koch for rushing it?

Sure she could. Damn it.

"Well, I guess the judge would have to decide if the evidence is admissible or not," she said sharply. It could go either way in court.

"If you're building your case around it—"

"Let's discuss something else. Mr. Swenson, I have your phone records here. It seems three months ago, you and Catherine Lamb called each other almost every day." She took out the phone records and showed them to him. "That's two months after the charity you two organized."

"She was my religious counselor," Swenson said. "She talked to a lot of people on a daily basis."

"That's true . . . but your conversations were quite short. None of them more than five minutes."

"My crisis of faith resolved fast."

"Your conversations occurred at the same period of time in which Terrence Finch photographed your relationship with Ms. Lamb. Since we already know you had a sexual relationship with her, and you now know I've already seen the photos, let's cut to the chase. You were calling her to meet up."

"Detective," Nelson said. "My client won't—"

"Yeah, okay, so what?" Swenson asked, raising his voice. "Is it illegal to fuck a pastor's daughter?"

"No, it's illegal to blackmail her," Tatum said. He folded his arms, his face imposing. Doing his job. Looking scary.

Swenson shook his head. "Are you out of your mind? I didn't blackmail her."

O'Donnell took out six photos from the case and laid them one next to the other. Swenson and Catherine standing close together. Swenson and Catherine kissing. Swenson holding Catherine as she tried to pull away. Swenson and Catherine—her crying, him almost smiling. Then, a photo of the cash found in Swenson's house. And finally, Catherine's body lying naked in a pool of blood.

"It tells an interesting story, doesn't it?" O'Donnell asked. "Let's summarize, and you can imagine how it'll sound in court, with the jury listening. Three months ago you began to have sex with Catherine Lamb. I doubt it was ever a real relationship. Maybe she enjoyed the rush or the forbidden fruit; I don't know. But after a few weeks, she decided to terminate your meetings. And then you told her that you were filming her the entire time. You had videos of your sexual encounters. You started blackmailing her. We saw steady withdrawals from Catherine's bank account. We can match the serial numbers to the cash we found under your mattress—"

"They can't do that, even if the numbers did match," Nelson said.

"The police maybe can't, but the FBI can," Tatum said. "We're willing to allocate a lot of resources to this case."

Tatum had actually told O'Donnell he doubted they'd be able to do it, but he bluffed well. O'Donnell continued. "*Maybe* you even insisted she keep having sex with you. I wonder what a jury would think about *that.*"

Nelson bristled. "Detective—"

"But recently something happened. You bled Catherine dry. Her account is almost empty. She told you she couldn't pay anymore and that she was about to tell her father. And you knew he would go to the police. Fortunately, you had an ace up your sleeve. Your good pal Rod Glover. As you know, we have Patrick Carpenter's testimony verifying that you two were good friends. Glover told you it was okay. He was *experienced* in that sort of thing. You went to Catherine's home and killed her together. You also raped her, for old times' sake."

Swenson shook his head. "That never—"

"Then you went and told Terrence Finch to delete any photos of you and Catherine. He can testify to it. What do you think, Swenson? If you were a juror, what would you rule? Guilty or innocent?"

Nelson turned to his client. "Don't tell them anything. We'll discuss everything later in private. They don't have anything solid, and they're trying to bully you."

"Rhea Deleon is what we really care about," Tatum said. "As far as we know, she's still alive. But every second wasted she might die. If you come clean now, give us everything you have, help us find Glover and Rhea, you might not spend the rest of your life behind bars."

"Their case hinges on inadmissible evidence," Nelson said, ignoring them.

"Really, Mr. Nelson?" O'Donnell asked. "Would you bet your client's life on it? Because it really depends on the judge. Besides, even without the DVDs, we have a pretty compelling case."

"Not to mention we still have the computer," Tatum said. "What will we find in there once we crack your password? And I promise you the bureau can crack your dumb password."

They wanted to confer again. O'Donnell stepped outside, Tatum following her.

Zoe was waiting for them out the door. "Nice work."

"What do you think?" O'Donnell asked.

"Your explanation is full of holes, of course," Zoe said. "It doesn't fit the pattern or the evidence, not to mention the profile. It doesn't explain Rhea Deleon or Henrietta Fishburne."

"Yeah." O'Donnell couldn't argue.

"But it did the job—he's scared." Zoe pointed at the monitor, where Swenson was whispering fervently with his lawyer. "Swenson doesn't have a criminal record, and it's probably his first time in a police station. He's freaked out, and his lawyer won't be able to calm him down. He'll give us something."

O'Donnell nodded. "Let's just hope that it leads us to Rhea."

"Or to Glover," Zoe said darkly.

The door opened again, Nelson standing in the doorway. His client wanted to make a deal.

CHAPTER 63

It took some convincing, but the state's attorney eventually agreed. The deal stipulated that Allen Swenson would give them everything he had on Catherine Lamb and Rod Glover. In return, they would not press charges unless he had participated in the homicide. Nelson and the state's attorney's office negotiated the various clauses for several hours. It did not matter that Rhea might be dying or that Glover was getting away, possibly planning yet another murder. The law had its own pace.

By the time they sat back down to talk to Swenson, it was dark outside. They'd raided the snack machine and O'Donnell's cache of nuts. O'Donnell was jittery with sugar and coffee, while a dull headache and nausea indicated her body wasn't happy with the abuse.

This time, she had an earphone so that Zoe could provide her own input from the other room.

"When did you first meet Rod Glover?" O'Donnell asked.

"I knew him as Daniel Moore," Swenson said. "He joined our community almost ten years ago. I don't know the exact date. But one afternoon we started talking about baseball. Daniel surprised me because he was a fan of the White Sox, like me. Most of the guys in the church were Cubs fans."

"Glover never gave a shit about baseball," Zoe said in O'Donnell's ear. "He just gave Swenson what he wanted to hear."

"We went to a game together. He seemed like a good guy. Fun to be with. He didn't give any weird vibes or anything, and I'm a good judge of character." Swenson's tone was defensive.

"Yeah, okay," O'Donnell said impatiently. "But your friendship didn't just focus on baseball, did it?"

"No. We talked about our jobs. About women. I went through an ugly divorce and told him about it. He liked talking about porn."

"What kind of porn?"

"He never got into specifics, and it was all in a sort of cheerful half-kidding sort of manner, you know? But he was interested in stuff that wasn't the usual internet vanilla."

"Was there a reason he talked to *you* about it?"

"I . . . I don't know. It must have come up somehow." Swenson seemed confused, as if now that he talked about it, he couldn't fathom how things had taken that turn. "Anyway, we were just joking around. Except a couple of years later, I met a few people online, on the dark web. They were starting a sort of marketplace for porn."

"Why would they need to go to the dark web for that?" O'Donnell asked, already knowing the answer.

Swenson glanced at Nelson, who nodded at him. This was covered by the deal. They wouldn't be able to charge him with that. "They sold illegal porn. Underage girls, fake snuff, bestiality, some really rough BDSM. People pay a lot of money for that shit. Not me. I'm a vanilla sort of guy."

"So you told Glover about it?"

"I mean, I was sorta joking, you know? We were drinking, and I told him I knew of a place where he could finally find anything for his weirdo fetishes. It's the kind of thing we'd say to each other."

"So you led him to the marketplace?"

"I first had to teach him all about Tor and bitcoin. He didn't know anything about it. He was kind of a dinosaur when it came to technology, which I always thought was weird because he worked in tech support. Anyway, he was really into it, so I showed him around a bit. Not just the porn stuff. Like, he told me he had a problem with his passport, that they always gave him a hard time when he went to Canada, so I showed him a place where he could get fake papers. I never used those services, but I knew about them."

"That's how he solidified his fake identity," Zoe said.

"What did he check out in the porn marketplace?" O'Donnell asked.

"I have no idea. It's not something we talked about, okay? Like, I asked him once, and he just told me he was into videos of my mom. That was the kind of conversations we had."

"What happened then?"

"Nothing. We kept drinking together, occasionally going to a game."

"Ask him why there are hardly any photos of him talking to Glover in church," Zoe said.

"What about church?" O'Donnell asked. "Did you talk there? Sit next to each other?"

Swenson shifted uncomfortably. "We both kind of avoided each other in church. Daniel wasn't the kind of guy I wanted around when listening to a sermon about God, you know?"

"So when did you notice Glover had a special interest in Catherine Lamb?"

"*Never.* I had no idea. Look, that's all I know about that guy, okay? A couple of months ago he disappeared. I called him a few times, he didn't answer, and I left it at that."

"You didn't have *any* contact with him after he left?"

"Absolutely not. I mean, I would have told you otherwise as soon as I saw his photo in the paper. But I honestly had no idea he was back in Chicago. You can check my phone records or whatever. I'm telling you the truth."

"If we find out you were lying, the deal's off," O'Donnell pointed out.

"I *know* that. I didn't have anything to do with him."

"Let's talk about Catherine Lamb."

A flicker of wariness, and he glanced at Nelson again. "They can't charge me for the sex thing, right?"

"Not unless you're involved with the actual murder," Nelson said.

Swenson turned back to O'Donnell. "Three months ago, Catherine and I began having sex."

"Who initiated the relationship?"

"I'd been flirting with her for a while, just for sport, you know? But one day I jokingly said we should meet in a motel. And she said yes."

With Swenson, everything was "jokingly." O'Donnell knew the type all too well. Men who would say anything with a smile, but you knew they always meant every word. They could tell you that you had nice tits, and why didn't you sit on their lap, and smile all the time, like you were in on the joke. And if you became even slightly hostile, you were the bitch who had no sense of humor. You couldn't win.

Why had Catherine fallen for that? It had probably been gradual. It hadn't happened in a single day. Maybe her way of dealing with Swenson's "jokes" was convincing herself it was actually some sort of love. Or maybe she felt a need to rebel. Or maybe she was actually attracted to the little goblin. They'd probably never know for sure.

"But you didn't always have sex in a motel."

"No, we never actually went to a motel. It was always my home."

"Where you took videos."

"I only do that for fun. And it wasn't like it was only her, you know? A lot of the women in those videos don't mind. They find it sexy."

Fun, sure. "Then what happened?"

"I wanted to try some other stuff with her. I mentioned the videos, and she flipped out." Swenson's eyes widened; his face looked hurt. "I wasn't going to *show* those videos to anyone. They were just for me. I told her I could make a copy for her, but that just upset her more." He paused.

O'Donnell didn't prompt him again. There was the cash, and they both already knew Catherine had given it to him. She waited him out.

He sighed. "*She* wanted to buy those videos from me. She said she had cash. I would have said no, except . . ."

There it was; let's hear the rationalization.

"My business was going under. I needed that money. I told her it would be a loan."

Of course you did. Asshole. Bastard. O'Donnell suddenly wished she could chuck the whole deal away. He'd given them almost nothing. And they couldn't even charge him for what he *had* given them. He was going to get away with it all.

"Did you still tell her it was a loan when she told you she had no more money? And how come you still had the videos? Wasn't she buying them from you?"

"She never told me anything about the money, okay? I just thought she had a bunch of money from her dad or the church or something. And . . . yeah, okay, I kept a copy of the videos. I mean, it was a loan anyway, and she didn't know I kept them. I wasn't even going to watch them again."

"And then what?"

"Then Patrick Carpenter called me to say she was dead. He called a lot of people that day, not just me. And yeah, I kinda freaked when I heard about it. I mean, I was sad, sure, but I was worried you guys might get the wrong idea. And when I saw the agent here at the church, looking at the photos, I remembered that I once saw Terrence take a photo of us when we were close. So I went over and told him to delete those photos. But that was *it*. I never had anything to do with Catherine's murder. I swear."

CHAPTER 64

Zoe sat in the task force room going through the interview transcript for the tenth time, hoping to spot something they'd missed. O'Donnell and Tatum were still with Swenson, grilling him. Trying to catch him at an inconsistency, at a lie. Searching for any tidbit that would shed light on Glover's whereabouts. Or Rhea's.

Every piece of evidence recovered from Swenson's house just solidified his testimony. Could he still be unsub beta? Glover's accomplice?

She tried to imagine a chain of events that fit the evidence they'd uncovered. Swenson had a short fling with Catherine, filming her in the process. Meanwhile his obsession about blood consumption grew. He began fantasizing about drinking her blood. Maybe he bit her during sex; Zoe would have to look through the videos. He went off his meds, becoming more and more volatile.

Then, when Catherine found out about the videos, Swenson began blackmailing her. Eventually she threatened to blow the whistle, and he killed her with Glover, also giving in to his urges and drinking her blood.

Once he did it the first time, he had to do it again. Already off his meds, he lost himself to his urges. So he worked with Glover, helping him to kill Henrietta. Then Rhea . . .

It was tenuous. It didn't work. The evidence didn't indicate that unsub beta had any sexual interest in Catherine Lamb. The blackmail didn't fit with the profile of unsub beta either, who wasn't one to take the initiative. Unsub beta didn't plan. He followed. He *reacted*. And, of course, it didn't explain all the missing pieces. The pentagram and the knife. Glover's agenda in all this.

But the thing that struck her the most was that Swenson kept it together throughout the interrogation. Sure, they rattled him, and he was scared, but he didn't exhibit any behavioral patterns that Zoe would expect from a man going through a psychotic episode. He was lucid and rational.

Had she been wrong about the whole thing? Could Glover's relationship with his accomplice be just that—a friendship between two cold-blooded killers?

No. The evidence didn't support it, and her gut didn't support it either. Unsub beta was spiraling out of control.

Which meant only one thing. Swenson wasn't the unsub. He wasn't a killer. And Glover's accomplice, the real killer, was still out there.

CHAPTER 65

"I'm sorry," the pharmacist said. "I can't give you antibiotics without a prescription."

"It's for an infection," he said again, battling the frustration, no, the rage that bubbled up in his gut. He had to stay in control. "From a nasty scratch."

"I understand, sir, but I need a prescription."

She stared at him strangely. Could she see the *real* him, beyond his facade of normalcy? Had it emerged through his skin? He reflexively touched his cheek, but it felt the same as always.

"Do you have something for cancer? Brain cancer?" He wasn't certain about the exact terminology. Perhaps he should have brought Daniel's latest test results. But he didn't even know if Daniel kept them, or where.

The pharmacist exchanged glances with her coworker. As if he couldn't see it. As if he didn't understand what was going on. They thought he was weird. Maybe they *knew*. Maybe they knew about Catherine, and about the woman in the train station, and about the third one currently in his house.

"Do you mean pain medication?"

"No . . . something . . ." Something that would fix the tumor. But that was idiotic; he should have known that. If there had been such a thing, Daniel would have taken it already.

It was the third pharmacy he'd gone to. *Third*. And that was after being delayed earlier. He checked the time, and a wave of dizziness made him lean against the counter, faint.

"Sir, are you okay?"

How was it possible? Could it really be the afternoon already? He tried to recall the day, remembered bits and pieces. Fragments of conversations. He'd panicked for a while and had been forced to catch his breath in the car. But that had been just ten or twenty minutes, right?

"Sir?"

He turned around and left. The man behind him in line seemed to shrink to the side to avoid touching him. They could all *see*. He'd finally lost control.

He'd go to a different pharmacy. The pharmacist was just a bitch, like the others. She didn't want to help him. Daniel had been right: some women were just bitches. They just wanted men to suffer. He'd talk to a male pharmacist next time.

And then he saw the newspaper stand.

It was as if someone had punched him in the stomach. There were pictures of that woman on most of them. Rhea Deleon, the headlines called her. And pictures of Daniel.

But it was the picture of Catherine that really got to him. One of the newspapers had a picture of her on the front page. It wasn't the usual picture the newspapers used, the pretty one from the picnic. No, they used one when she looked slightly sideways, with a tiny sad smile. A real-life version of the *Mona Lisa*. His dad had once told him, when he was a child, that the *Mona Lisa* always seemed to look at you, no matter where you stood. It had scared him back then. And he could see it now.

Catherine watched him.

The dark secrets. He knew what they were talking about. Catherine knew about him. About his craving for blood. She would tell everyone all about him. Just like Daniel had said she would.

That cryptic smile. He knew it all too well. How many times had she smiled like that when he'd talked to her? It was the smile of a person who saw right through all your facades. Saw your twisted, sick true self.

He stumbled away. Began walking hurriedly back home. All the people he brushed past followed him with their gazes. He wanted to shut his eyes so he couldn't see them staring. Halfway home he remembered that he had actually driven to the pharmacy, and now he'd left the car in the parking lot.

It didn't matter. He wasn't going back for it. He could walk; his house wasn't too far anyway.

It started raining.

He would get home and have a hot shower. And then maybe later, Daniel and he could watch some TV.

Except the woman was in the bathroom. And Daniel's brain had been consumed by a malignant tumor that wanted to infect *him* as well.

Was Daniel still in his own body, somewhere? Could he maybe still save him? Daniel had been there for him so many times. He owed it to Daniel to do everything in his power to save him.

He reached the front door of their house, unlocked it, stepped inside.

Something was wrong; he could feel it as soon as he closed the door behind him. Daniel waited for him in the kitchen, holding a bottle of beer, smiling warmly.

"You're drenched!" Daniel said cheerily. "You must be freezing. Go change—I'll make you a cup of tea."

The bathroom door was shut. He stepped toward it, and Daniel stepped into his path.

"We need to talk. Something happened while you were gone," Daniel said.

"What?" His voice was high. Panicky.

"That woman managed to free herself. She had a knife. I had to take care of it."

He pushed Daniel aside, lunged at the door, swung it open.

The woman lay in the bathtub, motionless, eyes staring at nothing.

It was then that he finally knew. Daniel was beyond saving. The tumor had consumed him completely. Because Daniel would *never* have done this to him.

"I know you're upset," the tumor said in a measured tone behind him. "And I promise we'll find someone else. With even better blood. But first we need to fix this."

He had to stay focused. Because the most important thing right now was to stop the tumor from infecting him as well. He saw the scalpel on the floor, bent, and picked it up.

"See? She had that thing with her. I don't know how she got it. I think you may have been a bit careless when—"

He turned around and thrust the scalpel at the tumor. The tumor stepped back, shouting, and the blade nicked its shoulder.

"What the hell are you doing?" the tumor screamed. "Put that down, you psycho!"

He swung it in a wild arc, cutting the tumor's chest. Panic and rage churned in his mind. He was truly out of control now.

"Jesus," the tumor blurted, stumbling back. It raised its hands in a conciliatory gesture. "Listen, put the knife down, we can talk about—"

Another swing. A spurt of blood from the tumor's hand.

The tumor turned around and bolted outside.

He stood there, staring at the open door. The rain had built up to a torrent, water pouring from the sky, crashing on the earth in a horrendous constant cacophony that matched the noise in his mind. He trembled with fury at the unfairness of it all. They'd been doing so *well*.

He shut the door, stumbling to his room, letting the scalpel tumble from his fingers to the floor. A feral, helpless sob escaped his mouth. It had all gone to pieces. He noticed the laptop on his desk. Abchanchu had sent him a message, asking him if he'd gotten what he needed. For a moment he panicked, thinking he was somehow talking about Daniel. About the tumor. How did he know? Did everyone know?

But then he recalled that chart. Useless now.

He put on his costume and typed a quick answer. Sure, thanks. Maintain that semblance of control. The costume. The disguise.

Suddenly, he couldn't see the point. The woman was gone. Daniel was gone. Everything had gone to hell despite his effort to stay in control.

Screaming, he tore his laptop from the few wires it was connected to and bashed it over and over on the desk. Storming out to the kitchen, he grabbed the beer bottle that the tumor had left behind and smashed it on the counter, feeling a blaze of pain in his palm as he cut himself. Dripping blood, he went through the house throwing and kicking chairs, books, discarded takeout boxes. He destroyed Daniel's computer as well, slamming it against the wall repeatedly until the screen was a spiderweb of cracks, the keyboard keys scattered everywhere.

Breathing hard, he entered the bathroom and touched the woman's cheek, leaving a red streak of blood on it.

She was still warm. He touched her neck and felt a weak, but steady, pulse.

He let out a shuddering, relieved breath. The rain poured on, great cacophonous torrents of water hitting the house's shuttered windows.

CHAPTER 66

"Guess what?" Tatum said, walking into the task force room. "I just talked to Barb."

"Who's Barb?" Zoe asked tiredly.

"The computer wiz. The one who made the Trojan horse? It turns out that Dracula2 answered in the chat and logged off an hour ago."

It took Zoe a second to catch on. "Swenson was still here an hour ago."

"Yup."

"Could he have logged off with his phone? Or—"

"I was *with* him an hour ago, Zoe. He didn't log off with his phone."

"Then that clinches it. He isn't Glover's accomplice. He's not unsub beta."

"You don't sound surprised."

She sighed. "The evidence didn't make sense any other way. What did Dracula2 say on the chat?"

"He wrote, 'Sure, thanks.' He was answering the question I asked him, if he got what he needed from the file."

"But he didn't open the file?"

"No. Maybe he figured out that it was a trap." Tatum shook his head and crossed the room, slumping into an empty chair.

Zoe groaned and leaned back. Looking at the task force room, it was impossible to guess that it was Saturday night. The majority of the investigators were in the room, talking on the phone, updating the whiteboards, tapping on their laptops. O'Donnell wasn't there, but Zoe could hear her talking outside the room on the phone. She sounded furious.

Martinez slid his chair next to hers. "I just got off the phone with Rhea Deleon's doctor," he said.

"Why?"

"I'm trying to figure out why she was returning home so late from work. The doctor was one of the people Rhea talked to on the phone that day. Anyway, it turns out Rhea had severe anemia. Do you think the unsub knew that? Perhaps that's why he targeted her?"

Zoe bit her lip. "The evidence doesn't look like he targeted her. It looked like a random abduction. But maybe it affected the taste of her blood. And that could change his behavior."

"That could explain why we haven't found the body yet."

That was one of the many questions they were grappling with. Catherine and Henrietta had been found soon after their murders. In Henrietta's case, Glover had made sure it would happen. But they were getting close to forty-eight hours since Rhea's disappearance, and there was no sign of her body.

"It's possible," Zoe said.

"Maybe they kept her alive."

"Or maybe the unsub decided as a result to eat her entire body," Zoe said.

Martinez sighed. "You sure can give everything a positive spin."

"Cannibalistic behavior among serial killers isn't rare, and it's a natural progression from blood drinking."

O'Donnell strode into the room, fuming. She stomped over to Zoe. "I need a cigarette break."

"Okay." Zoe frowned. "Why are you telling me that?"

"Because I want you to come with me."

"I don't smoke."

"Neither do I. But I still need a break."

Zoe shrugged and followed O'Donnell out to the hallway. They crossed it and stepped into a room with a small gray couch, a round table with several magazines, and a potted plant. A large window faced the highway. Headlights twinkled as cars drove past. O'Donnell trudged over to the window and exhaled loudly.

"What is this room?" Zoe asked, looking around her. It almost seemed like a waiting room at a doctor's office.

"It's an interview room," O'Donnell said. "For people we want to make comfortable. Family members, frightened witnesses, that sort of thing. It's also a good place to chill, late at night, when you feel like punching a wall."

"Do you feel like punching a wall?"

"I feel like punching my husband."

"Oh."

"And Bright. And Manny. And this entire damn department."

Zoe walked over to O'Donnell, unsure what she was doing there.

"It was my husband on the phone," O'Donnell said. "He was angry I left him with the kid on a Saturday night."

"It's not exactly your fault that Rhea Deleon got abducted," Zoe said.

"That's what *I* said. But it turns out some random detective from the department posted a picture of his children sleeping on Facebook an hour ago. And guess who's Facebook friends with him? That's right, my husband."

"So what?"

"My husband," O'Donnell explained, "thinks that this guy is maintaining a healthy family-work balance. He wants me to *learn* from him."

"You can explain to him that the entire task force is here."

"He doesn't want to hear it, Zoe. If you just had to listen to his endless bitching like I did, you'd know." O'Donnell shut her eyes. "Sorry for dragging you out like that. But I had to vent, and I have no one else in this damn place to talk to."

"It's okay."

"Besides, you're a shrink, right? You're probably used to it."

Zoe frowned. "I'm a forensic psychologist. When I talk to patients, they're mostly violent criminals."

"I'm pretty violent right now," O'Donnell said cheerfully. "So that works for me."

"I'm sure your husband understands."

O'Donnell shook her head. "He doesn't. Not that it matters. I'm probably on my way out of Violent Crimes. Bright pretty much told me that a few hours ago. My husband will be thrilled."

"Oh." Zoe recalled O'Donnell going to Bright's office to talk to him. "I'm sorry. Is this because of that thing with your ex-partner?"

O'Donnell shrugged. "It's part of it. For a while I figured I could just try to hang in there. The rumors would pass. And if I handled my cases well, then at least Bright would see it's worth keeping me. But two out of my five homicide cases in the past year are still open. And now this case is going nowhere. Bright isn't stupid. No one wants to partner with me, and I have that thing with Manny hanging over my head."

"Well, I doubt Bright is actually paying attention to the rumors about you being a rat," Zoe said. "Like you said, he isn't stupid."

O'Donnell broodingly leaned her forehead on the windowpane. "I informed on Manny to Internal Affairs."

"Oh." Zoe didn't know what to say to that.

"I didn't do it because I was sleeping with him or sleeping with the IA guy, and I didn't cut a deal. All the rumors are bullshit. But I did rat him out." O'Donnell's voice cracked.

She seemed to curl into herself as she talked. She suddenly looked like a tiny, lost child. Zoe hesitated, then put her hand on O'Donnell's shoulder.

O'Donnell glanced at her, eyes wet. "It's not like I have a stick up my ass. Some cops are dirty, but they're still good cops. When I was in uniform, I saw my partner skim five hundred dollars off a drug dealer we busted. He wanted to cut it with me, and I refused. But I didn't rat him out. This job . . . civilians don't even know how many times a day cops need to fight temptations. People slip. Especially when everyone assumes we're all dirty anyway. I *get* it."

"But with Manny it was different?"

"He had drug dealers paying him on a monthly basis. He had a whole racket with two different defense lawyers—he busted dealers, gave them a lawyer's card, and if that lawyer got the client, Manny got twenty percent. I saw him take money from a pimp twice. And he kept telling me I need to take some of it. That way, he'd know he could trust me. And you know what? I almost did. Because at that point it was either be a rat or be dirty, and I couldn't even figure out which was worse."

"But you didn't."

O'Donnell wiped her cheek with the back of her hand. "No, I didn't. You'd think I'd feel good about having a backbone or whatever, but frankly, half the time, I've regretted it. It would have been so much easier. Instead, I went to Internal Affairs and gave them what I had. And now I'm the department's rat."

"You did the right thing," Zoe said, feeling the hollowness of her words.

"Yeah? Well, they don't give awards for that."

Zoe squeezed O'Donnell's shoulder. Then, after a moment of silence, she said, "I sometimes regret going after Glover."

O'Donnell blinked, looking surprised. "Why?"

"After he got away, things weren't the same for me. Some people thought I'd made it all up. I didn't have a lot of friends. And it hasn't changed since. I didn't have to do it, not really; I was just a teenager. I could let the police do their job. It's not like he was arrested because of what I did. He stayed free. Kept killing. So I sometimes wonder what would have happened if I just did nothing. Grown up to do something else. Hanging around with friends, maybe have a family like you. Without this *thing* hovering over me. Without getting creepy letters from him, without putting my sister in danger."

Neither of them moved or said anything for a few minutes.

"I'm done feeling sorry for myself," O'Donnell said.

"Okay," Zoe said. "Let's go. I need to go over your transcripts of the interviews with the men from the list I gave you, in case you missed something."

CHAPTER 67

Sunday, October 23, 2016

His phone rang, making him jump. He'd been sitting in the kitchen staring at the morning sunlight filtering through the window. For how long? An hour? Two?

He vaguely recognized the name on the phone's screen. He needed to answer that call, just like he'd needed to answer the previous four, but he couldn't find it in him. Answering that phone meant wearing his "normal" costume. It meant that he had to contain all those emotions and impulses and fears behind a facade of calm.

And he couldn't. He had lost control.

"Aren't you going to answer that?" Daniel asked.

Daniel had returned last night, his face sheepish and apologetic. He'd taken one look at his friend's eyes and had seen it really was Daniel, not the tumor, in control. So he'd let him in. Daniel had apologized, and he'd said there was no need to be sorry. He knew the tumor had done that, not Daniel. Besides, the woman was still alive. Daniel had been happy to hear that.

"No," he said. "It doesn't matter. They'll call back later."

But it mattered, he knew. He was letting his life fall apart. At some point, someone would notice. Daniel had told him over and over to make sure he maintained his routines.

The phone stopped ringing.

"Want to go for a walk?" Daniel asked.

He gaped at his friend in surprise. Daniel never went on walks with him. It was too dangerous. "What if someone recognizes you?"

"That picture doesn't look anything like me."

That was true. Cancer had consumed Daniel's body. His face was almost a skull, the skin stretched on it like shrink-wrap. His hair was falling out in clumps. He looked terrible.

But at least no one would recognize him.

He got up and opened the door to the bathroom. "We're going out for a little while," he said.

The woman gave him a beseeching look. She didn't look too great herself. He tried to recall when he'd last let her drink. That morning? The night before? He'd have to do that when they returned.

They walked side by side, passersby ignoring them. He was relieved. When he was on the streets alone, people always stared at him. But when he was with a friend, they didn't pay him any attention.

Maybe people just thought that a man walking alone was strange. Maybe they liked everyone to be paired up. A man and his wife. A couple of friends. Boyfriend and girlfriend. A man and his dog. A mother and her child. Things had to come in twos. Just like in Noah's ark.

"We need to go hunting again," Daniel said.

"I know. But . . . can it wait? Just a few more nights?" He didn't like the idea of leaving the woman alone in the house just yet.

"You know we can't."

It was true; they couldn't. Daniel's time was running out. And besides, *he* had stopped drinking the woman's blood, giving her time to get better.

They strode by a kiosk, and his gaze was drawn to the familiar face.

Catherine, her eyes following him, a real-life *Mona Lisa*. He paused, transfixed. She knew his secrets. All his dark secrets.

"She'll tell everyone," he murmured. "She knows."

"Not if we stop her," Daniel said, just like he'd said two weeks ago. "Buy them. Buy them all."

The man in control approached the kiosk owner. "The *Chicago Daily Gazette*," he said. "How much?"

The vendor offered a copy to him. "One dollar."

"I want them all."

The man blinked, confused. "All?"

"All the copies of the *Chicago Daily Gazette*."

"I have more than two hundred here."

"I want them all." He took out his wallet.

"I'll have to count them."

That would take ages. And Catherine would be staring at him the entire time. "No. I'll pay three hundred. For all of them."

The man considered it, then nodded, looking pleased.

He took out three bills from his wallet. Daniel always insisted they carried enough cash with them. Plastic created a trail.

The bag with the papers was heavy, but it didn't matter. It felt good to be doing something about Catherine's stares. "Let's go home," he told Daniel.

CHAPTER 68

"We need to review the case from the start," O'Donnell said.

Zoe nodded. She was right. Their current path led them nowhere. They had to contemplate other possibilities.

The three of them sat in the situation room by themselves. It was Sunday morning, and several members of the task force hadn't shown up yet. Zoe wondered if Albert Lamb was at church, preaching. If the congregation had gathered. She'd wanted to go there herself, see the service, but O'Donnell insisted they stay away, that after the previous day, their presence would be problematic. Bright had sent a detective who wasn't related to the case to watch the proceedings and take a few pictures.

"Let's entertain the possibility that Glover's partner, our unsub, doesn't belong to the church at all," Tatum said.

An instant tug of rage. She almost snapped at him. *Of course* the unsub belonged to the church.

Except maybe he didn't. Did they actually have a shred of proof that he was a member?

A profiler's job essentially wasn't finding the killer. That was always the police's role. A profiler needed to point the police in the right direction. To reduce the group of suspects from *everyone* to a manageable crowd. But if the profiler made a mistake, if a part of his profile was wrong, the killer could be outside the tight group of suspects. And the cops would ignore him because he didn't fit with what the profiler had said. The worst possible thing to do then would be to cling to the existing profile.

"Okay," she said. "Let's assume I was wrong. The unsub is not part of the church community."

Tatum looked startled as she said it, almost as if she'd spoken in an alien language.

"In that case," O'Donnell said, "Glover chose Catherine as the victim for *his* reasons. Maybe she knew something about him. Maybe she'd seen him return to Chicago, and he was worried she would tell someone."

"And he met his accomplice somewhere else," Zoe said. "Like on the dark web."

"We know Dracula2 was on the dark web," Tatum said. "That's where the vampires forum is."

Zoe waited for the rush of ideas to manifest, but all she felt was frustration. She tried imagining it: Glover approaching a stranger on the dark web, abandoning all his real-life charm, replacing it with chat acronyms and emojis. And convincing a stranger to go on a killing spree with him. Sometimes, an idea felt so wrong its presence in your brain was almost like a pebble in a shoe. It distracted you, everything else becoming hard until you got it out.

"I don't like it," Tatum said. "It doesn't fit. Glover wouldn't put the cross on Catherine. He would take it as a trophy. And if the unsub didn't know her, he wouldn't have done it either, because he wouldn't be aware it existed."

"And those crime reports," O'Donnell said. "They do intersect with the area of the church."

Zoe exhaled, relieved. "So we think he's in the church."

"It does fit. But he wasn't on the list of names you gave me," O'Donnell said.

"Maybe he was and just had a good poker face," Tatum suggested.

"He is spinning out of control. It's very unlikely he could withstand a prolonged conversation, not to mention a police interrogation," Zoe said. "Could you have missed his odd behavior when you interviewed him? A facial tic? A stutter?"

"No," O'Donnell said sharply. Zoe recognized that tone well. She used it often enough when people suggested that she'd messed something up.

"Let's assume he wasn't, then," Tatum said hurriedly. "Who else do we have?"

"All the other people on the list are very unlikely," Zoe said tiredly. "But we can go over each one and discuss why."

"What about people who aren't on the list?" Tatum said.

"There *are* names on Patrick's list that don't appear on the list you got from Albert," O'Donnell agreed.

They had the lists printed out in three copies, and each of them went over them, looking for discrepancies.

"I've got twelve extra names," O'Donnell finally said.

"Me too," Zoe said.

"I have thirteen," Tatum said. "You missed one. Patrick Carpenter isn't on either of the lists."

He was right. Patrick's name wasn't on the list O'Donnell had gotten from Patrick. And when Zoe had written down all the members with Albert, they'd ignored Patrick, since obviously she already knew who he was. They stared at the lists for a few seconds in silence.

"It could be Patrick. It fits," O'Donnell finally said. "He knew Catherine well. He lives in the area we marked likely for the killer's address."

"He's married, though," Tatum pointed out. "Wouldn't his wife notice something strange?"

"She's been in the hospital for almost two weeks," O'Donnell said. "She was hospitalized just after we assume the unsub stopped taking his medication."

"He's been absent from church, supposedly because of his wife," Zoe said.

"Does he fit the profile?" O'Donnell asked.

"His age and physical appearance fit," Zoe said. "He might be obsessive. He would definitely have regrets after killing Catherine and would feel the urge to cover her body."

"Didn't his wife tell us something about being pure?" O'Donnell asked. "Just like that weird phrase of *pure blood* Dracula2 used. Maybe she got the idea from her husband."

"But is he someone who could be manipulated? A follower?" Tatum asked skeptically. "He seemed quite controlling himself. He has a lot of presence in the congregation. Would he be the kind of partner Glover would want? I don't think he'd follow instructions that easily."

Zoe nodded. That was a good point, except . . . "He didn't actually have a lot of presence in the photos," she said. "He appeared a few times, but it was Catherine who was the dominant one in all those pictures. Catherine and Glover. Maybe Patrick wasn't as important in the community as we thought. In fact, it could result in aggression toward Catherine, who *was*. He could view her as someone who was stealing his place."

Tatum seemed skeptical. "That doesn't mean anything. Didn't you say that Albert didn't appear a lot in the photographs either? Some people don't like their pictures taken. And maybe the photographer didn't like him. Or maybe he spent a lot of time in the church's back room or something. Those photos don't actually represent the whole truth."

That was true, and Zoe had a hard time imagining Glover approaching a religious counselor, trying to manipulate him into killing someone. Glover would want an accomplice who didn't draw attention.

Something Tatum had said niggled at her. She didn't like the idea of the unsub being Patrick. She wanted to move on. But there was one thing that rang true. That they'd overlooked. Maybe something Patrick had done? Maybe he'd covered for the unsub? Or . . .

She suddenly felt dizzy.

Those photos don't actually represent the whole truth.

She'd treated the photos as a straightforward representation of what went on in the church life, but that wasn't actually true, was it? Sure, Catherine Lamb and Rod Glover were clearly more dominant in the pictures than any other person, but that didn't necessarily mean they were dominant in the church's community.

What it could mean was that they were dominant in the photographer's perception.

In her years of working with murder files, Zoe had begun treating photographs as if they represented the entire case. Police photographers were professionals who didn't make actual *choices*. They documented everything. But this photographer wasn't a police photographer at all.

And there was something else.

"The photographer wasn't on my list either," she said, her voice almost a whisper. "He was in *every single shot*, but he was the one taking them. Albert and I never even discussed him."

"Does he fit?" O'Donnell asked.

Did he?

Like a glove.

"He's Caucasian, of average height. The photos he took demonstrate his interest both in Catherine and in Glover. He's definitely a follower. Tatum and I saw him following a client's instructions to the letter. And he gave us the pictures without a lot of argument. But he also folded when Swenson demanded that he delete *his* pictures. He does what everyone tells him. Glover would have easily noticed that. He's been in the church for years. Judging by the photos, he was close to Catherine. He's . . ." She was about to say he might be obsessive, but then she realized it didn't matter. She'd been reading the evidence wrong.

"Oh god," she groaned. "The pacing in circles. It's not an obsessive ritual. He took pictures!"

Those footprints. Three steps, turning to face the victim. Then again and again. She thought of Terrence Finch in his studio, circling the toddler he was photographing, taking pictures from all angles.

"And that was what the necklace was about, and the pentagram, and the knife. It was a *setting*. They were props for his pictures."

"She's too dark," O'Donnell said. "Remember? The drug addict, Tony, told us one of the killers had said, 'She's too dark.' We thought it was a racial preference, but maybe he was talking about how she appeared in the photo. He was looking through the photos and saw that they weren't good enough."

"That guy Tony also mentioned flashes of lights, right?" Tatum said. "We thought it was an effect of the crack, but maybe those were actual flashes, from a camera."

"Why would he take staged pictures of the murders?" O'Donnell asked.

"I don't know yet," Zoe said. "Killers sometimes took pictures of their crimes for later sexual relief. But this murderer didn't kill for sexual pleasure. And besides, if that was the case, he wouldn't use props."

"Hang on," O'Donnell said. "Didn't you talk to Finch yesterday?"

She had. And he'd kept the phone conversation short, agreeing almost too quickly to give her the missing pictures. Because, as she'd said just a few minutes before, he was spinning out of control and couldn't withstand a prolonged conversation. And maybe because she'd threatened him with a search warrant, and he knew they'd find a lot more if they actually came looking.

"I missed it," she muttered. "It was him, and I missed it. We need to get there."

"Hang on—we have nothing solid," O'Donnell pointed out. "Give me a few moments. I'm making a phone call." She stepped out.

Zoe shut her eyes. "I've talked to him. I could have seen it, but I was too distracted. What if Rhea—"

"We don't know anything for certain yet," Tatum said. "It's just conjecture."

Zoe didn't bother arguing. It was far more than conjecture. It *fit*. Like nothing else so far. She could imagine Glover spotting Terrence as he took photos. Maybe he could see a darkness there already, the way Terrence sometimes took photos when people didn't notice. Trying to catch them off guard, whipping out the camera. Glover would approach him, say he liked photography too. Befriend him. Find out the man's weaknesses.

Or maybe Terrence had gone to *him*, when Albert Lamb had told them anyone who was struggling with darkness could approach Glover. Maybe Terrence had needed to get something off his chest.

O'Donnell returned to the room, her expression grim and alert. "I just talked to Swenson. He never threatened to sue Finch. He threatened to expose Finch's secret. Something he'd heard from Glover on one of their guy-to-guy talks."

Zoe's gut sank. There it was.

"Apparently, Finch was obsessed with the notion of drinking human blood."

CHAPTER 69

He dropped the bag with the *Chicago Daily Gazette* copies on the floor, letting them spill out, Catherine's all-knowing eyes staring at him from multiple angles. She knew; she would tell. He had to fix it.

No. He had to focus. First he had to take care of the woman.

He went to the bathroom, crouched by her side. He gently removed the gag.

"Can you get me some water?" she whispered, voice cracking.

He nodded, went to the kitchen, and filled a glass of water. He put it to her lips and tipped it, and she drank. Some of it spilled, dribbling down her chin. He felt her forehead, relieved to see it was no longer burning. She was getting better.

Was she doing well enough? Could he drink from her?

He almost went to get a scalpel, but if he accidentally killed her, he would never taste her again. Now that he knew what actual pure blood tasted like, he couldn't afford to take any risks.

"I have to take care of something now," he told her. "But as soon as I'm done, I'll get you some food, okay?"

"Okay."

He left the bathroom and went to get the newspapers. He took a quick glance at the topmost paper, meeting Catherine's stare. "I'm sorry," he muttered. "I have to do it; I'm so sorry."

"You're only doing what you have to," Daniel told him, sitting on the couch. "Don't apologize. It's this country and the insurance companies. They forced our hand. *They* were the ones who did it, not us."

He placed the pile of newspapers on the table and picked up the top one. "I remember taking that picture," he said sadly.

"It was when we painted that shelter," Daniel said. "It was a nice day."

"The sunlight caught her face just right. It was supposed to be a profile picture, but she noticed me taking the photo, and she turned. And smiled that smile of hers."

"It's a great picture," Daniel agreed. "But you have to take care of it."

"I have to take care of it."

He tore the page and crumpled it, dropping it on the floor. Then he took the next newspaper, tore it as well. The sound of the ripping newspaper made him shiver. Almost as if it were Catherine's screams. As if by tearing her picture, he caused her pain.

"I'm sorry," he said again. "I'm sorry." He tore another paper and crumpled it. The papers piled on the floor around his feet.

"You should get the matches," Daniel said.

"How much longer?" Tatum asked, teeth gritting.

O'Donnell looked out her window at the lone house. "Twenty minutes. That's what they said."

He knew that. He was being the obnoxious kid, asking his parents repeatedly if they were there yet. But damn it, the house was right there. And they could see movement through the closed shutters. Terrence Finch was home.

But he was dangerous, even more so if Glover was there as well. And if they were holding Rhea Deleon in that house, it could devolve into a hostage situation fast. Waiting for SWAT was definitely the right thing to do.

Still, it was hard to fight the urge that kept prodding him to move, move, move. The house was right there.

"What if they're killing Rhea Deleon right now?" he asked. "We need to move."

"That's highly unlikely," Zoe said from the back seat. "Why would they kill her at this very minute?"

Tatum glanced at the other car, in which Koch and Sykes waited. Unmarked cars, and they were keeping their distance. But still, what if Glover glanced out the window? Or Finch? After all, Finch was probably highly paranoid. If he just saw an unfamiliar car outside his home . . .

He checked the time. Eighteen minutes.

The crumpled newspapers covered the entire floor. He lit a match and held it by one of the papers. It caught quickly, and he watched, fascinated, as the flame danced, the paper's color morphing from white to brown and finally black, the fire flickering.

And then it died, a wisp of smoke curling upward.

He tried again, lighting a second match. This time, the flame hardly seemed to take before it died.

"I think the paper may be too damp," he said.

Daniel didn't answer. He looked through the shutters, frowning.

"I'll get the cooking oil," he muttered. He went to the kitchen, got the bottle of cooking oil, and returned to the living room. He squirted the oil on the papers, emptying half the bottle.

Then he lit a third match.

It caught fast this time.

"Is that smoke?" Tatum asked, squinting.

"Damn it, you're right—it's smoke!" O'Donnell flung her door open. "Let's go, let's go!"

Tatum's body shot from his seat like a tightly coiled spring. He was out of the car and running, pulling his gun from its holster. Koch and Sykes were running as well, shouting.

They'd parked far from the house. Too far, it seemed now. Much too far.

Tatum sprinted for the house, the wind shrieking in his ears, praying they would get there in time. He glimpsed something bright and orange through a crack in the shutters. Flames.

"The back!" he shouted at Koch. "Cover the back of the house!"

Koch changed his direction, running toward the back of the house. Sykes slowed down and suddenly turned back. Tatum had no idea what the man was doing. He pointed his gun at the window, the muzzle wavering as he ran. He hoped Zoe had stayed in the car. This could turn into a firefight. Reflexes kicked in, his mind processing the scene, his own backup, the possible dangers, eyes intent on the windows, searching for movement.

One of the shutters shifted slightly, a figure beyond it.

Tatum changed his direction, staying away from the window, sprinting for the front door.

Smoke curled through several windows now. Flames flickered behind the shutters.

The smoke was thick in the living room, and he was coughing hard. He went over to the bathroom and closed the door, not wanting the woman to suffocate. He should open a window, let the smoke out. But Daniel had told him to keep the shutters closed ever since they'd taken the woman.

"Daniel, I'm opening a window!" he cried, though his voice cracked as he doubled over, coughing helplessly. The living room table had caught fire and was now blazing. It was hot and almost impossible to breathe. His eyes teared up from the smoke, and the world became a hazy blur.

But knowing the fire had finally silenced Catherine felt good.

He went to the window and opened it, letting the smoke out. He blinked, watching the street outside through his teary eyes. Someone ran toward the house. As his sight focused, he saw the gun in the man's hands.

"Daniel, cops!" he shouted.

"I can see them," Daniel said, standing by his side. "Listen, I have to run. If they catch me here, it'll be over. You know that, right?"

Of course he knew that. Daniel was a wanted man. "Go! I'll stall them." He slammed the window shut.

Daniel dashed to the guest room. Good, he could leave through the window. Get as far away as possible. But he needed time.

Was the door locked? He stepped toward it and stumbled, tipping the bottle of cooking oil as he tried to gain his balance. The oil spilled on his pants.

And the flames rose.

Tatum reached the door a second before O'Donnell, and gave it a solid kick. He heard the wood crack, and the door swung open, filling the air with smoke. The fire roared, feeding on the oxygen from the doorway, the heat driving Tatum to stumble backward, hand protecting his face. His eyes teared up from the billowing clouds of soot and ash, glimpsing vague shapes of furniture—an upturned chair, a couch, a coffee table.

Deeper inside, a voice screamed in pain. Finch.

"Run!" Finch shouted. "Daniel, they're here! Get out!"

Tatum stumbled into the room, coughing. Through billowing columns of smoke and hazy hot air, he saw Finch flailing, his clothes on fire.

"Run!" Finch screamed again.

Tatum lunged at Finch, felt the shock as he collided into the man, knocking him to the floor. Finch twisted and rolled, screeching in pain, the flames that had caught his clothes flickering. Tatum swatted at the flames on the man's pants, putting them out, vaguely feeling the scorching heat on his own skin.

"Tatum!" O'Donnell coughed behind him.

"The windows!" Tatum roared at her. "Cover the windows. Glover is making a break for it!"

She ran back outside. Tatum peered through the hazy air. Was Rhea Deleon here?

Sykes ran into the house, holding a red fire extinguisher. The air filled with particles of white foam as he sprayed. The flames died around them, the air becoming almost impossible to see through.

"Watch your back," Tatum said, coughing, peering through the haze.

"Is Glover here?" Zoe shouted behind him.

"I don't know," Tatum croaked. "Get out of here! Check outside." He got up, pulling Finch with him, forcing the man to his feet. He shouted at Sykes, "Cuff him! I'll check the rest of the house."

Heart pounding, he went through the first door, gun muzzle sweeping the room, his eye catching quick details beyond the clouds of smoke. Broken furniture. Bloodstains on the floor and the walls. One window, latched from inside. Glover hadn't gotten out through there. "Clear!"

Sharp burning pain on his palms and arms crept through his adrenaline-addled brain, and he forced himself to ignore it. He kicked through the next door, swiveling as he thought he heard something. It was another bedroom, with a single bed and a small nightstand. A large window, also shut and latched from inside. "Clear!"

Third door. Kicked it open, forced himself to sweep the bathroom, even as he saw the woman slumped in the bathtub. There was no one else there. He coughed again, this time not because of the smoke but because of the stench. The room buzzed with insects. He crouched by the tub, felt the woman's neck for a pulse. She was stiff and cold, her skin pale and sickly, flies crawling all over her.

"Is it Rhea?" Zoe asked behind him, her voice hoarse.

"Yes," he said. "She's long dead."

His entire body burned with agony. The fire had burned his legs, his arms. He kept coughing, his lungs full of smoke. He retched and doubled up, vomiting.

But Daniel had gotten away. He'd given him enough time; he was sure of it.

A man made him stand up, walk over to an ambulance. People were walking into his house, talking about backup, and techs, and dispatch. Police talk.

For some reason, no one was helping the woman out. He glanced back, thought he could still see her beyond the smoke. She nodded at him, almost a friendly nod.

"You should get her help," he croaked.

"What are you talking about, freak?" the man barked at him.

"The woman. I think she needs medical help."

The man looked at him, incredulous. "She's dead, you maniac. You killed her."

"No." He tried to explain. "She's alive—look!"

A woman stepped out of the house and approached them, looking at him quizzically with intense green eyes. "Terrence. You remember me?"

He did. It was *her*. "Of course. You're the profiler, Zoe Bentley. We met. And Daniel told me about you."

"Where is Daniel?"

He laughed and pointed at the guest room window. "He got away. Fled through the window."

"That window is latched from inside," Zoe said. "And we had a cop covering the windows. No one got out."

He frowned. A movement in the corner of his eye drew his attention.

It was Daniel leaning against the house, grinning. Terrence tried to catch Daniel's gaze. Tried to signal that he should get away before the cops noticed him.

"Who are you looking at, Terrence?"

He ignored her. "Run," he told Daniel. "Run."

"There's no one there," Zoe said. "And Rhea Deleon has been dead for more than a day."

There was no point in talking to her, or to any of them. Only Daniel really listened to him. Only Daniel understood him.

"You have to run," he told Daniel over and over.

But his friend just smiled.

CHAPTER 70

Zoe's throat still felt scorched, and when she took a deep breath, she began coughing. The paramedics who'd arrived at the scene had given her oxygen for the smoke inhalation. She'd stubbornly refused to go to the hospital for tests, saying she was fine. Tatum, whose arms were burnt, had been evacuated.

Now she stepped back into Terrence Finch's house, moving aside to let two men with a stretcher through. The air inside smelled of smoke and rot, and Zoe's breathing became even shallower.

O'Donnell stood in the living room, watching grimly as the men moved the body onto the stretcher. Zoe approached her.

"She was crawling with flies," O'Donnell said. "And the smell . . . and Finch seemed certain she was still alive."

"He was delusional," Zoe pointed out. "And was probably hallucinating as well."

"You must see this kind of thing every day."

"No. A psychotic serial killer is actually a rare occurrence. And most are caught very fast. The only reason we didn't catch Terrence Finch sooner was because he was constantly coached by Rod Glover."

"Dr. Terrel will do the complete autopsy tomorrow morning, but the victim's face was covered with smudged food, and there was some of it in her mouth. It looks like he tried feeding her after she died."

"When can we question him?"

"He was severely burnt and inhaled a lot of smoke. I doubt he'll be able to talk to us before evening."

The familiar impatience rose in Zoe. She wanted to talk to him *now*. She needed to hear why they'd photographed those murders. And where Rod Glover had gone.

"What was he burning?" she asked, looking at the charred scraps of black paper that were scattered everywhere.

"Newspaper. We found a pile of *Chicago Daily Gazette* copies. He ripped the first page of each one. It had a picture of Catherine Lamb. We found a few unburnt crumpled pages under the couch."

The *Chicago Daily Gazette*. This fire could be a direct result of her own work with Harry Barry. "All the same page?"

"Yup."

Zoe watched the photographer take shots of a few brown stains on the floor.

"It's blood," O'Donnell said. "There's blood almost everywhere. The bathroom, Terrence's bedroom, the living room. Oh, and over here." She walked over to the fridge and opened it. In the fridge door were a few vials full of thick crimson liquid.

She turned to the photographer. "Did you photograph the fridge interior yet?"

The photographer glanced at her. "Not yet."

"Do it now." O'Donnell held the door open, moving aside.

The photographer took a picture, moved sideways, took another picture. Then shuffled aside again for a third one. Zoe thought of the sideways footprints she'd seen in the crime scene photos and of her original interpretation—that it was the result of some sort of obsessive behavior. If she hadn't made that mistake, would Rhea Deleon have still been—

She forced the thought away. Plenty of time for self-flagellation later.

"In Terrence's bedroom we found something that looked like a sort of rodent's limb. Probably belongs to one of the hamsters taken from the pet shop." O'Donnell sounded satisfied. Another puzzle piece confirmed. "We found some fragments of plastic and a key from a keyboard. Probably belonged to a laptop. We didn't find the rest of the laptop yet; maybe he dumped it. We also found two jars full of urine."

"*Urine?* Not blood?"

"That's right. Maybe he started drinking urine as well."

"Maybe," Zoe said after giving it a moment's thought. "It's also possible he peed in jars because Rhea was in the bathroom."

"Could be," O'Donnell said. "Also, someone slept in the guest room for a while. I told them to leave it for last because I figured you'd want to have a look."

Zoe blinked in surprise. "Thank you."

"Just put on gloves and shoe booties before you step inside."

Zoe did as she was told and stepped into the other bedroom, the nylon on her shoes crinkling with her footsteps.

Like the rest of the house, it smelled bad. But underneath the smell of death and fire, she sensed another stench, somehow even worse. Sweat and sickness. The room was dirty, the bedsheets stained and rumpled, scattered around the room.

"No blood in this room, not as far as we could tell," O'Donnell said behind her. "And not a lot of possessions, mostly clothes. But we found a box in the bottom of the closet."

Zoe opened the small closet. There were underwear, shirts, and pants tossed on the shelves. A tangle of gray ties lay on one of the shelves, like coiled snakes. A rectangular box sat on the bottom shelf. Zoe crouched and pulled it out, her heart beating. She already knew what she'd find inside. For a moment, she was fourteen again, looking under Glover's bed. Her hands trembled as she lifted the lid.

"What do you think?" O'Donnell asked.

"His trophies," Zoe said. She hoped O'Donnell thought it was the smoke inhalation that made her voice hoarse. "I've seen some of them before."

Several pairs of torn underwear. A bracelet. A thin golden necklace. She lifted one of the underwear pairs. It had several holes in it, as if it had been eaten by moths. It was old. When she'd glimpsed it last time, all those years ago, it had been relatively new.

Underneath the trophies, she found newspaper clippings. The article about the arrest of Jovan Stokes, with a picture of the task force that had caught him, with her at the corner. Then a picture of her and Tatum at a crime scene. Another article, written by Harry Barry, covering the arrest of the Strangling Undertaker. And a few articles, again by Harry, covering the murders of Clyde Prescott in San Angelo. Unlike many serial killers, Glover didn't collect news articles related to his own crimes. He was interested in *her*.

CHAPTER 71

The hospital room had two beds, but only one was taken. Terrence Finch lay in it, his hands cuffed to the bed, dressed in a turquoise hospital gown. His arms and legs were bandaged, and he was hooked to an IV. The doctor had told them Terrence was getting some pain relievers, as well as antipsychotics. He was gazing at the wall in front of him and didn't turn his head as they walked inside. Zoe sat down on a chair by the bed, and O'Donnell sat next to her. Tatum remained standing behind them.

"Mr. Finch, I'm Detective O'Donnell, and this is Dr. Bentley and Agent Gray," O'Donnell said. "We need to ask you a few questions."

He blinked and woozily turned his gaze to them. "Dr. Bentley," he mumbled. "We've met."

"Hello, Terrence," Zoe said steadily.

"I understand you've been read your rights," O'Donnell said. "But I would like to do it again before we talk."

As she read Terrence his Miranda rights, Zoe scrutinized his face. He didn't seem to listen, and his eyes flickered at one point to look behind them. Zoe took a quick glance to see what he was looking at, but there was nothing there. Despite his medication, she suspected he still hallucinated. It was doubtful that anything said here could be used in court. But Zoe didn't care about that. Terrence Finch wasn't going anywhere, and only he could give them Glover.

O'Donnell nodded at her. Zoe leaned forward.

"Terrence," she said. "Tell us about Rod Glover."

He tensed, glancing behind her again. "Who?"

"You first met him as Daniel Moore. But you must know by now that he was really named Rod Glover."

"No," Terrence said. "He was Daniel. Rod is the tumor. He's trying to take over Daniel, to kill him. But Daniel is still in there. He's in there."

"Okay." Zoe decided to skirt the subject for now. "Tell us how you first met Daniel."

"I had thoughts," Terrence said. "I needed someone to talk to. Someone who understood. I tried to talk to Catherine, but she just said I should go to a doctor and pray. Praying didn't help, and the doctor made me take more pills. I hate taking pills."

"So you talked to Daniel?"

"Our pastor said Daniel could help. So I talked to him. And he understood me. He knew exactly what I was going through. He helped me."

"How did he help you?"

Shrug. Another glance over her shoulder. "He helped me. We talked. He showed me how to meet other people like me online."

"Okay. When did he move in with you?"

"When he came back."

"Came back from where?"

A shrewd expression flickered across Terrence's face. "He came back from a trip."

How much had Glover told this man? "Okay. So Daniel came back, and he moved in with you?"

"Yes. He was sick. He couldn't drive. He needed my help. And I was glad to help him—we were friends."

"And he wanted to help you in return, right?"

Terrence hesitated. "We were friends. Of course he did. But he was sick, so I was the one who took care of him. He had difficulties sleeping, and he couldn't drive. I wanted to help him get better."

"Do you know what he had?"

"A brain tumor."

Zoe nodded. "So you wanted him to see a doctor?"

Terrence shook his head, then winced, the movement causing him pain. "Doctors never tell you the truth. There's a cure. They don't want you to know."

"And what's that cure?"

Terrence thought about it for a long while. "You're a doctor, right?"

"I'm a doctor of forensic psychology."

"Daniel said you were clever. You know the cure already, don't you? Are you trying to trick me? Trying to make me say it? Like Catherine? I won't say it—I won't!" His eyes widened, the handcuffs clanking as he pulled against the restraints.

"Okay," Zoe said hurriedly. "You don't need to say it."

He relaxed.

"Can I say it?" Zoe asked.

"Doctors never admit it," he said derisively. "They don't want people to know. There'd be chaos if people knew."

"The cure is blood, right?" Zoe said. "Human blood."

He blinked in surprise. "Yeah."

Zoe smiled at him slightly, as if they were sharing a secret. "It'll remain in this room. Detective O'Donnell and Agent Gray won't tell anyone. Right?"

"We won't," Tatum said woodenly.

"So you wanted Daniel to drink human blood? So he could get better?"

"Yes. But he said it wouldn't help him. He had a different idea."

"What was his idea?"

Terrence's eyes shifted. "Nothing. He said he had no health insurance, so the doctors won't take care of him. Just like my health insurance didn't fix me. It's the insurance companies. It's their fault."

"Did Daniel want to hurt women? Was that his idea?"

"Daniel never wanted to hurt anyone." The tone was sharper.

"Okay, but he wanted to do something, right? To get better."

"No! It was all my idea. All of it."

"Okay, what was your idea?"

"I wanted to get some human blood, and Daniel told me *not* to." He met her eyes victoriously, as if he'd proved his point. "He didn't want any of this. He said it wouldn't work anyway, not if the blood wasn't pure enough."

Zoe paused, looking sideways, as if considering this. "So this wasn't Daniel's idea at all. He tried to stop you." Acting the caring friend, no doubt, while simultaneously planting the idea that they should start with Catherine. Catherine, who knew about Terrence's obsession with blood. Who could point the police in the right direction.

"He was right," Terrence said. "We needed pure blood. So I suggested we go after the only pure person we knew."

"Who was that?"

Terrence's eyes widened, and he seemed to be looking behind her shoulder again. His lips moved without uttering a sound, as if spelling out something for an invisible accomplice. Zoe repressed the urge to glance backward. "Terrence, who was the person you suggested?"

"Catherine Lamb," he finally answered.

Zoe nodded. "And Daniel agreed?"

Another furtive glance. "He . . . he didn't like it. But he agreed she'd be the only one pure enough. I wouldn't have done it for myself. But Daniel needed the blood."

"Was that his plan as well? To extract the blood so he could drink it?"

Terrence hesitated. "Yeah."

"So you went over to Catherine Lamb's house to extract the blood. And then what happened?"

"She died."

"Because you extracted too much blood?"

"Yeah, there was a lot of blood."

"But Terrence." Zoe feigned confusion. "Catherine Lamb was strangled to death. And she was raped."

"No, you're wrong. It was only the blood." He raised his voice. "*Only the blood!* That's why it happened. I took too much blood." He yanked his hands, the handcuffs rattling on the cot's metal bars.

"Okay . . . ," Zoe said gently, nodding. "And then you took photos of her, right? Why did you do that?"

"I'm a photographer." He looked defiantly at her. "I take pictures of unusual situations."

The photographs weren't Terrence's idea. They were Glover's. Why? Was it just for the sexual pleasure? But Glover didn't keep any photos in his trophy box. "Did Daniel tell you to take those photos?"

"No."

"You put a necklace on her throat, right? The necklace with the cross. Why?"

"She always wore it. It made the picture seem better."

"And did Daniel drink the blood?"

"No . . . he didn't want to. But I slipped some into his coffee. And into his food." Terrence seemed pleased with himself. "It made him better. It helped."

Did Glover know this was going on? Did he let Terrence put some blood in his food just to make him feel like he was the one calling the shots? She doubted it. More likely, the brain cancer played havoc with Glover's taste buds, and he hadn't noticed the taste.

"Then why did Daniel go along with it?" she asked. "If you went to provide him with pure blood, but he wouldn't drink the blood later, why did he go at all?"

"I . . . I'm confused. It's all those drugs they give me here. He did drink it; that's why we did it. It was my idea. But he drank the blood." He shook his head violently. "He wanted to get well. That's why we did it. For the blood."

369

"And three days later, you went and grabbed another woman, near the train station. You did that for the blood too?"

"Yes. I wanted . . . we were running out of blood. So we went there and waited for the woman. And we took her blood."

"But you also killed her."

"It was an accident."

"Why did you draw the pentagram? Drive the knife into her stomach?"

A note of hesitation. "Just props. For the photographs."

"Whose idea was that?"

He mouthed unheard words again, turning away from her, looking at something unseen. She tried to read his lips but couldn't make anything out.

"Terrence, whose idea was it?"

"It was mine."

"And Daniel went along with it? Spent an entire hour with a dead woman, preparing the set, taking the photos?"

"He's a good friend."

"And then you took Rhea Deleon."

His head wavered from side to side. "Who?"

"The woman we found in your house."

"Oh, right. Her. Yes. Daniel didn't want to take her. He was against it from the start." His eyelids flickered. "It was all my idea."

In this case, she believed him. "So he killed her."

"No. It wasn't him. It was the tumor. It was Rod."

She eyed him sharply. "The tumor killed her? What do you mean?"

"It tried to. She's still alive. But it tried to kill her. It drank her blood, and it strangled her and tried to kill her." His eyes focused momentarily, and rage flickered in them. "*It* did it."

Terrence was willing to take the blame for Daniel's deeds, but not, apparently, for the tumor's part in this. "What happened then?"

"I kicked him out. I thought Daniel was gone. That the tumor consumed him. So I threatened him with a knife, and he ran."

"Do you know where he ran?"

"No, but it doesn't . . ." He yanked his hand again, the handcuff clanging. "It doesn't matter. He came back. And he was Daniel again. He helped me. He helped me silence Catherine again. We didn't want her to tell about the blood."

"Is that why you burned the newspapers?"

"Of course. But it was my idea. Not Daniel's. He helped me. He's a good friend. I won't tell them. I *won't* tell them." His eyes flickered again, and he cocked his head, as if listening to something else.

"Terrence, can you tell us when Daniel first contacted you?"

"No. I won't answer anything more. I won't. I *won't*." Spittle shot from his mouth. "I told you everything. Leave me alone."

"Just a few more questions, and then we'll let you rest. When did Daniel first contact you?"

He whispered something, his lips moving emphatically. She leaned closer to hear what he was saying.

He lunged so fast she barely had time to pull back. His teeth snapped inches away from her cheek, and she felt his breath, smelled the rot that rose from his mouth. She pushed her chair back, revulsion and fear swarming her mind.

"*Leave me alone!*" he screamed, spittle spattering from his mouth. "Just leave me alone! Get out, get out, get out!" He bucked in his cot, the handcuffs screeching on the metal rails. "Get out get out get out get out!"

Zoe rose and stepped back, almost colliding with Tatum. He placed a steadying hand on her shoulder, and Zoe took a deep breath. They left the room, Terrence's screams in their wake.

CHAPTER 72

"So Glover's been gone since yesterday," Tatum said darkly. "Probably halfway to Canada by now."

They stood in the hospital's hallway, a few steps away from the door to Finch's room. The painkillers were wearing off, and his arms had begun to hurt like hell. He was half regretting not letting Finch burn.

"Maybe," O'Donnell said doubtfully. "He left most of his things behind, including some cash. He didn't use his credit card or go to the bank. According to Terrence, he can't drive."

O'Donnell looked at Zoe. "He was cagey about the photographs, so I'm guessing it was Glover's idea."

Zoe frowned. "I agree, but I can't make any sense of it. Glover gets off on violating and strangling women, not posing them in strange satanic ritual settings."

"Maybe the photos were just a weird excuse for killing women," O'Donnell suggested. "Glover tells Terrence that to get better, he needs to photograph those dead women because he gets some sort of psychic energy from it. Then he needs to follow through with that idea. There's no point in trying to understand the logic of a crazy person."

"But there *was* a consistent logic to it," Zoe said. "Terrence's delusion was all about the blood, right? Or it was at first, before he went haywire. Remember, other than that he was completely functional. So he wouldn't believe some sort of harebrained idea about photos drawing psychic energy. Whatever Glover said, it had to make sense to Finch." Her voice rose in frustration.

Tatum eyed Zoe worriedly. He knew his partner well enough by now to spot the pattern. When it came to Glover, her analytical ability faltered. She *tried* to understand what made him tick, but of all the killers she profiled, this one constantly eluded her. He stood in her blind spot.

"O'Donnell has a point," he said slowly. "The photos aren't for sexual gratification. So they must serve a different purpose."

"Maybe," Zoe said impatiently. "But I just don't think he could conceivably say that they would cure his cancer."

"He didn't tell Terrence that he needed a cure," Tatum said.

"What do you mean?" O'Donnell asked.

"Terrence said that Glover told him he had no insurance. He didn't say he was dying or that doctors couldn't fix him. He said doctors *wouldn't* fix him."

"Well, we discussed this," Zoe said. "Glover would make a way to paint himself as a victim."

"But he made it sound as if the problem was *money*. Photos of dead women can't be used to cure cancer." Tatum shook his head. "But they can be sold. Remember what Swenson told us?"

"He said people paid a lot of money for that kind of stuff," O'Donnell muttered after a moment. "And he mentioned fake snuff. But if they knew it was real . . ."

"We assumed that Glover only went on the dark web to buy illegal porn," Zoe said, her eyes widening. "What if he sold it as well? How much would someone pay?"

"Maybe a lot," Tatum said. "If they were authentic. If those crazies on the marketplace knew that these were the actual murder photos. If that's what he did, it would explain why he called to tip off the cops about Henrietta Fishburne. He needed the press to report her murder before he could sell the pictures."

"*That* was how he explained it to Finch," Zoe said. "He needed money, maybe for a treatment or for private hospital care, and that's why they had to kill those women and take those photos. I'm betting that the pentagram and the knife were actual client requests."

Tatum shook his head in disbelief. "Do what you love, and the money will follow."

"If that's true," O'Donnell said, "he might be receiving treatment here in Chicago."

"We've already gone down that road," Tatum said. "There are too many patients. And they wouldn't let us look at patient records without a warrant, which is impossible to get."

"But we can narrow it down now," O'Donnell said. "If our theory is correct, we can find out how much he sold those pictures for and when he got the payments. We can look for a clinic that accepts cash as payment and minimizes the paper trail. If those transactions really exist, the more we know about them, the easier it'll be to find the place and the patient name."

Zoe shut her eyes, looking pale. "We need to find him fast. If dead women are his lifeline, there might be another victim *very* soon."

"We'll make a few phone calls," Tatum said. "If he sold those pictures, there would be traces in those dark web sites. We'll get analysts to help us look."

CHAPTER 73

Laughing_Irukandji sat on his throne in his underwear, staring at the monitors, waiting. Lurking.

He halfheartedly skimmed the forum, checking a thread about a hacked dating app database and another one about a new exploit found in a popular webcam application. He didn't comment on anything, his face frozen in a sneer.

On Twitter, the hashtag #FindRhea was trending. He read some of the mind-numbingly boring tweets, a sea of hypocrisy, a multitude of people trying to outshine their peers with their so-called heartfelt prayers.

He set ten of his bots to spew rumors that Rhea was an illegal immigrant, tagging each tweet with #FindRhea and #DeportRhea, and yawned as the predictable outrage bloomed.

A few messages popped up, fellow trolls, guessing correctly that the rumors were his doing. Most were amused. One of them thought that he'd gone too far. Laughing_Irukandji smirked.

If he only knew.

Another message appeared, and he tensed, his heart rate picking up. Jack_the_Ripper. Finally. His finger trembled as he clicked the message.

> Jack_the_Ripper: I had a few setbacks, I won't be able to send you the last batch of pictures. But you

have the three images I already sent you, and you can check the press to see it's authentic. Those are the pictures of Rhea Deleon, minutes after she died. No one else has them

A wave of disappointment washed through him. That wasn't the deal. He'd given the man instructions, hadn't he? He typed his answer.

Laughing_Irukandji: That wasn't the deal. No pictures, no payment

The response came immediately.

Jack_the_Ripper: I need that money. I already sent you three pictures. If you won't pay me, we're done

Laughing_Irukandji: Fine. Then we're done

The man had already clarified that he needed the money, and fast. He wouldn't find someone else who would pay that amount. No way in hell.

Jack_the_Ripper: Okay, what if I send you something else? Something better? But if you want it you'll have to pay what you owe me, and extra for the new photos

Laughing_Irukandji: It'll have to be something pretty special

Power rushed through him again. Trolling people on social media didn't give him a fraction of what he felt right now.

Jack_the_Ripper: I can do a pregnant woman

Laughing_Irukandji smiled and let a whole minute go by before answering.

Laughing_Irukandji: That would work nicely. But I have specific instructions

CHAPTER 74

Monday, October 24, 2016

Tatum scrutinized the task force room, which was now at full capacity. Despite the bloodshot eyes and disheveled looks, everyone seemed sharper that morning. The thrill of the hunt kept them alert and on their toes.

Well, that and coffee. It seemed like they were having a cup-size contest. O'Donnell had shown up nursing a mug as big as her head, while Valentine held a large thermos from which he constantly refilled his Styrofoam cup. Even Zoe had abandoned her newly found hot chocolate in favor of a strong cup of Starbucks coffee.

"Good morning," Bright said. "As you all know, we arrested Terrence Finch yesterday and found the body of Rhea Deleon in his home. Detective O'Donnell and Dr. Bentley managed to interrogate him yesterday evening when he woke up, but he didn't give us a solid lead for Rod Glover's whereabouts. Detectives Koch and Sykes, you went there this morning?"

"Yeah," Koch said. "But he lawyered up."

"He's being medicated, so it's likely that his psychosis is diminishing, making him more careful," Zoe said.

"In any case, we'll go there later, see if he's more coherent. If he can lead us to Glover, we might be able to cut a deal with him."

"We also had some progress on Glover," Sykes said. "We talked to Finch's neighbors yesterday, and one of them had seen Glover just two days ago at Finch's house. She identified him when we showed her pictures but said that he looks different now. We sat her down with a sketch artist, and we have an updated likeness."

"Are we under the assumption that Rod Glover is still in Chicago?" Bright asked.

"Oh, yes," Tatum said.

The eyes in the room shifted to him. He paused for two seconds and then said, "Yesterday, following leads from Finch's interrogation, we theorized that Rod Glover might have been selling photos from his recent murders to fund his cancer treatment."

"Selling to whom?" Bright asked.

"To customers on a dark web marketplace dedicated to illegal porn," Tatum said. "We had a few analysts take a look during the night, going through sites we got from Swenson."

They'd spent the evening in the bureau's Chicago office. Tatum, Zoe, and Valentine had kept hovering over the analysts' shoulders until one of the vexed analysts had politely kicked the three of them out. The final results of the search had been emailed at four in the morning to the three of them.

"A month ago, a user named Jack_the_Ripper began talking about selling unseen photos of a murdered victim," Tatum continued, setting a folder on the table. "The people who responded mostly trolled him, but some were interested. He ended up selling images that were shared later in the forums publicly." He handed a photo from the folder to Koch, who sat to his right.

"It's a photo of Shirley Wattenberg, a murder victim from 2008, suspected to have been murdered by Rod Glover," Tatum said. "This photo looks like it was taken soon after she was killed. He initially wanted five thousand dollars for the photo, but because of the bad quality and the suspicion that the picture was fake, he ended up selling it for two hundred. However, after the forum members realized the photo was authentic, Jack_the_Ripper's reputation grew. He said he could come up with more."

Tatum took two more photos and passed them around. "Next came Catherine Lamb. All taken soon after the murder. We know he sold eight of those, but only two were shared with the rest of the members. The exact amount he got for those pictures isn't clear, but the analysts estimate it at above eight thousand dollars."

"Why didn't anyone find this earlier?" Bright asked angrily. "Those pictures were *online* for anyone to see?"

Valentine cleared his throat. "Not anyone. Just a few select members of this forum. Do you know how many Tor websites dedicated to illegal pornography are up at any given moment? Over eighty percent of the entire dark web. Thousands of websites. There are currently about thirty million images and videos, constantly exchanging hands."

Tatum knew the statistics well, but it always made him nauseous to hear them again. It was like lifting a rock in a field. You *knew* there would be critters underneath, but it wasn't the same as actually seeing them crawl and scuttle. The majority of those images and videos were of underage children. To actually find something *specific* in that mountain of depravity was a difficult and sickening task.

He took a moment to let them all understand what they were dealing with and continued. "The next time Jack_the_Ripper appeared in the forum, he sold the images of Henrietta Fishburne. He stated that most of those were sold to a private client who had commissioned certain specific props for the images beforehand."

"Props?" Koch frowned.

"The knife and the pentagram," Zoe said. "They never fit the profile of either Finch or Glover because it wasn't their signature. These things, and the ritualistic posing of the body, were the fantasy of a third person."

"Do we know who this private client is?" Koch asked.

"No," Tatum said. "We're trying to find out, but the entire thing was negotiated on a private chat on the dark web. I don't think even Glover can really tell you who he talked to. The private customer never shared the photos he bought, but other images from the murders *were* shared." He passed two more images around. In a way, these were the worst, because they had been taken when Henrietta was still alive. They were close-ups of her face, mouth open in a soundless scream, a tie wrapped around her throat. The arm holding the tie was visible. It belonged to a Caucasian man. The hand clutched the tie tightly, veins standing out, scratch marks on the skin. This fit the findings of the autopsy—skin cells underneath Henrietta Fishburne's fingernails. And since they had a DNA match for those skin cells, it could only mean that it was Glover's arm.

Tatum waited for the photos to be passed around and then resumed. "Because the press reported the murder on that very day, affirming the authenticity of the photos, they went for four thousand dollars each. Several of the forum members pooled their bitcoins together to buy the photos and share them. We don't know how much the private client paid for his photos. But they were tailored to his requests, and we're guessing Glover wouldn't have done it if it hadn't been worthwhile."

He glanced at O'Donnell, giving her a small nod.

"We believe the money earned from selling those photos was used to finance Glover's cancer treatment in a private clinic," O'Donnell said. "There are over twenty such clinics in Chicago."

Bright frowned. "Well, we're not likely to get a search warrant for those clinics. It's an interesting hunch, but without confirmation—"

"One of the clinics caught my attention," O'Donnell interrupted him. "The Celeste Cancer Center. It's an expensive clinic, with a high patient survival rate. Two things seemed to stand out. First, it's one of the smallest clinics; the regular staff is only six people. Glover would like that since there would be less people who could identify him. Second, it's one of the only clinics that will accept cash payments."

"We believe Glover has a contact in Chicago who converts bitcoin to cash," Tatum interjected.

"I went to the clinic this morning," O'Donnell continued. "I verified his cancer type was treated there and that the treatment could be done in payments that more or less match what we assume he had. It checks out. Following that, I showed our recent sketch of Glover around. I also explained to a very impressionable young nurse what Glover does to women he meets. She explained she can't break patient confidentiality but constantly stressed that there could be a good reason for us to get a warrant. She also mentioned that on November second, at half past two, it might be a great idea if we showed up in force. Patients go for routine treatments in the clinic, and I'm guessing this is when Glover's next treatment is scheduled."

O'Donnell had already told Tatum all this earlier, but now something caught his attention. Something about the sketch. What was it? He gritted his teeth, trying to focus. The nurse had identified Glover by the sketch. It was likely she'd seen his photo on the news before, but that photo had been taken months ago, when Glover was still healthy. So what?

There was something there.

"That might be good enough for a warrant." Koch smiled. "November second is next week. If he shows up for his treatment, we can nail him then."

"There's a problem with waiting that long," Zoe said. "We know Glover still searched for victims after Henrietta Fishburne. That's why they originally picked up Rhea Deleon. But I don't think Rhea's murder went according to plan, and I don't know how much time he had to take photos."

"None of Rhea's photos showed up on the marketplace as far as we could tell," Tatum said.

"If we wait until Glover's appointment, he might kill someone else to finance his next treatment," Zoe said.

"Point taken," Koch said. "I'll see if we can get a warrant for that clinic. Maybe once we look through their records, we can find a lead to Glover. A phone number, an address, an emergency contact. These places have endless forms people need to fill out. He must've screwed up somewhere."

"We'll also talk to Finch again, see if we can extract something else from him," Valentine said.

"And we'll send copies of the recent sketch to the media," Bright said.

Tatum was aware of some more talk, followed by the meeting breaking up. He thought about the sketch, about how Glover had changed. The participants filed out of the room, but Zoe noticed that he didn't get up and walked over to him.

"What's wrong?" she asked.

"How did Patrick Carpenter know Glover was sick?" he asked her.

"What?"

"When we arrested Allen Swenson, Patrick Carpenter showed up and said that it was impossible for Allen to do all this with a dying man. But we had never mentioned in the press that Glover was dying or that he had cancer. We never mentioned this to Patrick either. And Glover looked healthy in the photo."

"Maybe Glover told Patrick about his cancer a while ago," Zoe said. "Or he heard about it from someone."

"But we know he was diagnosed with cancer when he was in Dale City. So Patrick had to learn about it in the past month. So Patrick either discussed this with someone who'd talked to Glover recently . . ."

"Or he talked to Glover himself," Zoe said.

"Let's go have a chat with Patrick," Tatum suggested.

CHAPTER 75

Leonor Carpenter's days were an endless roller coaster of anxiety and relief. Her emotional state was completely in the hands of her unborn child. Or more accurately, in his feet.

Every time he kicked, she felt a surge of relief. He was still there, still alive. But then, as time went by with no movement, she'd start worrying. Had he choked himself on his umbilical cord? Had his little heart stopped? When she was in the hospital, the reassuring beeping of the monitor was worth the constant discomfort. But once they'd disconnected the monitor, she was at the mercy of little Bump's movement.

She shouldn't have given him a name; it had been a mistake. She should have known better by now. But after twenty-nine weeks, she couldn't call him *it* or *the fetus* any longer.

If he didn't kick her for more than two hours, the trepidation became too intense. She'd lie on her side in bed, tears in her eyes, whispering to him, "Come on, Bump. One little kick for Mommy. Just one little kick."

And he always listened, finally giving her the tiny kick she needed to calm down. He was already such a good boy.

He'd kicked fifteen minutes ago, so she was, like Patrick had begun to jokingly say, at kick-plus-fifteen. She felt calm, almost happy. She watched Patrick as he finished his cup of coffee before leaving. She knew he had to go; the congregation needed him, with Catherine gone and Albert in mourning. Their community was fracturing under the weight of the sadness and fear. The constant police persecution kept the congregation away from church, away from solace. They needed Patrick to help them recover.

She and Bump could spend a few hours without him. Besides, it wasn't like she was alone in the house.

Still, she saw Patrick's worried frown as their eyes met.

"Are you sure you'll be okay?" he asked.

"Of course."

"Maybe I should stay. Albert could . . ." The words faded. She could see the truth in his eyes. Albert couldn't. She wasn't sure Albert would ever heal enough to return to his duties in the church.

"Go," she said, smiling. "I'll be fine. I'll rest in bed. And if anything is wrong, Daniel will help me."

As if on cue, their guest stepped into the kitchen. Leonor's heart squeezed again as she saw how thin he was. Poor man, the cancer was rapidly eating him from inside. Not to mention being hounded by the police like that. A surge of anger blazed through her, and Bump kicked, feeling his mother's rage.

"Good morning," he said blearily.

"How did you sleep?" Leonor asked. She'd heard him tossing and turning in his bed. He'd told her the pain became difficult to bear at night.

"Like a baby." He flashed her a smile and winked. "Maybe not as well as little Bump."

She grinned, marveling at Daniel's good cheer. "He actually kicked me all night long."

"He'll be a feisty one," Daniel said. "Like his mama."

"I'll come back to make lunch," Patrick said. "I don't want Leonor cooking."

"Don't worry about it," Daniel answered. "I can cook. I'll make my special chicken à la Daniel."

Patrick still didn't seem at ease. "If anything is wrong, don't drive her to the hospital. Get an ambulance."

"Couldn't drive even if I wanted to, my friend," Daniel reminded him.

"Oh, right."

"Go." Leonor laughed. "We'll be okay."

Daniel left, giving them time in private. Patrick hugged her before going, holding her tight, as if he was afraid to let go. She pulled his palm to her belly just as Bump kicked again, and they smiled at each other. Then he left.

She gazed out the kitchen window, lost in thought, thinking of poor Catherine. She would never know the feeling of a growing life inside her. The sensation of those tiny kicks. The bond between a mother and her child.

Leonor wiped a tear from her cheek.

And to think the police believed Daniel could have done this. As if he could ever harm *anyone*, not to mention Catherine. The police didn't know him, not like Leonor and Patrick did. They hadn't seen him at the homeless shelter, talking to those men and women, giving them an encouraging smile along with a warm blanket for the winter. The police hadn't heard him pray fervently at church. They weren't there when he'd talked to her, shedding a tear, telling her about his violent childhood.

And they hadn't been there last night, when Daniel had thanked her and Patrick for letting him lay low and told them he'd decided to turn himself in. He was worried that the stress could affect the pregnancy, and he didn't want to risk that.

It was Leonor who'd managed to convince him to stay. They all knew if he turned himself in, he would probably never get the medical treatment he needed. The cancer would kill him. It would be a death sentence long before the acquitting trial.

She was about to get up, when Daniel stepped into the kitchen.

"I was just about to go and rest a bit," she said. "Feel free to grab anything from the . . ." She suddenly noticed he held something. It took her a moment to realize it was a pair of her stockings. He gripped it strangely, stretched tight between both hands. His eyes seemed distant.

"Oh," she said, embarrassed. "Did we leave that in the guest room?"

He gave her a small smile and took a step toward her. "I'm sorry, Leonor, but—"

A sudden knock on the door made them both freeze. Daniel's eyes widened in fear.

"It's probably the neighbor," Leonor reassured him in a soft voice. "She said she might drop by and give me a cake she baked. Go in the back; I'll tell you when she leaves."

He hesitated, then nodded and quickly left the room.

Leonor got up and shuffled slowly to the door, just as there was another knock.

"Just a minute," she called. She took a look through the peephole and instantly recognized the man and woman on her doorstep. For a second she considered not opening the door. But they'd heard she was there already. If she didn't let them in, they'd know she was hiding something.

She unlatched and opened the door. "Hello," she said frostily. "You're the people who showed up in the hospital last week. Tatum and . . . Zoe, right? You didn't tell me you were from the FBI."

Tatum looked appropriately abashed. "I'm sorry, Mrs. Carpenter," he said. "We didn't want to alarm you, considering your condition."

"How very considerate. I wish you'd have shown the same consideration to the rest of our congregation."

"Is Patrick home?" Zoe asked.

"No, he's gone."

"Gone where?"

"You'd have to call him and ask him yourself." He was at the church, but she wasn't about to tell them that.

"Mrs. Carpenter, can we come in?" Tatum asked. "We need to ask you a few questions."

"Patrick is probably at work," she said desperately. "I'm sure he'll talk to you."

"It'll only be a few minutes," Tatum said. "We don't want to take too much of your time."

She could tell them no. She was almost sure they needed a warrant to enter by force. She tensed, about to tell them to leave, but the words never left her lips. If she told them they couldn't come in, they'd be suspicious. They'd know she was hiding someone.

No, she had to let them in. They wouldn't start searching the place. They had no reason to suspect anything. "Sure," she said, feeling her gut roil. She moved aside. "Come in."

She led them back into the kitchen. Daniel was probably locked in his room. All she had to do was answer their questions and get them out of there. Despite there being four chairs in the kitchen, none of them sat down.

"Leonor," Zoe said. "Do you know Daniel Moore?"

"Sure," she said. "He was in our congregation."

"When did you last hear from him?"

Leonor shrugged. "Just before he left Chicago. He told me he was leaving because of a family crisis."

"Weren't you concerned about him driving, considering his medical condition?" Tatum asked.

"He could still drive—" She almost bit her tongue. She should have known better. She'd always been a lousy liar. It wasn't about keeping cool. She could do *that*. It was about thinking the alternative truth through. The reality and fabrication always got tangled. She *hated* it.

"What were you going to say?" Zoe asked. "That he could still drive despite his medical condition?"

"No."

"What then?"

"I just said that he could still drive."

"But you didn't seem surprised to hear about his medical condition," Tatum said.

"I just assumed . . ." She had nothing. "I'm very tired. I need to rest. I can't stand too long—it's not good for Bu . . . for the baby."

"Why don't you sit down?" Zoe suggested.

"I need to go to sleep," she said firmly. "Please leave."

"Just a few more questions, and we'll be out of your hair," Tatum said lightly. "When did you or Patrick *really* last talk to Daniel?"

She sat down and stared at him. She wouldn't lie any longer, but she wasn't about to say another word.

"Did he contact you after he returned?" Tatum asked.

The silence stretched. They thought she could be intimidated by silence? She put her palm on her belly. Bump gave her a small kick, reassuring her. She wasn't even alone.

"Did you know Daniel Moore's real name is actually Rod Glover?" Tatum asked. "That he's wanted for the murder of eight women, including your friend Catherine Lamb?"

She let her mind wander, as she did sometimes. Thinking of little Bump, of their family. Thinking of doing the right thing. This was when good deeds really mattered. When they were difficult to do.

Zoe glanced at Tatum, and he sighed. "Can I use your bathroom before we leave, Mrs. Carpenter?"

She almost said no. But then again, they had a small bathroom just across the kitchen's doorway. "Sure," she said. "It's just over there."

He followed her pointed finger, and she kept her eyes on him until she was sure he went nowhere else. Zoe sat down in front of her.

"Leonor." Zoe's tone was soft, just above a whisper. As if she didn't want Tatum to hear. "There's something important you need to know."

Leonor said nothing, but she found herself leaning forward to hear the woman's voice better.

"I knew Daniel back when I was a child," Zoe said. "He was our neighbor."

Leonor felt a flash of astonishment, followed by the sudden realization. "You're the Bentley girl!" she whispered, smiling warmly. "Daniel told me all about you."

CHAPTER 76

Zoe wasn't sure if she could hide the shock that shot through her as Leonor said those words.

Daniel told me all about you.

Leonor hadn't said it angrily or accusingly. In fact, whatever Glover had told her about Zoe made her seem more friendly.

She forced herself to smile lightly. "That's right. I was fourteen when he left Maynard. I knew him quite well."

"He *told* me you worked for the FBI, but I didn't make the connection until now," Leonor whispered, clearly intending not to be heard by Tatum. "He said you two stayed in touch."

Zoe felt dizzy. With Glover, it was sometimes impossible to know the purpose of his lies—or if he even believed they were lies at all. As a teenager, she'd caught him lying a few times, and he always made it seem as if he was just joking. But occasionally, he almost seemed to believe the fabrications himself. Did he really think they had "stayed in touch"?

Perhaps he had told Leonor that story to make him seem more approachable. It turned him from a single man with no family to a sympathetic man, caring enough to stay in touch with the neighbor kid.

Whatever the reason, she could use it. "So he told you what happened in Maynard? About the girls?"

"He *did*." Leonor's eyes widened in sadness. "He even said the police suspected him. But you were there, so you know what happened."

Zoe didn't have to make an effort to guess what Glover had told the woman. "They caught the guy who did it," she said. "A high school kid. He killed himself in jail."

Leonor nodded, and her eyes flickered to the hallway and the bathroom door. "But your partner thinks . . . "

"Never mind what my partner thinks," Zoe said smoothly. "I'm keeping this investigation *objective*. We don't want to make any assumptions."

Leonor seemed to relax slightly. "That's right."

Zoe chose her words carefully. "I'll be honest with you. There's some evidence linking Daniel to those crimes. But I get a feeling he was at the wrong place at the wrong time. But if we don't get his version of what happens . . . " She shrugged. "Things don't look good for him. The sooner we get a chance to talk to him and clarify everything, the better. That's why I need to know when he talked to you and what he said."

Leonor's eyes narrowed slightly. "Like I said, I haven't talked to him recently."

She was losing her. Zoe thought fast. "He'd be safer if he turned himself in. The Chicago PD are looking for him."

"I'm sure he'll turn himself in eventually."

Eventually? Then Zoe realized what the woman was talking about. "After he finishes his treatment?"

Leonor seemed to think it through. Finally she said, "I wouldn't know. But I doubt he'd get the treatment he needs in prison."

Zoe suspected that Leonor knew where he was right now. She had to make the woman see things clearly. "Do you know how he pays for the cancer treatments?"

Leonor's forehead furrowed. "No. Like I said, we didn't talk recently."

"He sells pictures on the dark web. Pictures of his victims." She opened her bag and drew out the pictures. She lay them down one by one.

"This is Shirley Wattenberg. She was twenty-two when she died. He raped her and strangled her and left her in the ditch like trash. This is the picture *he* took."

Leonor glanced away in disgust. "You lied to me. You already decided he's guilty."

"*He* is the one who lied to you. This one you know. Catherine Lamb. Look at the picture. *He* did this. He sold this picture online."

Leonor's body became rigid. "I want you to leave. Get out. Now!"

Zoe knew she'd blundered. She should have kept her cool. Leonor would have given her something. But she was committed to her course of action now. She laid the pictures of Henrietta Fishburne on the table. Leonor glanced at them, the color rushing away from her face. She looked sick.

Zoe pointed at the picture. "This is Henrietta. Daniel did this. But his real name is Rod Glover. We need you to tell us everything you know. We need to catch him before he does it to anyone else."

Leonor shook her head and shut her eyes. Her lips twisted as if she was about to cry.

After a few seconds, the toilet in the bathroom flushed, and Tatum stepped out. They exchanged glances, and Zoe shook her head. She then collected the pictures from the table and placed her card in front of Leonor.

"If you think of anything else, let us know," she said, getting up.

For a moment, Leonor seemed on the verge of saying something, but instead she glanced away.

Zoe strode out of the house, furious with herself. She'd been so close; she was sure of it. If she'd only said the right thing, the truth would have come out. Leonor had wanted to talk. But instead, she'd made Leonor close up, like she invariably did with people.

"Patrick is probably at church," Tatum said, unlocking the car. "Let's find him. If we need to, we can get them both into separate interrogation rooms at the station."

Zoe nodded, sliding into the passenger's seat. She gazed through the window as they drove away, leaving the house behind them. "She said Glover told her about me as a child. He made it sound like we had a good relationship."

"Glover lies. He says things people want to hear—you know that."

"But why talk about me at all?"

Tatum sighed. "I know you feel the need to explain everything those people do, but you know what? Sometimes there is no real reason. He just felt like talking about you, and he did. And naturally, he made it sound like you two are best friends, because everything he says is supposed to cast him in a good light."

"Yeah."

They drove in silence for a while.

"You shouldn't have shown her those pictures," Tatum said. "Not in her state."

"She *knows* something. I was trying to jolt her into talking."

"Still, showing her a picture of her dead friend took it too far. If she complains to the police—"

"She didn't seem to care about her so-called dead friend," Zoe said impatiently. "She hardly looked at the photo. She seemed a lot more upset about the picture of Henrietta Fishburne." She thought back to that moment. The way the blood had run from Leonor's face. She hadn't seemed disgusted or horrified. She'd seemed . . .

Scared.

"Well, I don't blame her," Tatum said. "If you showed *me* a picture of—"

"Turn the car around," Zoe blurted.

"What? Why?"

"She wasn't looking at Henrietta at all—she was looking at the *arm* in the picture." Zoe took out the picture just to verify. Henrietta Fishburne, being strangled, only the arm of her attacker visible. And his skin was scraped in several places, long red scratches.

Leonor had seen those scratches before. That's what had scared her. She'd seen them on Glover's arm, and when she saw the picture, she realized that he was the man who was strangling Henrietta.

But that could only mean she had seen him *very* recently. And it was possible he was in Patrick and Leonor's house right now.

CHAPTER 77

Leonor didn't budge until she heard the feds' car drive away. She'd heard of the phrase *frozen in fear*, but up until that moment, she'd thought it was just a way to explain that someone was very scared. Now she realized it was possible to be so frightened that the body didn't respond.

She tried to convince herself it had just been her imagination. She'd hardly gotten a glimpse of that photo. Those scratches she'd noticed on the arm in the photo could be just a trick of the light. And even if they weren't, it meant nothing, right? Scratches on the arm were hardly a rare thing. She'd managed to scrape her arms dozens of times just by working in the garden.

Still, there were three long scratches. Just like on Daniel's arm.

She'd asked him about them, and he'd explained in embarrassment that the cancer medication made his skin dry and that he itched all night and sometimes scratched himself until it bled.

Such a specific explanation. And he'd said it instantly, without hesitation. Surely if it was a lie, he would have taken a moment to come up with something. She'd even given him some of her moisturizing cream, and he'd later told her it was helping already.

She thought back to his earnest face when he talked. Scratching as he explained it and then laughing as he realized what he was doing.

No one lied so well. It was impossible.

He'd never tried to hide that he'd been living with Terrence Finch. It was the first thing he'd told Patrick when he'd called. He had been staying there and had recently found out that Terrence might be involved in something illegal. He also said that Terrence's behavior was getting more and more erratic. He said he just needed a place to stay a few nights, until the next treatment. And then, later, when they'd found out that Terrence had been arrested on suspicion of killing Catherine, Daniel had blamed himself. Saying he should have seen the signs. Pain and shame had shimmered in his eyes.

But now she wondered. Was it really possible for Terrence to kill those women while Daniel lived in his home without Daniel noticing it?

And whoever had taken that picture of the strangled girl wasn't the attacker. The angle was wrong. So if Finch had taken the picture . . .

Those three scratches.

She regretted not saying something when the agents were there. She didn't have to tell them Daniel was in the back room. She could have just suggested that she come with them to make a statement at the station. Or tell them to wait until Patrick came back.

Because she was now alone in her home with Daniel. And she knew him—he was a good-hearted man, but . . .

It was impossible to get those scratches out of her mind.

She was just overreacting. She saw a violent picture, and it affected her badly. But she needed help.

She picked up the phone and dialed Patrick.

"Hey," he said, picking up almost instantly.

"Patrick," she whispered, her voice cracking. "Can you come home?"

"Why, what's wrong?" He sounded alarmed. "Is it the baby?"

"No . . . I just really need you here."

"Sure, I'm already on my way. Hang tight." He hung up.

She exhaled. Even the short conversation with Patrick already made her feel better. And a bit silly. It was just a dumb overreaction.

The sudden feeling of a cloth noose tightening around her throat took her entirely by surprise.

CHAPTER 78

Tatum switched off the engine, already opening the car door. Zoe followed closely behind as he half ran to the door. He seemed about to knock when they heard a crash from inside the house.

Tatum pulled his gun and opened the door. "Wait here."

She ignored his instruction, stepping inside behind him. Tatum advanced silently, his movements fluid, his gun aimed forward, gripped in both hands. He stepped into the kitchen doorway and shouted, "Stop! Let her go, and put your hands up!"

Zoe looked over Tatum's shoulder, heart in her throat.

Glover was standing by the counter at the far end of the room, a sharp knife held to Leonor's throat. Leonor's face was red, and she was wheezing, eyes panicky and wide. A pair of stockings was wound around her neck, though the noose seemed to dangle loosely. Glover had probably let go of it when he'd heard their car parking by the house and had grabbed for the knife.

"I'll kill her!" Glover shouted. "Put down the gun, or I cut her throat."

"That's not going to happen," Tatum said. "Put down the knife, and no one gets hurt."

Glover barked a laugh. "I think we're beyond that point. Zoe, step inside the room—I want to see your hands." He moved his head slowly from left to right, like a snake.

Zoe slowly crept around Tatum, her palms held up. "I'm unarmed."

"Please," Leonor wheezed. "I need—"

"Shut up," Glover snapped. "Or I swear I'll drive this knife into your belly."

Zoe's heart hammered, her eyes locked on Glover's. She saw the darkness there, the emptiness. That same look he'd had all those years ago when he'd figured out she'd broken into his house. The same look he'd had when he'd attacked her months ago. A look that meant death. A face of pure evil. Death hovered behind him, waiting to strike. She had trouble breathing, mirroring the wheezing in Leonor's gasps. For a second, she knew they were all in Glover's control. Only he could decide how this was going to end.

No.

This was a child's thinking. The fear of the unknown. The terror of knowing the bogeyman was coming to get you. But Glover wasn't that. He wasn't a creature that crawled out of the swamp or hid under the bed. He wasn't a monster. He was a man. She forced herself to see him for what he truly was.

He was sick. If death hovered above him, it was because he was dying. His skin was drawn, eyes sunken. There was a bald patch on his head where someone had shaved his hair off, probably to perform a medical procedure. He was thin, almost skeletal.

This man was broken. It didn't make him less dangerous. He had nothing left to lose.

"Glover," she said, her voice soft and low. "If you hurt her, Agent Gray will shoot you."

"Maybe," he said, grinning insanely. "But I'll get to see the look on your eyes as you see this woman die. It'll be worth it."

He wasn't really afraid of Tatum's gun. Like many psychopaths, Glover's risk assessment was skewed. He was aware of the gun's existence, but the threat was abstract, distant. For Glover, real fear came with pain. She recalled his attack on her and the dismay in his eyes when she'd managed to stab him. And it had happened again, when Marvin had shot him. When Glover felt actual pain, the threat became real.

And now he was in pain all the time. That was what he was really afraid of. The cancer. He had time to process the pain and forge acute terror from it. The gun, in comparison, meant almost nothing. In fact, by this point he might welcome being shot, just to escape death by cancer.

"If you put down the knife," Zoe said, "we will make sure you get the cancer treatment you deserve." She stressed the word *deserve*. In Glover's world, he was entitled to everything he took.

"That's a cute story you're trying to sell me," Glover snarled. "I've researched prison hospitals. I've seen the treatment I'd get there. I'm afraid I'll have to pass on that generous offer."

Of course. He'd already contemplated the possibility. Checked it. She recalled what Leonor had told her earlier. *I doubt he'd get the treatment he needs in prison.* She'd repeated things Glover had told her. For him, being arrested was tantamount to a death sentence. Slow and painful.

No. He wanted something else here. To either escape or die. Perhaps all he was doing right now was building enough courage to force Tatum to shoot him, suicide by federal agent. And once he was ready for it, Leonor would die.

"What if we let you leave?" Zoe asked.

"Leave? When we finally get the reunion we wanted?" Glover shifted his head again. "After all those years we have an opportunity to talk, and you want me to leave?"

"What do you want to talk about?"

"A little gratitude would be nice."

Zoe blinked. "Gratitude?"

"I *made* you, Zoe. You owe everything to me. I am the reason for your stellar career. Jovan Stokes, Jeffrey Alston, Clyde Prescott. I've been following the stories. And meanwhile *I* need to hide in a shitty two-bedroom apartment, constantly making sure the cops don't look at me funny. Had to pay thousands of dollars to get a solid fake identity, just because a snotty kid once decided her nice neighbor was a killer."

"You *were* a killer."

"No! It was that kid from the school. The police said so. In fact, I helped them in their investigation."

She stared at him in amazement. It occurred to her that he'd said that so many times he might have started to believe it. Or maybe, in some insane corner of his mind, he thought he could still get out of this. Could somehow prove he was entirely innocent. Maybe he lied because currently he saw no better course of action.

"Say thanks," he snapped.

"What?"

"Thank me for your career, or I slit this woman's throat right now."

He kept shifting his head. Why was he doing that?

He had no peripheral vision. That was why he couldn't drive. He looked at her and Tatum as if through a tunnel. That was why he kept moving his head. He wanted to see them both.

She decided to test her theory. "Here's my offer. The agent and I move from the doorway. You can walk through it and get out of here, leaving Leonor with us. I'm getting the car keys from my bag now."

"Don't." His eyes widened, the knife-wielding hand tensing.

"It's just car keys," she said, very slowly taking her key chain out of her bag. They weren't even the keys to the car—Tatum had those—but it didn't really matter. "Here."

She tossed them, intentionally throwing them just a bit to the side. Glover moved his entire head to watch as the keys arced in the air, then clattered on the floor. He then whipped his head to look at Tatum and the gun, taking a step back.

"Don't move," he barked.

He hadn't been able to watch Tatum when he'd followed the keys.

"You can take them," Zoe said. "Drive away. Just leave Leonor behind." Had Tatum seen the way Glover's head moved? Did he understand what she was doing?

He did. She could almost feel it. Their minds thinking along the same lines, processing the moment together.

"I want you to thank me first," Glover said slyly. He was buying time. Maybe thinking of her offer. Maybe making plans of his own.

And maybe he really wanted her to thank him. It was possible he was intent on getting that from her before he died. He'd always been obsessed with her. And Glover's fantasies were what always propelled him. Perhaps this was one of them.

"Thank you," she said. "You're right. I owe everything I have to you. Now look: I'm moving aside." She took a step to the right.

He moved threateningly. "Don't—"

"What happened to you wasn't fair," she said. "You were a good neighbor. You were my friend. I was ungrateful."

"A bitch," he spat.

"I shouldn't have blamed you. The police already had a suspect, right? And because of me, you had to leave your home behind." Another step. And another. Glover's head moved, following her.

"If I hadn't done that, a lot of people wouldn't have gotten hurt, right?" Another step. Slow. Soft. Eyes constantly on him. "You didn't want to hurt Catherine. You *had* to."

"It was Finch! It was all Finch's idea."

"Right!" She talked faster, higher. Tried to sound panicky. A woman trying to accommodate him. "And I'm sure you tried to talk him out of it. But what choice did you have? Because of me, you didn't have health insurance. And those pictures could get you the medical treatment you deserved, right?"

Tatum shifted, moving slowly toward the wall. Glover didn't notice. In fact, she was almost sure he *couldn't* notice. Tatum was out of Glover's line of sight.

"You can still make this work," Zoe said. She didn't try to sound convincing. Glover wasn't interested in being convinced. He wanted to see her afraid. This was about him winning. "The car keys are right there on the floor. I won't stop you. I just don't want anyone to get hurt."

Tatum crept along the wall, making sure not to make a sound.

"Do you think I'm stupid enough to think you'll just let me walk out?" Glover asked.

"I don't care if you run!" she said, her voice cracking. "I'll fix this. Just don't hurt her! Tell me how to fix this!"

He smiled then. A victorious smile. "Sorry, Zoe. You can't fix this."

His hand tightened around the knife handle, about to slit Leonor's throat. Tatum lunged, crossing the space between them in two fast steps, and grabbed Glover's wrist. Glover's head whipped in surprise, and he let out a scream as Tatum twisted his arm, forcing him to drop the knife.

It all happened in a flash. Glover's movements were sluggish, confused. Zoe dashed forward and grabbed Leonor, who stumbled away, almost falling.

"You're okay, you're okay," Zoe told her repeatedly as the woman whimpered. She helped her sit down and turned to watch as Tatum cuffed Glover's hands behind his body.

Glover was crying.

It was strange to watch. This man who had frightened her so much, who had hounded her for years, beaten so easily. Tatum wasn't even sweating. The entire thing had taken three seconds, maybe four. And Glover's face seemed so pathetic.

Maybe this was the moment to say something victorious of her own. "I hope the cancer kills you slowly," or "You shouldn't have killed those girls."

Instead she said, "I'll call O'Donnell. It's over."

CHAPTER 79

Tuesday, November 1, 2016

Zoe's phone rang while she jogged down Birchdale Avenue. It was her first jog since she'd returned to Dale City, and she had to admit to herself that she missed Lakefront Trail back in Chicago. There were some nice forest tracks in Dale City but none as expansive and beautiful as the shores of Lake Michigan.

She glanced at the phone screen, the caller's name jumping up and down with her footsteps. O'Donnell.

"Hello?" she answered, breathing hard.

"Zoe? Is this a good time?" O'Donnell's voice came through Zoe's Bluetooth earphones.

"Yeah."

"What's that noise? It sounds like wind."

"I'm running."

"I can call later."

"It's okay—what is it?"

"I wanted to tell you that Terrence Finch tried to kill himself. He managed to palm and hide some of his pills and took them all at once. He's now on suicide watch."

Zoe slowed down, gasping for breath. "Did he say why? Or leave a note?"

"He had nothing to write with, and he didn't bother saying why. But the guards and the nurses that have been taking care of him said that for the last few days he kept begging them for blood. Specifically, he wanted Rhea Deleon's blood."

"Maybe he finally realized she was dead," Zoe said. "And with her, his hopes of ever getting another sip of her blood."

"Could be. His lawyer says they're pleading not guilty due to insanity."

"It probably won't work," Zoe said. "And I'll tell you why."

"Because the rules of legal insanity don't apply to him?" O'Donnell suggested.

"Because the rules of legal insanity . . . yeah, exactly. He knew his actions were harmful. There was premeditation and planning."

"Yeah, the state attorney already told me. He said they'll try to claim that the M'Naghten rule applies, but it won't fly."

"Right." Zoe wiped the sweat off her forehead. "He *is* insane, O'Donnell. He's suffering from delusions and hallucinations. He's medicated for schizophrenia. He should be in a hospital. But he'll go to prison."

"Well, it's up to the court to decide. The state attorney is after blood." There was a pause. "No pun intended."

Zoe exhaled, staring at the sunlight filtering through the tree branches. It was late afternoon; the sun was setting. She needed to go back home. "What about Glover?"

"The doctor estimates that he has maybe four months. There's a chance he'll die before his trial ends."

Just like he'd predicted. Did he blame her for his so-called death sentence? Probably. She wasn't sure how she felt about that.

"A couple of BAU agents showed up here yesterday," O'Donnell said. "They want to interview Glover. Weren't *you* supposed to do that?"

"I decided not to," Zoe said. She began walking back.

"Why not?"

"I doubt I could be objective."

"Still, it could give you closure."

"I don't need closure," Zoe said, annoyed. "And this interview should be done professionally. We need to know how, exactly how, Glover overcame his urges in the long stretches of times between murders. And it's important we understand the details about his childhood; it's still unclear if he was abused by his parents. The letters he sent me, were they part of his sexual fantasy, or did they fulfill a different need? And I want to know more about the function of the—"

"Okay, okay. I'm just saying if you talk to him, you could do a much better job. Those BAU agents look like a couple of dumb nitwits."

"They are not dumb nitwits. They're very capable."

"Uh-huh."

"Well, one is pretty capable; the other is, perhaps, a nitwit," Zoe conceded. "Still, I briefed them, and as long as they stick to my briefing, they'll do a good job. I . . . I can't do it."

"Because he hurt your sister?"

"That too." She was about to end there, but the truth spilled out. "And when I look at him, I'm just a little kid again."

"I guess that makes sense," O'Donnell said after a moment.

Zoe crossed the road, approaching her apartment. "Any news about you? Are they transferring you out of Violent Crimes?"

"I don't know." O'Donnell sighed. "Maybe. I still don't have a partner, and you can't be without a partner in Violent Crimes for long. But seeing as I was the detective who arrested Glover, I guess that buys me some time. My husband isn't thrilled."

"What do you feel about it?"

There were a few seconds of silence. "This is what I do best," O'Donnell said. "I like doing it. Even with all that shit with Manny and the department."

"I get that."

"What about you? Any new cases?"

"No. Just a few ongoing things." She stopped by the entrance to the building and exhaled. "I might transfer out of BAU. I've been offered a position."

"Really? What position?"

"They want me to take charge of the profiler training in the FBI Academy. I'd be working with new agent trainees, and I'll also be in charge of any agent assigned to the BAU."

"That sounds right up your alley," O'Donnell said. "Will you take it?"

"I don't know. Probably. It's a good job, and I'll be able to make some important changes. And I won't need to travel all over the country so much."

"Any downsides?"

"Uh . . . no. Probably not."

"Congratulations then," O'Donnell said. "Oh, one last thing. Leonor Carpenter didn't lose the baby. It was a close call, and she's being monitored at the hospital, but it looks like they're going to make it. So you probably saved *two* lives that day."

"That's good."

"Just in case you're still beating yourself about Rhea Deleon."

"I'm not," Zoe said. But she was.

"Okay, good. It's been nice talking to you, Zoe. I might give you a call sometime. You're a good listener. You're my own personal shrink."

Zoe rolled her eyes. "I'm a forensic psychologist."

"Yup. I guess that's what I need. Good night, Zoe."

"Night." Zoe hung up. She stared up at her building, feeling a slight stab of trepidation. The day was far from over. She was about to do something she rarely ever did.

CHAPTER 80

Zoe paced her living room, her hair still wet from the shower, Beyoncé singing in the background. Despite her recent jog, she needed to go out again, the walls closing in on her.

"You seem tense," Andrea said.

Her sister stood in the kitchen doorway, dressed in an apron, holding a ladle. Zoe smiled despite herself. Even though Andrea had flown in two days ago, Zoe still felt a jolt of pleasure every time she saw her.

"I'm not tense," Zoe said.

"There's literally a groove in the carpet from your pacing," Andrea said. "Are you worried about tonight?"

Zoe was about to deny it, then thought better of it. "I shouldn't have let you talk me into it."

"It'll be a nice evening."

"It's too many people."

"Five people, including us, Zoe." Andrea grinned. "How is that too many?"

Zoe sighed. "Fine, you're right," she said hollowly. "It'll be a nice evening."

"It will. Come help me in the kitchen."

Zoe obediently followed Andrea to the kitchen. There were three pots on the stove and lasagna cooking in the oven. The mixture of scents in the air was divine. Zoe paused by the pots and inhaled deeply.

"Wash and chop those vegetables." Andrea gestured at a pile of cucumbers, tomatoes, and peppers. "And I want them lightly chopped. Don't mince them. I'll tell you if it's too small."

"I think I can handle chopping a cucumber on my own."

"I'll be the judge of that."

Zoe began washing the peppers. "Mom called me today."

"Oh yeah? What did she want?"

"She said she wanted to hear how we're doing. But then she spent fifteen minutes trying to convince me to quit my job and come back to Maynard because Dr. Rozenberg's secretary just quit and the doctor's looking for someone capable to replace her."

"Those once-in-a-lifetime job opportunities are hard to pass up," Andrea said, adding salt to the mushroom soup. "She tried to convince me to take the same job. And by the way, that secretary quit two months ago, and Dr. Rozenberg is probably about to retire."

"And apparently there are some handsome single men in Maynard," Zoe said. She chopped one of the tomatoes. "She ran the entire list by me."

"So it was a nice conversation?"

"I don't know how you could stay there for so long. I would have gone insane."

"It was peaceful," Andrea said after a moment. "Sure, Mom can be . . . Mom. But she's busy most of the day. You're cutting the tomatoes too small. Staying there was just what I needed."

"And now you're done?" Zoe asked, trying to keep the hope away from her voice.

Andrea gave the soup one final stir. "Yes, but I'm not returning to Dale City."

"Oh." Zoe focused on the cucumber.

Andrea peered over her shoulder. "You're mincing it. I told you don't cut them too—"

"I'm doing it fine. Why don't you want to return here?"

"For one, I have a few very bad memories from here."

"Glover is in prison! He'll die in a few months; you can't let him ruin—"

"I didn't like living here, Zoe. I didn't! I'm sorry. I know you found your place, but it's not mine."

"Okay." Zoe blinked away a tear that threatened to materialize. "What will you do, then?"

"You remember Mallory? From Boston?"

"Is she the one with the touching habit?"

"She doesn't have a touching habit. She's a bit physical."

"She keeps touching anyone she talks to. She caresses their shoulder. It's clearly an obsessive habit."

"It's not . . . never mind." Andrea sounded exasperated. "She wants to open a restaurant."

"So you're going to work in her restaurant?"

"She actually suggested we open it together."

Zoe bit her lip. "You want to open a restaurant with Mallory?"

"I'm considering it."

"Where will you get the money?"

"She just inherited some money from her grandmother. And I thought I might take a loan."

"It sounds really risky."

"Said the woman who chases serial killers for a living. Look, you're cutting it too small. Let me just show you for a second."

"I am holding a very sharp knife, and this is *not* the moment to tell me how to cut vegetables," Zoe said, slamming the knife just a hair's breadth away from her own finger.

"Okay."

"How much do you need?"

"We need to figure it out, but it'll probably be between thirty and forty thousand."

"I'll loan you the money."

Andrea snorted. "With what? Your government salary?"

Zoe turned to face her. "Harry Barry's publisher is willing to pay me for the exclusive rights to my story." She'd told Harry she wouldn't do it in a million years, and he'd responded in that infuriating smug tone of his that he'd give her some time to think it over. "It'll be enough for your share of the restaurant."

"I can't take your money."

"You're not *taking* it. It's a loan. It's not like I have anything to do with it."

"Oh, Zoe." Andrea's voice cracked. She lunged at Zoe and hugged her fiercely.

"But I'm eating there for free whenever I show up," Zoe said, shutting her eyes and wrapping her arms around her sister.

"Okay."

"And you don't get to tell me how to cut vegetables."

"In your dreams."

They held each other for a few seconds, until a knock on the door made them pull away.

"They're here," Zoe said, wiping her eyes.

She went over to the door, Andrea following behind. She opened the door just as Tatum was about to knock again. Marvin stood by his side, Christine Mancuso behind them.

"We brought wine," Tatum said, then frowned, looking at her and Andrea. "Are you two okay?"

"We were cutting onions," Andrea said, sniffing. "Give me that bottle."

CHAPTER 81

Andrea had made a tray of cheese and fruit that she served as an appetizer until the lasagna would be ready. The five of them sat in the living room drinking wine, mostly listening to Marvin talk. The old man had an uncanny ability to hold everyone's attention.

"We were discussing it in my book club just last night," he was saying, turning to face Mancuso. "Did you ever go to a book club?"

"No, I can't say that I have," she answered, smiling.

"You should come to my book club—you'd love it. You'd fit right in." He frowned slightly. "You're a bit young; most of the women there are forty or fifty. But I think they'll like you."

"How old do you think I am?" Mancuso asked, arching an eyebrow.

"Well, I don't like to guess a lady's age, but in your case I'll make an exception. Thirty? No, hang on . . . twenty-nine."

Mancuso glanced at Tatum. "I like your grandfather."

"Everybody does." Tatum sighed.

Zoe felt strange. She was too focused on herself, on her posture, her behavior. Trying to look as if she was part of the conversation but doing her best not to say anything significant. Was she smiling too much? She placed her palm on her knee, but it seemed artificial, and she took it off. Then she tried to lean casually back, but the couch was somehow all wrong.

She *never* cared about what people thought. But inviting them over made her too conscious of everything. It was unnerving.

"Do you think we should tell Marvin that Christine is married?" Andrea asked her in a low voice.

"I don't think it would matter either way," Zoe answered.

She lost the thread of the conversation for a few seconds, trying to sit straight. When she tuned back in, Marvin was explaining to the chief of the Behavioral Analysis Unit how you *really* caught a killer.

"It's all about the eyes," he said. "Gotta look them in the eyes."

"Really?" Mancuso seemed to be having the time of her life.

"'Eyes so transparent that through them the soul is seen.' Gootier said that."

"It's *Gautier*," Tatum said, rolling his eyes. "And he was talking about women, not murderers."

"You know, Tatum, when I need French literature lessons, I'll be sure to give you a call."

Zoe got up. "The lasagna is probably ready. I'll go get it."

"I can get it," Andrea said.

"No, it's okay. I'll do it." Zoe hurried away to the kitchen. Once out of sight, she exhaled and leaned on the counter. She took a moment to steady her nerves.

"Need a hand?" Mancuso said behind her.

Zoe whirled around. "No," she blurted. "I'm fine."

Mancuso stepped into the kitchen. "Thanks for inviting me," she said. "I'm having a really nice time."

"Oh. Good." Zoe felt a surprising wave of relief.

"Do you have an answer for me yet? The assistant director of the FBI's Training Division is nagging me."

"I . . . I need another day to think."

"It's a good position Zoe. It's perfect for you."

"I know."

"The profiler training material is outdated and needs to be rewritten from scratch."

"I can't argue with that." Zoe suddenly remembered the lasagna. She quickly opened the oven and grabbed the tray with an oven mitt.

"That looks incredible," Mancuso said.

"Andrea made it. She's great with Italian food. She's actually opening a restaurant in Boston." The words felt strange in her mouth but not entirely unpleasant.

They returned to the living room.

"Look, I'm just saying, if the fish didn't do it, *who* did?" Marvin was asking Tatum.

"Marvin, you're being ridiculous. The fish isn't some sort of criminal mastermind—"

"Is that the fish I gave you?" Mancuso sat back down.

"*You* gave him the fish?" Marvin asked.

"Yeah," Mancuso said. "I love fish. I have a large aquarium at the office and another one at home. The fish I gave Tatum is named Timothy. He's a bastard."

"I should have known that fish got special FBI training before it moved in with us. That explains everything," Marvin said.

"It's just a goldfish, Marvin," Tatum said.

"It's not a goldfish, Tatum. It's a gourami. If you knew anything about fish at all, you'd know that."

"And *you* know about fish?" Tatum asked, incredulous.

"I know a lot about fish." Marvin glanced at Mancuso. "I love fish. They're fascinating."

"Really?" Tatum said. "Name three types of fish."

"Well . . . gourami. And tuna."

"That's two."

"You know what, Tatum? You're a pain in the ass. I don't want to bore the women here with our talk about fish names. We could be talking about much more interesting stuff. Like that geography teacher you had in eighth grade. And the thing that happened."

"Fine," Tatum said grudgingly after a second. "You're a fish expert."

"Damn right I am."

"I want to know about the geography teacher," Andrea said.

"Maybe later," Marvin said. "It's not something to talk about before dinner."

"Okay," Zoe said. "Let's eat."

"Can I make a toast first?" Marvin asked.

"Uh . . . sure," Zoe said.

"Marvin—" Tatum said irritably.

"Be quiet, Tatum. Your grandpa is talking." Marvin raised his glass. "Six months ago, my grandson told me he was going to Quantico. I wasn't thrilled, because I knew I needed to come along since he wouldn't manage a day without me."

Tatum rolled his eyes but stayed quiet.

"I always knew Tatum was a good man, but he never seemed happy in LA, and I thought he just wasn't the right fit for the bureau. But we came here, and he ended up with a brilliant, talented partner. And suddenly my grandson began to smile more."

Blood rushed to Zoe's face.

"He doesn't talk a lot about your unit. But when he does, it's with great admiration and enthusiasm, and I now see he ended up where he belongs. And you guys are lucky, because you won't find a better agent in the FBI."

Tatum's mouth hung slightly open, as if he was mimicking the previously discussed fish.

"So thanks, Dr. Zoe Bentley, for being such an incredible woman. And thanks to the three of you for getting those psychos off the streets so people like Andrea and I can sleep better at night."

He raised his wineglass slightly higher. "To the agents of the BAU."

CHAPTER 82

After Marvin's toast, the weight in Zoe's chest diminished. She was still tense and jittery, but she could also relish the wonderful meal Andrea had made. And to her surprise, she enjoyed the company. Mancuso left soon after dessert. Marvin regaled Andrea with suggestions and anecdotes about his own experiences with the restaurant business. Zoe went to the kitchen to get some peace and quiet while washing the dishes. Her small kitchen wasn't equipped to deal with Andrea's five-course meal, and the pots and dirty dishes towered over the tiny sink.

Tatum entered as she scrubbed one of the pans, cleaning a particularly stubborn patch of burnt tomato sauce. He grabbed a towel and began drying the wet dishes.

"It's okay—I can finish up here," Zoe said.

"I want to help." Tatum picked up a wineglass and wiped it. "Better warn Andrea. If she listens to Marvin's advice, her new restaurant might never survive the opening."

Zoe put the clean pan aside and started with the lasagna tray. "I wouldn't worry about her—she knows what she's doing."

"I'm sure she does."

They stood side by side in silence for a moment.

"Everything okay?" Tatum asked.

"Sure, why wouldn't it be?" She realized she was clenching her jaw tightly and forced herself to relax. "It was a very nice evening."

"Uh-huh." Tatum placed the dry wineglasses in a row. "You know, it occurred to me we actually had *three* different signatures in this case. Three profiles."

"Yes. Glover, Finch, and Glover's client, who gave him instructions."

"Is there a precedent? I don't recall a serial killer ever fulfilling requests."

"Serial killers sometimes interpret the media coverage that revolves around them as a request," Zoe said. "But of course, there's no point in profiling the media. This case was particularly interesting because there really were three individuals. We never tried to profile the third. But it would be worthwhile to try. It's fascinating to think of the internet functioning as a mechanism of victim obfuscation. Glover's client didn't need to actively depersonify the victim, because seeing her through the filter of his computer screen already did that. It's very similar to the process with other internet trolls. The BAU should definitely research this topic more. We should talk to Mancuso . . . what? Why are you looking at me like that?"

Tatum had a tiny smile. "No reason."

"Okay." She laid a few washed spoons aside just as he reached for another wet plate. Their fingers brushed. Zoe was suddenly aware of their proximity. Tatum was much taller than her, and her head was inches away from his shoulder. If she tipped her head just slightly, she could touch it. Put her cheek against it. She recalled the feeling of him holding her in the motel room, then later, falling asleep with his reassuring presence beside her.

She took a tiny step away and cleared her throat. "I'm not used to having guests over."

"Oh? I can give you a few tips. First of all, Rihanna usually isn't the right background music for dinner."

"Oh yeah? What would be better?"

"Almost anything. But jazz could be nice. Miles Davis or Duke Ellington . . ."

Zoe snorted.

"Oh, I'm sorry," Tatum said, annoyed. "Obviously Rihanna is better than a couple of the most acclaimed jazz musicians of the twentieth century."

"I was trying to say, before you pretentiously lectured me about my taste in music, that it was . . . better than I expected."

"Well, I'm glad."

"I'm happy you came."

"Sure. Anytime."

She wanted to say more. It bubbled up in her, and she tried to get the words out. How she was glad he'd transferred to the BAU and that they'd ended up as partners. That when she worked with him, everything felt smoother, as if he had a knack for softening the sharp edges of reality. That in a way he completed her, because he could nudge her off her one-track pathways she sometimes got stuck on and could give her a different point of view. That she'd never worked with someone so well before. That she had been offered a promotion she was about to turn down because it meant she wouldn't be his partner anymore. That she was really upset her sister was leaving for Boston because for a long time, Andrea had been the only one who understood her. But now she felt like she didn't need to hold on to Andrea, because she knew he was there. That the FBI agents were no longer a single hostile cluster, because someone finally had her back.

"You know, we work well together," she blurted.

"I think so too," Tatum said brightly. "Look how fast we finished cleaning the dishes."

"Right." She smiled at him. "Best dishwashers in the bureau."

ACKNOWLEDGMENTS

This book was the hardest to write out of the three Zoe Bentley books. Figuring out Terrence Finch's downward spiral while maintaining the correct pacing of the book *and* weaving a satisfying mystery? It was almost impossible. And would have never happened without the people who supported me every step of the way.

My wife, Liora, first and foremost. She helped me think through the plot and figure out how to plow through difficult scenes, and then she read the mishmash of a first draft I had and told me what I had to do to shape it into something more coherent. When people ask me how I can write books, Liora is always a large part of the answer. Anyone who wants to write should have a Liora of their own.

Christine Mancuso, who read the next draft, had to do the most difficult thing of all—to tell me that it didn't work. There was a serious pacing problem (those are the worst), and if I didn't fix it, the book would suffer. This prodded me to do several huge changes that made the book so much better.

My dad read the final draft, just to make sure that I got Terrence Finch's state of mind right. It's been useful to have psychologists as parents over the years, and this was one more perk.

Jessica Tribble, my editor, received the final draft and gave me her thoughtful notes, which later helped me correct some serious issues. The whole Allen Swenson subplot was rewritten from scratch due to these notes, vastly improving in the process.

Kevin Smith, my developmental editor, stepped in and helped me figure out how to rewrite several of the central moments in the book, with thoughtful comments and suggestions that were invaluable to the final draft. O'Donnell, Finch, and Glover all became much better under his guidance.

Stephanie Chou did the final editing on the book (and, like Jessica, has been there for the previous two). Her sharp eyes caught a torrent of mistakes, and she taught me something about pumas and gazelles in the process.

Sarah Hershman, my agent, was the one who first helped this series get published and has been there to support me since.

Hagar Cygler helped me with a bit of photography advice, assisting in getting Finch's character just right.

Gali Lior helped me figure out some details in Catherine's autopsy that were almost impossible for me to find by myself.

To my friends in Author's Corner, without whom my entire writing adventure would never have taken off: You are the best friends I could hope for. Thank you for helping and cheering me every step of the way.

ABOUT THE AUTHOR

Mike Omer has been a journalist, a game developer, and the CEO of Loadingames, but he can currently be found penning his next thriller. Omer loves to write about two things: real people who could be the perpetrators or victims of crimes—and funny stuff. He mixes these two loves quite passionately into his suspenseful and often macabre mysteries. Omer is married to a woman who diligently forces him to live his dream, and he is father to an angel, a pixie, and a gremlin. He has two voracious hounds that wag their tails quite menacingly at anyone who dares approach his home. Learn more by emailing him at mike@strangerealm.com.

Printed in Great Britain
by Amazon